The

RIVALS
of
VERSAILLES

Praise for *The Sisters of Versailles*

"An intriguing romp through Louis XV's France, filled
with lush backdrops, rich detail, and colorful characters.
Fans of historical fiction will enjoy this glimpse into the
lost golden era of the French monarchy."

—Allison Pataki, author of *The Accidental Empress*

"A stunning breadth of period detail,
offered in a fresh, contemporary voice."

—Juliet Grey, author of
Becoming Marie Antoinette

"A wickedly delightful read."
—*New York Daily News*

The
RIVALS
of
VERSAILLES

A NOVEL

SALLY CHRISTIE

ATRIA PAPERBACK

New York   London   Toronto   Sydney   New Delhi

ATRIA PAPERBACK
An Imprint of Simon & Schuster, Inc.
1230 Avenue of the Americas
New York, NY 10020

First Atria Paperback edition April 2016

ATRIA PAPERBACK and colophon are trademarks of Simon & Schuster, Inc.

For information about special discounts for bulk purchases, please contact Simon & Schuster Special Sales at 1-866-506-1949 or business@simonandschuster.com.

The Simon & Schuster Speakers Bureau can bring authors to your live event. For more information or to book an event, contact the Simon & Schuster Speakers Bureau at 1-866-248-3049 or visit our website at http://www.simonspeakers.com.

Manufactured in the United States of America

10 9 8 7 6 5 4 3 2 1

Library of Congress Cataloging-in-Publication Data

Names: Christie, Sally, 1971– author.
Title: The rivals of Versailles : a novel / Sally Christie.
Description: First Atria paperback edition. | New York : Atria Paperback,
   2016. | Series: The mistresses of Versailles trilogy ;
   2 Identifiers: LCCN 2015041813 (print) | LCCN 2015044989 (ebook) |
Subjects: LCSH: Pompadour, Jeanne Antoinette Poisson, marquise de,
   1721–1764—Fiction. | France—History—Louis XV, 1715–1774—Fiction. |
   France—Kings and rulers—Paramours—Fiction. | France—Court and
   courtiers—Fiction. | BISAC: FICTION / Historical. | FICTION / Literary. |
   FICTION / General. | GSAFD: Biographical fiction. | Historical fiction. |
Classification: LCC PR9199.4.C4883 R58 2016 (print) | LCC PR9199.4.C4883
   (ebook) | DDC 813/.6—dc23

ISBN 978-1-5011-0299-8
ISBN 978-1-5011-0301-8 (ebook)

To Douglas

Contents

The

RIVALS
of
VERSAILLES

The year is 1730.

France is at peace and King Louis XV is a handsome young man of twenty, with all the promise and potential in the world.

In Paris, at a fair on the edge of the great Bois de Boulogne, a young girl meets her destiny in the shape of a prophecy and starts a journey, one that will see her scale to heights few women have obtained, driven to depths few women would have dared to go.

Act I

Reinette

Chapter One

The gypsy's hair is as red as blood, I think in astonishment. She catches me staring and starts, rabbitlike, as though she recognizes me. But she does not, and I certainly don't know anyone quite so dirty.

"I pray you not to touch me," I say as she comes toward me, but still there is something familiar about her. My mother bustles over, carrying a pastry in the shape of a pig, and pulls me back from the filthy woman.

"Just look at those perfect eyes," says the woman. She takes my hand, a coarse brown mitt over my own, and I smell a mix of smoke and sweat. "And that heart-shaped face. She is as pretty as a miracle, though no wonder with such a handsome mother. I'll tell you her fortune."

"We have no need of counsel from the likes of you," says my mother harshly and pulls me away into the crowd, almost colliding with a pair of shepherds reeling in a drunken dance. The fair is in full swing, a riot of festivity and noise billowing around us:

"Fresh lemons and fresh lemonade, sugared or not! Fresh lemons, straight from Provence."

"A pair of dancing ducks! A pair of dancing ducks!"

"Come see the white bear, only fifteen *sous*!"

"No, no," wheedles the gypsy woman, appearing once again at our side. "I will tell her future. I know it already." She catches Mama's curiosity and deftly pockets it. "But I have no need to tell you how special she is. A princess with a queen for a mother."

Mama inclines her head, softened by the compliment.

"Come to my tent and I will tell you of the wondrous future

that lies ahead for little . . ." She leers keenly at me, sees the engraved *J* on the porcelain pendant, tied with a ribbon around my neck. "Little Julie . . . Jo— Jeanne?"

"Oh! But Jeanne is my name!" I exclaim. How did she know? My mother wavers. "No more than fifty *sous*, mind you."

"Eighty is my price, but none has ever been dissatisfied."

The two women stare at each other and I stomp my foot, impatient to be away and see the dancing ducks. I have no need for my future to be told, for what nine-year-old ever doubted their happiness? They reach an understanding and reluctantly I follow the red-haired woman into the gloaming of her tent. Something slithers in the dirty rushes at my feet and the foul odor of uncured leather swamps the air. Smoothly she pockets the coins my mother gives her and her hands, as coarse as bark, fold over mine again.

"No cards?" asks my mother imperiously.

"No need," says the woman. The outside world fades and the gypsy seems to grow in stature and dignity. Brown fingers steal over my palms, and up and around my wrists.

"Your daughter is a pearl." She speaks as though in a trance. "So rare—open hundreds of oysters, but you'll find only one pearl." Soon we are lulled by the soft stream of her voice: "Your future extends even beyond the ambitions of your mother. You will be loved by a king, and be the most powerful woman in the land. Your future glitters like the stars. A little queen: I see it as though it passes in front of me."

She snaps out of her trance and smiles ingratiatingly at my mother. "And there, madame, the fortune of your daughter."

"How do I know it is true?" asks my mother, and her voice comes from far away; she is as spellbound as I.

The gypsy snorts and spits neatly into the rushes. "Because I can see what is to come. This little girl is special. She will be the lover of a king."

My mother flinches. I know vaguely what a lover is: a nice

man who brings gifts and compliments, like my Uncle Norman.

"The way is not all clear," the gypsy continues, stroking my palm lightly. "I see several great sorrows, three men on dark horses riding across the plain."

"None of that," says Mama sharply. "She is much too young."

"Three is a number far less than most will know," retorts the gypsy.

We emerge back into the crisp sunshine of the October day, the world bright and noisy after the confines of the dirty tent.

"Mama," I ask timidly, uncertain of asking for a trifle after such momentous news, "can we go and see the ducks now? The dancing ducks?"

My mother looks down at me and for a second it is as though she knows me not. Then she blinks and squeezes my hand.

"Of course, darling. Of course. My Reinette," she adds. "My little queen. What wonderful news! Come, let us go and see these ducks you have been pestering me about all morning. Anything for my little queen."

℘

That night Mama's lover Norman comes to visit. Papa is away in Germany, disgraced for some business no one will explain to me, and it is Norman who takes care of us. Uncle Norman, as I call him, often spends the night. I'm not sure why, for his house is far grander than ours. We don't keep a single manservant, only Nurse, and Sylvie in the kitchens. Perhaps he is lonely—he is not married—or his sheets are being laundered. Mama is very beautiful and Sylvie once said that we only live comfortably because of Mama's friends. It is good she has so many.

Mama and Uncle Norman closet themselves in the salon and I eat alone with Nurse and my little brother, Abel, who fusses and spits out his milk. I think of the fortune-teller and her hands, like dried old leather—how did they get so rough?

"Marie, do you think our king is handsome?"

"Of course he is, duck. The most handsome man in France, as is fitting." We have a portrait of the king in the salon: a small boy, stiff in a magnificent red coat, with large eyes and thick brown hair. I think he looks sad, and quite lonely. He was only five when he became king. That must have been difficult, with still so much to learn, and who would play with a king?

Of course, the king is older now—he turned twenty this year, more than double my age—and is married to a Polish princess. Sylvie says the queen looks like a cow and I imagine her to be very beautiful, with large, soft eyes and a peaceful expression. How lucky she is to be married to the king!

Later that evening my mother comes to say good night. She pushes a strand of hair back into my nightcap and strokes my cheek. I love my mother with all my heart; the nuns at school say the heart in my chest is no bigger than a chestnut, but how can something so small hold so much love?

"Dearest, your Uncle Norman and I have come to a decision."

"*Oui, Maman.*" I am fighting to keep my eyes open but what Mama says next opens them wide.

"Jeanne, darling, we have decided you will not return to the convent."

Oh! "But why, Mama?" I sit up and duck her caressing hands. "I love the convent! And the nuns! And my friend Claudine, and what about Chester?"

"Who is Chester?"

"Our pet crow!"

"Darling, these things are for the best. You must trust Uncle Norman and me."

"But why?" I ask, tears pricking my eyes. I love the convent and had secretly been counting the days until my return. Only twelve, but now that number has become forever.

"Darling, you heard the gypsy woman. You have a great future ahead. My little Reinette."

"Why do you care what that smelly old woman said? It's not fair!"

"Reinette! Never speak like that about other people. No matter how dirty they may be. Now, listen, dearest. Uncle Norman has agreed to take care of your education. This is a wonderful opportunity and you will learn far more than the nuns could teach you." My mother imparts her desires through her tightening grip on my hands. "He promises you will learn with the finest musicians in the land. We'll buy a clavichord! And take lessons in painting, and drawing, and singing. Anything you desire."

"Geography?" I ask.

"Certainly, that too, darling. We shall order a globe from Germaine's. And elocution as well, I think. Though your voice is very pretty by nature."

Mama leaves and I snuggle down to sleep, happy, dreaming of my very own clavichord. I will write to Claudine very often and we will always remain friends, and they will take care of Chester and all will be well. As I drift down to sleep, I realize I forgot to ask why Uncle Norman is suddenly taking such a strong and expensive interest in my education.

From Claudine de Saillac
Convent of the Ursulines
Poissy, France
March 10, 1731

Dearest Jeannette,

Greetings to you, my esteemed friend, and thank you for the letter you have done the honor of writing me.

Do you like my new handwriting? The nuns praised it—even Sister Severa! I am very sad that you will not be coming back. I miss you a lot a lot a lot. There is a new girl here, her name is Madeleine but the nuns made her change her name because Sister Severa doesn't approve of Saint Magdalene, on account of her Sin. Well, she—Madeleine who is now called Marie—is very pretty but not as pretty as you.

Chester is well but he lost one of his feathers. I wanted to wear it on my sleeve, but Sister Severa made me offer it instead to Saint Francis, though why Saint Francis needs a feather I don't know. How lucky you are to have dancing lessons! Who plays the music? I am sorry your mother does not allow you the harp, but it is true that playing it will give you a hunched back.

Write soon!

I remain your most respected and esteemed servant.
Claudine

Chapter Two

A steady stream of tutors flows in and out of our house on the rue des Bons-Enfants. Apart from singing, my favorite subject is history. I now know that a lover is a mistress and I have studied the mistresses of kings past. My favorite is Diane de Poitiers, who was one of the most beautiful women in France. King Henri II loved her faithfully all his life.

Imagine—one day our king will love me as King Henri loved Diane! When I am allowed to daydream, which is not very often—Mama says I am like a bird, always up in the clouds—I imagine the king . . . but it is hard to imagine what he does, when he loves me. He will want to kiss me, and perhaps pull up my skirts, but then . . . I am not sure what it is that men seek beneath our dresses. The garters that married women wear? Mama has a beautiful pair of cherry silk ones trimmed with beaver hair. Perhaps that is what they like.

I do know that when a man loves a woman, he is very kind to her and will give her anything she wants. Last month Mama asked Uncle Norman for a new marble-topped table for the salon, and he was happy to buy it. If I were his mistress, the king would give me anything I wanted! I'm not sure what I would ask for; perhaps some new drawing books? Or, I think one day when I am in the kitchens and Sylvie is busy shooing away a beggar woman, I could ask the king to give all the poor people something to eat.

On Wednesdays I cross the river in Uncle Norman's carriage for dancing lessons. I love dancing—it makes me feel as though I am on a swing, flying high and free—but I do not care for the other girls, mostly relatives of Uncle Norman. His family is far grander than Papa's, who was only the son of a butcher and who gave me my last name of Poisson, which means fish.

The little girls—Mama says I must call them cousins even though they aren't—sneer at me and make cutting comments.

"Oh, it's Jeannette Poisson. Do I smell something fishy?" asks Elisabeth, an older girl wearing an unfortunate mustard-colored dress. The others snigger, then remember they are supposed to be elegant, and titter behind their little fans.

"Your dress is very beautiful," I reply to Elisabeth. Mama says one must never return rudeness; instead swallow it whole and offer only charm in return. Lying is a sin, but it is far more important to be polite. In truth, Elisabeth's gown makes her face the color of morning ashes.

"A fish! A fish!" parrots Charlotte, a younger girl. She frowns, as though she wishes to add something, but cannot think what.

"Why aren't you in a convent?" accuses Lisette. She is very pretty and has a beauty spot shaped like a star, placed under one eye. I am envious, for Mama says I may not wear them until I am sixteen, four long years away.

"I was at the convent at Poissy. My aunt is a nun there."

"The Dominicans at Poissy? My cousin there never mentioned a bourgeois fish."

"No, with the Ursulines," I say softly. The girls say bourgeois as if it were a sin only to be mentioned in the confessional.

"So bourgeois! So dreadfully common!" shrieks Elisabeth. "As common as a . . . as common as a . . ." She flounders, chewing her lip.

"As common as a cold?" I say helpfully.

"Yes, as common as a cold." She glares at me and takes a step back, as if my humble roots are contaminating.

"Your hairstyle is most becoming," I reply in an innocent voice. Elisabeth narrows her eyes: thin frizzles of hair have escaped from their pins and one of her bows has fallen out.

"Enough chatter," says Monsieur Guibaudet mildly. "Form into pairs and walk in front of me. Demoiselles, two at a time, and

one, two, three, and one, two, three . . . Mademoiselle de Tournehem, a little lighter on the feet! Mademoiselle de Semonville, do
not bob your head so—you are a young lady, not a duck. Mademoiselle Poisson—beautiful, beautiful. The rest of you—notice
the carriage of her head as she glides, arms at her sides, grace implied in every step."

I pass Elisabeth and the other girls and smile lightly.

Back at home I run to Mama's room, sobbing. Mama is on the
bed with Abel, who is attacking our cat Freddie with his tin soldiers. I fling myself down beside them and burst into tears.

"Why do I have to go there? They are so hateful. They look
down on me!"

"Now, dearest, no complaining. We are grateful to Norman for
introducing you to his family, for they are very well connected."

"They called me a smelly fish."

"Even I will admit your father's name is unfortunate, Reinette,
but you must learn to bear cruelty with grace. The world can be
a hard and hateful place."

I bite my lip. "I don't want the world to be a hateful place!
Why can't they just be nice to me? I'm nice to them!" Well,
mostly, I think, remembering Elisabeth's hair. But she probably
didn't even know I was mocking her.

"Don't bite your lips, dearest, you will wear them away to
nothing and then they'll be as thin as Madame Crusson's upstairs." Mama sighs and runs her fingers through Abel's hair. "I
know how you like to be admired, dearest, but life is not always
a fairy tale."

"We should change our name, and then they won't make fun
of me anymore."

Mama laughs, bitterly. "Never think that would change anything; they would just find something else to torment you with."

"Fish are excellent creatures," observes Abel. "Silent, and
smart." Abel is seven and is as annoying as little brothers are wont
to be.

Mama leans over and fixes one of my pins back above my ear.

"I fear you are too soft, dearest Reinette. But don't worry, one day you'll make a brilliant marriage and then you will change your name."

"I'll probably marry a *Monsieur Poulet*—Mister Chicken," I say glumly, thinking of my drawing master. I hate having a horrid name.

"Reinette! Don't be so sulky. Smile, please. Now, I must go and find Sylvie—it's almost six."

Mama leaves but Abel stays behind and continues to besiege the cat with his tin soldiers. Despite his protests I grab one away and throw it on the floor, the hateful words of the girls still caught in my head. I chew my lips. And I have to go there again Wednesday.

I lie back on the bed and think about crying, but then I think of the king and I brighten. Those silly girls, they aren't called *Reinette* and they don't have a special destiny like mine. And when I am the king's lover, they will have to be nice to me, and won't ever call me nasty names again.

The clock strikes six and I roll over on the bed. Tomorrow the famous opera singer Monsieur Jelyotte comes for my singing lessons and I have four new songs to practice. He wants me to learn one hundred songs; I'm already at fifty-nine or sixty—I can't remember which.

Chapter Three

I wear my best dress, so stiff and formal I feel like I am being hugged by an iron mother. Uncle Norman has arranged a special dinner with my godfather, the great financier Jean Paris de Montmartel, who is also a good friend of my mother's. My father used to work for Montmartel before he was exiled. An escaped goat, Sylvie in the kitchens told me, but I'm not sure what that means, and besides, Papa used to sell grain, not animals.

Uncle Norman is also in business with Montmartel; they lend people money and collect taxes, and own ships and companies. According to Uncle Norman, my godfather and his three brothers are so powerful they have all of Paris in their pockets. Montmartel is very rich and always splendidly dressed; tonight he wears soft white boots and a fine velvet coat embroidered with crimson lace. He brings with him the scent of a grander, more luxurious world.

During the meal Montmartel compliments me on my table manners and the dainty way I eat my asparagus.

"Thank you, sir." I smile—Mama always says a pleasant smile is the best of dress and should be worn on all occasions. "I admire the way you boned your duck."

The men laugh.

"She's no shrinking violet, is she?" says Montmartel to my mother. "And fourteen: what a delightful age."

Mama smiles at him, almost as widely as she smiles at Norman, and says that I am very independent, though soft when occasion demands. When the meal is over she turns to me and says, "Now, Reinette, as we prepared."

"*Reinette*—I always thought nicknames vulgar, but this one suits our little girl entirely." Uncle Montmartel settles back with a spear of asparagus in one hand—he didn't let the footman take the plate away—and a pinch of snuff in the other. Uncle Norman doesn't like snuff; he says it causes excessive sneezing and he once knew a man who sneezed out his brains, right through his nose, and all because of too much snuff.

"Dear sirs, I shall now sing an aria from *Hippolyte et Aricie* for your pleasure."

I stand and curtsy, then launch into the song, using my arms to declaim the most important lines, looking to Heaven and clasping my hands when I sing of my invincible heart.

I note that the men are staring at me with parted mouths and glazed eyes; I hope I am not boring them. Oh no—Mama also looks worried.

"Did I not do well?" I whisper when the evening ends and Norman is showing the great man to his carriage.

"No, darling, you were charming. But that dress—it is getting a little tight."

I blush and turn away. It is true: I am starting to grow small breasts but I hoped no one had noticed.

"And that," says Norman, reentering the room, "was the most powerful man in France."

"Surely you jest, Uncle! The king is the most powerful man in France, and then there are his ministers, and all the dukes and princes? The cardinals?"

Norman shakes his head and sits back at the table, popping a grape into his mouth. He takes a gold coin from his pocket and spins it on the cloth.

"He certainly liked his asparagus, didn't he?" says Mama in disapproval. "There's hardly any left." She takes the last stalk and drags it delicately through the spice dish before chewing it thoughtfully.

"You see, Reinette, that man, that man who ate nearly all the asparagus, as your mother has so rightly pointed out, well, he and his brothers have more of these"—Norman catches the spinning coin, glittering in the candlelight—"than anyone else in France.

Including our king. And so that makes him, and his brothers, the most powerful men in the country. Titles, birth, rank . . . those do not matter as they once did. Their power pales before the power of this here coin."

Mama shakes her head and pours herself a glass of brandy.

"In my youth," says Norman, flicking snuff grains off the tablecloth, "the great financier Crozat, as rich as Croesus but the son of a peasant, sold his daughter in marriage to the Comte d'Evreux. Poor girl—the comte refused to make, ah, I mean kiss her, saying he'd never debase himself with the daughter of a commoner. Though he did make full use of her enormous dowry."

"Oh! Poor little girl!" How horrible: her husband would not even kiss her, and just because she was not a noble. Like me. But while the little Crozat girl was a great heiress, I am penniless. As enchanting as a sunset, Uncle Norman likes to say, but I don't have any money.

"Those high nobles—they have their own way of looking at things. They are very resistant to change." The old nobility are disdainful of the rich bourgeois like Uncle Norman, but also envious. Uncle Norman likes to say the starved old nobles carry their prestige and their birth around with them, as though it would feed and clothe them. Which it won't, he always adds with a smirk. "But one day we will intermarry and rule, in a nobility based solely on merit."

"Oh, tush, Norman, you do talk nonsense!" says my mother.

I am doubtful as well; everyone knows that rank and birth are very important. I think of the loathsome Poirot sisters at the convent and the special way the nuns treated them, and all because their uncle was a marquis with a position at Court. The way the nuns shunned the poorer girls. The shame I feel at the dancing lessons with the better-born girls.

I explain these things to Norman, but he just guffaws and over my mother's protests plies me with brandy that makes me glow and giggle.

From Claudine de Saillac
Convent of the Ursulines
Poissy, France
June 10, 1737

Dear Jeannette,

Greetings to you, my esteemed friend, and thank you for the letter you have done the honor of writing me.

I am sorry to report that Chester flew away after that loathsome Julie Poirot forgot to close his cage. Now we have a new bird that Sister Ursula bought for us, but he has white feathers and is much smaller. Then he laid an egg. And he with no wife! Marie said that the Immaculate Conception might even happen to birds, but Julie said that if a bird has no soul, then how could it have an immaculate conception? No baby has come from the egg, yet, though we keep it warm in a nest of ribbons.

I am to leave the convent in September and return to Honfleur. My sister is staying behind; she wishes to consecrate her life to God and my parents have finally agreed. How I should love you to visit me in Honfleur! What I wrote last summer about the leaking roof and how boring it was and the wolves that ate my dog, I didn't mean it; it is really very nice there and you must visit.

Write soon!

I remain your most respectful and esteemed servant.
Claudine

From Madeleine Poisson
Rue des Bons Enfants, Paris
September 2, 1738

Dearest Daughter,

Norman will send the carriage for you and it will be in Honfleur by next Thursday. The coachman brings a box of candied chestnuts that you must present to Claudine's mother. Do not be remiss in thanking them once again for their hospitality, and of course insist that we would be honored to host Claudine in Paris (though the news that she is now betrothed to her uncle makes that possibility rather remote).

While you may be flattered that both her brothers have declared themselves to you and are threatening tears and more over your departure, you must not encourage them. We have higher hopes for you than a petty provincial family (and I am sure their parents have higher hopes for their sons than you). Assure the boys that if they write, their letters will be returned still sealed.

Your brother, Abel, was fitted for his first wig last week! It was a very proud moment for myself and Uncle Norman—he is growing so fast. Abel, I mean of course, not Norman. He leaves for school next month, but you will be back in time to say goodbye. Try to bring him a shell from Honfleur that he may add to his collection.

I must finish up; the candle is about to snuffle and Sylvie has already gone to bed. I wish you safe travels.

With much love,
Mama

Chapter Four

There are private meetings and strangers visit the house. I catch whispers, fragments:

"She is already nineteen and to look at her is to fall in love."

"You've been in contact with Montmartel; what does he say?"

"De la Portaille's cousin is a fine man and astoundingly rich, but he's almost seventy."

The most important event of my life is being discussed: my marriage. When I think of my future husband my thoughts turn, as they often do, to the king. My mother bought us a copy of the king's latest portrait and his face is so handsome I feel like crying when I look at it. My husband must be a Court noble who will bring me to Versailles, where the king will fall in love with me. And I with him.

But of course the choice is not mine.

Then I learn my husband is to be Uncle Norman's nephew Charles, a young man only a few years older than me. As our wedding present, Norman is giving us land and a château, enough for the title of count.

"And so you will be a countess, dearest! And such a beautiful name for the estate: Étiolles, almost like Étoiles—*stars*," says my mother.

I meet Charles; he is sulky and his father comes with him to register his disapproval. But by the end of our meeting Charles is enchanted with me and cannot stop declaring his eagerness for the match. Even his father is mollified: Norman has no children of his own and Charles will be his sole heir. We will have 40,000 *livres* a year, a great sum and large enough to keep us in all the gowns, instruments, and books I desire.

After the meeting I retire to my chamber and stare blankly at the ceiling. Mama comes in and kisses me on the head.

"You made a conquest today, my dearest."

I bite my tongue. A conquest—he's just a boy. And an insignificant one at that.

"He's not very handsome," I say finally. Charles is barely taller than I am and his small, fine features remind me of a rat. When he said goodbye he gave an awkward bow and stumbled over his words: *Mill we tweet again.* I think of my favorite portrait of the king—his curved mouth, the dark eyes and the kind elegance of his gaze. Charles has no position at Versailles and probably never will.

"Now, Reinette, since when does beauty in a man matter? You will be married, dearest. An important first step in your life, and one that we hope will lead to greater things."

"He stepped on my skirt when he bowed goodbye," I continue. "And what was that awful orange coat he was wearing? It looked at least a decade old."

Mama softens and takes me in her arms. "We could not work miracles, even though you are known throughout Paris as the most desirable and accomplished of young women. We wish for a dazzling match for you, but we must also face reality."

"He stutters. Couldn't even say one sentence correctly."

"Enough, Reinette! We must all do things we do not wish," she says crossly. A hard look passes over her face; I wonder what past hurt she is considering. Mama keeps her pain bottled up inside her and always says sorrow is never to be shared.

"*Oui, Maman,*" I say in defeat and hold my smile until she leaves, when I burst into tears.

After the wedding Charles and I move to Uncle Norman's house on the rue Saint-Honoré, just around the corner from my mother's house. Our private life is not very satisfactory; I am not sure that we have accomplished all that we are supposed to, for there is some impatience on his part and I cannot bear to assist in any way. Besides, fumbling and stickiness outside is infinitely preferable to being probed and parted by heavy fingers, or worse, it would be like searching for meat inside a crawfish tail.

When he sleeps—he insists on sleeping in my chamber—I listen to him snore and think how strange it is, this thing that men and women do together. Mama and Uncle Norman have done what I do now. Or at least what we are trying to do now. How extraordinary. And this is what I will do with the king, when I become his mistress. It will be different with the king, of course; more like the mating of angels described by the poets. It must be.

From Madame de Tencin
Rue Quincampoix, Paris
June 15, 1741

My dear Comtesse d'Étiolles,

Let me be the first to congratulate you on your marriage. Your husband is a man of fine family, and your accomplishments are known far and wide. The singer Jelyotte, a good friend of mine, cannot stop boasting of your talents.

I would be honored if you would attend one of my little gatherings. Nothing grand, but a place of good wit and conversation, fine manners and bold discourse. If I may be so blunt, my salon boasts a more refined yet varied selection of society than the salon of Madame Dupin; the goal of *my* salon is to drive away the boredom, not encourage it.

You may attend alone. Your uncle, though I love him dearly, is no asset to a gathering of wit and conversation, and your husband occupies that sad place where desire to sparkle outstrips talent, and it would be best if he stayed there.

Wednesday next; many ladies enjoy dressing in an informal style.

Please reassure me that you will attend, and do not doubt my sincerest regards.

Tencin

Chapter Five

At the Parisian salons all classes and ranks mingle—poets and peers, writers and dukes, beautiful women and young men with nothing more than their wit—and this raises the most important of questions: Why is a man inferior simply because he doesn't have a title? Can one really say that the Marquis de Villemur, renowned for his stupidity, is a better man than Voltaire?

Now that I am married, I may attend these gatherings and seek the answer myself.

"You came! Wonderful. We must see this little gem that all of Paris is bubbling about," says Madame de Tencin, running her closed fan over my cheek. She is an older woman with lively, darting eyes and a face as wrinkled as a roasted apple. A perfume burner sends wafts of lavender and geranium throughout the elegant room, papered with pastoral scenes for an enchanting effect.

"Yes, yes, this is the future and she is here," she says, laughing rather hoarsely. "Younger, blonder, prettier. Three words to sum it up."

"Ah, but, Madame, does she have the wit and the conversation? Youth and beauty are fleeting, but wit outlasts us all," says the Chevalier de Rohan, coming to her side. They inspect me as one might a horse before purchase, Rohan stroking his sword handle in a slow, suggestive manner.

"Well, that we shall find out, shan't we, my dear?" says Madame de Tencin.

I hide my nervousness as she takes my arm and leads me around, introducing me as the Comtesse d'Étiolles, niece of Monsieur le Normant's, goddaughter of Montmartel. No mention is made of my husband or Mama. I meet Cassini, the astronomer, and Crébillon, whose plays I love, and a young British woman, reputed to be his lover, who sits with a yellow finch perched on her silken shoulder. An ancient gnarled man, introduced as the Duc de Broglie, claps his hands in delight and inquires, lustfully, as to who is paying me gallantries.

"Why, no one, Monsieur. My husband is a wonderful man," I answer.

Tencin snorts, a delicate puff of air. "That won't last long, darling, let me assure you."

"I shall be first in line once you decide to avail yourself of the joys of society," declares the old duke gallantly, his eyes creeping down my bodice.

"Then you must wait behind the king," I say, unsure, but then the words feel natural and right. "I shall not deceive my husband with any man, unless that man is the king."

The assembled group twitters and snickers.

"Well said, well said," says Madame de Tencin. "A pleasant way of handling admirers, which you'll sorely need. But don't forget, little fish, fidelity is far too bourgeois for this crowd."

෬

I clamber into Mama's room, flushed. "Oh! How I wish you could have been there."

"Dearest, you know how tired I am these days." I do, but I only spoke kindly; Mama is not received in such places. She is of too low a birth, and is known to have had too many friends. Lovers.

"I met Cassini! And the Polish ambassador said my eyes were spring skies before a storm. Apparently he is a poet. Though very shortsighted."

"And your gown?"

"Quite suitable. Well, no one commented on it. Madame de Tencin's gown was very plain, just some cream linen, and one of the other ladies wore a *belt* around her waist." I finger the bow at my throat and remember how Broglie said my voice was a nightingale's, one that he would like to fall asleep to. I sit down on her bed and kick off my shoes. One of them lands in the ashy fireplace.

"You must be tired if you cannot scold me," I say lightly, caressing her hair.

Mama doesn't answer, so I burble on about the conversation, the entertainment, and the food. "A pyramid of cream meringues in different colors! I never would have thought, but the combination was exquisite and so pretty! I must tell Cook. And so many compliments! The Duc de Broglie said I was as pretty as a peach, and that he would like to be my first lover! And the Marquis de Merquin compared my hair to a . . . well, I mustn't repeat that."

I can't stop myself; I feel alive and invigorated. To be at the center of ideas, expressions, writers, art! And attention.

Later when I am alone I think back to the nasty undercurrents I missed or ignored at the time: the grain of jealousy in Tencin's voice when she admired me; the desperate, quavering voice of the Comte de Nangis, whom everyone ignored and pretended they couldn't hear. The overly sweet inquiries about my mother. So many people, so much self-importance. The Chevalier de Rohan sniping that the Polish ambassador was just a staircase wit, someone who only remembered the right words when he had already left and was in the stairwell. What had they said about me behind my back?

Following my debut, scores of flowers and a fine painted fan arrive, along with several invitations. The next week I meet the great Voltaire. When he sees me he pretends to fall down in ecstasy, saying he has been struck with the gunpowder of love, for one must update Cupid's arrow to our modern times. We are soon discussing what this new missile should be called. It is unanimously decided that Cupid now carries *the rifle of rapture* in his quiver.

Soon I know I am a success by the train of admirers I attract, as well as by what I hear. Some of the rumors make me laugh, but others are more cruel:

"So that's the little bird reserving herself for Our Majesty? I'd say she was his type, she's rather delicious really."

"Any type is his type—look at those Mailly-Nesle trolls."

"Beauty as well as substance; apparently she has brains, buried beneath the fluff."

Despite the fashionable whirlwind my life has become, when I am alone my thoughts still yearn for the king. What I would give for one day at Versailles, one day at the center of his world. At the salons I meet members of the Court; among others the Duc de Duras and the Duc d'Ayen, both intimates of the king. They are courtiers who straddle both worlds, attending the Paris Opéra and mixing with commoners in the salons, then returning to their gilded lives at Versailles.

Though they proclaim my loveliness, I doubt they talk about me to the king—why would they? To them I am just a lovely nothing. Sometimes in my glummer moments I think Versailles is the ultimate salon, but one to which I will never be invited. I am like a fly, on the wrong side of the glass.

They say the king is very sad these days, for his mistress, Pauline de Vintimille, died giving birth to his son. I felt a flare of hope when I heard the news, but then quickly we hear the king is once again in the arms of her sister Louise. I think of Louise often— they say she is not very pretty but is kind, and the king treats her as both a lover and a nurse. Is it possible to be jealous of someone you've never met?

Then we hear he is courting another Mailly sister, the youngest one, the cleverest and most beautiful one.

Her name is Marie-Anne.

From Emmanuel-Félicité de Durfort, Duc de Duras
Hôtel de Duras, rue de Duras, Paris
December 10, 1742

My dear Madame d'Étiolles,

I thank you, dearest Madame, for the invitation which you so
thoughtfully made mine. Your château at Étiolles is divine, and
the supper you hosted shall long remain in my memory. What a
time it was! The carp in jelly broth—as without compare as your
hospitality! The denseness of the liver pie—as sublime as your wit and
conversation! And what a charming idea to match your dress to the
yellow canaries that fluttered around the room as we dined. If I may be
so bold, Madame, I would compare their fluttering to the fluttering in
my loins as I beheld your perfection.

And what a wonderful idea to put on a play in your little theater—
it was as if the role of Ariadne was written just for you. What joy it
would give me to perform with you one day, both on the stage, and off.

My dearest Madame, you have the making of a great hostess, and
soon you will be a threat to the grandest of the Parisian *salonnières*. I
shall be the first to abandon the trite convention of their rooms, should
you desire to start your own salon.

I await the new year, Madame, that you might condescend to offer
me the favor of your regard and the warmth of your embrace. We know
of your fidelity to your husband, but hope rests in my soul as eternal as
the waves and the winds.

Your devoted admirer,
Duras

From Adeline de Villemur, Marquise de Villemur
Château de Chantemerle, Loire Valley, France
April 12, 1743

My dear Comtesse d'Étiolles:

How wonderful that you have agreed to be part of our little gathering next month here at Chantemerle! Society is an insatiable beast, constantly demanding new flesh and distractions, and what pleasure it would give me to host you. Our dear and mutual friend Monsieur de Montmartel—now what would I do without his little loans to insure me against the vagaries of the gambling table?— insisted I invite you and I am indebted, in so many ways, for his wonderful suggestion.

Amongst our guests will be the Duc de Richelieu, an intimate of the king (we like to joke that he is an old friend of the royal family, for he was once found underneath His Majesty's mother's bed). I am sure we will become friends and so I offer you words of advice: Be wary of the duke and his designs. He is a charming man, but also known as the scourge of priests for his ways with women. But no doubt you have much experience fighting off your many admirers—I heard Duras complain last month that you remained unmoved, despite his presentation, bound in calfskin, of his entire illustrious genealogy, dating back to 1050.

We will be performing Marivaux's *The Game of Love and Chance*. In anticipation of our collaboration, I enclose the script; I have chosen the part of Sylvie for you.

Your future friend,
Adeline

Chapter Six

The Marquise de Villemur greets me warmly and leaves me in the care of the wonderfully attentive Duc de Duras, a genial man with a small mouth who always declares himself in raptures when he sees me.

Then I am introduced to the great Duc de Richelieu. The man who could be the key to my future, the man with a reputation for supplying mistresses to the king. He is shorter than I expected and his face is an interesting mixture of arrogance and charm. I remember everything I have heard about him, about all the wicked things he has done with seemingly all the women of France.

"Madame la Comtesse d'Étiolles. Your fame has spread far and wide." His bow is extravagant and obsequious.

With those few words I dislike him; this is a false man, I think, as I curtsy and smile brilliantly at him. He regards me with lecherous eyes and doesn't hide his appraisal of my chest or his examination of my waist. Suddenly I feel naked—a rather extraordinary feeling. I take a step back.

He steps smoothly forward. "Madame d'Étiolles, I have heard so much about you. The most enchanting bird in all of Paris, they say."

"Thank you, sir. You are very kind." I note his choice of words. A bird, if said in the right tone, could mean a loose woman.

"Well prepared for this little trifle, are you?"

"I hope my performance will not disappoint."

"Of course it suits you to act on the stage, being of a more humble caste than the other guests."

I accept the insult and realize that our dislike is mutual. But I must charm him; he must talk of me and praise me to the king. I open my eyes wide and give him the look that sometimes causes Charles to attempt improprieties in the afternoon. "Oh, but sir, it is a most enjoyable pastime, performing. You should try it."

"I? I do not think so. Indeed."

"But, Richelieu, my good man, it is well known that you love actresses," says Duras, clapping him on the back. "And your less than illustrious ancestors included judges and lawyers; perhaps there were some actors in there too? I for one am acting, and am delighted to be doing so."

Richelieu accepts the gibe with a thin smile, then appraises Duras' fussy pink waistcoat, embroidered with swans, that clashes with his yellow stockings. "Don't tell me your eyesight is failing, my dear duke. Mercury and carrot juice! Just the thing."

"But my sight is fine," replies Duras in confusion.

"Come, gentlemen," I say, smiling at both. "Put away your swords and let us see if Madame de Villemur has some supper for us."

The play is a decided success and afterward I am flush with triumph. I love acting: there is nothing finer than to be onstage, channeling beauty through words and song, escaping from my daily life into another world.

"I would talk with you awhile," says Richelieu the next day after Mass, offering me a blue sleeve trimmed with gold lace, the elaborate cuffs almost reaching his elbows. He steers me out into the gardens and down a path lined with hundreds of blooming rosebushes, all in various shades of cream and white. The gardens at Chantemerle are as generous and splendid as the rest of the château.

"I have a friend, who I am sure would be delighted to meet you," he starts.

"Any friend of yours, dear sir, would be a welcome friend of mine." We both know who he is talking about, and suddenly I want to jump in happiness and twirl in the roses. It is only with effort that I keep my stride sedate.

"I have a house in town—to clarify, the town of Versailles. I could welcome you there and arrange for this great friend to meet you, perhaps even a little supper."

While I express my delight and thanks, inside I am sinking. A little town house in Versailles? A midnight assignation? I must not be brought into the king's path like a little *grisette* from the streets, shameful and hidden away. How humiliating. But, really, what was I expecting? Richelieu helped put Marie-Anne in the king's bed and wants to keep her there. He's just looking for some added amusement for his master.

Richelieu notices the change in my demeanor. "Is anything wrong, my dear Madame d'Étiolles? Did I say something amiss?"

"No, of course not, Monsieur." I stop and pick an enormous white rose and inhale its fortifying scent. "You see, my mother is unwell and I am not planning any more journeys this year. You understand?"

"Oh, I do understand," he says, his eyes glazed with hard amusement. "I understand perfectly. Perhaps my invitation will be considered in the future?" We stop before a statue, her stone eyes reflecting my distress. "You are just to the taste of my great friend, for he is a fine gourmand."

"Of course."

After we part I sink down on the bench by the statue and bury my head in my hands. How humiliating. And I have the distinct impression that for all his pretty words, I have not charmed him as much as I should have.

From Charles Guillaume le Normant d'Étiolles, Comte d'Étiolles
Caen, Brittany
August 20, 1743

Dear Wife,

I trust this letter finds you in good health. Thank you for the news of the party you hosted at Étiolles last month and of your performance of *Agrippina*. You know well I wished to see you act, but I suppose it is true that September is too cold and you could not wait for my return.

Please write to me more often, wife. Bardot, Uncle Norman's man here in Caen, says his wife sends him notes daily, informing him of her devotion and duty, and it would give me much joy were you to do the same.

I leave at the end of next week. I will bring you a present, a very handsome cheese I am convinced you will enjoy, though the smell leaves something to be desired.

No, I did not give Bardot my orange coat as you suggested. I have told you, many times, that it is quite my favorite coat and it is not embarrassing, as you claim. Coats cannot be embarrassing.

Here I enclose a verse that I composed. It is efficient in portraying my emotions for you:

> *Darling wife,*
> *You are my life*
> *I will return to you*
> *For now, adieu*

I remain your faithful servant and devoted husband.
Charles

Chapter Seven

Charles does have one redeeming feature: our estate at Éti-olles is in the Forest of Sénart, one of the royal hunting grounds. This is the forest where the king hunts when he stays at the nearby Château de Choisy, and any of the gentry that live in the forest or surrounding areas may follow the royal hunt.

Now I understand better the choice of Charles for me.

Geography will provide an alternative to Richelieu's insulting proposition and smooth sneers. It is here, I decide, it is here in the forest that I will meet him. He would be alone, chasing a magnif-icent stag and intent on his quarry. Then he would come across me, wandering along a sun-dappled forest path, and I would look up and . . .

I shake my head. Time to stop daydreaming and time to start preparing: September approaches and that is when the hunting in Sénart is at its best.

I have a new chestnut mare I name Carnation, her long white mane a few shades lighter than my own. I twine apricot ribbons in her hair to match my dress. Norman gifts me a charming little chaise in the modern style and I have it painted blue with apricot trim on the wheels.

The king arrives at Choisy and this year the deer are abundant and the royal party hunt almost daily. The local gentry are out in force, all of us trying to catch a glimpse of him but seeing only his beaters and hound handlers.

In the evenings I return home dejected, imagining what the king is doing while I sit in front of the fire, eating my supper: Stopping for a drink at the lodge at Mongeron? Riding in a car-

riage with his mistress Marie-Anne, now the Duchesse de Châteauroux? Yesterday I caught a glimpse of her, her perfect face
partially obscured by a gauzy cream veil in the Venetian style. All
of Paris buzzes with their affair. They say the king has never been
so in love, and that she is wrapped around him as tight as a swaddling blanket.

Even if I am at Étiolles and the Court is at Choisy, not a few
miles away, I must accept the sad truth that distance is not always
measured in miles.

Then, a break in the clouds and a ray of hope. The young dauphin joins his father at Choisy and one of his equerries is a distant
relative of Uncle Norman. This man Binet writes to let us know
that father and son will be hunting on Wednesday, and he promises to do his utmost to guide the king to a clearing by the stream
that runs past an old mill.

On the designated day I drive through the forest to the little
clearing by the river, the old stones of the ancient mill lining one
edge. I pull up and wait and Carnation leans down to pick at the
wildflowers by her feet. Something so long anticipated—could it
ever come true?

I wait. And wait. Clouds threaten and an insistent breeze her-
alds a coming storm. It must not rain. Please, God. My nerves
are frayed as the wind whips the ribbons on my hat. Please, no
rain.

Then the sound of hooves to mimic the pounding of my
heart. Binet canters out of the forest, followed by another man.
That it is the king I have no doubt: his face is at once both wonderful and familiar.

"Well, if it isn't the charming Madame d'Étiolles. What an excellent surprise!" declares Binet, as if I am the most unexpected
thing he has ever had the pleasure of seeing. He performs an elegant half bow from his saddle.

"Sire, might I introduce you? The Comtesse d'Étiolles."

"Madame d'Étiolles," says the king, bringing his horse up
alongside my chaise. "So, Binet, this is the doe you thought had

come this way." His voice is low and husky, the tone amused. "Delightful."

"Indeed, Sire, this is the lady that is enchanting Paris, as well as these forests."

"And I can see why. A singular beauty," murmurs the king, looking at me with intense dark eyes. I am staring at him open-mouthed. The face I gazed upon constantly . . . he is even more handsome than his portrait.

"You make a most charming picture, Madame. A veritable Flora."

"A Flora to serve Your Majesty as she did Hercules," I say, fighting to keep my voice steady and light. I want nothing more than to reach over and touch him. He's here, not two feet distant. He's *here*. My king.

Thunder in the distance, bringing the storm closer, then the sound of a hundred hooves as the rest of the hunt closes in. A passel of bloodhounds bursts from the forest, barking loudly. The king's horse wheels around and my horse snickers at the scent of the kill they bring with them.

"All will be wondering where you are, Sire," says Binet, winking at me.

The king canters back to my side and reaches over to take my hand, the suede of his green hunting gloves as soft as moss. He presses my pink-gloved hand to his lips and I can see him inhaling the rose oil I have rubbed over the leather.

"A pleasure, Madame. I do hope we shall meet again." His grip lingers and we stare at each other, holding hands like two little children.

"As do I, Sire." I can barely breathe, or blink. An understanding passes between us, or do I only imagine it does?

Then he releases my hand, catches my heart and spurs his horse. The two men canter out of the clearing, followed by the blood-crazed dogs, calling out to the rest of their party.

Carnation whinnies to be gone but I am frozen as if in enchantment. I am trembling inside and though I want to dismount from my carriage to jump in joy, I fear my legs would not support the weight of my emotions. *I do hope we shall meet again,* he said. I bury my face in my hands and take great gulps of air to satisfy the tightness in my lungs. Something so longed for, so anticipated . . .

Too soon darkness closes around us and reluctantly I turn back to Étiolles. I will remember this day, every detail and every minute sensation of it, forever, even if . . . even if I never see him again.

But such a thought is unthinkable.

&

The next day a brace of hare arrives, their little feet bound with a thick crimson ribbon, a short note attached. *Bearing the compliments of the king,* with a scrawl under the formal words—his signature? I run the ribbon through my hands and sniff the silken skeins, read the note again and again. Was he thinking of me when he signed it?

Cook braises the hares with onions and I lock the ribbon and the note in a small box. My first gift from him. But not the last, I am determined.

Mama is delighted and Uncle Norman is in touch with Binet and others he knows at Versailles, working to find out if the king is talking about me.

Charles is the only one who does not share our delight. One evening he catches me daydreaming by the window, twining the red ribbon in my hands. I smile at him and try to hide my irritation; Norman has promised me that soon he will return to Brittany.

"You've quite lost your silly little head." I don't like it when he calls me silly. I am smarter than he is, and certainly more educated. "He sends such a parcel to all he greets. Do you think he selected the ribbon himself? Do you think he chose four of the hoicest chare, choicest hare, and bound them with his own hands?" As always when he gets flustered, he fumbles his words.

"Darling, jealousy doesn't become you."

"I am not jealous!" explodes Charles. "I am simply tired of this endless talk of the king."

"Then I shall talk no more about our king, if you so wish," I say primly.

He sinks down into a chair and tugs ineffectively at his cravat. "When are you going to give up this childish fantasy, Reinette?"

"It's not a fantasy." From the beginning I have been clear with Charles. I will never be unfaithful to him, except with the king. He knows about the gypsy and the prophecy, and all my hopes.

Suddenly a harder, meaner man emerges. "Prophecies like yours are as common as fleas," he spits. "Was she going to tell you that you'd marry a fishmonger?"

I stare at him.

"Or a lowly comte like myself?"

It is the first time he, or anyone really, has spoken to me so harshly. "I see you think me a fool," I say stiffly.

"Yes, I do. You're just a woolish foman, I mean a foolish woman, a deluded girl. From now on, I call you Jeanne. Or Jeannette, a common name for the common woman you are. Anything but that stupid, idiotic nickname, *Reinette*. I should never have put up with this."

Despite his cruel words, I soften. He has never been anything but good to me, and to be so trifling in all that he does must be difficult. And I have news for him. I waited to tell him in case he forbade me to ride out, but now my goal is accomplished and this news might keep him from my bed tonight.

I clasp his hands. "Darling, enough of this talk that distresses you. I have wonderful news for us." I whisper the words that will make him happy: "You are going to be a father."

My own emotions are uncertain.

Chapter Eight

I am enormously pregnant and I sit and knit and twine and brood and feel as though life is passing me by. I am already twenty-two years old, and here I am, as far away as ever from the king. Since the meeting last year, no word from Versailles. Norman talked with Binet, as well as with Monsieur le Bel, the king's valet, but they had nothing to report—the king never inquired after me. We also heard that Marie-Anne, the Duchesse de Châteauroux, forbade mention of my name and even stomped on the slipper of the Duchesse de Chevreuse, hitting a painful corn, when that lady dared to mention me. But that is all.

Norman is optimistic; he insists the seeds are planted and now we must seek only ways to water. Water, I think grimly, but how barren the earth is beneath my feet.

Now the king is away at war and there will be no hunting this fall, no chance to see him again, no chance for him to clasp my hands and promise that we will meet again. Next year, perhaps, but then I will be another year older, another year more bitter and sad. Is it all over, my chance gone as surely as yesterday? Was that to be the height of my happiness?

Foolish woman, said my husband. Foolish—perhaps I am. Was it foolish to believe in that gypsy woman, foolish to think myself destined for a king?

My little daughter, Alexandrine, is born in early August but her birth does little to raise my spirits. Soon she is sent away to nurse. When I am well enough I visit her, walking through the forest to the village where she stays. I don't daydream anymore, or even linger in the clearing where I met him.

The king, far away in Metz, falls sick unto death. I pray for him, night and day, and wish with all my life that he not die. Then he recovers and the priests read aloud his confession in all the pulpits of France: he has repudiated his mistress, confessed his sins, and now intends to live honorably with the queen again. I allow myself to breathe and hope. Marie-Anne, gone. Cursed woman who has all that I long for.

But then comes the shocking news that the king has renounced his sacred vow and *she* is recalled. Marie-Anne will return to Versailles. She is ink that cannot be erased, a mountain that cannot be moved.

൦ഃ

I pull myself from the dark pit I find myself in. I must accept that my stage is Paris, not Versailles. I decide I will return to the city, enjoy the New Year's festivities, and look to 1745 to bring me some happiness and cheer. And forget my foolish dreams of a destiny I don't deserve.

I gaze out the window at the swaying trees, their gnarled branches curled like the fingers of an old, old man. Cold rain splatters down and I shiver at the bleak landscape. A horse canters up the drive, narrowly missing a swaying beech branch. I note the colors but can't place them.

The footman enters with a letter. "From the Duc de Richelieu, Madame," he announces with a bow. Richelieu. Of course, the white and red chevrons of the rider's habit. What—a cruel note to rub salt in my wounds, to remind me I will never be at the king's side?

I tear open the seal and read the contents. The note slips from my hand and falls to the floor, and I follow it quickly in a faint. When I revive, blinking and disoriented, I remember.

Marie-Anne.

Marie-Anne is *dead*.

I look at the letter again.

I write this before her blood is even cold, says the hastily scrawled note. *I wanted to be the first to tell you. She is dead, suddenly, from a high fever. The king is inconsolable, but the way is now clear.*

The way is now clear.

ↄ৲

"There is no time to be lost. We must strike while the iron is hot," declares Norman.

"That is *entirely* the wrong metaphor." My mother is lying on a chaise by the fire, swaddled in white woolens, her face wan and tired. "We are talking about a dead woman whom the king adored. He is no doubt in deep mourning, and will remain so for quite a while." She coughs and I watch her anxiously; she denies all mention of her illness.

"The king has a history of rebounding rather quickly," Norman insists. "Wasn't it only a few months after Vintimille's death that this last one replaced her sister? And there are rumors he is back already with the fat one . . . what is her name?"

"Diane," I say. Not beautiful, but reputed to be kind and funny. It is only eight days since the news; surely he is not taken already?

"Yes, Diane de Lauraguais—a whale of an enemy," Norman remarks. His jest falls flat. "But with his predilection for that family, and his love of the familiar—"

"What are they saying about Louise, the Comtesse de Mailly?" I ask anxiously.

"Nothing, as far as we know; she is still in Paris and is excessively religious now. As is her sister Hortense, though she remains at Court."

A carriage rolls into the snow-covered courtyard. Charles is due to return this week and I do hope it is not him. A footman enters and announces the Duc de Richelieu.

"Madame," he says, bowing as the footman brushes snow from his enormous silver-furred cape. Richelieu is now my friend—his note showed that. When he said the way was clear, he could not have meant to his house in town, for I could have gone there anytime. After a few terse pleasantries, I decide the bold course is the best course.

"And pray, sir, what do you think the right move is?" I ask.

"Why, the opportunity is now," Richelieu says. "As I indicated in my note. I do believe the king would be most delighted to meet you."

"And we are only talking about a meeting?" asks my mother sharply.

"Certainly, to pique the curiosity." His tone is as frosty as the night outside as he lays his gloves on the table. "But then . . . I am not sure what you expect."

The gauntlet sits, pristine and untouched, for all to see.

"We expect the king to fall in love with our charming daughter," says Norman mildly, as if anyone would be a fool to think otherwise.

There is silence into which Mama eventually speaks: "They must meet in a proper fashion. Our Reinette is not to be treated as a little bit on the side."

Richelieu raises his brows but says nothing. He walks around the room, lifts a stuffed duck from the sideboard, puts it down quickly, runs a light finger over the wooden mantel. Presently he turns back to us: "I will be frank. There is no question of our dear Reinette being presented at Court, no question of any *official* liaison. Had I known that you entertained such lofty, and, might I say, *deluded* ambitions, I would not have wasted my time. Your daughter is delightful"—he bows to Mama—"and the king is a fine gourmand who makes it his business, and pleasure, to sample the most delicious morsels—"

"Do not speak of my daughter as a piece of food," interrupts Mama.

"I speak in the metaphors you might understand, Madame *Poisson*."

"Are you suggesting," continues my mother stiffly, "that Madame d'Étiolles is—"

"No, no, no," Richelieu interrupts with a voice as mild as milk. "You misunderstand me, Madame. I'm not suggesting she is a fishmonger's daughter, or the granddaughter of a butcher. No—not at all. Did you hear me say that? I'm merely saying she is not of the nobility. Of that, there can be no doubt." He raises his eyebrows. "Despite her current . . . what shall we call it? Title?"

The atmosphere in the room has grown sour and poisonous. So Richelieu has not changed his mind about me. Cursed man. I notice for the first time how heavy his nose is, the row of moles stretching down his left cheek. If he were not Richelieu, he would not be the most attractive of men.

"Sir, my mother is unwell, I do not think we need to discuss such things at this time," I say, but my voice wavers more than I want.

"No, Reinette," says Norman firmly, raising his hand. "We *do* need to discuss this now. There can be no better time."

Richelieu shrugs, irritation straining his features. "We cannot change birth, and we all know this modern talk of equality is just a fairy tale. There has never been a bourgeois mistress at Versailles, and there never will be. As the king's oldest friend, I make his happiness my business. Your charming daughter would be just the thing right now to cheer him of his sorrow. But dreams of Versailles and something more official . . . *never.*"

Norman is watching Richelieu with amused indulgence, a look that I can see lies sorely with the duke, who turns to me and continues: "I am sorry if I have misled expectations. I mean you no disrespect, Madame; I am one of your keenest admirers, but the reality is that you are simply not suited for Versailles."

My husband comes in, kicking the snow from his boots. "Six feet high, the drifts were uncommon, we passed a frozen cow . . ." Charles slows down, the tension in the room sharp enough to pierce his thick head. "Two, actually. Two frozen cows." He looks around and stammers: "Gat is who-ing on?"

"Nothing, I believe," says Richelieu. "Absolutely nothing." He reclaims his gloves and leaves without bothering to bow to my husband. Norman hugs me tightly as I lean against him, sobbing.

"Don't mind that trumped-up popinjay," Norman says kindly. "We have powerful friends that the duke sorely underestimates. You must not worry, dearest."

From Jean Paris de Montmartel
Quartier de Marais, Paris
January 2, 1745

My dearest Goddaughter,

An exceptional alignment of the stars that would impress even the great astronomer Halley. The infanta arrives from Spain next month and there will be many festivities to celebrate her marriage to the dauphin. An invitation for one of the Court balls will be secured for you. There is no need to impress upon you how important this chance is, as the king struggles to overcome his sorrow and fill the hole left by the death of Châteauroux.

Much is expected of you; we will support you in whatever way you require and we are confident that our investment in your education and upbringing will bear fruit. I dine at Norman's on Saturday. If your time permits, join us that we may discuss this fortuitous development. I am envisioning a cozy dinner and there is no need to inconvenience your husband to attend.

Yours respectfully,
Paris de Montmartel

Chapter Nine

"No, no, no," says Mama when she sees my intended costume. "Your colors are pale and pretty, Reinette. Black and white are colors of death and mourning! Do you want to remind His Majesty of his grief?"

"Everyone else will be wearing light, pretty colors," I say mildly. I must stand out. I am modeling myself on the mistress of Henri II, Diane de Poitiers, who always wore black and white. And Diana, the Roman huntress who so skillfully captured her quarry. A saddler has made me a supple leather quiver of silver cloth, which I will fill with real arrows.

"Reinette is right," says Norman, watching the dressmakers bustle around me. "I predict a surfeit of shepherdesses and nymphs. And birds, no doubt, wanting to nest in the royal tree." Rumor from Versailles is that the king and his entourage are planning to dress as Yew Trees. "Mesdames de Brionne, de la Popelinière, de Portaille, and those are only the ladies of Paris. I needn't remind you of Antin, Périgord, Rohan, not to mention that fat Diane and her sister Hortense." He ticks them off one by one on his fingers. "They all have their sights set on the king, and they are all bound to be in some frothy light costume."

Norman's predictions are soon confirmed; through spies and friends we learn that the Parisian ladies will be birds and shepherdesses. Our friends Binet and the king's valet Le Bel provide us news from Court: the beautiful Marquise d'Antin, known as the Marvelous Mathilde, is keeping her dress a secret, but rumors abound she will be a Canary. Diane de Lauraguais is dressing as a Cat, and her sister Hortense as a Rosebush.

We swear our dressmakers to silence and put out word that I

will be dressed as a Pink Dove. I know I have planned correctly: simplicity is what will stand out. And, I remind myself, I do have some powerful friends.

☙

Versailles, at last. I have been here for six miserable hours already, trying to keep sweat and flying wine from ruining my white bodice, and my arrows from being stolen. From my quiver I take a small bottle of scent to rub on my neck. The press is extreme, the rooms a fog of billowing silks, crushed flowers, and wax fumes from the thousands of candles burning in the chandeliers above.

Versailles, at last, but I cannot even enjoy my first glimpses of the splendid palace: the richness of the rooms, the startling perfection and symmetry, the impression that one is walking through a world made entirely of crystal and gold. All is lost beneath the crush and scrum of a thousand people or more.

A Turk pushes rudely past. A Potted Flower faints and is carried from the room by a Chinaman and a Roman. Three Dancing Nymphs look on in amusement as a stampede erupts: they have opened another buffet room. Through the enormous gold-paneled doors I catch a glimpse of tables piled with food: all manner of fish dishes, for it is still Lent, and hundreds of cakes and sweet pastries, including, I overhear a rotund Cat say, some twenty-seven varieties of pie.

The king has not yet arrived. Only the dauphin and his new wife are here, dressed as a Shepherd and Shepherdess. The new dauphine is impressing no one with her looks or her stilted manners. I hear the nasty whispers that float around me, mostly about her aversion to rouge and her red hair she refuses to hide with powder.

As foreseen, there are a great number of birds, including a particularly ravishing Yellow Finch, as well as a sense that time is running out—where is the king?

"Come," brays a Donkey softly. Binet? He guides me through to the Hercules Salon and pushes me through a door, concealed in the paneling next to the chapel entrance. I find myself in a small, dark room, no wider than my skirts. I sink to the floor, glad to be free of the crowds and the noise, terrified of what will happen next, or not.

An hour or more passes.

A Devil and a Cat crash through the door and the woman—at least I think it is a woman—shrieks in horror to find their tryst hole occupied. As they back away I can hear the commotion from outside—the king and his entourage have finally arrived!

Then Binet opens the door of the little room to tell me that Madame de la Popelinière left gleefully with a Yew Tree—but she will discover only the Duc de Nivernois beneath the leaves. Another Yew was seen chatting with the queen; all agree that one couldn't possibly be the king.

"Don't worry, charming one, we are taking care of you. Wait," he says, then he is gone.

The room is hot and dark and it closes around me. Can I trust Binet and Le Bel? What if they keep me here until the king, and my chances, are gone? I am about to go and find him myself when the door opens again and the Donkey trots back in, followed by another man holding a candle. He is leafy but unmasked, and instantly I recognize him.

"Sire, as promised, the Huntress of Sénart."

"Flora from the Forest," the king says, bowing low over my hand. "Now transformed into Diana the Huntress. How lovely you are." His voice is a well of admiration, warm and honeyed.

I have anticipated this, planned this, dreamed of this for so long; now all I can do is gaze at him in wonder. Binet leaves and we are alone with only a solitary candle flickering. Though we don't speak, something passes between us: an understanding, a beginning, a destiny.

He raises the candle closer.

"I remembered correctly how beautiful you are," he says in his glorious voice, rasping velvet. "You are ravishing, Madame." Though he is as handsome as ever, I see sadness in his eyes.

"You are not so well," I say, and without thinking I reach out a hand to touch his cheek, then snatch it back in horror. He smiles and takes my hand, returns it to his face.

"I think you may be my tonic," he says, then brings my hand to his lips. Gently he takes one of my fingers in his mouth, and I want to faint at the sensation.

Too soon there is a scratch at the door and this time it is Le Bel, dressed as a Bat. The king releases my hand and reaches over my trembling heart to pluck one of the arrows from my quiver. He whispers in my ear, close and intimate: "Until Paris."

"Until Paris, Sire," I echo, and then he is gone and the force of anticipation and desire overwhelms me. I sink once more down to the floor. It is beginning. I'm going to faint, or—God forbid—vomit.

Chapter Ten

News of my rendezvous with the king quickly leaks and throngs of well-wishers crowd our house. I greet all the visitors and listen politely to their advice. My stomach is bound in knots and I am surviving on bouillon and the knowledge that I will see him again soon.

Last night Sylvie from the kitchens replaced my tea with a glass of milk, and solemnly told me the story of her cousin, used and abused by a horse trader who, already having the horse, did not bother to buy her a bridle. I drank the glass of milk defiantly, down to the last drop.

Binet brings tidings from Court and pulls me into a corner: "Now, who would buy the chicken if they're eating eggs every day? The Duchesse de Châteauroux held off on the eggs, and received the farm, as well as a castle."

"You don't feed the fish you've already caught, now do you?" says Madame de Tencin, waggling a gnarled finger at me.

What? I want to say, but instead: "I am sorry, Madame, but I am not sure I catch the way of your words."

Others chime in.

"No one wants the beaver if they already own the hat."

"Why purchase the book if you can borrow it? Libraries—the brothels of the literary world, my dear."

"Who would buy the whole hog if all they want is a little sausage? No, wait, Madame, ignore those last words; I spoke ill."

I flee the salon for the peace of my chambers. I want them all to go away, to do anything but give me more of their tiresome advice. I cannot explain, even to my dearest mother, what I know in my heart: strategy, subterfuge, plans and plots—I do not need them.

I reach under the mattress and pull out the note, so secret that no one else has seen it. I received it three days ago and the words make real his whispered promise: *Until Paris.*

Fairest Flora, it is with delight and anticipation that I write this note. I must see you again—the ball at the Hôtel de Ville. Be by the back door, and wait for Ayen.

℘

My gown, a gift from my godfather de Montmartel, is a diaphanous gray-blue silk, the skirt three floating layers of gossamer that match my eyes perfectly. No one can stop staring at me. Tonight there is an added ingredient, and one that draws my beauty to the highest peak: love.

The rooms of the magnificent Hôtel de Ville are draped with vines and flowers and crushed with people. This ball is without invitation and soon the slim barricades are overturned as the masses flood in. I narrowly miss a jug of ice falling off a water bearer's shoulders and strangers shove me more times than I can count. I receive homage from some; dark gray looks from others.

Then I recognize the Duc d'Ayen battling his way toward me, his wig rising above the close-hatted crowd like a majestic white tower. Without a word he throws a thick black domino over me and ushers me through a back door, out into the magical night, thick snowflakes falling slowly through the cold air.

I climb into the waiting carriage and there he is, also wrapped in a black cloak and wearing a three-cornered hat and a red mask. He kisses me on the cheek and puts his arm around me and I settle beside him. It is the first time we are in such proximity and I wonder at how there is nothing more natural in the world than sitting thus, as though my body were a rib carved to fit with his. I have come home, I think. The world has come right.

"Where to, my lovely?" he whispers in my ear. Nowhere: I want to sit like this forever, but the carriage has already started, the driver crying out to the crowds to part for us as we enter the main road.

"Rue des Bons Enfants," I say, and give directions to my mother's house and childhood home, not far from where we are. The carriage crawls slowly through the clogged streets, the whole town drunk on festivities and fireworks, the snow and the moon illuminating the scene.

"By God, but the way is slow," complains the Duc d'Ayen, sitting opposite us, trying to free his tall wig from the upholstery on the coach ceiling.

"I can think of no finer way to pass the time," says the king, his hand tightening round my waist. "We could be trapped until next Tuesday for all I care."

I am floating, I am free, I am euphoria unbound, tethered only to this world by the gentle pressure of his arm encircling me.

"What an adventure, my dear, what an adventure," says the king, burying his face in my neck. "Twenty-four bodyguards, and not a one of them knows where I am."

I say nothing, for nothing needs to be said.

As I have planned, the house is empty but for the few servants who stay in the shadows. The king enters, curious and excited; I am sure he has never before been inside such a humble house. But he knows what I am, and what I am not; I will not be ashamed of where I come from.

"What a delightful room!" he exclaims. "So small and cozy. So small," he repeats, looking around. "The ceilings hardly higher than my head! What a cozy effect." He wanders around, picks up a wooden candlestick, peers curiously at a small oil painting of a dog that hangs above the mantel. "And the carpet—now would that be a *cow skin?*"

I quietly lock the door; the servants have strict instructions but it may be hard to keep them out. I note in satisfaction that all is in readiness: the decanter filled with Madeira, the plate of pickled eggs, the heavy felt blanket on the table beside the sofa. I take a glass of milk, sitting in isolation on a sideboard, and pour it into a potted plant.

"I'll light us a fire, Sire."

"How interesting that you know how to light a fire, my dear, you quite astonish me! What other skills might you have that I do not know of?"

I blush and he laughs too, regretting the double entendre.

He settles on the sofa to watch me.

Soon the fire blazes and I sit on the floor in front of it, warming my hands, aware that he is behind me. Louis—*my* Louis. At last. I untie the great cloak and it falls around me in a velvet lake. I take a deep breath, then look back at him with all the hope, happiness and love in the world, written plainly on my face.

He joins me on the floor in front of the fire and the enormity of what is about to happen dawns on me: I have to admit my daydreams have never gotten quite this far. With soft fingers he reaches for my nape and at his touch an exquisite pain shoots through me. Then his fingers are on my neck and my hair and his breath is coming in shallow, ragged waves.

"Oh my dear, you are so beautiful," he breathes, running his hands over my bodice, grappling and kneading my flesh with urgency. Suddenly I am in his arms, burying myself beneath the wonder of his body, my hands all over him, and I too am tugging and pulling him toward me and we are both straining with my clothes—the undressing was not something I had considered fully—but at long last we are naked in front of the fire. Then I am caressing him, pulling at his hair, urging him inside me, pushing him toward his rapture.

When it is over and he lies on top of me, I don't have any desire to push his sweaty body away; instead I want to lie like this forever, him still pulsing inside me, buried by his body and the force of his desire for me.

Making love with the king is unlike anything I have known before, so hard where Charles was soft, and so soft where Charles was hard. But one does not compare a stallion to a pony or a candle to the sun, I think in satisfaction. We lie together all the night, safe in each other's arms, and once again I have that strange feeling that I have known him all my life, and that I have come home at last.

From François Paul le Normant de Tournehem
Rue Saint-Honoré, Paris
March 5, 1745

Reinette,

Your silence is simply unacceptable. We hear you are lodged at Versailles in a room under the attics, where all the world knows the king brings his little fancies. We are dismayed by the news that, despite our best advice, it appears you have kept nothing back from him.

We fear you have made a grievous mistake and one that cannot be undone. How can you be in ignorance of that rule of nature which causes men to lose interest once they have too easily achieved their heart's desire? Are you so full of feminine silliness that your head is turned by a few words of flattery from an important man?

Your mama is worried sick. Her health is suffering and Charles is demanding to know where you are. If you do not increase your communication, or return to Paris and put an end to this disgraceful behavior, I cannot promise I will keep him away as I have in the past.

To ignore our counsel, after all we as a family have worked for, is simply unacceptable. Please come back to Paris, though I fear the king will tire of you and return you soon enough. We still love you dearly and want only what is best for you.

Norman

Chapter Eleven

I crumple Norman's letter. I know I have been remiss in not writing, but I cannot explain what they will never understand.

The week after the ball at the Hôtel de Ville I traveled here in a covered coach, entered through a back door, and made my way up a staircase too narrow for panniers. Now here I stay in this little room that love has made perfect. I am closeted, cosseted, somnolent and dreaming, only coming to life when he is with me.

And though I am secluded from the rest of the palace, I am at the center of everything, for this room holds his heart. I know this, but can't explain it to Uncle Norman or Mama and so I hide away from them, like a little girl playing peek-a-seek.

The king and I are hopeless in our infatuation; never have I felt such a deep connection. I am besotted by him and I tell him so frankly, and he tells me the same. There is no need for artifice or coyness, the shy and light lies that can fill the world of courtship. In our love, there is no room for doubt.

He says I am Nature's most angelic creation, and that my eyes are the most beautiful he has ever seen. Eyes are the window to the soul, he says, and so I must be the kindest woman on earth. When we make love—I had no idea a man could perform with such frequency and intensity—I feel as though I am lost in enchantment.

And as the man behind the myth that he always was for me comes slowly clear, I find only more to love: he is gallant, tender, eager to please, intelligent and thoughtful.

"From two different worlds," he says one night. He had been in tiresome ceremonies all day, and the look of relief and joy on his face when he was finally able to join me transported me straight to

Heaven. "Two such different worlds." He traces my breasts with one light finger. "They say there are some twenty million people in my kingdom, yet I know only a small fraction of them."

"You live a narrow life," I murmur. "Yours is a confined world."

"Ha! I would not have described my life thus, but you see the truth in ways I do not."

It is because I am an outsider, not of your world, I want to say, but don't.

"Yet out of all those millions, how do two people like us find each other?" he muses, his fingers now twirling in my hair, gently tugging my face to his so we can kiss again. "There you were, in the forest, and then again at the ball—that fate could have thrown us together in such a way. Indeed, God exists."

I am silent. Surely he knows there is intrigue surrounding his every step? But I adore his delight in the universe that threw us together. And why not? It was an improbable, impossible leap from where I was, to where I am now.

"Such slim strands of fate," he continues. "There was a delightful Finch at that same ball—I was tempted by her, but then she appeared to lose one of her wings, and I was distracted and then led to that little room. When I saw you again . . ." He pauses and takes a deep breath: "It was as though I found a dream I could believe in."

"I knew we were going to meet," I say before I can stop myself.

Louis sits up and looks down at me in astonishment. "How did you know? There were a thousand if not more at that ball. I daresay there were others that wished to make my acquaintance?"

"I knew we were going to meet long before the forest or the ball," I confess, uncertain how he will react. "When I was a child, a fortune-teller told me I would have the love of a king. I decided it would be you."

"You believed her?" He chuckles. "And you knew it would be me? And not some other 'king'? My hound handler's name is Le Roi."

I laugh. "I hoped it would be you. We had your portrait in our house and I looked at it every day. I would stare at your face and think: One day, this man will love me."

"How wondrous," he says in amazement. "How wondrous a thing is love, is life indeed."

He loves to be cuddled after we make love; his need for affection, in all its forms, is insatiable. I stroke him until he falls asleep in my arms, then I trace his cheeks and lips, lightly brush his forehead, all the while marveling at my fortune. Yes, there was intrigue, yes there were plans, but none of it would have come to anything if this one thing had not been true: Louis and I are made for each other. There were others that could have filled his bed, but he chose me.

And I chose him.

☙

"I'm off to war," he announces after we have made love for the second time. "Those scurrilous Austrians will take the world if we do not contain them, and the Maréchal de Saxe assures me my presence will turn the tide." We are at war with the Austrians; almost four long years now as France battles the succession of the empress Maria Theresa to the Austrian throne.

My thoughts fly to the last time he was with the army, at Metz—he almost died. And how could he go and abandon me?

"You would leave me," I say quietly, removing myself from his embrace and sitting up. I look out the window: it stormed all night and now the dawn rises brilliantly, the vast sky rife with pink-tinged clouds.

"Now, now. Come back here, lovely. I have a plan for you," Louis says, his eyes twinkling, an impish grin lighting his face. "While I am away, you are to spend the summer preparing yourself. For this world. It would amuse me to undertake your education; I shall be your Pygmalion, my fair lady."

I lower my lashes. He wants me beside him, at Versailles, out in his world. A tremendous step, but his love is stronger than convention and history. My happiness is overshadowed only by the knowledge that this intimate world of ours is coming to an end, that the strands of the silk cocoon are starting to unravel.

"I'm afraid," I whisper. Down there, in *ce pays-ci*, this country, as they call it, there is malice and spite, tests and challenges, hurdles and pitfalls. All waiting for me. "What if they don't love me?"

"Don't be afraid," he whispers back. "They will love you, because I do."

"You will come back to a changed woman," I declare, covering his face with kisses.

"Not too changed, I hope," he replies lightly. "Just someone who . . ." He can't express to me directly what the change is, but we both know: someone who will not embarrass him with her bourgeois ways.

"Say no more," I say, placing a finger against his lip. "I know what you mean. And I promise: I will not disappoint." I am an excellent actress, I want to add. Then I decide he doesn't need to know that, not just yet.

∽

"Come." It is three hours past midnight; too late for the revelers, too early for the servants. He leaves for the front next Thursday and I have seen little of him these past few days. We follow a footman through the great halls of the palace, draped in the silence of the night, empty save for a few guards obscured in the shadows. We climb a back staircase to a wide, plain corridor and he ushers me through the open door.

"No need for candles," he says, and it is true: the room is bathed in silver moonlight. "You will be very happy here, I believe."

I explore the apartment: five large rooms, three small ones, a delightful bed in a niche, draped now in white curtains.

Marie-Anne, the Duchesse de Châteauroux—the previous occupant of this apartment—had good taste. I look out one of the tall windows over the quiet of the North Parterre, farther still beyond to the Fountain of Neptune. A faint smell of carnations lingers in the air. Though the rooms are empty, traces of her presence still remain. I shiver when I realize she must have stood in this same spot, looked out this same window.

Many claim she haunts the palace and they say the queen is afraid of her ghost. The courtiers scoff that if Marie-Anne were to come back, it would be highly unlikely that she would seek out the company of the queen.

No, she might not visit the queen, but she would come back here to these rooms, to the site of her life and her triumph. And she would want to see her replacement, the woman who took the life she should have had. I shiver as the ghosts of dead mistresses swirl around me. Pauline, dead in childbirth; Marie-Anne, dead so suddenly and in such agony; Louise, banished and all but dead.

"They will be redecorated, of course," says the king, "to your tastes." Then he is silent and a sad, empty look fills his face. We haven't talked about Marie-Anne, but I know he still mourns her. I must let him; she is no rival. Not now.

"Come away, this is not the time," he says suddenly, and turns abruptly to leave.

From Madeleine Poisson
Rue des Bons Enfants, Paris
May 2, 1745

Darling Daughter,

    You cannot know how happy we are with your news! Our faith in you is restored; we should never have doubted. Uncle Norman is ecstatic and your godfather Montmartel sent me a handsome fire screen, worked entirely in silver, along with a kind note expressing his delight. He wrote that while the king is away at war consolidating France's future, you will be consolidating your (and our) future. Of course you will not forget him, Montmartel, I mean, now that you have the king's favor.

    I won't write much; I am tired today. Whilst at Étiolles do not forget to visit Alexandrine—I enclose a little wool chemise I knitted for her. Norman will visit frequently and ensure you have all you desire.

    How strange and wonderful it is that the woman's prophecy should have come true, and in such a way. I did not tell you this before, but now I will: I know who she is. She is settled on the rue Saint-Martin, with a respectable name, and we must not forget her as you rise in this world.

    Much love,
    Mama

Chapter Twelve

"You must consider etiquette as you would your catechism. No, no, Madame, I say nothing of sacrilege, for etiquette is like the word of God: we ignore it at our peril."

My new tutor is the Abbé de Bernis, a moon-faced young man with kind eyes and delicate little hands, exquisitely refined, more courtier than cleric. Though his lineage is impeccable (as he does not fail to remind me) he is as poor as a rat in winter, and so has condescended to be my tutor.

We are in the dining room at Étiolles, papers strewn out on the vast table before us: lessons, vocabularies, lists of dukes and peers, names to memorize.

"Stools and low chairs: certainly the rules are very clear and we have been over them at length. But, Madame, what about high-back chairs, or armchairs with ears? And oh! Don't get me started on those newfangled reclining chairs, an innovation I may value in terms of comfort, but what problems they present in terms of everyday life and usage! What anarchy will reign amongst us now? Oh my!"

Bernis reaches for a handkerchief and delicately pats his face; occasionally he is a little overdramatic. He takes a deep breath, and we continue our discourse on chairs and seating.

"Do not underestimate the power of the *tabouret,* the sacred stool that inspires respect when seated. The Rohans, for example, do not allow the wives of their younger sons to be present at Court, as they may not all be seated as befits the pride of that ancient family." Bernis sighs and shakes his head, though whether he is upset with the wives, or the stools, it is hard to tell.

"As well, where one sits in a carriage is of the utmost importance. The Duc de Luynes is very adept at all matters concerning carriage seating; should you have any doubts, he is the man to ask. And I remind you again: to break the rules of etiquette for advantage is permissible; to break them from ignorance is barbaric."

In addition to chairs, I learn about fingers and hats and tones of voice; about precedence and the correct procedure for greeting a duchess, and then a duchess who is also a peer. I learn about opening doors, and having doors opened for you; who may take a chair through which rooms, and who may not. Who may dance with a princess of the blood, and who may never, under any circumstances, approach one. When to wear a mantle, when not to. The words I may use, the words I must never say.

"And the Prince de Monaco, a man with no rank in France, petitioned to be allowed to dance with Mesdames, the king's daughters, and the question of the most vexing sort was whether his application should be viewed through the lens of his standing as a prince of a foreign principality, or through his lack of title in France . . ." As Bernis drones on I think about the labyrinth that is my new life. Like a lace handkerchief of the most intricate design, made up of a thousand delicate threads forming a pattern I must memorize.

"And the Comtesse de Noailles," counsels Bernis. "Another excellent source of information. Married to the Duc de Noailles' second son. Though young, she has a very rigid sense of occasion, not to mention precedence."

"Indeed," I say. Much of it—all of it?—sounds convoluted and against all common sense. But if I can learn one hundred songs by heart, I can certainly learn how to address a duchess.

In addition to my lessons, I greet an endless stream of visitors; everyone with the faintest strand of connection makes the pilgrimage to Étiolles, either to remind me of our affiliation or to inspect the king's latest fancy. Everyone is admitted; I have been counseled that I must not foster enemies. Enemies—I don't think I have had one in my life, and I don't intend to start now!

Everyone is welcome except my husband.

Poor Charles is now tucked away safely in the provinces, apparently prostrate with grief. Though he may implore me through a hundred letters, my conscience is clear. I am breaking no promises, and certainly he will prosper from his connection to me. I must look to the future and poor Charles is but a remnant of the past.

The faces of those visitors that consider me no more than a passing fancy are marked by a cool demeanor and flat eyes, their readiness to sneer and turn away. I catch whispers and comments:

"Certainly pretty, but the Lord knows beauty can never overcome the taint of blood."

"What is he thinking? I mean really, what is he thinking? She's a *bourgeoise*."

"Didn't the Comte de Carillon marry a coachman's daughter? And then he went mad?"

"Don't worry, she's just a passing fancy. She can't compare to the Marvelous Mathilde, or even to Hortense de Flavacourt."

Along with visitors, every day brings long letters from the king, wrapped in red velvet ribbons and sealed with the gallant words *Discreet and Faithful*. He declares his love ever stronger as he keeps me updated on the course of the war, including our triumphs at Fontenoy and other faraway places. This summer France can do no wrong and the king says I am as a charm, both for him and his country.

Voltaire visits and we sit in the garden, surrounded by the heavenly scent of hyacinths, and I compose a verse for the king.

> *My longing is true and pure and blue*
> *I sigh for you, for the memory of you, for simply you.*

"Passable, Madame, passable," chuckles Voltaire. "I like the first line—longing is indeed blue—but I believe we can make it better."

Beside me Bernis stiffens; he does not approve of the man.

Voltaire is a dreaded *philosophe,* and all *philosophes* are considered atheists and therefore not welcome at Court. I nod gravely but pay him no mind; when I am established at Court, I shall invite Voltaire and cultivate all the great writers and philosophers. Bernis fancies himself a poet—his specialty is light, spontaneous verse—and I sense he is jealous of Voltaire. In turn, Voltaire once called him a fat flower girl.

"Let me suggest, Madame . . ." Voltaire sucks on his quill; his tongue is permanently stained black with ink. A pause, then the wheels of genius rumble into motion:

> *My longing is true and pure and blue*
> *Forget-me-nots; cobalt; the sky in June*
> *That is my desire for you.*

&

"My darling Jeannette! Cousin!" The voice is high-pitched and affected. A small fleshy woman with plump cheeks, like two lumps of melted cheese, descends on me. "To see you again, and after all these years! How precious you look, darling. As pretty as ever. I came as soon as Bernis told me."

I step back, uncertain, then realize it is Elisabeth, one of the girls I took dancing lessons with.

I look around for Bernis but he is nowhere to be found.

"You look enchanting, my dear, simply enchanting!" The woman has taken my arm and is steering me down the steps of the terrace, away from the safety of the house. "I heard of your great good fortune, and I thought to myself: Now, what does a young woman need, at such a time, about to embark on such an adventure? A friend, of course, a bosom friend. I have decided that I shall be the sister you do not have!"

Elisabeth prattles on and I force myself to forget the old memories and focus on her endearing words. It was so many years ago, after all. And it is true that I will need friends at Versailles. Bernis' lessons are becoming more complicated, and underneath all the pretty words and attention is the question that no one is asking: How will the interloper fare at Versailles?

So I let her hook her arm in mine and soon I am answering her questions, telling her about the visitors to the house, skillfully avoiding her rather too direct questions about the king, and by the time we arrive back at the house, we are chattering away like old friends.

Bernis meets us on the terrace and kisses Elisabeth. "I see you have met our dear cousin," he says, holding Elisabeth at arm's length and beaming at her. "The Comtesse d'Estrades is a member of one of the oldest families in our country. 'Of ancient lineage is she / France forever in her thrall will be.'"

Elisabeth inclines her head. She is wearing a pale gray gown with white stripes. Though it is unkind, I note that the two colors perfectly match her skin.

"Madame d'Estrades has been living a life of virtuous seclusion since the death of her husband in '43, but at my urging she has forgone her widow's weeds to come and help us with our mission."

"You have a position at Court?" I ask politely. I don't remember Bernis mentioning the Comte d'Estrades; he was obviously not important enough to be included in our lessons.

"No, no, not at present," says Elisabeth airily. "Though my husband was there, when his military duties allowed."

"So you are not presented?" I ask, confused. How will she be of help?

"Elisabeth will provide us with a unique feminine perspective," says Bernis in satisfaction.

I look at Elisabeth and nod, still confused. Then I feel a rush of sympathy: it must be awful to be so unattractive.

❧

In the middle of summer the most important letter of all arrives: the deed to the lands and title I will bear. The title that will enable my presentation at Court, the title that will open all the doors of the kingdom to me.

"At last," says Elisabeth. "A good title is like a bar of soap: it cleans up even the basest grubs."

I laugh, a little drily. Elisabeth is forthright and funny but her words can be rather jarring. At least she speaks the truth; no doubt her frankness will be useful at Versailles.

"The Marquise de Pompadour. A wonderful title!" I am delighted, already thinking of the literary possibilities: Pompadour rhymes with *amour*! My coat of arms is three silver castles on an azure field. Three castles to bury the fish forever.

"Pompadour . . . I know the daughter of the last marquis," says Elisabeth. "The old woman has a very keen sense of what is proper and the news that the ancient family title is to be held by one of such inferior birth will surely vex her."

"The estate is in Limousin," adds Bernis. "Unfortunate, that. But do not fear, my dear comtesse—ah, forgive me! A thousand pardons. Do not fear, my dear *Marquise,* there should be no call for you to visit the patronymic estate."

I smile and think: This morning I woke as the Comtesse d'Étiolles, a poor title and one with no history, yet now I go to bed a marquise, with one of the oldest titles in the land.

From Louis-François-Armand de Vignerot du Plessis, Duc de Richelieu
Bruges, Austrian Netherlands
August 5, 1745

My dear Marquise,

You must allow me to offer you my congratulations on your new title and position. The marquisate of Pompadour is certainly fine, and one can easily overlook its location in Limousin and the slight taint of madness that ran through the founding family.

After the strain of our last meeting, I shall not apologize: to do so would besmirch my own character, and such an action is unthinkable. But I forgive you and wish you nothing but the best. Though friendship must be reserved for those of the same pedigree, fond acquaintances can be had across all manner of society, no matter how low or varied.

I am with the king and he has never been happier; our military victories delight him so. I must stress to you our connection that dates back many decades to his very youngest days. He considers me at once a father, a brother, and a cousin.

Surprising things are happening: here a hailstorm in July, there a lamb born with five feet; all signs that the world is turned on its head. But why would I bore you, my dear Marquise—what pleasure it gives me to call you by your new title—with such trifles? Surely you have bigger things to worry about, for I fear your reception at Versailles will not be an easy one. Ah, my dear madame, such trials you will be forced to face! I regret that my military prowess must keep me here at the front and not beside you at Court.

Let me now close with a saying I am fond of:

> Friends are like melons.
> Shall I tell you why?
> To find one good, you must a hundred try.

I remain your humble servant,
Richelieu

Chapter Thirteen

The day of my presentation the throng outside the doors and around the palace is enormous. Bernis is controlling access, though he declares it to be like herding cats, and says that such a scrum of notables has not been seen since the death of the last king.

"The Bible said the world would end, but who would have thought the day would be September fourteenth, 1745?"

"Who's next? My chambermaid? My chambermaid's maid? The kitchen girl? The starving scruff from the side of the road?"

"If this is a sign of the modern times, then pray return me to the last century."

The hairdresser is a haughty man who regards me with ill-concealed disdain. "She's not as pretty as the other one," I hear him say in a loud whisper before he sets to work.

For once in my life I let go and leave others to decide; I am too nervous to think, let alone make decisions about my hair. I wish Mama were here with me for this most important day, but she is too ill to travel from Paris. I must rely on Elisabeth and others whose names I can't remember.

A brief note arrives from the king: *Courage—champagne later.* I smile and bite my lips. I have not seen him for several days and a keen swell of anticipation rises in me for tonight, when I will be in his arms and this dreaded ordeal will be over. Then tomorrow, I will be of this world, a woman openly loved by the king.

The elderly Princesse de Conti, a granddaughter of the late king, will be presenting me. She sits in the corner of the room, dripping distaste. She has made a point of telling me over and again that she only agreed to this humiliating duty because the king promised to pay her gambling debts. I am reminded of Uncle Norman's words, the twirling gold coin, the power of money over those who think their blood and rank should put them above such petty concerns.

"I was there at the Hôtel de Ville ball in Paris, but I do not remember seeing you," says the princess. She peers at me in dreadful accusation. I smile in return while the hairdresser tugs at another strand of hair. Something sizzles in his tongs but I dare not look.

"It was dreadful, dreadful, such rude people, crowding the buffet table and not letting me pass, though I desired a slice of the orange pie." She looks at me with piggy eyes. "Even when a footman announced me, no one allowed me to pass. *No one moved,* I say. Tell me, why are your people so rude? Mmm?"

"Perhaps they did not know who you were," I offer softly.

"Why would they not know who I was!" she huffs, fanning herself vigorously, her three chins wobbling in disapproval. "I told you, I was *announced*. Such insolence! And then one of the men, dressed as something resembling a rag, said that I might be the Princesse de Conti, but that he was the Prince de Ponti. Oh, I feel faint at the very memory of it. Marie! Rose! Salts, and quickly."

"Look what you've done to my sister," accuses Mademoiselle de Charolais, shaking her head. She is a frightful woman; an inch of face powder and a dress in violent shades of lavender. Her voice, though tiny and girlish, simply aches with opprobrium.

The Prince de Conti, the old woman's son and the head of this powerful family, arrives to lecture his mother on the impropriety of what she has agreed to. In his words, she is bringing eternal shame to their family, consorting with a bourgeois nothing. The prince is as tall as his mother is fat, with bulbous blue eyes and a stooped countenance. He does not speak to me. His every movement, every gesture tells me that I am nothing. Soon, soon, I think. Soon they will love me.

My hair finally finished, the seamstresses sew me into my presentation gown, the heavy fabric dripping with silver gilt, the hoops wider than my arms.

"Hold still," snaps the princess as a woman laces the bodice from behind. "One would think you've never worn a Court dress before."

"I never have," I say quietly as the stiff bodice closes around me, a cage without bars, an invisible prison. I bow my head: in a few hours this will be over. I flex my fingers: two, three at the most.

"Stop wiggling your fingers!" barks the princess. "Are they maggots?"

It takes a small army of Conti's footmen to clear a path for us through the crowds as we slowly wend our way to the King's Apartments. I look neither left nor right, careful to keep my face neutral. My gait is perfect, slim sliding steps; the tilt of my head just so, accentuating the pearls and silver filigree in my hair. I have the power of youth and beauty on my side and I know that one day, they will love me.

"Something to tell our grandchildren—the day we saw the daughter of a fishmonger being presented at Versailles!"

"Her father wasn't a fishmonger, that's just the unfortunate name. He was a butcher, I believe, or the son of one."

"Are you suggesting a difference? Daughter of a taxpayer, they are all the same."

At the King's Apartments we enter and I am announced: *The Marquise de Pompadour.* I perform my curtsy to the king, but he looks miserable and mutters something I cannot make out. The room is hot as Hades on this September day and I know this is difficult—anything that makes him uncomfortable in front of his courtiers is a trial for him. Not soon enough I am backing out, on next to the Queen's Apartments. Our torturous progress continues, as does the sibilant, evil drone that surrounds us:

"All this fuss over a nobody. As if we'll even remember her name by next year!"

"Don't curse me, Isabelle, but I do have to admit that it would scarcely be possible to be prettier."

"Quick, Séraphine, let's take the east stairs and see if we can get to the dauphin's apartment before the crowds—we'll miss the queen but his should be more amusing."

The queen receives me gently, and even inquires after a mutual acquaintance from Paris. At her unexpected kindness, my worries evaporate and the future opens up, bright and happy. I will do whatever I can to serve her. We might even be friends! I float out on a cloud.

The dauphin and his wife shatter my nascent hopes as surely as an egg cracks on the floor. They are frosty and silent and as I turn to leave I see in the reflection of a mirror the dauphin sticking his tongue out at me, like a petulant child.

Chapter Fourteen

"We are in our honeymoon, my dearest," says Louis. He wants to carry me over the steps, in the Italian style, but etiquette demands that a footman fill the role, and he decides he would not like that. Instead we enter the marble halls of Choisy hand in hand, laughing like children.

With a small group of guests, we retired here after the presentation. My chance, Louis tells me, to meet the people who will be important in my new life. Some I know from before, including Elisabeth and the Duc d'Ayen. Others I meet for the first time: the Marquis de Gontaut, with a lazy eye and pleasing blandness; the pretty Comtesse de Livry and the very elegant Françoise, the dowager Duchesse de Brancas, who is, rather confusingly, Diane de Lauraguais' step-grandmother. Frannie, as I soon call her, serves in the household of Mesdames Henriette and Adélaïde, the king's two eldest daughters. She is a tall, elegant woman about a decade older than me, with the palest skin, a nose as long as a slipper, and an elegant, languid manner.

"Eight months," she whispers to me during supper. "Eight months married to the old duke and then—poof! Too many spiced radishes one night and he sadly departed, leaving me a duchess. A dowager one, but still, a very satisfying state of affairs." She looks at me with one raised eyebrow, waiting on my response. I burst out laughing and from that moment on I know I have a friend and an ally.

Frannie's step-granddaughter Diane, the Duchesse de Lauraguais, is also with us. She is not as fat as I had heard and though I like her laugh and easy manner, it troubles me the way the king's eyes sometimes linger on her. Perhaps the rumors—that she was once his mistress—are true. I confess myself amazed, for though I am still learning about the king, I know him to be a fastidious man.

During the day Louis hunts, and now I often ride alongside him, through the same forest where I used to roam and daydream. When we cross paths with the carriages of the local gentry, seeking to greet the king, I think how strange it is that I was once there, looking on enviously at the magic inner circle. And now, here I am.

In the evenings we sup and play games, but my happiness is complete only when the day is done and we may be alone.

"Your breasts are perfect," declares Louis, admiring them with the proud look of someone surveying his own creation. "How I should like a cup made in their shape! I would drink only the finest champagne from it. We shall make a mold."

"Hot wax on my breasts—a painful thought!"

"A small consideration in pursuit of perfection."

I gaze at him in adoration. The dauphin hasn't yet consummated with his dreadful dauphine—her red hair and freckles are partially blamed—but his father suffers from no such fault. He is always ardent and always ready; often we make love three or four times a night. Though the motions of love do not produce for me the liquid lust the poets promise—male poets, mostly, I note, so perhaps those pleasures are reserved for men?—I adore being in his arms and the joy that I so obviously bring him. He is a magnificent man, and twenty times a day I thank God and my stars he is mine.

He runs his hands down my back. "Not a blemish, not a one. You are like a goddess created fresh from perfection, and only for me. Are you even mortal? Wait, I think I spy a freckle, beneath your right armpit." His fingers stop and he tickles me there.

I take his hand and guide it to a small scar on my shoulder; he kisses it softly. "One faint scar, given by the gods to remind us you are human. What happened?"

"I fell on the sharp end of a wick-trimmer and it cut me rather badly. I was five, I think."

"A wick-trimmer? And what is that?"

"Ah, Monsieur, but you have a lot to learn in life. I fear you have been far too cosseted." I lean in and breathe in his ear, as though to reveal the greatest of mysteries: "A wick-trimmer is used to cut the wick of a candle, to ensure a proper length for burning."

"Ah!" replies the king, whispering back: "You are an oracle, revealing secrets every day." I try to pull away but he doesn't let me. The intensity of his affection is flattering, but occasionally overwhelming.

Less than a week passes before a more bored and irritable king emerges. He dislikes the cello quartet that the steward of the *Menus Plaisirs* has arranged for us. At Versailles such entertainments are the domain of the First Gentleman of the Bedchamber—the most prestigious of all appointments that rotates amongst four of the highest nobles of the land. This year, thankfully almost over, is the year of the Duc de Richelieu, but he is not with us at Choisy and I am uncertain who is responsible here. Louis yawns through the first performance and then complains vociferously that he must listen to them again the following night.

"It will quite ruin the hunt for me," he snips, pursing his lips and refusing to catch my eye. His attendants hang back and I gather from their silence that they are used to such outbursts.

"But then we must find something else to amuse you! We are not bound to listen to them again."

"Well," says Louis, hitting his hunting boots with his crop, "these things are decided and—"

"Nonsense! You must listen to what you will; you can't be bound by silly customs if you don't want to be."

Louis laughs, a trifle harshly. I am not sure if he is angry with me, or with the steward, or with the world in general. I think—hope?—it is the with the steward. "Traditions rather rule my world."

I gaze at him, unsure what to say or do. He's acting a bit like a child, but of course I don't admonish him.

He sighs and turns away. "Do what you will, dearest," he says and motions the groom to bring his horse. He mounts, then viciously kicks his heels into the animal's flank and they gallop off in a flurry of dust and discontent. The rest of the courtiers and attendants scramble to their mounts and I am left alone, with only his words to ponder.

Do what you will? Does that mean I may contradict the orders of the steward and cancel the concert? Bernis said, *To break the rules of etiquette for advantage is permissible; to break them from ignorance is barbaric.* Unfortunately, Bernis is not with us at Choisy, and I don't think Elisabeth would know.

I wander back from the stables to the château and on the terrace overlooking the Seine I find Diane, the Duchesse de Lauraguais. She is enjoying a bowl of goose livers fried in almonds that I recognize from dinner yesterday.

"I had my man follow the dish down to the kitchens with strict instructions to save the remainder; I could not bear to think of those overfed kitchen girls enjoying them." Diane motions with her hand and I take a place on the stone bench beside her. This is the last of the warm days before winter finds us; today it is almost as hot as August. I should wash my hair, I think, and dry it out here before the sun disappears and the men return from the hunt.

"Have one?" offers Diane. "I believe they are even more delicious than yesterday. Funny, isn't it, how some food benefits from a little aging? Like people and wine, I suppose, well, wine more than people. Cheese, certainly. And some meats, like these livers of course, and chicken, now that is something—"

"The view is remarkable from here," I say, to stop the rush of words. At the foot of the garden the Seine flows placidly, the warm sunlight and the autumn leaves reflected in the water.

"Mmm, I suppose so."

"Dearest Madame, I would ask your advice," I say boldly. We are not fast friends, and I doubt we ever will be, but she knows the king well. Perhaps too well.

"Yes? Very nice gown you are wearing, Marquise. I normally

don't like embroidered birds—they make me hungry—but the pattern on your shawl is divine. Reminds me of a green shawl I used to have, though where in the Heavens it is now I couldn't say."

"Thank you, Madame. I shall have my seamstress send over some of the same fabric, if you so desire." Diane is wearing a magnificent but faded yellow gown, with what appears to be a mustard stain on one sleeve. I take a deep breath. "I would ask your advice on keeping the king amused."

A fleck of liver splutters out of her mouth and lands on her skirt.

"Amused?" Diane looks decidedly uncomfortable.

"Yes, to keep him amused," I repeat carefully. "In the evenings and such."

"Well . . ." Diane recovers her composure and chews thoughtfully, avoiding my eyes. "Well, he likes . . . ah, what is it I want to say? Funny, words rarely fail me. He likes . . . he likes it when you hold . . . ah, hold . . ."

"Balls?" I ask as Diane pops another goose liver in her mouth.

"Yes." Diane looks as if she is straining against every known convention. Is she choking? What a strange woman, I think and not for the first time.

"So the king likes balls, and such festivities. And masked balls?"

"What?" says Diane in confusion.

Abruptly I realize what she thought I was asking.

"Oh, no, Madame! I did not mean advice in any particular—ah—personal fashion." I feel a blush creeping over me; Diane is stark red and giggling. "I meant amusements . . . in the evenings . . . but before bed! Plays and such. Concerts."

Diane breathes a huge sigh of relief. "Oh, of course, Madame, of course. You wouldn't ask me about, well, you know, that wouldn't be proper. I mean I do *know*, I have some ideas, it's not a long history but occasionally, oh, no, not since you, dear, no, of course not, but, well . . . Well. He likes the theater. And songs.

And sometimes silly games. Marie-Anne tried to get him to enjoy literary evenings, discussing books and such, but he doesn't like writers very much."

"Ah, indeed, very interesting. Thank you." Though I am glad we are on firm footing again, I wonder if there is something wrong with her: there appears to be no barrier between her thoughts and her words. Extraordinary.

"Marie-Anne was very clever, she always made him laugh, she was frightfully witty. I don't think you're as witty, though you're certainly nice . . . He likes funny stories, you probably have lots of stories of . . . of bourgeois people? I suppose they are funny, though our lawyers are quite the most dreadful people . . . everyone knows the bourgeois are really the *bore-geois.*" She giggles at her own witless joke, then casually pops the last of the goose livers into her mouth.

I regret initiating the conversation; I must extricate myself if I am to have my hair washed and dried before the sun loses its strength. I take a chance, because sometimes chances are luck, and lean over to hug her, avoiding her messy fingers and the spot where the spat-out liver still lingers.

"My dearest Duchesse," I say, "I do hope we shall become friends!"

"Mmmm," says Diane, smiling, but she does not return my hug.

೧೨

Then the worst of all news finds me at Choisy and shatters our idyll. I return to Paris in time to say goodbye to my mother, and one cold December day she dies, leaving Norman and me bereft. How cruel she should be taken at this time, after all those years of love and support. How cruel of this world to deny her the chance to see me in my triumph, and to share in the bounty I will bring my family.

Three great sorrows, said the gypsy woman, and I have no doubt that this is the first.

Louis is consideration complete and forbids me to return

from Paris until I have fully grieved. But I doubt that time will ever come, so, shortly after the New Year I dry my tears and ride back to Versailles through a landscape as hard bitten by frost as my heart.

Norman returns with me, looking as lost as I have ever seen a man. He will take up his new post as the Director General of the King's Buildings, and I know his presence at Versailles will be a comfort to me. On the road we pass a mournful parade of black-cloaked monks, then hear the bells pealing for a village birth. "A funeral and a birth," says Norman, seeming suddenly old and frail beneath the furs; the loss of Mama has robbed him of half his life. "The alpha and omega of our existence."

Tomorrow I must dry my tears, hold my head high and take my place at Versailles beside the man I love, on the great stage where my life will truly begin, and where all of my dreams will come true.

Act II

Marquise

Chapter Fifteen

"And for the walls?" inquires Collin, the man in charge of my ever-growing household.

In addition to the love of the king, I now have all the trappings of a powerful woman. My First Woman of the Bedchamber is Nicole, a distant relation of my mother's with a calm, competent demeanor. I also have several other women to help me with my toilette, wardrobe, and daily needs, as well as my own cook and chaplain, and numerous valets and footmen.

I look around at the beautiful white and blue paneling of my new apartment, framed with delicate gold gilding. The overall effect of the room is charming, but it must be changed. I cannot be thinking of her, nor can Louis.

"A pale green," I say, recalling a room I loved at Chantemerle. "With a strong hint of gray."

Collin motions and the draper springs forward with a pile of fabric samples.

"No, no," says Elisabeth, fanning herself in a corner. "I would choose a light mustard; I have a gown I could share with you for inspiration."

"This one," I say, choosing a satin brocade, embroidered with gray and white flora against a background of soft green. I ignore Elisabeth; her taste in colors simply does not exist. "These for the curtains and this color here, by the vine, for the walls. What do you call that color?"

"Fairy Moss, Madame."

"A beautiful choice," gushes Bernis. "And Fairy Moss—what a delightful name!" My tutor on etiquette also has exquisite taste;

we tease that he knows precedence and order both for princes of the blood and for colors of the rainbow.

"And for the upholstery? The same?" inquires Collin.

"No." I shake my head. Something different, a little unexpected. "Pale blue," I say, decisive. "Also with gray undertones."

The draper raises his eyebrows. "A tad somber, Madame, do we not think? Might I suggest a stronger tone for the seating, a red or a rich pink? I have a lovely shade I call Persuasion that marries those two colors nicely."

"No." I want to feel as though submerged in the cool waters of a lake, bathed in an early-morning glow. "Pale blue-gray for the upholstery. And I would have six—no, ten—celadon vases, as high as the window seats, filled daily with . . ." I think, then snap my fingers and Collin's eyebrows almost rise off his face—I won't be doing that again— "with brunia berries. They have a delightful silver-gray shade."

Bernis clucks in consternation. "So many flowers inside, such a strange notion! 'Flowers belong outdoors / Not inside, over the walls and floors.' I am not sure it's completely proper. And what if they harbor spiders?"

"And?" I say, laughing, "is there etiquette against flowers inside? Must they be taken off the table if a duchess should pass by?"

"Oh, my friend, do not mock, do not mock!" Bernis sits down heavily and produces an enormous yellow handkerchief, matching his cravat, and dabs it delicately against his brow.

Collin bows. "I will ensure the hothouses are stocked immediately."

Though I can see doubt in their eyes, the men obey me. But no matter: if I am wrong about the décor, I will simply redo it. I am experiencing the first touches of power, grander even than love. Money is suddenly in dazzling abundance and I have decided that I will use it, and lots of it, to create a beautiful life for the king and me.

☙

Louis bounds up the stairs and enters my salon. On days when the demands of ceremony allow, he greets me after Mass, then drops by in the afternoon before the hunt, escaping from what he calls the tiring trifles of governance.

"Darling, how wonderful to see you." I saw him just a few hours ago, but when we are apart my stomach turns, and I am filled with a rare restlessness.

The courtiers in the room reluctantly melt away, all hoping for a last-minute reprieve. But the king cares to see only me and he waits impatiently by the mantel, fiddling with a pair of pink china ducks. When everyone is gone we embrace and he kisses me passionately, then flings himself down on his favorite chair.

"Orry," he complains, speaking of the finance minister. I rub his back and caress his neck, lean in and inhale the sensual scent of musk that rises from his wig.

"What is it, dearest?" I murmur.

"Ah, that feels good. Richelieu always contends that there is nothing that a little rubbing cannot cure."

I blush and reach for the bell, ring it as Louis continues with his woes.

"Orry is intractable, simply intractable," he complains. "A war requires money! How else are we to fight the Austrians? It is not as though God will send them an earthquake, once and for all, and be done with them."

A footman comes in bearing two plates, a pigeon tart on one, a few slices of jellied hare on the other. Louis gestures to the hare and the servant sets it on a small table. On days when he is not dining in public, Louis likes to take a light luncheon here with me. Today he doesn't seem very hungry. I watch him closely but take pains to hide my gaze: a life on public display has led to a horror of being stared at.

As he eats I entertain him with the gossip.

"As you know, the poor Abbé de Rouen passed suddenly Tuesday night, while dining at Fontenelle's house in Paris. Fontenelle had just received the best of the early asparagus, and being an excellent host he cordially offered the *abbé* the choice of having it cooked in butter or oil."

"Mmm . . ." Louis is enjoying the jellied hare; I must remember to compliment my chef and have him prepare it again.

"The *abbé* chose it to be cooked in oil, which disappointed Fontenelle, as he is partial to asparagus in butter. But he could not ignore the wishes of his guest and so instructed his kitchen to cook half in butter, half in oil. Now, as we know, the men were enjoying drinks before dinner when they all fell down dead from a fit of apoplexy—as quick as a wink, as Voltaire so wittily described it. Immediately, Fontenelle leapt from his chair, jumped over the body of his dead friend, and raced to the kitchens, hoping against hope that it was not too late, crying: 'All of it in butter! All of it in butter!'"

Louis roars with laughter, then inquires if there will be asparagus at supper this evening.

"There will be, darling," I say, delighted he enjoyed the story. The king often compliments me on what he calls my "keen Parisian wit"; when he does I smirk inside at Diane and her scathing words about the *bore-geois*.

"You look lovely," he says, finishing his hare and appraising me. My gown is of the palest yellow, matching the primroses gathered in great sprays around the room. He does not recognize the art, but the overall effect pleases him.

I know by the look on his face that he is becoming aroused. Quickly I offer him a dish of lemon candies, which perfectly match the flowers and my dress, and share a little gossip about the Marquis de Gontaut, who delivered them this morning. I am about to suck on one myself when I realize there may be unintended consequences.

"I'll save mine for later," I say. "My time with you is sweet enough."

Last week he insisted on making love on the carpet, a soft Aubusson woven with a pastoral scene in seven shades of green. I had a very hard time communicating to Nicole what had transpired on the face of the shepherdess, and what needed to be cleaned.

"Tonight, darling, a surprise," I say to distract him. Louis loves surprises and I have very quickly taken over the task of organizing his pleasures and entertainments. The Duc de Duras is this year's First Gentleman of the Bedchamber and is only too happy to oblige. Sometimes I think with amusement of Duras' overwrought declarations of love from my Parisian days. Now? Discretion personified: the king's touch makes a eunuch of even the most lecherous of men.

"Tell me." Louis pouts in mock indignation.

"Later, my love: it is a surprise. Do not be a curious boy." I have noticed Louis sometimes likes it when I scold him; I oblige, but only in a very gentle way. "You will be well pleased, I promise."

He smiles at me fondly. "Ah, my dear, what would I do without you? You have done such a fine, fine job of making a home for yourself, and for me, here at Versailles." He reaches for my breast and I pretend he is reaching for the dish of candies, which I hand him with a smile.

"I knew you would like these," I say lightly. "Gontaut told me his apothecary swears by them, both for pleasure and cure. But now, back to work—you're being as lazy as Gontaut's eye."

He gets up with a show of reluctance and chortles as I push him toward the door. I kiss him goodbye, but not too ardently; too much and we will end up on the carpet again. I have no desire to redo my hair before the afternoon, nor give the ministers more to grouse and gristle about.

When he is gone I sink down on the sofa and lie awhile staring at the ceiling. I have decided against a traditional heavenly scene and the cherubs have been whitewashed, awaiting my instructions. Only their faint outline remains, and for some reason I am reminded of a wood in winter. I would take a nap, like this, lying on the sofa: my life is becoming quite exhausting. But I cannot rest for long.

"Nicole," I call, and she bustles in from the left antechamber. "Have one of the men check with Monsieur Richard that the asparagus is up, enough for a plate. If not . . . send Gérard to Paris, posthaste, he can just make it there and back in time."

Outside the comforting cocoon of my apartments, the rest of Versailles buzzes and hums and purrs. I am becoming like Louis: detesting all that is public and ceremonial, preferring to be in my private rooms, surrounded by friends. But venture out I must, and when I do, people are remarkably rude.

In the more egalitarian atmosphere of the Parisian salons, the Court nobles were somewhat polite, but here in their native habitat . . . well, I have never met such smug, rude, and ignorant people. Their snide comments about me continue to float through the vapid air of the palace like a Greek chorus gone wrong.

"I can't understand why the king continues eating fish, now that Lent is over," I heard someone say yesterday. Last week I slipped on a slick stone in the gardens and almost fell into one of the Lizard Pools; for days the Court shrieked about my return to the water.

Certainly, I expected some resistance, but this virulent torrent puzzles me. Then I realize they think I am just a passing fancy; an intrigue, not a mistress. Why waste kindness—or manners—on someone who will soon be gone?

I have enemies, I think sadly, real enemies; men and women who hate me for my birth, for my influence with Louis, for simply being me. An unpleasant truth, but one I must shoulder. It will not do to flake apart like a well-cooked fish in the face of these obstacles.

A tribute to the French Crown arrives from the Emperor of China. Louis assures me the gift was sent long before my presentation: a pair of delicate red-and-gold fish, prettier than any I have ever seen. The Chinese envoy insists they are meant to be admired, not eaten, which only confirms the Court's opinion of the barbaric Chinese. I adore the fish and have a pond stocked that they might multiply. I commission an enormous glass bowl, which I place on my mantel. In it, the fish swim serenely around above a bed of stones and pebbles, untroubled by the woes of the outside world.

From *François Paul le Normant de Tournehem*
Director General of the King's Buildings
Rue Saint-Honoré, Paris
May 10, 1746

Dearest Reinette,

Do not trouble yourself if the courtiers do not respond to your overtures. There is little you can say or do to change their hearts, and this is especially true of the ministers who seek to discredit anyone who has the king's ear. They will use your birth as a rationale for their hatred.

Maurepas, the naval minister, is the essence of evil and a self-proclaimed hater of mistresses. He's also a terrific snob, despite—or perhaps because of—his own less than illustrious ancestors. Argenson, the minister of war, is tricky but has the king's trust. Luckily that peacock Richelieu is in Flanders with the army, and though the Prince de Conti seeks a place on the council, the king refuses and his influence is minimal. The king has not chosen a prime minister since the death of Cardinal Fleury three years ago and keeps all his ministers vying with each other for the privilege.

The king is surrounded by many false friends and advisers. Reinette, you offer the king the greatest gift of all: pure love and friendship. You must not worry, for his love will insulate you against the machinations of those petty men.

I will be at Versailles again Tuesday to supervise the repairs in the Marble Court. Rouget forwarded me your thoughts concerning the new fabric for the king's winter upholstery. I am in complete accordance and will relay your instructions immediately upon my return.

Fondly,
Norman

Chapter Sixteen

I eat a fifth pickled egg and consider having a sixth. Perhaps some quince jam instead? I smile as I caress my belly. Even though it is early, I swear I can feel a slight curve. If it is a girl, I will name her Madeleine after my mother. But it won't be a girl; it will be a handsome boy, the very image of his father.

This summer Louis is again off at war. The dauphine, despite her looks and some mechanical difficulties on the part of her husband, is also pregnant. My Louis will return soon, for the sovereign must be present for the birth of a future King of France.

In the meantime he writes every day, and I to him. I also correspond with the venerable Maréchal de Saxe, commander of the king's army, who has become a good friend. It is sometimes true that the enemies of my enemies are my friends, and I find supporters amongst those who despise Argenson, or Maurepas, or Richelieu. As mutual hatred is the natural order at Versailles, my list of friends grows daily.

Before he left Louis gave me a present: the château of Crécy, a delightful palace overlooking a small river. Though many clamor for an invitation, I do not want carping courtiers infecting my sacred retreat. Only Elisabeth, Frannie, Bernis, the Duc de Duras, the Marquis de Gontaut, a few other friends and intimates of Louis' are admitted.

At the center of the château at Crécy is a beautiful octagonal salon. There, the great Boucher is painting eight large panels with scenes of children playing music, dancing, gamboling in gardens. I watch his progress and delight in the little faces that emerge to greet me from the walls.

The last king legitimized many of his children and the addition of those new princes of the blood caused much upheaval in the norms of precedence and ranking, the reverberations of which, Bernis confides to me with the hysterical tone he reserves for only the greatest of etiquette tragedies, are still being felt today.

My Louis is adamant that he will never do the same and has not acknowledged paternity of the Comte de Luc, his bastard with Pauline de Vintimille. But I doubt he loved Pauline as he loves me, so it will only be natural that he will want to claim our children. They will have the rank of princes and princesses of the blood, and will be treated with reverence, make grand marriages. And of course my darling Alexandrine will also marry well. I actually think that the perfect match would be the Comte de Luc, now five years old: my child, with Louis' child.

On the third panel, the one that catches the light of the afternoon sun, Boucher paints a little boy with adorable chestnut curls, dressed in a red velvet suit and holding the bridle of a pony. This child, I decide, is Louis, our firstborn, and I watch in contentment as he is slowly painted into life, surrounded by his future brothers and sisters.

∽

The day is hot and muggy. The land below Crécy is slightly swampy and the mosquitoes are out in force. I am with my landscaper, planning the back gardens from the terrace. Bernis and Elisabeth trail along after me, Elisabeth complaining about the insects and the heat, Bernis wobbling on a new pair of shoes that he is determined to break in before returning to Versailles.

"Madame, I suggest we remove that village," says Monsieur d'Isle, my landscaper, gesturing to a cluster of houses in the distance.

"Oh, no, we cannot do that." I am shocked at his suggestion.

"My dearest Marquise, why ever not?" says Bernis, scrambling to regain his balance after almost tripping over a cobble. "A wonderful suggestion. If the village and those unsightly—huts—I don't know what else to call them—were moved, then we would have a clear view beyond the river and could enjoy the sunset without it being marred by—what are those things? Surely not houses. Cow houses? Do cows have houses?"

I waver. "Such a displacement. The people . . ."

"Jeanne, do not think of such things. You must learn to think as one born to this place and station," Elisabeth chimes in. "You must learn to be *grand*. It is beneath your dignity to think of such petty concerns. Oh, get off me, fly! What—do they travel in pairs?!"

I stare at the little houses in the distance; despite the heat of the day, a curl of smoke rises from one. But it is true—the view would be vastly improved if they were removed. And the point is perfection, is it not?

"Very well, have them moved," I murmur to d'Isle, who bows in approval.

We continue along the terrace to inspect progress on the stone staircases that will lead down to the river. White limestone from Limousin, the riser of each step carved with curved waves and fish.

"I shall walk down, and up, twice. Observe me," says Bernis, setting off in teetering determination. We laugh at his progress and after a wobbly descent, he gives up and takes off the offending shoes, their red heels almost two inches high.

"These mosquitoes, really!" complains Elisabeth, smacking one against her cheek, leaving a faint smear of blood that blends with her rouge. "That's the fifth one today. Never mind that village—what can be done to get rid of these flying fiends?"

But soon those petty concerns fade before my own private sorrow: the baby is no more. A mess of blood and tears, and a retreat into my bedchamber to cry the pain in my soul away.

From Maurice de Saxe, Maréchal de Saxe
Commander of the King's Army
Brussels, Austrian Netherlands
June 24, 1746

Madame,

I thank you for your latest missive as well as for the bottle of Madeira wine—however did you discover my fondness for that particular drink?

Madame, the king continues in excellent health; you will have heard by now of our victories in Flanders and of the continued glory of France. All our triumphs have put His Majesty in excellent humor, but if I may be so bold, Madame, I avow our victories account for only a small portion of his happiness.

I assure you, Madame, of his continued devotion. He delights in your letters and keeps the ribbons that bind them; an affectation expected of a convent girl, and in our sovereign one that is both touching and enchanting. If you permit me, Madame, I will blink back a tear, as such tender scenes remind me of my youth and when I first met my dear wife, and then my dear mistress.

I am ever in your charge and in your employ, Madame, and I will continue to keep you informed of all that concerns Our Most Christian Majesty.

Madame, I remain your faithful servant,
Louis de Saxe

Chapter Seventeen

Versailles, full to the rafters, holds its collective breath as the dauphine's labor begins. I stay away from her crowded chambers and pass the hours in my apartment with Elisabeth and Frannie. I try to read my book—a new French translation of *Pamela*—but my thoughts constantly drift over to Louis, far away in the grand staterooms, trapped in the ceremonial machine surrounding the birth of a future king. He has only been back four days and our reunion exceeded my expectations. I cried, as did he.

Even if I had the entrées to the dauphine's apartment, I would not wish to be part of the throng of spectators, crowding around, chatting, even playing cards. The rawness of my miscarriage still haunts me and I have no fond feelings for the dauphine. She has been nothing but cold to me since her arrival, and her husband has continued to metaphorically stick his tongue out at me. But, for Louis' sake, and for France's, I wish her well.

"The poor dauphine," I remark, thumbing to the back of the book to see whether Mr. B achieves his seduction of Pamela. "Those crowds in her rooms—how frightful."

"Oh, Jeanne, don't be so bourgeois. People may not care who your father was, or wasn't"—Elisabeth arches an eyebrow at me—"but amongst the best families this is the way things are."

I do not like the way Elisabeth constantly reminds me of my roots, as if I do not get enough of that outside my apartment. Still, she is a good friend and I value her frankness, for truth is a rare commodity at Versailles.

Frannie shudders. "Luckily my husband was seventy-four when we wed, and congress was an act that required a perfect constellation of wine, health, and, oddly, a new moon. I escaped the horrors of childbirth, but with his first wife it was done in the old public style. Two hundred people, they say, attended the birth of the fourth Duc de Brancas. Thank goodness such old customs are passing, for all but royalty."

"You'll come with me to the chapel, later? To pray?" I ask her. Frannie is a soothing aloe ointment; she always knows what needs to be done and said. She is wearing a pale white dress, wrapped with a white wool shawl, and with her ivory skin the overall effect is of an elegant, albino swan. She once told me she leeches her skin, occasionally, to achieve the right paleness.

"Of course, darling, of course. The poor dauphine, they say she is terrified; the dauphin comforted her by saying the pain would be less than a tooth pulling."

"Men!" snorts Elisabeth.

I think of the birth of Alexandrine nearly three years ago, the agony and the burning thirst, the anger and the rage that had surprised both myself and the midwife—but somehow, all quickly forgotten, the fruit erasing the pain.

I flip through my book, trying to determine where Pamela went wrong, then think again of our future King Louis XVII, if they name the baby Louis. Which of course they will. So far into the future, if I live to see the day.

Of course I won't see the day, I think in alarm: it would mean I had outlived my Louis.

Eleven hours later the dauphine is delivered of a baby girl. Madame de Tallard, the governess of the king's children, comes out with the infant in her arms and a grimace on her face. Excitement evaporates like dew on a hot morning and the palace quickly drains of courtiers. The bells ring for only a few minutes, and all fireworks are canceled. There is of course much mumbling that the curse of daughters, famously begun by Queen Marie—six daughters and only one son who survived childhood—is to be revisited on this generation.

Louis comes briefly, kisses me, and leaves; despite it being a girl, there is still protocol and order to attend to. But all ceremony around the unwanted baby grinds to a halt when the dauphine, just turned twenty and in seemingly excellent health, dies three days after the birth.

e∕ა

In the wake of a royal death, etiquette dictates that the king and his household must leave Versailles. At Choisy, Louis finds solace in my arms and barely leaves my side for two days and nights. Despite his strained relationship with his son—the dauphin is a perfect prig who overtly disapproves of his father's lifestyle—I know Louis cares deeply for all his children. He grieves for his son, who is inconsolable, and for the fate of the Spanish alliance this marriage was supposed to ensure.

"Death—death," he says to me, lying in my arms. "All around us, springing at us from the dark corners of every room. That poor, poor girl."

"You are so kind," I say gently, and it is true—hardly anyone spares a thought for the Spanish princess, dead in a foreign land, so young and so alone. If she had produced a son it might have been different, but as it is she will quickly be forgotten, just a cipher for the history books.

"Only you, Pomponne," he murmurs to me. "Only you understand me. I feel so close to you—we are one soul in two bodies."

"One soul in two bodies," I repeat as I cuddle him to sleep. I kiss his tearstained face and stroke his brow. I am beginning to understand that despite being surrounded by people, Louis is an intensely lonely man. His need for me and his dependence are touching, I think, gently licking away the salt tears that stain his cheeks.

The next day Louis invites me to sit beside him at an impromptu council, called for this national emergency. With the dauphine's body not even opened or buried, quick decisions must be made.

"Shall we wait for Monsieur le Dauphin?" inquiries Maurepas, the naval minister.

Louis shakes his head. "He is overcome. We shall leave him to his grief."

Though disapproval hangs as heavy as the black velvet cloths that are everywhere since mourning began, no one dares say anything about my presence. And this room is filled with an absolute cabal of my enemies: both Maurepas and Argenson are present, amongst others of lesser importance but equaled hate.

Argenson, the minister of war, clears his throat and starts on the list: "The daughters of the King of Sardinia must be considered." The man has darting goggle eyes and appears unable to keep them off my bodice. I surreptitiously check I do not have a stain there—the noodles at noon were rather messy.

"A request will be prepared," says Puysieux smoothly. The Marquis de Puysieux, with the Ministry of Foreign Affairs, has declared himself a friend; curiously, he is also rumored to have been the first lover of Louise, the Comtesse de Mailly. A good-looking man, I often find myself thinking.

"Sire, what about her sister?" suggests Maurepas, in his high-pitched, whining voice.

"Whose sister?" says Louis, looking longingly out the window, and I know he wishes he could be out hunting.

"The late Madame la Dauphine, she has a younger sister."

"An ugly dwarf, with dark skin and a hump, here," interjects Orry, the finance minister, patting his left shoulder.

"Well, the looks are not important—we saw that with poor Thérèse—but sisters—no. We French are not fond of incest," declares Louis, picking at a bit of skin hanging off his thumb, ignoring his own well-known predilection for sisters.

Silence.

I speak into the uncomfortable void. "The Maréchal de Saxe spoke highly of the daughters of the King of Poland?" The death of the dauphine presents an opportunity: a new dauphine, more disposed to my interests, could help me gain favor with the rest of the royal family. And the King of Poland is also the Elector of Saxony, where they make the most magnificent Meissen porcelain: French artistry would benefit.

"That king is an ex-Protestant!" spits Argenson. "And he is married to an *Austrian*. And grossly obese." Though his look and tone ask me if I am mad, I note he dares not say it.

"No, no, Argenson, you're wrong and the Marquise is right," says the king.

Ha! I feel a surge of pride and bite my lips to hide my smile.

"The Saxons should be considered: new friends in times of uncertainty. I'm somewhat tired of these Spanish princesses and their dour airs. No offense, of course, to my departed daughter-in-law." Louis looks around the table. "The mother, despite being Austrian, is excessively fertile, if I am not mistaken? How many children does she have?"

"Eleven children living, Sire, out of fifteen pregnancies so far, and five of them sons."

"What excellent fecundity," remarks Louis in approval.

"Still, Sire, six daughters—"

"Five sons," adds Puysieux, warming to the idea.

"But consider the queen," says Maurepas in a voice that is overly shocked, for he is no real friend of the queen's. The previous Elector of Saxony deposed the queen's father from the throne of Poland and the queen is said to hate Saxons so much that she never eats potato dumplings and once even slapped a chambermaid for wearing a cap in the Saxon style.

"How must I consider the queen?" asks Louis in sharp bewilderment.

Maurepas flushes and examines his quill with great intent and shaking fingers.

"The queen may be gently coaxed to see the advantages," I offer helpfully, but receive nary a sign of gratitude from Maurepas.

"She'll come around," says Louis, nodding. "And if she doesn't, no mind. I like this idea. Excellent, my dear."

Puysieux and I smile at each other as Maurepas drops his pen in disgust.

"Any other ideas, gentlemen?"

"The King of Portugal's niece . . ."

From Françoise, Dowager Duchesse de Brancas
Palace of Versailles
August 1, 1746

Dearest Jeanne,

All is dreary here with little to report. My step-granddaughter Diane de Lauraguais, as *dame d'atour*, had the unpleasant duty of carrying the dauphine's heart on a platter after the autopsy. She fainted and fell straight to the ground and the heart slipped alongside her. There was not much love between her and the dauphine, so all are curious as to why she would faint. It was quite dramatic—I'm sure had our dear Bernis been here, he would have composed a little verse, something to do with *heartache* and *earthquake*.

More pleasant duties are of course the division of the dauphine's possessions, which by custom Diane has the right to. She made me a present of a very fine fur cape, you remember the one of white weasel the dauphine wore at Easter? I know how much you admired her garnet necklace, that day in the gardens, and I will press Diane to make you a present of it.

Darling, something a little darker: the Comtesse de Périgord, a friend of the king's, is back. She was pursued by him after Marie-Anne's death, but she refused him and fled the Court in a whirl of virtue. Her husband is an idiot whom the king can't abide, not since that incident with the fleas, but unfortunately his wife does not share her husband's disgrace.

Let me know when our new dauphine is decided! Gontaut told me the odds are now four to one it will be another Spanish princess. I shall see you at Choisy next Sunday when I join Mesdames for my week on duty.

I remain, ever your friend,
Frannie

Chapter Eighteen

"Smallpox," murmurs Louis in a piteous voice as we contemplate the rough stone church on the hill, flanked by black-clad mourners. "I too had it as a babe, but by the grace of God survived. Not so my family, killed by measles: father, mother, brother."

We are still at Choisy—it has been raining for five days now, and instead of hunting we are riding out in this carriage, following village funerals, inquiring as to the manner of death. It is a strange pastime, and one I do not approve of. I am learning that Louis has a morbid side, which fits well with his natural inclination for melancholy.

Elisabeth and Bernis are in the coach with us and they murmur their sympathies. Bernis offers up the tale of a cousin who died of smallpox, capped with a quick poem: "'Fresh as a dewy morning leaf / Dead by sunset, spots all a-grief.'" The day is gray and overcast, matching the mood in the carriage, the rain still drizzling down.

"Touching words," I murmur as I caress Louis' hands. It is all I can do to hide my impatience. I am no fool—I know death comes for us, as certain as taxes for peasants—but I see no point in dwelling on that fact whilst there is still life to enjoy.

"There, over the hill—can you hear the funeral bells?" Louis perks up and snatches his hands back. He points eagerly out the window. "Bernis, quickly, tell the coachman to take the path to the left!"

At length I am able to persuade him to turn around and head back to the palace, but there the atmosphere is no better. Despite fond memories of our honeymoon last year, I decide I don't like Choisy. There is too much history here, too many ghosts, and the pink-patterned panels in the west salon are simply wrong. I must talk to Uncle Norman about having them changed.

Thanks to Frannie's letter, I am well prepared when I see an addition to the list of guests.

"The Comtesse de Périgord is coming tonight? I thought you disliked her husband."

"You see her husband's name is not on the list," says Louis shortly, shaking his head at a stack of papers that Puysieux is offering him. "Later. Tomorrow."

"Certainly, dearest, I see that. But Madame de Périgord . . ." I trail off, remembering Frannie's words. I do hope Louis' pursuit of her was before he met me. Surely so?

"She is back from Mareuil and I remembered how fine her company is," Louis says. He flings down a stack of papers Maurepas has left for him. "I cannot read this scribe's handwriting. I cannot!"

"Of course, dearest." I stare in despair at my love's face. I am uncertain how to manage this new king: melancholy, often curt, even occasionally rude. I feel as though I am walking on a pond in winter, yet don't know how thick the ice is. I give him a warm smile.

"You must excuse me, I did not realize she was back at Court, or I would have included her myself!" I lie. "Here, darling, let me read those for you." I take the stack of papers from him and with a kiss send him off for a rest.

At supper that night Madame de Périgord is the center of attention and her stories of the painful deaths of a variety of relatives interest Louis immensely. I am irritated by her sugary way with words, yet have to admit that her combination of beauty and purity strikes just the right note for this melancholy house party. My efforts to amuse the king were all wrongheaded; rather than fight the sorrow, I see, I must indulge it.

"Her lace sleeve caught fire, then quickly the rest of her, and then my dearest Gabrielle expired. But we took comfort that the fateful candle was to light her way to the chapel; such favor to die on the way to Him."

"Really, my dear Comtesse, we must have more of you, and of your stories. You are a credit to this kingdom," says Louis in appreciation.

Madame de Périgord blushes and lowers her eyes demurely. Her simple gray mourning gown is covered with a lovely pink mousseline shawl, just the right shade to bring out her delicate complexion. She had declared herself cold and then claimed this was the only wrap her maid could find.

"Watch her," warns Nicole when she undresses me and helps me into my night robe. There is no formal sleeping ceremony at Choisy and the king will be here at any moment. Not that Nicole's presence would present a barrier; he once said he thought of her as my dog. Nicole almost barked in pleasure, but his sentiment troubled me.

"I am friends with her equerry's cousin. Hold still." Nicole picks the pins out of my hair and brushes it out. "She says that the countess is as sly as a dove. You know what they say: vice follows virtue."

I frown and rub myrtle cream on my hands. Delicious, I think, inhaling the deep scent.

But Louis doesn't come that night.

It is the first night when I expect him that he does not come.

I lie awake as the hours pass, wondering where in the maze of rooms and intrigue he might be and what he is doing. The perfect smiling face of the Comtesse de Périgord swims around and around in my mind, like fish in a bowl. That delightful dimple on her right cheek, the elegant way she passed the king his coffee cup, that obviously false story about the gruesome death of her uncle in a well.

Though I live in dire fear of losing him, I won't say anything. Reproach is like lye to love, wearing it thin, my mother used to say. I repeat her words in my cold bed. Piety and death are a troubling combination. Was this day inevitable? I must, I think as slumber overcomes me, I must . . .

§

"She refused him. Again!"

Elisabeth brings me the news at my morning toilette. While I often enjoy the gossip she shares, this time I don't and my heart stops—one can refuse only if a proposition has been offered.

"Who?" I say quietly, smiling at Elisabeth and noting with distaste the overlarge bow she wears at her neck. She should remember she is not fifteen. I dab a tiny dot of rouge on my cheek and rub it in; a new shade my perfumer calls Mosquito Blood.

Elisabeth doesn't answer, only shakes her head with a pained look.

"Surely the king did not . . . ask?" My words falter, as does my world.

"Well, not in so many words, but apparently there was a letter."

"A letter? When?"

"Well, a note, a few words, from the king. Informing her of his admiration."

Admiration is not a proposal. A trifle. I can breathe again. "He is a generous man and the comtesse's piety is much admired." I dab a little rouge on my lips and smack them; is it my imagination or has my complexion sallowed slightly? Perhaps in sympathy with the king? I need to get out of here, I think suddenly.

"But this was *after* their tryst," says Elisabeth, moving away so my woman can start on my hair.

"Their tryst?"

"Well, not exactly a tryst, but they did talk after supper. He made her a coffee himself."

"I saw them," I say coolly. "In the salon, with the rest of us." I hide my irritation. Elisabeth is like a cat licking an empty plate, looking for scraps where there are none.

"And then she left. In her carriage, early this morning and watched by the king. Vowing eternal fidelity to her husband. But she is set to return, Tuesday next."

I look down at my lap and smooth the dark gray damask of

my skirt. Mourning will end soon and I have the most beautiful winter gown, of patterned blue velvet lined with white satin, that I am looking forward to wearing. I imagine pouring lye on it— ruined. I will not reproach him.

When I greet him later it is with my customary warmth. By small, almost imperceptible attentions I see he is sorry for whatever happened, or didn't, with the Comtesse de Périgord. These little gestures—a compliment on my hair, an order to the kitchen to prepare the stuffed eggs he knows I enjoy—reassure me more than any words could.

I am coming to see that Louis is a man fairly well led. Not to say he is weak; he just hates making decisions. Perhaps he has had to make too many decisions in his life? Or not enough? Regardless, he likes others to take charge, and I am amazed at how tractable he can be. I can lead him where I want. Not quite manipulation, I think, chewing my lip, more like *maneuvering*.

I decide this mourning has gone on far too long.

"Darling," I say to him after Mass, "I'm inviting you to Crécy. You must see the progress and I would so love it if you could give me your input on the billiard room I am planning. Will you? Please? For me?"

Chapter Nineteen

I have an idea. It's just a seed of an idea, one that still needs to be watered and given time to grow. But I like my idea—it is a good one.

An idea, something to help with the endless task of keeping my beloved amused. Recently I have felt despair creeping over me. There are only so many concerts to stage, only so many games of charades or cards that can be arranged. There is a surfeit of leisure in the palace, but Louis loses interest in almost everything, and almost immediately. My beloved is only really happy during the vigor of a successful hunt, or in the act of love. Frannie once said—with elegant candor—that he is the Great Unamusable, and I must admit she is right.

The days and years start to stretch ahead of me in a long line of demanding activities. How exhausting it is, to plan every evening and every amusement, to try and keep Louis ahead of the demons of boredom that snap at his heels. And as I worry about how to occupy him during our public hours, I am also afraid that his boredom will extend to the bedchamber. Am I Scheherazade, only staying alive by my ability to keep him amused?

Then—my idea.

I know well the effect actresses have on men, the thrill of seeing a woman they think they know become someone different. Change, the greatest of all aphrodisiacs.

Why should I not start my own theater group here at Versailles? I imagine my Louis watching me, applauding me, anticipating me.

I share the idea with my friends.

"We could all participate!" says Frannie. "It would be fun for the king to see his stiff courtiers prancing around onstage. We must ask my step-granddaughter Diane to help; I believe her sister Marie-Anne tried something similar."

"I don't know if you remember but you took dancing lessons with us as a child, Jeanne," says Elisabeth. "I am sure you have improved since then."

"Sacrilege, sacrilege," mutters Bernis, shaking his head and rootling through a bowl of potpourri. "It is one thing to perform in a private house, but here, at Versailles, for all the world to see?" His delicate hands flutter in consternation as he pulls a desiccated leaf from the bowl and sniffs appreciatively. "Mmm, orange blossom."

"Not for all the world to see," I say, refining the idea as I speak. Louis must feel it is all for him. He will be the audience, with perhaps a few select friends. And as for the cast . . . if a courtier has talent, yes, but I will fill any gaps with professionals. There shall be nothing amateurish about my productions.

Bernis dolefully shakes his head, still sniffing at his fingers. "But do you not think you are on the stage enough, already, my dear? One could say Versailles is like a theater. 'All the world's a stage / All the men and women merely an appendage.' An original poem; I so hope it pleases you. But you must give me the name of your perfumer—this mixture is simply divine!"

The next day Frannie invites Diane to stop by while the king is out hunting. Diane rolls in, looking frazzled.

"This trip to Saxony is so tiresome. How would I know how many horses are required? And they say it is so dreadfully cold there, but am I receiving an allowance to update my winter wardrobe? Apparently, no."

She kisses her step-grandmother on the cheek and nods at me. All positions from the previous dauphine's household were smoothly transferred and she is soon to leave for Dresden to bring the new dauphine—from Saxony, as I proposed—to France.

"I've heard this one is amiable, at least. And Françoise, dear, we must see about your accompanying us—you are such a comfort on long carriage rides," Diane continues, settling herself down on a delicate little sofa that wobbles precariously. "The other one, well, I mustn't speak ill of the dead, but oh my, she was so stiff and humorless. The Bishop of Rennes, who is an expert on the Spanish, told me they are intrinsically incapable of laughter. I'm not sure what *intrinsically* means, but it sounded serious."

She is distracted by Nicole coming in with a plate of fig tarts. They are for the king on his return from the hunt: six miniature tarts, each with a perfect Calimyrna fig in the center, covered with a delicate lattice of spun sugar, carefully arranged on a beautiful porcelain platter.

Nicole does not see my frantic eyes. I have no choice but to offer them to my guests and I watch in dismay as Diane quickly gobbles down two, ruining the perfect symmetry of the arrangement.

But I must concentrate on the task at hand and this time I am determined to be very clear. Carefully, I explain the theater project to Diane. "And I understand, my dear Duchesse, that once such a thing was undertaken, under the direction of Ma—the Duchesse de Châteauroux?"

"The Marquise is thinking of a similar venture, and is eager to learn from your experience," clarifies Frannie in perfect perception, even though I had not shared with her the troubles of my last conversation with Diane. But her perception does have holes; she too reaches for a tart and I nibble my lip anxiously.

Diane begins a long-winded and rather confusing description of past theatrical efforts. It all sounds dreadfully base and disorganized. The king dressed in a sheet? An untested play by that sodomite Thibouville, when Paris is full of writers of immense talent? Staged in the Duc d'Ayen's small salon, with its dreadful dark wood paneling?

"And once during a rehearsal Gilette got an arrow in her foot! And on the night of the play Soubise knocked into a large candelabra and one of the candles fell down on the bush that had been brought in to be, well, the bush, and it caught fire. The burning bush! We laughed for days." She sighs in nostalgia. "It was so much fun. If you are thinking of doing something similar, I have much experience being a maid, if one is required," Diane offers, then takes the remaining tarts.

"Thank you, Madame, it all sounds delightfully entertaining. And so many good ideas. I will certainly lean upon your expertise."

I bid the two duchesses goodbye, then quickly call to Nicole: "Fresh peaches from the hothouse. Go now, we haven't much time; it's almost five. Have them sliced and arranged on the blue—no, the pink platter, the one with the stars. And don't forget to peel them!"

⁓

I propose my new idea to Louis.

"Well, it could be a bit of an undertaking," he says, his face a well of worry. "And with the hunt promising to be so strong this winter. The deer have been amazingly fertile, something about the rains over the summer . . ." He trails off sadly.

"No, dearest, no. I propose that I—we—perform for *you*. It will be purely for your enjoyment."

"Ah! Well, that could be rather pleasant! No lines to learn—Marie-Anne was rather apt to scold if I forgot them."

I laugh. "I do not seek to add to your cares, when you have so many already. No, dearest, this is all for you." And for me, I silently add.

With the unstinting cooperation of Uncle Norman, we erect a small theater in the Little Apartments, complete in every detail. The scenery is painted by Perot and the costumes designed by Perronet, the most fashionable of dressmakers. Everything is beautiful and luxurious: I have the resources of a nation at my disposal.

Those not involved pretend to be shocked by the idea. A thick rumor circulates that the king will soon be dismissing me, for never, it declares, has the monarchy been brought so low: "She proposes actors alongside—alongside, I repeat, the noble participants! Great ladies cavorting with grimy theater girls! Counts mixing with comedians!"

I am happier than I have been all year and can ignore the snarls and whispers. How I miss performing! What joy to lose oneself in the scenes of another world, to pretend for an hour, or an afternoon, that I am somewhere else. We decide on *Tartuffe* as the inaugural play. Bernis urges something less controversial, but I insist; the play is no longer banned, and done right, it can be so amusing.

I audition my friends and find a few surprises: Frannie has beautiful elocution and the Duc de Duras' tiny mouth produces some excellent notes. The Duc de la Vallière is very talented—he shall be my Tartuffe. Though his craven voice is devoid of talent, to please Louis I give his old friend the Marquis de Meuse a small part. I shall play Dorine, the maid.

Diane is most put out by my refusal to allow her to play that part and is calling me a tone-deaf *grimple* behind my back. I don't know what she means by *grimple;* nothing complimentary, I am sure. Elisabeth also turned out to be terrible onstage, as awkward as a cow on ice, and will not be participating. I put her in charge of overseeing the tablecloth. I fill the rest of the roles with competent members of my staff, and professional actors from Paris.

At last the night arrives. I float on the stage in a simple gauze costume, virginal white belted with a sash of blue, and I can feel his eyes on me. He watches with a select audience that includes my brother, Abel, finally coaxed to Court; Uncle Norman and Elisabeth; the Maréchal de Saxe; a few other intimates. Invitations, it is whispered, are as rare as blue steaks, and the Court empties as the uninvited claim urgent business in Paris that they could not miss for all the world, or for an invitation to *Tartuffe,* had one been offered.

De la Vallière excels as Tartuffe, as do I as Dorine. Later we hear that the Marquis de Gontaut laughed so hard during the infamous table scene that he wet his new pea-green breeches.

After the success of the evening, Louis insists I wear my costume to bed and his passion is fourfold and forceful. As the night edges toward dawn, I am exhausted by everything—the play, the lovemaking—but I am utterly content. I have found something unique to offer him and the future unfurls in a whirl of comedies and light farces, perhaps the occasional tragedy, with me at the center.

From Françoise, Dowager Duchesse de Brancas
Dresden, Saxony
January 20, 1747

Darling,

New Year's greetings to you too, my friend. It is as cold as a winter sea here and my hands are chapped beyond repair. Apart from a large nose—perhaps too much snuff in childhood?—I believe our new dauphine compares favorably to the previous one. Richelieu has joined us here and declared he would be quite prepared to poke her, were she an actress. (That is going a little far, even for him; I hope his words do not reach the king.)

We are looking forward to the festivities upon our return. A good idea not to hold a masked ball, even though we know the king loves them. And do keep the guest list limited: don't invite the Parisian bourgeoisie but keep it confined strictly to our little Court. One can always find out about Court intrigues, but the Parisian wives are another matter. I remember how everyone was desperate for information about you at the beginning, and all the fabrications that flew around!

On that note, I must warn you about the Comtesse de Forcalquier—the one they call the Marvelous Mathilde, married now to a cousin of mine. The last time she was at Court she was feted as though she were the Madonna herself. She's just a child with an irritating laugh—to listen you might think her twelve, not twenty-two—but she is ravishingly fresh and beautiful. I heard that Maurepas has been singing her praises, and you know how the king depends on that man. I will say no more.

The Saxons are rather gross in many respects but their women do have lovely complexions. I have found an excellent skin cream, made from lard and lead, and I plan on filling half my carriage with it. Do satisfy Bernis that I have not forgotten him: he shall have his share.

With the fondest of embraces,
Frannie

Chapter Twenty

A new sound greets my ears. Well, not a sound so much as something far sweeter: silence. If not kindness and friendship, then at least now I command respect. After two years at Versailles, my enemies are resigned that I am here to stay, at least for a little while.

But though there is silence within, outside the palace walls there is vitriol and hate. Songs and poems abound; *Poissonades,* they are called, because they are about me, always about me, endlessly about me.

> *This whore who insolently rules*
> *It is she who decides at what price the honors of the*
> > *Court*
> *In front of this idol all must curtsy and scrape*
> *The greatest in the land suffer this disgrace.*

"It's because you're so powerful, because all know you hold the king's heart in your hands," murmurs Frannie in her soothing way. "Why, you could even see it as a compliment: 'In front of this idol.' They are calling you an idol."

Before the ritual of my public morning toilette I like to drink a cup of coffee alone, to fortify myself before I face the day and the many decisions and entertainments that will come with it. Frannie has joined me; Madame Adélaïde, the second-eldest of the king's daughters, was up all night crying with a toothache and Frannie has just been relieved of her duties.

"The word *whore* in the first line rather detracts from any compliment," I say drily, taking the paper and looking at it again.

Maurepas hand-delivered it at dawn; he is diligent in keeping me apprised of these poems. For my safety, he said gravely, and barely bothered to turn around before he started laughing.

I know Maurepas is behind many of these songs and they say he employs writers just for that purpose. Fool. I stare into the black void of my coffee cup and add another nip of sugar—I'm filled with a sweet craving and hope I am pregnant again.

"This is an interesting set, dearest—is it new?" asks Frannie, stroking the coffeepot with one long alabaster finger.

"Yes, I can't decide if cups shaped like cabbages are vulgar or perfect," I murmur, swirling the coffee around, distracted. They say you catch more flies with honey than vinegar, but I'm beginning to doubt that. Men like Maurepas have too much pride to ever be my friends, no matter how sweet I may be to them. Perhaps I should strive for fear, rather than trying to win them over?

"Well, I've got to go," says Frannie, getting up to kiss me. "Catch a few winks before that miniature powdered tyrant starts howling again."

She leaves and I go to stand by the window and look out over the peaceful dawn. *This whore who insolently rules.* The whole of the gardens and parks stretches before me, magnificent and vast, covered with a faint sprinkling of spring frost. I'm not an insolent whore, but I do rule. And I know a lot of writers, I think, remembering Maurepas' savage smirk as he delivered the note, just in time to ruin my day. Well. Two can play at almost any game.

The next week a caustic ditty about Maurepas circulates, comparing his alleged impotence to a frog's, his reedy voice to a chicken-seller's. I set it to music and one night at supper I sing it for the king, and our little crowd convulses with laughter. Maurepas will learn of our concert, of that I am sure. Vice can be overlooked, but at Versailles, to be ridiculous is death.

თ

"Charming, absolutely charming. This room is delightful. And what a handsome writing desk—is that pear wood?"

I greet Uncle Norman and my godfather, Paris de Montmartel; the days when I travel to do homage are long past. I indicate that they may be seated and feel a rush of excitement. I now know how intricately Montmartel is connected to the running of the country; they say that he and his three brothers are the four wheels that make the gilded carriage of France glide smoothly forward. And it seems they need my help with the steering.

"Madame." Montmartel flicks out the long skirt of his damask coat as he seats himself. We make small conversation—he admires a set of paintings by Liotard; I inquire after his wife—but soon he rolls round to the reason for his visit.

Orry, the king's finance minister, must be dismissed.

Norman nods in approval. Montmartel is impassive; only his eyes, small and dark, brim with expectation. Expectation that I will understand and not make this interview more awkward than it has to be. There have been previous requests from him—easily granted—but this is the biggest yet. He gets up to walk around the room; he is almost sixty but still cuts an elegant figure. I remember how dazzled I was by him when I was younger.

"He is refusing our bills and insisting on cheaper options. Impossible. War must be funded, and we have the best prices on all ammunitions and supplies." The war over Austria's succession, begun in 1740, grinds interminably on, into its seventh year now.

"I understand, gentlemen. The war cannot be won without ample provisions. How else will France triumph?" Secretly, I am pleased. Orry is becoming more vocal about my expenditures, especially as they pertain to my wardrobe and the theater.

I look down at my hands, waiting for what will come next. This is new territory for me. This is not the appointment of an equerry for the dauphine's household, or a tax-farmer in Toulouse—small favors for family and friends Louis grants me without thinking twice. Even Claudine, my friend from my convent days: her husband is now a magistrate in the Norman Parlement.

"Corners must not be cut—corners are like foundations, Madame, and the whole of the army risks tumbling if ill-advised economies are made. Or if our bills are not paid."

"Such a pity Orry is so intractable," I say politely.

"I speak for my brothers: our pique is such that we are considering putting an end to loans to the Crown. There will be no more money for wars, or other entertainments, as long as that man Orry remains in place."

The king comes in, unannounced, and walks over to kiss me. Was he listening at the door? Surely not. Norman jumps up and Montmartel sweeps down in a deep bow.

"Darling, Uncle Norman brought my godfather to see me."

"Of course, of course. Monsieur de Montmartel, always a pleasure."

"We were talking about the plans for the plumbing at Crécy. Montmartel has a strong interest in plumbing and drainage. He is thinking of installing a . . . a . . . at his new house . . ." I am babbling, suddenly afraid. Louis may be easily led, but does not like to *know* that he is being easily led.

"New plumbing at my brother's house in Plaisance," says Montmartel smoothly. "The Marquise has become quite the expert and the faucets of Crécy are the talk of the architectural town."

"Ah yes," agrees Louis, "that room at Crécy with both hot and cold water is quite the marvel! Delightful."

When Uncle Norman and Montmartel take their leave, I let them know with my eyes that their message has been received.

* * *

Dining in public is usually a trial for Louis—when he is required to do so, he often claims a headache—but today his young daughter Madame Adélaïde, fifteen years old, attended for the first time and he is in a good mood, a proud and happy papa. After the formal *couchée* he comes directly to my apartment and settles in a chair by the fire to enjoy his new hobby: the engraving of gems. The little sharp knives and a vise are laid out for him on a marble-topped table, and I sit next to him with some wine and a plate of roasted walnuts. I have a gem I am working on as well, but am rather mindlessly tracing a circle.

Occasionally I stop and look at the fire. I take a sip of wine and think of my daughter, Alexandrine. She is still at Étiolles, in the care of a nurse; soon we will find a place for her in the finest Parisian convent. Thinking of her makes me smile, but also sad. I run my fingers over the fur robe that covers my stomach: there have been other scares and sorrows, but nothing has come of anything. But I never cease my prayers.

One day. Soon.

And then my happiness will be complete.

Louis works away, humming an aria from *Agrippina,* performed here last week. I look at him fondly; he loves these cozy evenings together, blissful hours when he can pretend he is not the king.

"You're nibbling your lip, dearest, are you worried?"

I start, and realize he has been watching me. I smile and take a deep breath, quelling the sudden flutter in my stomach.

"Darling, Orry was rude to me again. About the expense of the new flying carriage for the theater. I know how you admire him, but he has no understanding of the demands of art."

"I'll talk to him," murmurs Louis, frowning at his piece of agate. He is engraving a ship; his instructor had deemed the angular lines more attainable than the rippling petals of the rose he originally attempted. He likes this pursuit, the focus and the concentration required. I take another sip of wine. The time is now.

"I think another man might do a better job, and be more amenable. Orry has alienated the Parisian bankers and it seems he goes out of his way to cause trouble."

"But Orry is honest, and efficient. A friend. Did you see the Comtesse de Livry's ruby choker? The stone was engraved with a likeness of her dead son. Of course, it was hard to see who it was, but I thought it a splendid concept." Louis pauses and looks at the fire, his features closing in as they do when he thinks of death. A log snaps in the hearth as though in sympathy.

"What a touching idea!" I exclaim. "And such skill required." I know Louis as well as he can be known; like the back of my hand, I sometimes think, but with the gloves still on. I must pull him back from the abyss he is about to fall into. "Have the last one. Catch."

I lob a walnut at him.

"What? Oh, thank you."

"So we should consider replacing Orry?" I take up my piece of agate and rub it nervously between my fingers, feeling the rough indent of the circle. An *O*—for Orry.

Louis frowns and chews the walnut. He peers at his little gem, turns it over by the candle flame. "'I saw the angel in the marble and carved until I set him free.' Michelangelo, I believe. I am not sure I can see the little ship in here that desires its freedom. And whom do you suggest, dearest?"

"Machault, the Intendant of Valenciennes," I reply promptly. The instructions came by post after my godfather's visit. I don't know Machault but I know he will forever be in my debt for helping him rise. I feel a frisson of excitement. This is not the traditional power of a woman over a man. No, this is entirely different, this is power over policy, over the fate of a nation. I am, I think in amazement, the most powerful woman in France, exactly as the fortune-teller predicted. Well.

"Ah, yes. Machault. A fine man. An interesting proposition, indeed. Now, let me show you this; the first sail is almost complete."

As I rise my piece of agate falls and rolls under the fire grate. Someone will find it in the ashes in the morning. I lean over Louis to admire his sail, then kiss the back of his neck and run my hands softly through his hair. He sighs in pleasure and pulls me closer.

The next day I remind him of his desire to see Orry replaced with Machault, and the wheels of change rumble into motion. One of my women finds my piece of agate in the hearth and returns it to me. My little *O, O* for Orry, soon to be gone. I feel a smidgen of guilt—he is an honest and efficient man—but really, he brought this on himself. Somewhat. On a whim I drop the gem into the glass bowl where my goldfish swim. The stone floats down and nestles at the bottom amidst the drabber rocks and pebbles. Above, the fish swim serenely on.

Should I add more stones, one engraved with a *P* for Périgord? She hasn't returned to Court yet, though rumors still abound. And another with *MM* for Mathilde? A stone for each of my rivals, I think, then smile at my foolishness. And besides, they aren't vanquished yet.

From François Paul le Normant de Tournehem
Director General of the King's Buildings
Rue Saint-Honoré, Paris
September 5, 1747

Darling Daughter,

A quick note before the carriage departs. At Fontainebleau I shall oversee the changes you requested to the Queen's Apartments. The six Aubussons are in hand and Dubois will take charge of the paneling. All will be done in secret as requested, but the rooms will be magnificent when finished—surely such a thoughtful gesture will dispose Her Majesty toward you?

Though your brother says he cares not for such trifles, I am sure Abel is delighted with his title of Marquis de Vandières. I am entirely in agreement that we must seek a wife for your brother, from the highest family in the land. The Princesse de Chimay is an ambitious but intriguing idea.

Also an excellent idea for him to work with me, in anticipation of my retirement—my gout is progressing and I have periods of fatigue and worse.

I received your request for a position in the Water Department for Nicole's aunt's cousin's son—consider it done. My dear sister-in-law's cousin Madame de Tournoy has asked me if you would be disposed to receive her daughter next month? I assured her you would be delighted.

'Til Fontainebleau, dearest one,
Norman

Chapter Twenty-One

There is one domain, only one, where I do not wield the influence I would wish. One domain that remains stubbornly impervious to my growing power.

His family.

The new Saxon dauphine has not proved any friendlier to me than her predecessor. When I was presented she gave me the bare minimum of courtesy and the dauphin remains my implacable enemy. That couple, along with Mesdames their sisters, form a priggish religious faction at Court known as the *dévots,* while those with more liberal leanings are known as the *philosophes.* Frannie tells me that the dauphine even called me a heretic, due to my support of the *Encyclopedia.*

A heretic! I have to laugh. The new book they call the *Encyclopedia* aims to capture the sum of man's knowledge in this world, and challenges ideas held by the Bible. It has become a rallying point for those who support new ideas and who believe that Versailles, despite its profusion of chandeliers and candles, could be more enlightened. And so she called me a heretic! Apparently the king only raised his hand, and counseled prudence.

Despite these setbacks, I continue my efforts to ingratiate myself with his family. I send the queen flowers and compliments almost daily but I am never allowed the entrées to her apartments I desire. Even my redecoration of her rooms at Fontainebleau did not succeed: all her gratitude was directed to the king.

Elisabeth calls me naïve, and Frannie asks me why I would walk down a path that is strewn with thorns. Bernis reminds me that even Jesus knew when to give up.

"And why this constant need for approval from the queen?"

snaps Elisabeth one afternoon when I am despondent over the return of a magnificent basket of snapdragons, fresh from the gardens and unrivaled for their size and color. "Isn't half the Court in your thrall enough for you?"

"Half," I murmur. And not exactly in my thrall; it is more acceptance than adulation.

Elisabeth snorts. "Cousin, the queen is entirely inconsequential."

"Shhhh." There are far too many servants in the room: Nicole is directing a parade of women carrying my gowns and accessories. My wardrobe has long since spilled out of the confines of my apartment and into a house I rent in town. I find it easier to schedule my weekly wardrobe ahead of time, rather than to wait until the desired gown is retrieved.

"Certainly the orange *saque* for the little supper on Wednesday," I say to Nicole, who directs the beautiful gown, a cascade of gossamer and silk, over to the dressmaker.

But it is true what Elisabeth says. While I endeavor to be kind to the queen—what harm has she ever done me?—she is rather inconsequential. Poor woman, I think, as I have thought more than once.

"And besides, dear," chips in Frannie, stroking a pair of delicate toile sleeves, real gems twinkling in the folds, "the queen recently presented the Comtesse d'Egmont with a watercolor of a bush and now she is obliged to display it and had to redo the décor of her entire salon! Oh, but that one is beautiful!" She gestures to a lovely yellow jacket sewn with stiff rosettes of silk that is being held out for inspection. "Exquisite—is it new? It would be perfect with your pearl-crusted petticoat. The silver one, I mean."

"The fit is a little uncomfortable—it stretched not quite the right way the last time I wore it. Or perhaps my stays were at fault."

"Well, cousin, if you are not partial to the jacket, you must give it to me! Yellow is quite the best color for my complexion," Elisabeth chips in.

"Of course, dearest." I am happy to oblige but stricken with a slight ethical dilemma: yellow is certainly *not* Elisabeth's best color.

Louis is away today at Marly, hunting with a group of close companions. They will spend the night there. Men only. D'Ayen has sworn he will let me know if female guests, of the uninvitable sort, are invited, but I'm not sure he will.

I feel rather distracted and anxious: the disorder in the salon, strewn with robes and gowns and packing baskets, is making my head hurt. Louis left me a long list of naval promotions that I must review and comment on; the stack of papers looms ominously on my lap. While I am thrilled that he seeks my input on everything, it is almost a full-time job. I run my pen down the list of names. I make a check mark against the Chevalier de Sillery— related to Puysieux, now the minister of foreign affairs—and run a line through a name I don't recognize.

"And Mesdames?" I ask Frannie, turning back to the vexing subject of the king's family. "Did they enjoy the casket of smoked pigeons?"

Frannie stops stroking a pair of pale lavender gloves. "Now, don't make me repeat any ugliness," she says kindly, avoiding my gaze. "Madame Henriette is a gentle soul, but her sister Adélaïde . . . well, the less said about that one, the better. But the leather of these gloves is so soft! Fetal calf, am I right? Who supplied this fine stuff?"

The king's youngest daughters, ranging in age from fifteen to eleven, are soon to return from the Abbey at Fontevraud, where Fleury sent them years ago to save on the expense of their upbringing. Perhaps Mesdames Victoire, Sophie, and Louise will be more disposed toward me, I think, nodding at a straw hat that Nicole suggests matching to the calico I will wear in the gardens on Friday. Then I have to laugh at myself: of course they won't be any kinder to me. Why would they be? They'll be under the sway of their elder sisters. I heard that Madame Adélaïde likes to call me *Maman Putain*—Mother Whore.

I confirm the mulberry-and-cream robe for my Tuesday toilette, then confirm the Marquis de Cremore on my list of promotions. I wonder what Louis is doing at this moment, at Marly. Safely returned from the hunt, and hopefully looking forward to a small supper with his friends. He returns tomorrow, and we will attend the Opéra in Paris—*Tamerlane,* by Handel. Oh, I must remember to invite the Prince of Monaco to join our party—Louis mentioned him favorably last week. Or have I already done so? I frown and rub my temples.

"What's the matter, dearest? Is it your head?" inquires Frannie kindly.

"No, no." I wave away her concern. "Oh, no, Nicole, I am not dismissing the blue brocade. It is perfect for my audience with the Marquis de Saint-Clair. Perhaps a relic from a saint," I muse, thinking again of the queen and turning back to the list of names. "I must see if she has a particular favorite that her confessor recommends . . . perhaps that would be better received than the Comte de Frugie?"

"Cousin?" asks Elisabeth in confusion.

"Better received than flowers and fruit, I mean." I peer at the stack of suggested appointments; the scribe's handwriting is hard to decipher and the afternoon light is fading.

"Oh, but that turquoise silk is divine!" exclaims Elisabeth as a woman holds the magnificent gown up. "Are you sure it fits you?"

"Do any of you know a Chevalier de Fabrique? The Marquis de Velours?" No, surely those cannot be the right names; I must be seeing things. I sigh and rub my temples.

"The turquoise is blissful, indeed, and paired with your rose taffeta petticoat it will be just perfect," says Frannie, getting up and coming to stand in front of me. She lays a cool hand on my brow. "Darling, why don't you take a rest? Go and lie down. I'll finish the wardrobe decisions and those silly naval appointments can wait for another time. Come."

I allow myself to be guided into my bedchamber and lie down gratefully. I call out, "The green mousseline for the meeting with the cardinal? With the matching train?" but Frannie has already glided out; I don't think she heard me. I close my eyes. I'll rest but only for an hour or two, just until this slight headache passes. I promised Bernis I would dine with him and his cousin then, and I've already canceled our meal twice this month. Perhaps he will have an idea for a suitable relic that will dispose the queen toward me—he is an *abbé,* after all.

Chapter Twenty-Two

"The poor have it; the rich need it; you will die if you eat it," says the Duc d'Ayen.

Nothing, I think, but allow the other guests a chance to shine. Riddles are the latest craze; the wine flows and the level of irreverence rises as the bottles empty. Rarely have I seen Louis laugh so hard as he does this night at supper, enjoying the foolery and the wit.

I'm in a good mood too; I can't stop smiling at Louis and when he smiles back I feel my insides flutter. Recently I have found myself tired after our nights together, and sometimes even wish for a night alone, but not tonight.

"Rotten bread!" cries the Marquis de Meuse, asinine as always.

"The rich don't need rotten bread," dismisses Louis. "What about . . ." He looks around for inspiration, at the detritus on the table, at the glossy faces of the guests by candlelight. "What about servants? One could say the poor have it, as they *are* servants, and we certainly need them. I'm not sure one would die from eating a servant, but it would be most unpleasant."

"Excellent choice, Sire, and very, very close. But not quite, I am sad to say," says the Duc d'Ayen smoothly. He is wearing a rather ridiculous pigtailed wig; he once dressed as a Chinaman for a masked ball and now keeps the wig for regular wear.

"I believe I know," says the Princesse de Robecq, turning to the king. "It is a riddle within a riddle; the answer is *nothing*."

The other guests clap and the princess smiles serenely.

When we retire, Louis holds me in his arms and whispers with moist champagne breath: "Far more attentive than Marie-Anne, far kinder than Pauline, far more amusing than Louise."

Oh. I can't believe he said their names.

He kisses me passionately and says my name over and over, then mercifully passes out from the wine. I sigh in relief and peer at the clock on the mantel; in the shadow of the remaining sconce I can make out the little hand at three. Enough time, if I can fall asleep now.

❧

The next day the rains settle in and I feel a migraine approaching, the outline of a dark beast on the distant horizon, its shadow coming closer and closer. I lower myself into bed and soon the beast arrives, armed with a little hammer, and starts to chip away at my head.

Supper is in two hours, but I cannot. I cannot.

Elisabeth is at my toilette table, having her hair done. Please go, I say silently.

"Did you see Anne-Marie last night? I would not worry, dear Jeanne, but those eyes! Enormous—larger than yours, most definitely. And clever too: 'Taller than Duras, fatter than Ayen, smaller than Soubise—the Marquis de Gontaut.' That was a good one!"

She is talking of the Princesse de Robecq, a willowy widow, back at Court after a lengthy absence. Nicole tells me I mustn't worry, for apparently she is madly in love with the Comte de Stainville. That is no consolation and I would laugh if I could: Who would choose Stainville—a decidedly mediocre man with an ill-deserved reputation for intelligence—over the king? I think of Louis' passionate kisses last night. Was he thinking of someone else when he whispered the names of his previous lovers in my ear?

"You must curb your enthusiasm, Elisabeth," I murmur, a particularly vicious blow with the hammer making me wince.

"It is not *my* enthusiasm," she grumbles, "but rather that of Maurepas that should concern you; he declares the Princesse de Robecq the wittiest woman in France. You know how the king listens to him." She pats her hair in satisfaction. "What do you think, Jeanne? Perfect, or perfect? Your woman is very skilled."

"Delightful," I say, taking a peek at a riot of chartreuse bows. "Please tell the king I will not be down. You do the honors, or let the princesse—no, you must do them—we can't give the gossips . . ." I trail off as my head is run over by a carriage that squashes everything, including the beast and the hammer.

Elisabeth leaves and closes the door rather loudly. Nicole presses a wet cloth, bathed in jasmine oil, against my temples but the smell is putrid to me and I push her away. Below, life is happening; up here I am a wounded animal, hiding in darkness.

Shortly Elisabeth returns, trailed by a nervous Bernis.

"Cousin, the king says if it is not a fever, you must come down. You are expected."

I keep my eyes closed. No, no.

"The king insists," adds Bernis, his face sweaty with distress. "And in such a cold manner! But my dearest Marquise, it is because he cannot be without you. Oh my, oh my!"

Louis is a barnacle, I think, clinging to a hull, so heavy it drags the ship down and everyone aboard drowns. I muster all my will and slide out of bed. One hour—two at most? Then into the peaceful oblivion of sleep. I can do this. May he never know what he does to me. Barnacle. I vomit into a bowl, then let myself be poured into my gown.

I make it through the evening but the next day I collapse and cannot leave my bed. The Court journeys on to Fontainebleau without me and it is only a week later that I am well enough to follow. My lassitude continues, touched with fever. Nicole massages my temples and prepares cool drinks of milk mixed with sugar. I hold her hands and smile at her gratefully; she is the quiet constant in my life, dependable and reliable.

∽

"Dearest," he says, coming into my chamber though I know he is supposed to be meeting with the Dutch ambassador. He is looking very handsome and pleased with himself, and I cannot resist his smile or the look of pleasure on his face when he greets me. It has been a hard few months; the endless war with Austria is finally over but the Treaty of Aix-la-Chapelle that ended it was not favorable to France. All we gained from eight years and thousands of deaths was the dusty little dukedom of Parma, while the Empress Maria Theresa remains firmly on the Austrian throne.

"As stupid as the peace," they are saying in Paris, and of course it is all blamed on me. An engraving appears showing me holding the king in chains, with him being whipped by foreign countries. Louis is indignant, and insists that he made peace as a sovereign and not as a lowly merchant, bargaining for advantage. I told him that was not the right sentiment, but for once he did not listen to me.

I am glad for the peace, of course, but the idea that there will be no more expeditions to the front fills me with hopelessness. I will never be alone, never able to rest properly.

"Darling. That coat looks wonderful on you," I say as he leans down to kiss me.

"You knew it. I was afraid the cut would be too tight, but it is as comfortable as a slipper." He sits on the bed and strokes my arm.

"Darling, there is someone I would have you meet." He calls to the antechamber and a stout man with bushy eyebrows enters and bows before us.

"Madame la Marquise, allow me to introduce you to Dr. Quesnay, the finest doctor in the land. He will ensure your health improves, that it might not drag on our happiness."

I start crying, touched and exhausted. Louis looks uncomfortable and elated at the same time, then mumbles something about Amsterdam and leaves.

Dr. Quesnay bows again and places his furred hat on the side table, where it sits like a small animal. "Do not fear, Madame, we shall have you back on your feet in no time." He has a kind face and an unfashionable mass of thick brown curls. I know him vaguely as an economist.

"I thought you were interested in matters of economy and commerce, Monsieur," I say as he examines my ears.

"The body, the country, all are in need of succor. Now, Madame, if I may be so indelicate, I should have a look at your armpits."

Soon we progress to more intimate matters. I tell him about the miscarriages and then I take a deep breath. "Even when . . ." If I can't confide in him, then whom can I confide in? "Even when I am in good health I am not so strong . . . under the sheets, as they say."

"Ah, such delicacy of expression. Delightful! Sadly, such problems are common with the females, as our Lord Creator did not see fit to endow both sexes with, shall we say, an equal capacity for rapture? But we will overcome this. When the body is well rested, the urges return."

I nod, unsure.

"I shall comb France for remedies to restore your delicate constitution. A good place to start: rest, and celery. An excellent vegetable; Celsus the Roman recommended it highly."

I try not to let my disappointment show. I am partial to celery, but only for its color—Heaven in long vegetable form. As a food it is bitter and I dislike the strings that get caught in my teeth. But I will follow his advice; my chef might prepare it in a soup, peeled.

And rest from this endless show that never ends—how I wish I could.

From Louis-François-Armand de Vignerot du Plessis, Duc de
Richelieu
Château de Fronsac, Fronsac
October 1, 1748

Madame,

It is with the utmost concern that I heard the news of your failing health. Surely not, in one so young, and from such sturdy stock? The butcher in the kitchens at my château here in Fronsac is of an immeasurable strength, and his wife as well.

I prescribe hot water and duck's blood—quite the thing for your indispositions. While you may recoil at the idea, I assure you it has been used with great effect on the wives of my peasants.

Bordeaux is delightful this time of year and acclaim accompanies me wherever I travel. The locals are a delightful folk, full of superstitions characteristic of the ignorant. The other day my hawk handler told me a local legend, about a foolish girl who aspired well above her station, and was then eaten by a wolf. But why should I think you interested in such trifling folk stories? Forgive me.

It is with the utmost sincerity that I assure you, dear Madame, of my continued allegiance and fidelity. I eagerly anticipate my return to Court in January to take up my year as First Gentleman of the Bedchamber. I am sure your anticipation is as keen as mine.

I remain your humble servant,
Richelieu

Chapter Twenty-Three

"This theater," says Bernis, his eyelids fluttering in concert with his hands, "is a peg upon which all may hang their grievances." A craze for theatricals has swept the country and I am blamed for everyone, including convent girls, wanting to take to the stage. Preachers fulminate against me as though I am single-handedly corrupting the morals of the country.

There are also grumblings about the expense, and outrageous sums are rumored.

"How could it cost two million *livres*?" I demand, crumpling the pamphlet and throwing it in the fire. "That is ridiculous. Perhaps ten theaters might cost that sum, but not just one."

For our second season, a new theater is constructed near the Ambassadors' Staircase, with room for a proper orchestra and seating, the stage wide enough for six horses to ride across. Perfection does cost but I believe it is money well spent if it amuses the king.

All of my faithful theater troupe return and there is fierce competition over even the smallest part.

"It is now more important to be a member of the cast than to ride in the king's hunting group," observes Elisabeth. I fancy a note of jealousy; this year Elisabeth is in charge of a stuffed duck that is required for one scene.

Frannie persuades me to give Diane a small walk-on part as a silent sea-nymph, in consolation for the death of her daughter earlier in the year. I reluctantly agree, and the next day I send for my daughter. Alexandrine is already four years old and as perfect as a peach, with light brown curls and blue eyes, and thankfully she has not inherited the sharp features of her father. She has a stuffed lamb she adores but the thing is filthy. I give it to Nicole to wash but Fanfan—my pet name for my daughter—is inconsolable.

"Little Agnes must be clean and washed, just like you."

"She will drown!" insists Fanfan, fighting back tears. "Agnes doesn't like the water."

"The women will make sure she doesn't drown." I hug her tightly and breathe in the sweet scent of her childhood innocence. "Now, Nicole is going to take you to visit Marguerite de Livry's new puppy. The little dog's hair is curly, like a lamb."

"Like a lamb?" asks Fanfan in wonder, allowing herself to be pried from my arms by Nicole. I close my eyes and cling to the memory of her warm shadow. She is all of my life; I would be lost if anything were to happen to her.

Our first play for the season is an adaptation of Handel's opera *Acis and Galatea*. During rehearsals Diane confirms my fears by constantly missing her cues and even when pushed onto stage at the right time, she often forgets where she is to stand. At the final rehearsal, she trips on the blue fabric that ripples across the floor as our river, falling and entangling herself in the stream of velvet.

When the night comes, I perform as Galatea in a magnificent costume: shimmering silver and green satin over a pale rose bodice, my long hair loose and entwined with seashells. I sing against a glorious backdrop of clouds in sunset, surrounded by my faithful Nereids, one of them struggling to stay upright.

After the performance Louis joins me onstage, accompanied by two footmen carrying the most enormous basket of red roses the world has ever seen. In front of everyone he kisses me. "You are the most delicious woman in France, and I wish to spend all my hours and my days with you," he whispers softly in my ear. I am suddenly deliriously, absurdly happy. *He* is my tonic, my celery, my medicine.

He will keep me strong.

Chapter Twenty-Four

In January 1749 the Duc de Richelieu returns to Court to take up his year as First Gentleman of the Bedchamber. His return is greeted with cheers from my enemies, for it is assumed that Richelieu will torment me until I have to leave. He bounces smugly around the palace with a huge pack of courtiers following him like hounds after their master.

"Still here, Madame," he says when he offers me greetings, his bow an exaggerated, sweeping flounce. I regard him coolly: Still my enemy, I think. But I am no longer that young girl playing on a provincial stage, hoping for a scrap of access to his master. Now I am on center stage and stride confidently across the plain of power. But still, appearances must be maintained.

I smile warmly: "Gone such a short while, Monsieur! It feels as if it were only yesterday you were here. We have had no time to miss you."

Richelieu is not the only unpleasant new arrival to mar a winter that grows colder and more miserable with each passing week. Louis' eldest daughter, Elisabeth, married off at twelve to an infante of Spain, returns to Versailles on her way to Parma. Thanks to the peace treaty that ended the war last year, her husband is now the Duke of Parma, and she will be its duchess.

Of course, Paris is not on the road to Parma, but Madame Infanta, as she is known, is in no hurry to see her new home; Parma is a dusty city in the middle of nowhere.

Louis is elated. "Four of them," he exclaims when he stops by, beaming, to see me after dining in public with his daughters. Madame Victoire returned a few months ago from the Abbey of Fontevraud and though uncouth—she didn't know how to curtsy properly or even how to eat an artichoke—he is very proud of her. "And I shall sup with them tonight, you don't mind, do you? There is so much to talk about."

"Of course not. What a delightful family reunion!" From which I am excluded.

"And Sophie and Louise coming home as well, within months."

"Our happiness knows no bounds," I murmur, thinking, not for the first time, that my rivals for Louis' affection take many forms. Soon there will be five daughters at Court, six if Madame Infanta stays. How frightening. We must start on marriage projects, and quickly. I allow myself a pleasant little daydream: me comforting Louis as his daughters depart, one by one, for foreign courts, and then five small pieces of coral, engraved with a variety of initials, floating down to the bottom of my fishbowl.

Soon, but not yet.

Madame Infanta installs herself in the magnificent ground-floor apartment of the Comtesse de Toulouse—now mostly retired from Court—and quickly worms her way into the king's routine. The wits wag that the king has the choice between going up in sin (to my apartments) or down to the delights of his family.

I should be happy that his daughters, and no one else, are keeping the king occupied. I feel the old fatigue return, coupled with a worrying cough.

Quesnay prescribes chocolate and I grow a little plumper but still feel tired and droopy most of the time.

"Crawfish," insists Frannie, and for two days I eat nothing but crawfish boiled in butter.

"Vanilla and ambergris," prescribes Elisabeth, saying it did wonders for her sister's heart. It's not my heart, I think as I down the sticky but delicious mixture. Or perhaps it is.

"To gain strength, you must be physically strong. 'A body as strong as wood / Is all that is desirable and good,'" declares Bernis, and forces me to lift solid blocks of iron he has procured from the stables. At the end of each hour, I am exhausted and not any stronger.

"And don't forget the celery!" chirps Quesnay. "And rest!"

"Of course," I murmur. My sleeping chamber is repainted to rid it of the light yellow-green that reminds me too much of that vile vegetable.

And rest—how can I, when there are appointments to be made, pensions to be considered, tax affairs to understand, new houses to be built and furnished, the theater to oversee and plan, as well as a king to take care of, day and night: to keep him busy is to keep him happy. His dependency is flattering, of course, but sometimes . . . sometimes I wish someone would take care of *me*.

Quesnay also wants me to limit the nights I spend with Louis, but that is not something I can easily do. The Princesse de Robecq has not returned to Court—I carved an *R* on an amethyst and dropped it into my fishbowl, feeling a little foolish—but I know there will be others. I live in fear that I will cease to please him sexually, though I am increasingly exhausted, and even disturbed, by his incessant demands.

He comes one night, late; he went out with Ayen after his official *couchée* to visit a new horse in the east stables. He climbs the stairs to my apartment, and while I serve him a glass of wine and chat about the new horse, he starts to kiss me and caress my neck. I kiss him back and lead him over to the bed—the quicker the better, then I can get some sleep. He fumbles with the buttons of his jacket and finally rips it half off, but it's still wrapped around him and somehow he manages to get his hands caught in the sleeves.

"You are helpless, Monsieur." I giggle and kiss him.

"Damned buttons," he sighs, defeated. "I feel like a baby in swaddling blankets."

"Now, don't be so silly," I scold, kissing him again.

"A baby! Or a little boy, Madame."

"Not at all," I say lightly. "Just twist your left arm and get your right arm out of the sash. Here, let me help you."

He rolls away onto the bed and looks up at me with a strange look I cannot place. "Bound!" he says. "I am completely in your power."

I am not sure what he wants me to do. I go again to free him but he squirms away. "I am in your power," he repeats, and I smile as much I am able, suddenly hating his look of childish greed mixed with arousal.

"And I have been rather naughty, haven't I, getting all caught up like this?"

I am reminded of a dog, panting for something from its master: not a bone, but a kick.

"Nonsense," I say quickly, and reach over and yank the coat off him. I give him a quick peck on the cheek and stand up, my hands trembling, feeling oddly sick inside.

"I . . ." I stagger away. "I do not feel well. I must ring for some, some . . ." I put my hand on a table to steady myself. I remain rigid by the table as he gradually snuffles himself to sleep, complaining of the cold. Only when he is firmly asleep do I slip in beside him, careful not to disturb him.

I lie awake all the night, listening to the clock ticking mercilessly forward, the threat of dawn closer with every minute. That look—so childish, so greedy, so strange. What did he want from me? I give him so much. Why does he always want more?

From Abel de Poisson, Marquis de Vandières
Rue Saint-Honoré, Paris, France
February 10, 1749

Dearest Sister,

Of course I am promised to silence! How happy I am for you:
I know how much you desire a child with the king. A child would
certainly further your position, but you must know you are already
well secure. Be content with what you have—there are many
misfortunes tied to ambition.

I am sorry to report I saw your husband last week at the Opéra,
where he has taken a box for the season. I was surprised as he is not
a cultured man, but he was blunt with his motivation: his presence
will prohibit you from attending. A petty move, for you have only ever
treated him with dignity, and he has certainly profited well from your
situation.

I shall be at Versailles next week, working with Uncle Norman; his
gout is better but I fear he is slowing down, just a bit. We will be busy
with the new apartments for Mesdames Sophie and Louise—what a
situation, to find housing and budget for five grown princesses! But I
am sure their marriages will happen in due course.

And do not think that by writing so, I wish you to consider *my*
marriage; as we have discussed, there is no lady I seek to take into
my affections. An alliance with a great family would not bring me
happiness and even if by some happy constellation of affairs I were
in love with the lady, and she with me, she would eventually come to
despise me for my lack of pedigree. That, I would find intolerable.

    Much love,
    Your brother,
    Abel

Chapter Twenty-Five

A child between us will be the glue that will never wear thin, impervious to lye or the passing of time. When I tell Louis the news his eyes fill with tears, then he turns away and mumbles something about the fumes from the new colza oil lamps irritating his eyes.

As I count down the months to October I occupy myself with a new project: a military school I propose to endow. It will be a school for young boys of good family but no fortune, similar to the one for girls established at Saint-Cyr by the previous king's mistress Madame de Maintenon. Her legacy is burnished; mine shall be the same. I am discussing the building plans with the Maréchal d'Estrées, when a sudden stab in my abdomen doubles me over. I feel something running down my legs and suddenly I know. I know.

Oh, my God.

I need to leave but Estrées' antechamber is full of courtiers, watching me, ready to tear me to bits with their sharp teeth. My equerry is instantly by my side; I reach for him gratefully. "My rooms," I murmur, and he leads me slowly through the avaricious crowd that parts before me. I hear someone whisper that I would still smile, even if my insides were falling out.

℘

Sadness and sorrow bundle up in my empty womb. It once was, but he or she no longer is, the child I would have had with Louis.

"I don't want to see him," I whisper to Nicole. "Tell him I am sleeping."

But I know it is useless, for he will come. He always comes. I take a deep breath and wipe my face and Nicole rubs cloves under my eyes to take away the sting of tears. I sit up and greet him in a bed perfumed with jonquils, surrounded by large bouquets of roses.

"A mild indisposition," I say—I have not told him about the miscarriage. I can't bear to, for speaking the words will make it real. My eyes remain dry: a small triumph.

"My dear Pomponne," he says, "how I have missed you. It has only been a day, but a day without you is like a day without the hunt! We cannot have you sick. So much has happened. I need your advice on this new tax—Parlement is resisting again—as well as another matter. And how delicious you smell! Where do the flowers end, and where do you begin?"

"Dearest," I murmur. "You look worried."

"I am, I am," he says, walking aimlessly around the room.

Selfish, I think, then shake my head: Where are these thoughts coming from? From a wounded soul, comes the answer.

"What is it, my love?" I ask, patting the bed beside me.

Louis sits and tells of a scandal in his daughters' household, so secret that neither Frannie nor Elisabeth has come to me with the details. The undergoverness of the royal princesses was found with a lewd book she had the temerity to show to Madame Adélaïde. Adélaïde then showed it to her brother and sister-in-law, who apparently fainted on seeing some of the pictures, and the dauphin's nose began to bleed.

"A serious matter," frets Louis, shaking his head. The virtue of these daughters of France must never be in doubt; even the tiniest speck of smut could squash royal marriage chances. A terrifying thought.

"A dreadful book. Of course I had to read it, that I might understand what filth my daughters had been exposed to. I had no idea such books existed! Marie-Anne did allude to them, once, and I believe Richelieu has several, but I had never considered there might be *pictures*. Engravings—extraordinary. I was going to bring it here, dearest, that we might look at it together, but I decided you might not appreciate it as I did."

"You did right," I murmur.

"Yes, I am glad I did not share it with you," Louis continues, picking at an embroidered flower on my coverlet, his face slightly flushed. "Those pictures—Richelieu called it a children's book, but I am not as worldly as he is. Some of the engravings shocked my sensibilities. The positions! And the quantity of people involved!" His fingers start shaking as he worries the coverlet, his cheeks reddening. "And in a church! There was one, a row of female bottoms, quite large ones, lined up as though to—"

"Darling, we must think of their marriages," I say quickly, forcing his mind away from the images that have captured him. "I know you don't want to see them gone, but they must marry. They must know the joys of marriage and of children." My eyes threaten tears, but instead I cough delicately into my thin handkerchief. "And the advantages to be had for France. Madame Henriette is almost twenty-two."

Louis sighs and looks up at the ceiling. "Mouths," he muses, "mouths on everyone, on everything. Extraordinary."

"And Madame Adélaïde—such a willful disposition, she needs the softening hand of a husband." I'd like to marry Adélaïde to the chief of the Iroquois in our North American colonies, but unfortunately he's not Catholic. Spain, with its dour court, or perhaps Portugal, might be suitable.

"She's in the Bastille, of course," Louis says, referring to the Comtesse d'Andlau, the woman found with the book. "As we speak, Chief of Police Berryer is working on her to find out exactly how this filth might have affected my precious ones."

"I'll talk to the Russian ambassador," I say, imagining a Court free of venomous princesses; perhaps a mass sale of all his daughters to a collection of Italian states? "And to Salieri, the ambassador from Sardinia."

"Oh, that man is tiresome and his breath annoys me. I'm off to the hunt this afternoon," he continues. "The Comte de Gaillac wants to ride and I will grant him that favor. But his breath is equally bad; you could not wish two such trials on me."

He gets up and meanders around the room in discontent.

Louis is surprisingly evasive when it comes to his daughters' marriages; certainly, there is a shortage of suitable Catholic grooms in a Europe overrun with revolting Protestants, but I am sure we could find some if we looked hard enough.

෴

Within days I am out of bed, but something is still dreadfully wrong. I devour a bottle of verjuice and rub vinegar between my legs in hopes of drying out, but still I leak a thick white liquid, mixed with blood. Like raspberry cream jelly, I think, then lean over and vomit into a vase.

"*Fluor albus,*" announces Quesnay. "The 'white flower,' as we say colloquially. A slight effluvium, common after birth or miscarriage. Also a sign of the gonorrhea, but in your case, Madame, unthinkable. I predict it will cure of its own accord, and rest, dear Marquise, rest is as always and ever recommended."

At the wedding feast for the son of the Maréchal de Montmorency, I can feel the king's eyes on me. He praises my gown, compliments my complexion, and laughs at my jokes. I know he misses me and I know he will come tonight.

When he does, I am a tangled mess of frayed knots. I feel the awful dripping and pray he won't come any closer. I am a deer frozen as the hunter approaches for the final kill. He unties my robe and when I see him recoil from the smell, something inside me dies.

"I believe you are somewhat indisposed," he says in a stiff voice.

I cannot reply; I do not trust my voice.

He leaves and I fall headfirst into the black abyss of my despair. Oh, my God, such wretchedness, such horror.

The next day I summon all my skills and step onto the stage of yet another day. I am light and airy, and I can see Louis is relieved: he hates unpleasantness almost as much as leaking women.

Chapter Twenty-Six

The note is tucked in a teacup on my toilette table:

> *By your noble and free manners*
> *Iris, you enchant all hearts,*
> *Under your feet you scatter flowers*
> *Always and only white flowers.*

No, no. White flowers. Oh, no.

"What's wrong, Jeanne?" asks Elisabeth in concern.

I pass Elisabeth the note. She instantly understands the allusion, confirming that the world knows what I have tried so desperately to hide. Nothing remains a secret here for long.

"Perhaps Maurepas has gone too far," Elisabeth says thoughtfully, avoiding my gaze.

"He always goes too far," I say. Louis did not come this morning; it is Adélaïde's birthday and he wished to spend the morning surrounded by his family. He will visit this afternoon, and on the table sits the plans for a new château I am building at Bellevue—he loves floor plans.

"You must not ignore this," advises Elisabeth, and though sometimes I question her advice, or her loyalty, this time I know she is right. "He has gone too far. This is insupportable."

Is it her love for me, or her hatred of Maurepas, that motivates her kindness?

I read again the spiteful words and imagine the whole of Paris and Versailles whispering in delight over this new mortification. Though I want to hide, I cannot. After the torment of the day I spend a restless night, circling my rooms. I go up to the roofs and stare into the blackness of the moonless night, Nicole beside me with a solitary lantern.

I never deliberately aim at anyone. But if they persist in coming into my line of fire and provoking me—what can I do?

The next morning I decide it is time to take up the sword and go to war.

"Madame la Marquise." Maurepas rises in surprise and dismisses the two men he was conferring with. He has a vase of large, flowering white hydrangeas on his desk. I hate hydrangeas—vulgar, overdressed blooms. I sit without being invited and he takes his seat again.

"What a delightful surprise, Madame." Never have I hated his high, reedy voice more. "You only need to express a desire for my presence and I—"

"When shall you know the author of this?" I throw the note on his desk and he reads it with a falsely furrowed brow. I note with distaste his mustard coat, last year's cut, his wig askew with threads of greasy black hair peeking out.

"Despicable. Utterly despicable. We must get to the bottom of this, and soon. But these authors . . ." He waves his hand in a gesture of hopelessness and I appreciate what a good dissembler he is. Perhaps even a better actor than I. "But rest assured, when I have the answer, I will not hesitate to inform the king."

Enough.

"You make light of the king's mistresses, Monsieur. Both now and in the past."

We stare at each other, all pretense of a polite façade gone, our emotions and our voices naked with hatred. It is frightening, exhilarating, real.

"You are wrong, Madame! I have always respected the king's mistresses, no matter of what sort they were."

"There is no further point to this conversation, I see." I want to hurl the vase of hydrangeas at him, see the sodden blooms dripping off his head. "But there is limited space at this Court, and soon there will be changes."

"Madame, you are overwrought. I do hope you suffer from no further . . . medical ills." He smirks, the oily sheen of politeness returning to coat his hateful words.

News of our meeting spreads and his supporters take to wearing white—fools—while those who profess my friendship eschew the color in all its forms, even for stockings. I am touched when the Duc d'Ayen wears orange silk stockings, ordered especially for the occasion, and Bernis appears with red ones, though it is clear that white would have better complemented his pink coat. Even Frannie forgoes her beloved white and wears a pale gray; *I hope it is dark enough,* she whispers.

Richelieu visits, bearing a bouquet of dazzling red geraniums, matching the red flowers patterned on his green velvet coat. Geraniums, the flower of friendship. I greet him and dismiss my women.

"He has gone too far," he says without preamble.

I watch Richelieu carefully. He hates anyone that has Louis' trust. Including myself, but also including Maurepas.

"He has," I agree.

"Yesterday he dined with the Duchesse de Villars." Villars is an evil woman and a fast friend of the queen. "In Paris, at her *hôtel.* Lobster and fresh butter lettuce, I heard."

I know he has not come to talk of food.

"Maurepas told her your dismissal was imminent." The words, said so baldly, threaten to stop my heart. "He crowed that he was the curse of all mistresses. He implied he had done away with Madame de Mailly, and even poisoned the Duchesse de Châteauroux. 'I bring them all bad luck,' he said."

I laugh shortly. "That man is an outrage."

"They were fatal words, Madame. The king will be shocked when he hears of them." Richelieu pauses, then continues, giving the impression of a man stepping lightly on stones over a puddle: "Sometimes, Madame, a little heat is needed. All men, including the king, and certainly myself, have a horror of what we like to call 'feminine flaps,' but used effectively they can be very rewarding."

"You know women very well, Monsieur."

"You flatter me, Madame."

I realize he is giving me advice and though my pride resists, I see the truth of what he is saying.

"Thank you, sir. I am glad you are my friend."

He rises to leave. "Madame, it is as Aristotle said: 'Friendship is a slow-ripening fruit, but nonetheless a sweet one.'"

ᘓᔆ

I am by nature calm and clearheaded and my years at Versailles have only heightened this tendency. Coolly I plan my next move. Someone once said timing is everything; I think they were talking of cooking, but it can be considered a maxim for any occasion.

The scene is set: delicate drooping foxglove flowers in gray vases, sad and cheerless; a plate of myrtle candies shaped like teardrops; scented handkerchiefs hidden in my sleeve and behind the cushions of the sofa. The note dramatically in the center of a little marble table.

Next to a half-eaten pie. My heart pounds with nervous exhaustion: it is opening night and I don't know how the audience will receive the play.

I am weeping uncontrollably when Louis visits, moaning about Parlement refusing to approve a new tax the Crown needs to overcome its deficit. Certainly, Parlement's resistance is worrying—they exist to support the king, not oppose him—but this time I'm not going to help him. This time, he will listen to me.

"My dear." He stops short, confusion and horror evident in his eyes.

"Poison! He says he will poison me! How can I think of eating—of doing anything—when he will poison me!" I almost fall off the sofa with the force of my wailing. Instantly he is beside me and through sobs and kisses I tell him the whole story. I grab his arm: "I would offer you some pie—cherry, your favorite—but I cannot, I cannot. Oh! I am so afraid."

"Please, please stop crying. Dearest. Darling. Pomponne."

"I cannot live constantly afraid for my life, surrounded by

hate." I flick the poem on the floor and Louis watches it sadly; he already knows the contents. "I would retire to a convent! That I might know some tranquillity and not this constant fear."

"Dearest, please. Calm yourself."

His voice is still full of concern, no hint—yet—of annoyance. I heard he left Louise de Mailly crying on the floor when he banished her, but now he cradles me in his arms and covers my face with kisses. Gradually I allow my tears to subside.

"I cannot tolerate this anymore," I hiccup. "I am suffering. I would leave."

"No, no. Versailles could not be without you," he stammers. He is a closed man, a man unused to emotion, but his words light my soul. He doesn't promise me anything, but I know I have done all I can. Without ever mentioning that detested man's name.

The next day Maurepas is gone, dismissed with a glorious *lettre de cachet.* He vomited on hearing the news; it is the hour of my greatest triumph. One less rival, I think in satisfaction, but any hope of a new alliance is shattered when Richelieu declines my invitation to a concert I am giving, citing a grievous earache. He sends a large bunch of extravagant white carnations as a gesture of his regret.

A little piece of turquoise, engraved with a simple *M,* sinks nicely to the bottom of the bowl, the fish swimming placidly on above it. And one day, I vow, there will also be another stone— perhaps a ruby—engraved with an *R.* One day.

From Abbé François-Joachim de Bernis
Saint-Marcel-d'Ardèche, Languedoc
May 2, 1749

Dearest Marquise,

No, no, no! I cannot have missed it! What woeful timing of my uncle to die, and a thousand curses on his funeral that caused me to miss such a historic event. And it is dreadful here: there are chestnuts in everything—even the wine. Such savages! I hold a grudge against my forebears for settling here in the wilds of what must resemble Mongolia.

I dined with the governor last night—a boorish man with pretensions of sophistication, and I could have sworn I found the hindquarters of a mouse in my pie. You were the subject of conversation, dear Marquise. I declared, in your honor, that you held both the love of the king and the reins of the country in your ever capable hands.

Though self-indulgent, I was proud to tell him of the role I had in your success. To think you didn't know a peer and duke from a simple duke when I met you! Or the proper form of address for greeting the granddaughter of a prince of the blood married to a count! How things have changed, my old friend.

Adieu, dear Marquise, I count the days until I am once more in civilization. And what sweet civilization it will be, now that you have so expertly removed that large and badly dressed thorn from your side.

I close with a light verse:

> *May you, dear friend, in your victory*
> *Never know another moment of misery.*

Ever in friendship,
Bernis

Chapter Twenty-Seven

"My dearest Marquise. Let me give you a kiss, in the Spanish style," says Madame Infanta, lounging on the sofa, her yellow robe spread around her like melted butter. In her features I can see Louis, but only faintly, drowned by the heavy nose and cheeks of the queen.

I lean down and endure the uncomfortable closeness of an avowed enemy. She is very stout for someone still so young and her heavily oiled hair gives off an unpleasant odor. One of her Spanish ladies, her upper lip sporting a moustache, stands silently behind her. With the arrival of the Spaniards and their overly hairy women, one wit declared he could not pay his usual gallantries to the ladies, or what he hoped were ladies, for fear of making a mistake and being imprisoned in the Bastille for crimes against God and nature.

I greet the dauphine more formally and then the Princesses Henriette, Adélaïde, and Victoire, all sitting together on a curved sofa. The two youngest ones, Sophie and Louise, have not yet been deemed couth enough to attend even informal gatherings with their family.

They leave me standing and I feel as though I am in a nest of cotton-clad vipers. In the crowd of ladies behind the princesses I see Elisabeth, newly appointed as their *dame d'honneur*, fanning herself nervously. She must have known of this invitation before I received it, yet she told me nothing. Frannie is not on duty this week; she would have warned me. I think.

"Oh!" I exclaim as a small child, in a blur of blue, dashes by and brushes my skirt with a rod of sticky ice.

"Isabelle!" reproves Madame Infanta lightly. "Look what you've done to the Marquise's dress."

"Not a worry, Madame, not a worry." The cherry ice is the same color as the tulips embroidered on the chintz and the stain blends in perfectly.

"Almost as though she planned it!" Adélaïde titters. "What a clever child you are, yes you are." She holds the reluctant little princess for a kiss, then the child squirms out of her grasp and dashes off into an adjoining room.

"What a pity *your* daughter, Marquise, could not be considered a suitable playmate for a granddaughter of France. I believe they are almost the same age," observes Madame Infanta.

"Madame Isabelle is a delightful child, most well-mannered," I murmur. "To your credit, Madame."

Madame Infanta regards me lazily. A cat, toying with a mouse, patting it around while deciding her next move. "You are looking pale, Madame. A slight indisposition?"

The side tables are burdened by vases filled with white roses.

"I am quite well, thank you. And I must thank you again for the Spanish tonic you sent, most helpful." Nicole took a mouthful for a headache, and promptly slept for seventeen hours.

Madame Infanta inclines her head as her daughter barrels back into the room, holding her ice stick to her forehead. "I am rhinoceros! *Soy* rhinoceros!" *Whump!* She trips on the edge of the carpet and she and the ice go flying. A nursemaid quickly removes the wailing child while the ice melts into a sticky red pool on the parquet.

Madame Victoire laughs. "She saw the rhinoceros in Paris and can't stop talking about it."

"I always thought unicorns would be far more attractive," observes Madame Henriette in her dreamy, faraway voice.

"Now, I have decided on a singing of *Armide,* in honor of our newest lady," says Madame Infanta. "Madame: may I present the Comtesse de Narbonne. You have met before, I am sure?"

Françoise, the young Comtesse de Narbonne, steps forward,

ravishing in a simple light blue robe, her complexion all white peaches. I remember Elisabeth gushing to me about the new lady in Madame Infanta's suite. What did she call her? A delicious dahlia. Yes, indeed.

"Our dear Comtesse is now married," says Madame Infanta smoothly. "And, if I may be so bold, as we are among women here . . . she now knows the joys of the marriage bed." Her words are pointed and sly: all the world knows the Comte de Narbonne lost his manhood at the Siege of Namur in 1746.

Since that awful scene when he untied my robe, Louis and I have spent only rare nights together and there are rumors about this young countess. Something sways inside me, though outwardly I remain calm. I greet the young girl and murmur congratulations on her recent wedding.

"I thought to have her sing to us."

Françoise de Narbonne smiles at her mistress and clasps her hands in front of her as she starts to sing. The violinists in the corner take up the melody. I study her even as I continue smiling; she is tall and slender, and oh so young, with flawless skin and surprisingly thick lips that give her face a seductive air. And—though surely not—there appears to be a slight curve to her stomach. I shake my head; no, I must be imagining things.

She chooses the aria where Armide celebrates her triumph over her lover, and as she sings she looks at me in defiance. Her voice is low and husky, as though she has a sore throat.

"'At last he is in my power,'" the young duchess sings, and I close my eyes. They will do anything to get rid of me, even support another woman in their father's bed. I feel as though I will faint, and sway slightly.

"Madame," says Madame Infanta in oiled concern, raising her hand to stop the music. "You look gray. So very gray. Are you not well again? What can we do for you?"

I regain my composure, and look around at Louis' daughters, lounging like malicious monkeys as I stand in the summer heat. They will not win. I will not let them.

"Thank you for your concern, Madame, but I am perfectly fine." A thin sheen of sweat starts to coat my cheeks and neck, and underneath my skirts my legs are trembling. "I am perhaps just a little overcome with the beauty of dear Madame de Narbonne's voice. Truly, my dear"—I turn to her—"your voice is a marvel. How I would love to sing a duet with you." Yes, there is a curve under her robe, a slight protrusion.

"A duet!" chortles Madame Infanta. "What a funny notion! I do believe Narbonne's voice carries just fine. Alone." She raises her eyebrows at me.

I smile back at her. "Then I too will sing *alone*," I say, and without waiting for permission, I launch into another aria from the same opera:

> *Flee this place, where Armide reigns,*
> *If you seek to live happily*
> *She is an indomitable enemy,*
> *You must avoid her resentment.*

No one dares interrupt and when I am finished, I curtsy deeply and smile at my hostesses. I *am* indomitable, I think, a sudden rush of confidence sweeping my body. They may play their little games but they underestimate the depth of the connection between Louis and me. The depth of his dependence on me, and the width of my reach. Nothing can touch me, not even a beautiful fifteen-year-old girl.

෨

My sources soon confirm that indeed, Françoise de Narbonne is sharing the king's bed. I don't believe this is the first time he is unfaithful to me; I know that his valet Le Bel sometimes brings young girls from the surrounding villages, and houses them under the eaves of the palace. But they are dirty *grisettes,* not Court ladies. And Mathilde, Périgord, Robecq—all are enigmas, though I suspect all have graced his bed.

My doctor, Quesnay, is increasingly concerned about my

health and finally tells me I must have no more miscarriages. The implications of his words are clear. I am only twenty-eight but it is as Quesnay says: I will be dead before thirty if I try to please this man physically.

He is all I live for, yet he is killing me.

When I tell Louis, he embraces me sadly. We both know this is the end. The end of so much, including my hopes for a child with him. I cling to him and through the night he comforts me tenderly.

"How safe I am in your arms, Pomponne. How safe." He falls asleep beside me and I think to the future. A future without children, without his arms around me. I kiss his sleeping brow, breathe in his familiar scent. When the dawn comes to take him away, he rises and takes my hands in his.

"I must go, my dear," he says, and there is true sorrow in his eyes. "But I do not go far, be assured of that. You are my friend, dearest. I would be lost without you."

And I without you, I think, staring up at him in mute misery. He leaves and I lie back in the empty cocoon of my bed. Friend. The worst of words, the best of words. I trail my hand over the warm indent where his body was, roll over and inhale the lingering shadow of his scent. I will no longer be the mistress of his five senses, paramount in all his affections. A friend.

And, though my bed may be empty, I know his won't be. A dangerous situation, though Frannie reassures me: "Remember, darling, it is *your* staircase the king goes up and down. We all know the king is a master of habit, and you are the greatest habit of all. It is with you he seeks comfort, diversion, cuddles."

I'm a habit, I think sadly, then shake my head. No, not a habit—no one loves a habit. But everyone loves their mother.

Chapter Twenty-Eight

At the end of 1749 Madame Infanta finally departs for Parma, taking the Duchesse de Narbonne—I worked hard on a sapphire engraved with a flourishing *F de N*—and much of the king's buoyancy with her. My brother, Abel, also travels south with them. He will spend a few years studying Italian art and architecture; though many scoff and say that Italy is good for nothing but pasta and poison, I know that what he learns there will benefit French artistry.

Madame Infanta's departure leaves a magnificent empty apartment. I now have almost fifty servants in my household, from my beloved Dr. Quesnay to my steward, my equerry, my chef and all his kitchen; footmen and porters, valets and torchbearers; numberless female attendants headed by Nicole; women for my wardrobes and clerks for my accounts, not to mention my coachmen and all the men in my stables. And two Senegalese pages, sent by the governor from the island of Gorée.

I need a new apartment.

I need to tell the world that though things are changing, I am going nowhere.

Louis' daughters and their growing households also covet Madame Infanta's apartment, so I must work fast. Versailles has changed me: I have become craftier and less forgiving of my enemies. There are limits to natural goodness and I now understand that once I am ahead, most everyone behind is my enemy. Sometimes I think of the trusting girl I once was, that naïve young woman who thought that everyone would be charmed by her. How wrong I was, how *foolish*.

Louis has more than once complained of the stairs leading up to my apartment, so I have Collin, my faithful steward, lever up a stair board when I next expect the king. As anticipated, Louis arrives grumpy and limping, complaining of a stubbed toe. I wrap him in sympathy and a clean white bandage, then insist I move somewhere more convenient for him, with no more of these dreadful accidents.

Louis agrees. "Yes, I did slip last year, didn't I? But whose apartment? Villemur died last month—he was inoculated three years ago, and there you see the danger—but his rooms are far too small. You need a table for at least sixteen, and of course your own kitchen."

"There must be a— Wait, I have it! The apartments of the Comtesse de Toulouse! With our dear Madame Infanta leaving, it is the perfect solution. Just a short trip down the marble stairs, well lit and spacious. No more dreadful accidents."

"Still small," observes Louis. "Perhaps we could add a few rooms from her son's suite?"

The news astounds the Court: the exile of Maurepas and now this. The largest suite on the ground floor, traditionally reserved for princes of the blood and royalty.

Those magnificent rooms will announce most solidly that I am still at the center of his world, despite what is happening, or not, in the bedchamber. And on the surface things remain as they always were. He still adores me and flatters me and defers to me. I am still the most powerful woman at Court and I control all access to the king, all appointments and all preferments.

I have woven, I think in a moment of clarity, a soft and invisible net around him. The net is very fine and very tight, and so is his illusion of liberty.

☙

"The coldest winter since '09," says the old Duc de Broglie. He regales us with stories of frozen peasants and icicles on cow udders.

It is the second hard winter in a row and the peace, after so many years of war, has not afforded any economic relief. Crops have failed for several summers and famine stalks the land.

Amidst continued grumblings about the expense, I cancel the Little Theater. In truth, I am glad, for it had become more and more exhausting. I also increase my charity and continue to support French craftsmen and artists, but my efforts are just little drops in an enormous ocean of need. Even if I am the most powerful woman in France, I am powerless against the waves of poverty and discontent that grow stronger with each passing year.

In Paris, street children disappear and rumors spread that they are taken to be drained of their blood, used to cure leprous princes. When the king travels to Paris to celebrate the Feast of the Conception at Notre Dame, the mobs call him Herod and accuse him of bathing in the blood of the disappeared children.

He is not the only target. I visit the Paris convent where Alexandrine is to be educated, and my carriage is pelted with stones and we must flee through backstreets to Uncle Norman's house.

There is even talk of burning down Versailles.

The king strides into the council room, white as a bone and shaken. Rarely have I seen him so upset. I take the note from his trembling hand: *You travel to Choisy and Crécy; why don't you travel to Saint-Denis?*

Saint-Denis is the traditional burial place for French kings. This is a direct threat, not a witty joke or a cruel sally, full of allusions and mostly directed at me.

"Now, now, Sire, not to worry," soothes Argenson. "Berryer will find the author of this outrage." Berryer is the head of the police, a man of great loyalty but still unable to stop the flow of vitriol that continues unabated in the wake of Maurepas' departure.

"On the mantel. In the Wig Wardrobe! Who put it there, I say, who would dare?" Louis' face is yellow and waxy and there is an emptiness in the lovely deep eyes that once so delighted me. In five short years he has become a far cry from the handsome man who took me in his arms in front of the fire at my mother's house. He is only forty but in tired moments appears a decade older.

"What insolence! Everything, all of it, the names, the accusations," the king continues to rail. Rarely does he show anger and the ministers watch him carefully, following his movements like apprehensive hawks. "They called me Herod—a madman who murdered his family!"

"Perhaps they were alluding to Your Majesty's many architectural achievements. I believe Herod was also a great builder?" offers Machault hopefully, but he is quickly silenced by an almost lethal glare from the king. I give him a grateful smile for his efforts: Machault, as predicted, has remained a loyal friend.

Argenson suggests seeking a scapegoat to divert the ugly rumors about the missing children.

"Any man, we can say we found the bodies of ten children in his cellar—that would exonerate Your Majesty completely." The evil of his words chill me, as do the murmurs of assent from the other men.

"But to even react to these rumors—no, I cannot have it," I say firmly. "To engage them is to give them credence."

"They already have credence," says Argenson quietly, staring at me with his hooded eyes. For once his eyes do not lower to my chest but remain firmly fixed on my face. I am struck by the menace in his voice and the tension in the room, as thick as unswept dust.

"They are like children, believing in fairy tales." The king sits down and starts to fiddle angrily with a button on his cuff.

The men watch him silently.

"They are indeed your children," Machault finally ventures.

"I will not hesitate to punish my children," says the king grimly.

"I am not sure, Sire, that that is the right—"

"From now on I shall not visit Paris if I need not! Not ever. No more opera or balls or ceremonies. I shall not travel there unless I am required at the Louvre. Or at Saint-Denis, as they so ardently wish."

"But, Sire, the capital of our great country, they need to see their king. As your illustrious predecessor once said, 'We owe ourselves to the public.'"

"No."

Only the futile buzzing of a wasp against a window breaks the silence in the room. I jerk my head in irritation to a footman and there is silence as we watch his attempts to kill it. He finally brings it down with a well-placed swish of his tasseled cane.

Louis turns to me. "Then how will we get to Compiègne?" he asks, referring to one of his favorite summer hunting places.

"A consideration, dearest, for one must pass through Paris to get there." I know he is overwrought and I don't want him to say anything he will regret later. Louis is already far too removed from his people, perhaps more so than any king before him.

"We'll build a road, a road around Paris," says Louis with the spite of a spoiled child. "Yes, that is what we will do. And it will shorten the time between Versailles and Compiègne. Most satisfactory, really."

"The expense . . ." says Machault quickly. "What with all the murmurs against extravagance that surround us these days—"

"The expense is nothing compared to the outrage I have suffered. Herod! A Herod they called me."

Louis gets up again and stalks around the room, looking for something, anything, to hit with his anger. He pushes a footman out of the window alcove and stands to look out over the snow-covered gardens. I know there is grief and sorrow there too, buried beneath the anger. Once they called him Louis the Well-Beloved; now, not six years later, they talk of Louis the Well-Hated.

From the Reverend Mother Marguerite of the Angels
Convent of the Assumption, Rue Saint-Honoré, Paris
April 1, 1750

To the most esteemed Marquise de Pompadour,

Honored greetings to you, Madame. Your daughter is well settled, the room furnished as provided, and the kitchens have their instructions. We do not usually allow stuffed toys, as the good Lord prohibits the worship of idols, but a lamb is a holy animal, next only to doves in saintliness. We scoured the thing and one of the eyes fell off, but as soon as it was replaced your daughter ceased her crying.

As per your instructions, she is to be called Madame Alexandrine. One of the younger nuns complained, saying that such a mode of address for a young girl should be reserved only for royalty. You can imagine, Madame, the punishment she received for her insolence. Also as instructed, only the most select of the other pupils will be considered as her playmates. Her education will be in the hands of Sister Anne, of the Noailles family; a more suitable tutor could not be found.

She will be learning her letters and I am confident she will soon be able to write her beloved mother a letter of her own.

I am, Madame, your most humble servant before God,
Mother Marguerite

Chapter Twenty-Nine

Summer mercifully arrives and I invite Louis to my new château at Bellevue. It is the first house that I have built from the ground up, the first one that is truly my own. It will be our perfect retreat, away from the worries of Court, far even from Choisy, which has always been poisoned for me. And Crécy: even if Boucher's panels were repainted, I would still know what ghosts and sorrows remain behind the whitewash.

The grumbling continues; critics say Bellevue is too small and lessens the majesty of the king, yet at the same time it is deemed too expensive. I will never satisfy everyone, and perhaps I should not even try.

But there is one man I do need to satisfy.

"Darling," I say as he weighs racquets for a game of *paume* he will play with the Duc d'Ayen, "I should tell you—the Comtesse de Forcalquier is coming tonight, for a few days. Alone. She needs a respite from her ape of a husband."

The Marvelous Mathilde is back at Court and her delightful face never seems to age. I think of the words of Racine: I embrace my enemy, but only to strangle him.

Louis stares at me with such astonishment and gratitude that I want to laugh and cry at the same time.

"She's coming?" he asks.

"Yes, she is."

He shakes his head as though dazed.

"Is that the right racquet, do you think?" I say, pointing to the one in his hand. "What about this one?"

"No, this one is perfect, absolutely perfect," he says, and

comes over to embrace me with a tender touch that thrills me as it drowns me in sorrow.

As the men play, a ball flies off Ayen's racquet and hits Frannie on the arm. Elisabeth and I retire in sympathy with her to the terrace to fan the hot afternoon away. One of Argenson's men, waiting since this morning to see the king, leaps forward in anticipation as we settle on the terrace. I shake my head at him.

"Where are your Senegalese?" asks Frannie. "They should be fanning you. Us."

"Sick and died, poor savages," I say. "Both of them." We fan in silence awhile and from the corner of my eye I can see the messenger tapping his foot impatiently.

I take a deep breath and ask aloud what I have been wondering all day: "Was it courageous of me, or stupid? To invite Mathilde de Forcalquier?"

"It was very courageous," says Frannie, nursing her arm. She is wearing an enormous straw hat, the size of a small table; she claims she has not a single freckle and doesn't intend to start now.

"Well, let's just hope her violent husband keeps her in black eyes," says Elisabeth lightly.

I try not to smile. I am nervous. The benediction I gave Louis was wrong, yet right at the same time. Is this what resignation feels like? All I know is that if I am not in his bed, someone else will be. Must be. Making love for Louis is like air to other men; he would die without it.

"I think it had to be done," I say. "One needs a certain . . . acceptance." I lean back and close my eyes. The sun is high overhead and I feel as though I am melted to my seat.

Argenson's man coughs loudly.

"Come here." I wave him over. "Unless it concerns the dauphine"—after a series of miscarriages, the second dauphine has finally carried a child to term and is due next month—"His Majesty is not to be disturbed today. You may see him tomorrow after Mass."

"But, Madame—"

"Tomorrow."

He departs, reluctance dragging his feet.

"Was that a *moustache* on his face?" asks Elisabeth, squinting at his departing form. "Who does he think he is, one of Madame Infanta's Spanish ladies?"

I am silent. I have a sudden premonition that something dreadful is going to happen. I listen anxiously for the sound of the ball in the distance, the shouts of the men. I pick up my fan again. Something is coming, something far worse than Mathilde. Or is it just my nerves over her arrival?

"You have nothing to worry about," soothes Frannie, seeing me chew my lips. "Mathilde is my cousin by marriage, and so, in allegiance to my family, I should be plotting your demise." Here she smiles, and I recall what a good actress she is. "But Mathilde is too silly for words. She'll never keep his interest for long and she has the most irritating laugh. I cannot imagine the king tolerating her for more than a few . . . sessions."

"But that complexion!" gushes Elisabeth. "The artless way she speaks, so charming in her innocence."

The men come up the stairs and collapse down on the stone benches.

"Ayen has the most powerful back swipe," says Louis, laughing at some private joke.

"Not as long as Your Majesty's stick," retorts the duke.

I rise in the heat and go to fan Louis. "Now, gentlemen, inside to change, for the guests arrive shortly. There will be cool drinks, and more, waiting in your rooms."

After a week at Bellevue we return to Versailles, and as Frannie predicted, Mathilde does not last long. When I see Louis' ardor for her is cooling, just a touch, a letter is intercepted by the police. Berryer shows it to the king, who does not recognize the writing as my own.

The anonymous note claims the young countess is seeking a divorce from her husband. There are still certain things that shock Louis, and divorce is one of them. The next day he is cold to Mathilde and the girl, not knowing what she has done, bursts into tears and thoroughly embarrasses herself in public. She leaves Court, to flee both her disgrace and her violent husband. I drop a piece of tourmaline, carved with two double *M*s, entwined—my most intricate engraving yet—into the fishbowl.

It could get quite full in there, I muse, feeling slightly queasy as I look at the pretty array of stones winking at me through the water. But will there come a day and a rival who can't be vanquished?

Chapter Thirty

I close my eyes and breathe in the memories and the ghosts, the sadness and the triumphs. My new apartments, redecorated to my taste, are finally ready. And so I leave the beautiful upstairs apartment where I have lived for four years, the rooms now as bare as when Louis first brought me here on that moonlit night. I was so young then, and the story of my life at Versailles, my improbable, wonderful, terrible story, lay still to be written.

Has anyone ever loved the way I loved my Louis? The way he loved me? The way we still love each other: not with the starry eyes of our first days, but rather with the deep true love of long years. I take one last look around, then carefully close the door and descend the stairs, heading for the great unknown on the ground floor.

After the zenith, is there only decline?

A statue of Philote, the Greek goddess of friendship, is placed in prominence in my new antechamber, beautiful and symbolic in her cold marble beauty. Another one graces the gardens at Bellevue. Love is a pleasure for a season, while friendship lasts an entire life. And it is friendship, I clarify to myself; this is no statue of Gaia, the Greek mother-goddess. Certainly, the mother bond is stronger than the bonds of friendship, but I still want to respect Louis, still want to believe that some of his weaknesses are no more than mere trifles.

So, Philote it is.

I know this is a terrible tightrope I walk, across the deepest gorge. To try to secure the love and loyalty of a man without that physical glue which binds two people together. We will be together as friends, but not entwined as lovers. Yes, I am friend, minister, companion, entertainer, nurturer, but will that be enough?

Or have I just made the biggest mistake?

If they write a book of my life, long after I am dead, will it just be a litany of one rival after another, until I am finally defeated?

I trace the eyes of Philote but the sightless marble orbs of the statue offer back no answers to my many questions.

Act III

Rosalie

Chapter Thirty-One

The first glimpse of the Marquise is like the first time you make love: something so anticipated must surely disappoint. The lauds of the poets lead you to expect making love to be like strumming on the harps of Heaven, but when the actual time comes, the reality is rather a disappointment. Lovemaking certainly improves with time and practice, but I am not sure the same can be said of the Marquise.

Of course, I am prepared. For the Marquise, I mean, not for making love, though I am well versed in that art. My aunt Elisabeth, the Comtesse d'Estrades, is the Marquise's most favored friend. Aunt Elisabeth says that without her guidance, the Marquise would be just another Parisian housewife, eating fish for dinner far too often.

I meet the Marquise at my wedding, arranged by the great woman herself in appreciation for my aunt's friendship. I will give that she is fairly attractive—Pompadour, I mean to say, not my aunt. Poor Aunt Elisabeth is living proof that God makes both flowers and weeds. But the Marquise de Pompadour—well, her eyes are lovely, large and a perfect blue gray, and her complexion still fine though she approaches her thirtieth year. She is fair enough, to be sure, but overall the effect is more of elegance than beauty.

Of one thing I am certain: she is not nearly as beautiful as I.

When Aunt Elisabeth speaks of the Marquise, resentment turns her words rancid and I know she is desperately jealous. It must be hard to be so plain, yet constantly at the side of one so elegant and pretty, if a little faded. I know well the jealousy that beauty can inspire in other women; I myself have few female friends.

My wedding is held at the Marquise's Château de Bellevue, though *château* is a rather lofty word for such a small place. It's more of an overgrown farmhouse and I would have expected something grander from the most powerful—and richest— woman in France. Small rooms, rather plain; not enough gold for my liking. I suppose it suits her humble roots.

The king and his family condescended to attend the wedding. The Mass was tolerable and the entertainments amusing; the fans and pots of pearls given to guests were well received. Only the choicest of courtiers from Versailles attended; I understand that these days, a certain acceptance of the Marquise is expected. I make the acquaintance of the highest in the land, including the Ducs d'Ayen, Duras, and Richelieu, and several princes of the blood. Invitations to Bellevue are sought after; Choisy was fashionable last decade but these days is frequented too often by the king's family.

Today I also met my husband. He does not interest me, for I saw instantly that I do not interest him. Such a thing is strange, of course, and entirely unnatural, but I have met others like him. One can usually tell by how many layers of ruffles they wear at their cuffs, or the way they hang their swords. Apparently their mothers, when pregnant, ate too many courgettes and that is what caused such an abomination.

After the dancing and a rather pedestrian ceremony featuring some singing shepherds and twenty local peasants marrying twenty village girls (though one stood out, a boy a head taller than the rest, with ginger hair and a strong, hard body), and after the royal family had departed, I was led to the bedchamber the Marquise had prepared.

There was a flush of romance in her eyes as she showed me to the room, quite stuffed with roses and violets. Roses are fine enough, though these were a lurid purple color, but frankly the smell of violets makes my head hurt.

"My darling girl," says the Marquise, clasping my hands and pulling me toward her. I am so startled I cannot even pull away—

has she no manners? "You cannot know how this day has caused me pleasure."

"Likewise," I reply crisply, and extricate myself with a curtsy. Aunt Elisabeth likes to say that the Marquise lowers the entire majesty of France with her manners.

Though the Marquise is undoubtedly elegant (I must admire her yellow satin dress, sewn with hundreds of pink pearls), there is a smack of sadness and strain about her that makes me uncomfortable. Finally the two women leave, but not before my aunt blows her nose twice, complaining of the pollen in the air, and the Marquise happily rearranges the bouquets on the side table.

Then I am alone in the small room.

I take a rose and toss a few purple petals in the air. He loves, he loves me not, I say, though I already know the answer. I wonder who is going to undress me? I can't get out of this uncomfortable formal gown myself. I pour myself a glass of something from a decanter on a side table, but it is not the weak wine I am expecting. I splutter a great gulp out over the floor. Ugh. Some strong and vile liqueur.

My husband, François, opens the door, and music and laughter float in. He closes it behind him and banishes the gaiety. We are alone.

He bows. "Madame." I suppose I should be happy; he is a Choiseul, and that family can trace their roots back to 1060. The head of his family is the great Duc de Biron; another cousin is the Marquis de Gontaut, an intimate of the king's. I gaze at François and he gazes back. He's older than I, thirty-four to my seventeen years, with hooded, rather mournful eyes and a thin, erect little body. He is wearing an overly fussy cravat of raspberry lace.

He gestures around the room. "This mess—why are you strewing the petals? And what is that awful smell of alcohol in the air?"

I fight the urge to shrug but instead I wave a hand, inspired. Even if women are not generally his preference, surely he can't resist me?

"I was just playing a little game," I say, and lean over to pick up a few of the discarded petals, affording him a full view of my wonderful breasts, which were once described as a pair of perfect angel cakes. I come up with a handful of petals, some wet and smelling of gin. I throw them in the air and as they flutter around me I smile at him, a smile thick with promises and dimples. "I was just playing a little game, asking the Fates what our love would be." I catch one of the petals and slowly place it on my tongue, then curl in and swallow. Oh—I hope rose petals are not poison.

His lips tighten in distaste. "Your manners are very bold."

"Gay and charming," I correct him. I sit down on the bed and wait to see if he joins me.

"You are expecting something, Madame?"

I laugh. "I don't think you have to be quite so hostile, really. This match was not of my choosing either."

"To insult me thus! Madame, the Duc de Biron is a Maréchal de France and my cousin the Marquis de Gontaut is an inti-mate—"

"I know who your cousin is," I snap.

"Madame, I should inform you he was against the alliance: he suspected that the morals of your mother were not of the high-est order."

I giggle.

"And you yourself appear to be very forward," he continues in distaste.

"I grew up in Paris, not this village! And I would wager it was in the family interests to get you married as quickly as possible, or you'd probably be shipped off to the colonies." Or put in the Bastille, I want to add. Both of François' brothers live in Saint-Domingue, miles away in the Caribbean. It was a definite article of my marriage contract that I was not ever, under any circum-stance, to join my husband should he decide to go there.

"Perhaps a preferable fate."

"I doubt it," I say airily. His hooded eyes have a certain charm and I have a sudden strong desire to make his mournful face smile. I am very beautiful and one is always attracted by beauty—who hates a rose? Strange, really.

"Why are you so cold?" I ask. "We could still be friends."

"You are my *wife*." He stays rigid by the door and I regard him under lowered lids. The night outside is completely black and the candles in the sconces won't last much longer. I don't think they're sending in a maid.

"Would you undress me?"

"I am your husband, Madame, not a chambermaid."

"Well, you must please yourself. But don't you think it would benefit both of us if there was at least some evidence of—of . . ." Perhaps I shouldn't be quite so forward, but the man is starting to irritate me. "Of a defloresting?" I pluck a rose from a vase and chuck it at him. François winces.

"Fine."

I lift up my heavy skirts and awkwardly untie the panniers as my husband turns away in prudish aversion. I step out of them in relief and lie back on the bed. My head is starting to spin rather quickly—what was in that decanter? The ceiling of the room is painted with shepherds and shepherdesses, how odd to have peasants where Greek gods should be . . . quite déclassé, really, the Marquise has *no* taste at all. Though that dress she wore was rather beautiful, especially the little flowers sewn entirely of seed pearls that decorated the shoulders.

Perhaps in the morning I'll have enough energy to tackle this bodice, I think as my head continues to whir like a weathervane. We could claim he was so eager, all he could do was lift my skirts. I have to chuckle at that. At least there won't be any awkward moments while I pretend to whimper in pain, unless he tries . . . no, he wouldn't dare. Though I would be intrigued to try that myself.

Presently François lies down beside me, declaring himself tired and needing rest. My mind still races and I wonder again what was in that decanter, then worry about the rose petal I swallowed, still leaving a singular taste in my mouth.

Next week I'll be presented at Court and take up my duties

with Mesdames, the king's daughters. I accepted the wedding and the position with gratitude but no fawning, as all that was due to me, the great-granddaughter of a Maréchal de France and the niece of the Marquise's favorite.

My thoughts dart back and forth over the events of the day and the coming of my exciting future. Today I saw the king for the first time. He is a fine-looking man, though a trifle old and jowly. I certainly wouldn't call him the most handsome man in the kingdom; perhaps twenty years ago but not now. The Marquise hung off his arm the entire day, as sticky as a leech—does she not know how embarrassing she is? His son the dauphin was looking quite handsome, a somewhat pudgy beauty but there was something pleasing about his face, and his blue velvet coat.

The dauphine was also there, with her large, ungainly nose. I've heard she is an absolute termagant and keeps the dauphin on a tight leash. I wonder if my dog Schneepers should come with me to Versailles, or should I leave him in Paris with my mother? Traveling with a dog in a carriage can be insufferable, especially in summer when it's hot. They say it is hot in Saint-Domingue; one of François' brothers, visiting from that island, was floating around morosely at dinner.

"What do they call him, that, uh, servant of your brother's?"

"What?" François asks in surprise. I wonder, briefly, what he was thinking about, lying in the dark beside me.

"Your brother the marquis. His black servant there, the tall one with the white and yellow jacket. Not livery; a handsome coat really."

"How curious for you to comment on the attire of a servant, Madame. Of a slave, no less."

What a tiresome prig. How disappointing his groom's gift was a place in the dauphin's household, and not in some remote regiment. Aunt Elisabeth really should have thought things through better.

"What is his name?" I ask again.

"Antoine calls him Caliban. Says he is a Mandingo from Senegal."

Caliban from *The Tempest*. How exotic. "'Misery acquaints a man with strange bedfellows,'" I quote.

"You know Shakespeare." François' voice holds a faint, grudging respect.

"I do." Some might accuse me of being uneducated, but I like reading. Such large eyes and lips; a high, aquiline nose, and that shiny black skin . . . one cannot help but wonder if all of him is that color, strange to imagine a dark snake in place of one red and pink. He must have fine muscles, from all that sugar he has to make. "Will your brother be leaving again for Saint-Domingue?"

"He has no plans to sail again this year, he travels now to our estates in Languedoc, then will seek favor at Court. He is a most accomplished man, why he . . ."

François, suddenly talkative, drones on about his brother and soon I doze, thinking of the ginger-haired peasant boy, and then the slave Caliban, and then the dauphin's rather shy, squishy smile. I fall asleep before I have time to be disappointed that there will be no ravishing, pleasant or otherwise, on this most special of nights.

Chapter Thirty-Two

"**D**id you see it? Did you not see it?" asks the Marquise. No, I didn't see *it*, I think in irritation, my head throbbing rather wildly. What *was* in that decanter?

"Did you not see how happy he was—the king? He does love it here, almost as much as I do." The Marquise looks around in contentment. "All of these flowers, how lovely. I was worried about transplanting such mature bushes, especially with that awful storm we had last month, but d'Isle did a wonderful job and now they are blooming to perfection, and so early."

She inhales deeply as my aunt and I watch her. The Marquise is flower mad and decorates her rooms every day with fresh ones. She also has hundreds of porcelain flowers crafted, then scented with the appropriate perfume. Extraordinary. I suppose I should be glad I married in the spring, and not November, otherwise my room might have been filled with china violets, not so easy to toss around. My aunt wears a look of droll indolence on her face—she often says the Marquise must be humored like a child—and I attempt to copy her expression but the Marquise only looks at me, briefly, as though she does not quite understand.

We are walking through the gardens at Bellevue, down a lengthy terrace from the château. For myself, personally, I am not a fan of gardens: always the insects, and disagreeable winds, the sun rather hurting one's eyes, the risk of freckles or bug bites. The Marquise has a perfect sun hat, made of pink-dyed straw, tied with a matched ribbon. A little vulgar and peasanty—straw—but I must admit it suits her admirably.

"And did he not look perfect, in that green coat and the matching stockings? He did not favor the idea but I convinced him to try them, I do believe his legs are shown more finely by a dark color, instead of a lighter one . . ." The Marquise burbles happily on about the king. Aunt says she has been worshipping the king for so long she can no longer see his faults, or remember there is a way other than adoration.

"He has been so melancholy lately," sighs the Marquise, as though she herself were afflicted. "The death of Louise, the Comtesse de Mailly . . . The death of a friend always hits him hard."

"She was hardly a friend," I say sharply. "And she was banished a decade ago."

"Almost nine years," murmurs the Marquise. She has a soft, sibilant way of speaking that draws one in with the promise of revealing something exciting. I might model my speech after hers, for though the content of what she says disappoints, her delivery is perfect. She waves her hands over another row of rosebushes. "Aren't these wonderful—look at that perfect shade of pink, like the lip of a seashell."

"They are saying the king's mistresses are cursed, all dying so young," observes Elisabeth, swatting at a large bee that is circling her with intent. "Why doesn't it leave me alone? I would swear it is the same one that has been following me since we left the terrace!"

"Forty-one is not so young!" I retort. Really.

"Still, before her time," murmurs the Marquise. "Are we all cursed? Ah, but I must not think such thoughts." She shakes her head and smiles to muffle the sudden sadness that floods her face. "Now, dearest Rosalie, you must tell us how your husband delights you."

"Oh, Madame, he is delightful," I say.

"Apparently he plays the horn," says the Marquise eagerly. "I was hoping to have him play yesterday, for the king's amusement, but the village ceremony took a long time and then the moment passed."

"Mmm . . ." Elisabeth says I must not worry too much about pleasing the Marquise, for she won't last long now that she and the king are just friends. Apparently she *leaks* and the king is repulsed by her.

On our way back to the house we are greeted by the Abbé de Bernis, a friend of the Marquise's who leaves soon to take up a post in Venice. Venice—full of Italians! If that's where she sends her friends, imagine where her enemies are sent.

" 'Though to far lands I go / Never will I forget those I know,' " the *abbé* spouts lightly. He has delicate, womanly hands and plump cheeks, and I suspect he might be friends with my husband. There is no recognition in his eyes when he looks at me, but that is just Court manners: until you are someone, everyone pretends you are no one.

"Ah, my dear Bernis," sighs the Marquise sadly. "It is bitter that the needs of France should trump our friendship, but I am sure you will do well in Venice. Though how I will miss your little poems!"

The Marquise links arms with her beloved *abbé* and back we all go to the little château, *the setting sun throwing shadows across the lawn / the company mixed, some in peace, some forlorn.*

Chapter Thirty-Three

Shortly after my wedding I am presented at Court and take my place in the service of Mesdames Henriette and Adélaïde, the king's two eldest daughters. It is strange that the princesses are not married, but Aunt Elisabeth says it is perfectly understandable: Who would want to leave Versailles? And besides, too much of Europe is in the hands of foul Protestants and there are very few suitable grooms.

My new mistresses are vastly different: Madame Henriette is twenty-three, lanky and sad, rather pretty but dreary. Even though it ended a decade ago, Aunt Elisabeth tells me she is still mooning over her forbidden love with the Duc de Chartres. I'm surprised; the duke is hardly a handsome man but I think I will like his wife, reputed, despite her youth and rank, to be as loose as a drawstring bag.

If it were only Madame Henriette, I would be well content. Unfortunately her younger sister Madame Adélaïde is cut from an entirely different cloth. She is just nineteen but already carries herself as though she were the queen of Europe. She is arrogant and despotic, and bosses her elder sister around terribly.

They both despise the Marquise and they associate me with her. Most unfair. I must find a way to show my new mistresses that my allegiance does not lie with that faded woman and her uncertain future.

Aunt Elisabeth, who also serves in Mesdames' household, told me that in her first week she entertained the princesses with stories of the Marquise's penchant for sardines, wholly invented: how she ate them for breakfast and even carried dried ones around in her sleeves, to have a little familiar nourishment on hand at all

times. The two princesses pealed with laughter, and since that
time they appear to trust her.

"Madame la Comtesse de Choiseul-Beaupré," Madame
Adélaïde says as I curtsy down. "What a pleasure to have you in
our service." Her tone implies the opposite. "You may show your
devotion by fetching me a glass of water from the fountain in the
North Wing, next to the Luynes' suite—known as the best water
in the palace."

"Madame?"

"Civrac, you explain it to her," says Adélaïde, turning away, "if
she doesn't understand. Now, back to our lesson. Henriette, read
the passage again." The two princesses are studying Greek, even
though there are no Greek kings to marry.

Henriette looks down at her Bible. "'Do not spare them, but
kill both man and woman, child and infant, ox and sheep, camel
and'—oh, I can't remember how to say *ass*," she says in distress.

"*Onos,*" snaps Adélaïde.

"Fetch a glass of water from the fountain in the North Wing,
by the Luynes' suite—known to be the best water in the palace,"
repeats the Marquise de Civrac, another of the ladies on duty this
week, guiding me by my elbow toward the door.

"But surely there are servants to do that? The footmen . . . the
women?" I whisper back in astonishment.

"Quiet!" Civrac runs a thin finger across her lips. "If Madame
Adélaïde desires it, you will do it. She always chooses her most
disliked lady for such honors." The young Marquise, frightfully
pretty—a direct descendant of Athénaïs de Montespan, the love
of Louis XIV's youth—gazes back at me with impassive dislike. I
am not sure what I have done to offend but she gives no evidence
that she is jesting.

Confounded place, I think, my cheeks burning in humiliation as I walk stiffly out the door. I—the great-granddaughter of
a Maréchal de France, and married to a Choiseul, being asked to
fetch water!

"You," I say to one of the Swiss guards outside the door. "Fill this glass with water from the nearest tap."

The man hesitates, but then I break into a dazzling smile and timidly he smiles back. I incline my head, indicating that he may go, and he does. The other guard does not move, or even look at me. I stare at him until a faint red blush creeps up his neck.

No one else is about. I wander over and peek up an ornate staircase but all is empty and quiet. The king is away with the Marquise at Bellevue and no courtier bothers to be out or about when he is gone; during the day the palace has a resting, somnolent air. But at night . . . yesterday there was a rather naughty party in the apartments of the Duchesse de Chartres, ending in a game of cards where the only chips were clothes.

Eventually the guard comes back with the glass of water. I reenter Mesdames' apartments and hand it to the Marquise de Maillebois, an old bat with a trembling head, who then presents it to Adélaïde, who, without even taking a sip, hands it to one of the waiting women, who then places it on a side table. I slink back into the shadows.

"Smite is *chetypo* and kill is *scotosay*. Not the same! Really, sister, you must pay more attention," scolds Adélaïde, shaking her Greek Bible at Madame Henriette.

Shortly the dauphin and his wife arrive, accompanied by their attendants. We shuffle and rearrange as they settle down to listen to Henriette and Adélaïde give a recital from the book of Samuel, in Greek.

Is this to be my life at Court? Certainly, the nights are fine—I think again of the pile of clothing at Chartres' last night—but oh! The boredom of the days when I am in attendance on the princesses.

As Henriette falters on with her oration, I study the dauphine. Such a drab woman. Apparently the dauphin is faithful to her—extraordinary. Her skin is rather sallow and she spends her days being carried around in an enormous armchair or resting cautiously in bed, fearful of another miscarriage, or worse, another daughter.

I turn to the dauphin, remembering how handsome I thought he looked at my wedding. He showed me great favor at my presentation: he spoke six sentences to me, rather than the customary two. Really, if you took away the large head and overly thick features, he is a fine-looking man. And young—but a few years older than I.

The dauphin catches me looking at him and I wink, instinctively, then immediately regret my action. He colors as much as his thick skin allows and turns abruptly away.

"Ferdie," whispers his wife, "pay attention!"

Oh! What was I thinking? That was rather forward. But I am quite sure he must be as bored as I. Surely this piety is just an act, to please his wife and future subjects?

I turn my attention to safer fields and study the head of the dowager Duchesse de Brancas, seated in front of me. Her hair is neatly packed under an enormous silver comb, shaped like a bird, a trail of rubies dangling off each wing. I have a sudden and overwhelming urge to pluck it off the nest of hair and set it free. I wonder, if we became friends, would she lend me it? It would be just the thing to wear with my red-and-pink-patterned silk.

※

"Ah," sighs the Marquise, waving the letter sadly. "How I do miss my dear *abbé*! And his little poems. Hear how he closes the letter: 'Farewell, Marquise, woman and friend / Never shall I forget thee, to the end.' Such lovely words."

"I'm sure he's enjoying Venice and has made many new friends," offers Elisabeth.

Fanfan, the Marquise's little daughter—I suppose no one has told her that nicknames are vulgar—is visiting from her convent in Paris. She is sitting on the carpet in front of us, playing with a stuffed gray lamb. Aunt Elisabeth tells me that the child is spoiled rotten and that the Marquise dotes on her in her typical bourgeois fashion. The Marquise's pet monkey, Nicolet, sits beside Fanfan, watching intently as the little girl swaddles her lamb in a napkin. Occasionally the monkey takes a strand of Fanfan's hair and pulls on it.

I watch the strange creature with distaste; I think I prefer cats. Nonetheless, monkeys are quite the fashion and the Marquis de Villeroy keeps two, one of which plays a passable tune on the harp.

"And how are you finding the ways of our Court, dear?" asks the Marquise kindly. She and the king returned from Bellevue last night and now we are seated in her salon, enjoying coffee and the serene view over the North Parterre. Her apartment is certainly fine, I think sourly. Though I knew Versailles to be a crowded place, nothing had quite prepared me for the humiliation of the little room that I am expected to share with my husband. With half-height ceilings, a smoking chimney, and the heavy footsteps of the enormously fat Duchesse de Lauraguais clomping over-head. I much prefer to spend my time with Aunt Elisabeth, away from my sad room and my equally sad husband.

"Mesdames are very kind," I reply. When Aunt Elisabeth heard of my humiliating treatment, she suggested stealing one of the Marquise's letters, preferably one where she talks ill of the princesses, and showing it to Madame Adélaïde. But I do not have the courage for that. The Marquise has spies everywhere and they say her vengeance is swift and terrible, and as perfectly orchestrated as her evening entertainments.

"His daughters are truly women of culture and appreciation," the Marquise says, pouring some more coffee and passing around a plate of jelly squares neatly arranged in a pyramid. "I must be careful," she says, laughing as she hands a cup to Aunt Elisabeth. "Last week I was pouring for Alexandrine de Belzunce and I spilled a few drops on her lap. Most clumsy, and unfortunate: I'm sure the gossips will transform that harmless little incident into something far more malicious!"

She rings a bell and her equerry—a fine man, his calves bulging strong under pale blue stockings—comes in with quill and paper.

"Now, we are planning a small faro party for tomorrow night: Ayen; Livry and his wife; Soubise, if his ears are better; and possibly de la Vallière. Would you like to attend, dear Rosalie?"

"Faro tomorrow—oh, yes, Rosalie would be charmed to attend," says Aunt Elisabeth enthusiastically, taking a red jelly square from the bottom of the pyramid, causing it to partially collapse. "Mmmm. Strawberry, I hope."

The Marquise frowns slightly, a single fine line etched on her smooth forehead. She does have rather a beautiful complexion, I think, nervously touching a small nubbly tag on the back of my neck. I think of the old Marquise de Maillebois: her neck positively swarms with little skin growths, alongside scars where she tried to burn them off. I hope this one doesn't grow.

The king enters, unannounced and unheralded. "Dearest," he murmurs, bending down to kiss the Marquise. The monkey is quickly whisked away, for the king has a horror of such creatures. He greets Aunt and myself and indicates that we may stay, then picks up Fanfan and twirls her around. He steps on the gray lamb and Fanfan starts crying, and then she too is quickly whisked away.

"I would have you look at this," the king says to the Marquise, taking a letter from his pocket. Elisabeth motions to me and we move to the fireplace at the other end of the room.

"I heard," whispers Elisabeth as the Marquise and the king become engrossed in a conversation over tomorrow's state council, "that the dauphin was singing your praises to his man Binet."

"Really?" I ask in astonishment. "Who told you that?"

"Your husband."

"I did not know you talked to my husband."

"I do."

Well. Perhaps my wink was not as misplaced as I had feared. "Oh! What are those?" I say, my attention caught by a pair of red-and-gold fish circling aimlessly in a large glass bowl on the mantel.

"A present from China. The Marquise displays them proudly, as though to flaunt her origins. Extraordinary. Though why they are called goldfish, I don't know; they are more like *redfish*," says Elisabeth, looking at them with distaste.

The bottom of the glass bowl is filled with pebbles and a variety of gems and precious stones, some of which appear to have carvings on them. Is that an *A*? And an *M*? Perhaps the names of the fish—it would be totally in keeping, I decide, for the Marquise to name her fish as though they were *pets*.

"So," I say, turning back to Elisabeth, "has the dauphin ever been unfaithful to his wife?"

Elisabeth taps her finger on the glass and one of the fish darts off. "It is not known. There were rumors about a certain Madame de Boudrey, but her husband packed her off to Lille and the dauphin was too scared, or too lazy, to order her back."

"Do you think . . ." I let the words dangle. "It would be rather intriguing, you know, to have a dalliance with royalty?"

"Well, if you are interested in that, better the king than that henpecked ball of lard!" Elisabeth whispers back. "You must be more discerning. And you'd get no public acknowledgment with that wife of his."

"The king is too old," I mouth back as I hear the Marquise chuckling and cooing to him from the other end of the room. "He has *jowls*."

"Really," hisses Aunt Elisabeth, holding up her hand, "we must stop this conversation and save it for later. A faro party tomorrow night!" she says more loudly. "An excellent choice. Niece, you know the rules, do you not?"

A Letter
From the Desk of the Marquise de Pompadour
Château de Versailles
July 10, 1751

My dearest Bernis,

It is as you wrote: *Friendship plucks the strings of the harp / Always soft, never sharp.* Though we miss you, Venice is worthy of your talents and France does thank you.

Life continues here as it always does, both exhausting and exhilarating. Which is it more? Perhaps these days a little more on the exhaustion side, but such is the life I have chosen.

His Majesty is still greatly saddened by the departure of our dear Madame Infanta. She leaves behind an empty space, on the large side, that cannot be easily filled. Do send all news you have of her, that I might share it with him. We did hear that one of her ladies, the Comtesse de Narbonne, was brought to the bed of a boy. His Majesty, always wishing to commend his subjects, sent the Duchesse a fine pearl choker as a gesture of his admiration.

A dinner party last night; a bat came down through the chimney and there was much shrieking and fear—Frannie slipped off her chair and sprained her wrist, poor dear—but then the Maréchal de Noailles killed it with his sword. There was much hilarity, and puns comparing the Austrians to bats. If you had been here I am sure you would have thought of something very witty and spontaneous to add. How we miss you!

We are all eagerly awaiting the dauphine's confinement—will this year be the glory of France?

Ever in friendship,

J

Chapter Thirty-Four

"I heard the Marquise had a sore throat yesterday," whispers Alexandrine, the Marquise de Belzunce, and the only one of Mesdames' ladies who has made any effort to be civil. "And a cough."

"It is true," I say airily. Madame Adélaïde may still despise me but my proximity to the Marquise has gained me some friends. "A trifle sore and dry, but my aunt prescribed a most excellent tonic of peppermint and lead."

"I would recommend mercury water," says Alexandrine. "My sister was stricken with a swollen throat, and the doctors prescribed thus."

"Was she cured?" I ask.

"No, she died," replies Alexandrine, turning away to congratulate the old Duc de Luynes, who has just won the round by betting on the 2. "The number of times he has scromped his wife," she whispers back in a malicious hiss.

We are at a *cavagnole* party in the Queen's Apartments. The game is a hundred years old—the average age of the courtiers in attendance, I note sourly—and completely stale. The family sit and play, along with a few courtiers; those who are not at the table may watch or circulate as they please. My mother informs me that *comète* is fashionable now, at least in Paris, but change comes slowly to Versailles, I think grimly: a thin trickle of water through a crack in the wall, firmly plugged by tradition.

Mesdames don't gamble but sit with their mother, Henriette looking as though she has been crying all day and Adélaïde jingling a bag of coins in a manner designed entirely to annoy.

The crowds shuffle and a new party sits down. I pick at a loose thread on my sleeve, then see to my horror that the entire lace flounce is unraveling. Drat my woman Julie—she is entirely unsuited to the exigencies of palace life; I shall write to my mother tomorrow and demand a replacement. Or perhaps that is now my husband's concern? I'm sure *he* would be appreciative of my fashion woes. To hide my disintegrating sleeve I move to the window and stare out at the night.

Court can be exciting—so many new faces, so many new men—but the weeks I must be in attendance on Mesdames are rather dull. The only intrigue comes from helping Henriette in her secret correspondence with the Duc de Chartres—I have shown her how to skillfully slice the seal off a letter, then reseal it with a dob of clear wax, spread with a small knife; how to reply in miniature code at the upper-right corner, where any swain worth his salt will know to look. I also suggested she embroider one of her garters with something to remind her of her love, though the chances of any man ever seeing Henriette's thigh are very dim—the princesses are ferociously guarded.

But apart from such small reliefs, service is a dreadful routine of ceremonies, Mass, formal meals, too much standing, and too many dull afternoons, supposedly earmarked for pleasure but rather more focused on outlandish pursuits like learning Greek or algebra.

But when my duties are over—well. I was invited to sup last week with the young Duchesse de Chartres; she is a princess of the blood yet a kindred spirit flows between us. At our intimate meal in her town house we were served by a particularly handsome footman and as he turned to leave she winked at me and held up two fingers—*twice*.

On the days when I am free I sometimes walk down by the canals where the more informal young people of Court and town go. I wear a veil and indulge in some harmless flirtation. It's all rather free, even more so than in Paris, where my mother did occasionally try to keep me in the house. Just yesterday I met a very handsome young man, one of the handlers in the kennel. Not the Governor of the Kennels, unfortunately, but he told me his name was Pierre and that he knew how to make bitches squeal.

I blush at the memory. Of course, such dalliances are common, for I am constantly pursued by men of all classes and stations. Even the humblest footman cannot help but admire me if I open my eyes wide and smile.

"It is a dark night," says a voice beside me, cutting through my daydreams and bringing me back to the dullness of the queen's card party. I am about to make a cutting remark about nights often, if not always, being dark, when I see in the window reflection who is beside me.

Oh.

"Monsieur," I say, dropping down in a deep curtsy. The dauphin looks and even smells like pudding—extraordinary. Could he be soft all over? "It is indeed dark outside. Black as the night, in fact."

"You are not playing?"

"No, I am not."

There is a silence. Before he can remark that the window has glass, I take a bolder step: "Your coat is very fine, Monsieur. What a nice shade of . . . um . . . brown." I reach over and twiddle one of the buttons. No one is watching us; no one ever watches the dauphin.

He blushes but it is less of a blush than a look of intense stupid surprise that blooms over his face and squishes his eyes.

"You have beautiful hands," he says finally, in the voice of one being strangled.

"Oh, thank you! They are very white. And I have fingers." I wiggle them for his benefit and lean a little closer.

"Yes—fingers," says the dauphin, now sounding as though his fat throat has entirely closed over.

"Ferdie!" His wife waddles over. She is past her due date and has been allowed out of bed in the hopes that movement may induce labor. I shudder; when I am pregnant I shall not waddle around like an obese duck, but take to my rooms and spare others the pain of looking at me.

Though married for nearly four years already, the dauphine has only managed two stillborn sons and one daughter to replace the daughter of the first dauphine, dead a few years ago. So, almost four years and still no son and heir; the Saxons are as disappointing as the Spanish.

She leads the dauphin away and I remain by the window. What was that? Was that his attempt at flirting? Astonishing. Finally the queen announces she is tired and will retire—the old Cardinal de Luynes startles awake and before he can remember where he is, commands everyone to open their Bibles to Genesis, verse 2.

After Mesdames' *couchée,* Alexandrine leads me to her cousin's rooms for the real entertainment of the night. To my astonishment my husband is there, his horn in one hand.

I am suddenly happy to see him. "Play for us, oh, play for us, dear François!" I cry, clapping my hands. He obliges and starts a mournful dirge that promptly puts two members of the group to sleep, the lovely young Comtesse de Forcalquier—the one they call the Marvelous Mathilde—snoring with the slack mouth of a whore.

I tap my foot and study my husband, marveling at the way melancholy flows off him. A footman comes to pour me more champagne and I note with appreciation his deep blue eyes and handsome mouth. Then I realize by his dress and manners that he is not a servant, and I smile even wider. He is wearing an extravagant red coat, with a sword in the new curved style.

"You are very beautiful, Madame."

I incline my head. Bold, but his words are true. "And who has the pleasure of serving me tonight?"

He executes a sweeping bow, still balancing the champagne bottle in one hand. "The Chevalier de Bissy, Madame. Of the family of Bissy."

"What would you say," I ask him, suddenly desperate for some firm flirting, "if I wiggled my fingers at you like this?"

I mimic the motion that had so entranced the dauphin earlier.

"I would say, my fair lady, that you are flexing the fonts of desire, ready to coax the genie from the bottle."

Ah. Now, *those* are sweet words of love.

Chapter Thirty-Five

A son at last, a little Duke of Burgundy, an heir for his father and grandfather: the future Louis XVII. The whole Court is in celebration, and it is rumored that the Marquise fainted with happiness when she heard the news. My nascent flirtation with the dauphin—despite my Aunt Elisabeth's advice, I was intrigued—disappears in the joy surrounding the birth.

The country does not appear to share in the jubilation. At the official celebration ceremonies in Paris, the king was booed and the reception chilly. The birth of their future king, yet the faces in the crowd sullen and angry!

Despite the economies that are supposed to be happening at Court, a lavish ball to celebrate the birth is held. The ball is extravagant: the food beyond compare, the company select, the rooms draped with hundreds of blue and green lanterns. The Marquise decided it would not be masked, declaring such balls an extravagance not needed in this time of fiscal restraint, but everyone knows it's because she doesn't want a luscious Pineapple or masked slinky Cat flirting with the king.

Back in the bosom of his family, the dauphin is beaming like a bourgeois and quite ignores me. I am not too disappointed: Aunt Elisabeth repeated again that he will never take an official mistress and that I am quite wasting my time. But still, the walls of a challenge are irresistible. How fascinating it would be to capture a future king and not just some unimportant courtier. Or dog handler.

At the ball I meet my husband's cousin Étienne, the Comte de Stainville. My husband admires him and says he is the future of the family, but I instantly dislike him. He has a bulbous nose and bulging eyes and brings to mind a deformed fish, something blobby that lives on a riverbed and rarely sees sunlight. One so unappealing should really limit his social interactions. His wife is the granddaughter of a common financier, and surprisingly both she and the Princesse de Robecq are rumored to be wildly in love with him.

"Madame la Comtesse de Choiseul-Beaupré," Stainville says, bowing low over my hand. "Cousin. I trust married life is treating you well?"

I incline my head.

"My dear cousin François was most certainly in need of a wife," he says lightly, then moves away rather abruptly. I sense his disapproval, though I don't know why he would disapprove of *me*. Never mind, he is so inconsequential he scarcely exists.

The Marquise is looking, if possible, slightly frayed, and everyone is interested to see the king rather ignoring her. Despite his delight in his heir, he was shocked by the reception in Paris and as the evening progresses he sinks into a dark and melancholic mood. "His *black blankets*, we call them," Aunt Elisabeth tells me. "Because they cover him and everyone else in gloom."

The Marquise is entertaining a group with a tale about a fortune-teller in Paris. In the middle of her story the king walks by and says rather loudly, "And what old wives' tale is she telling now?"

"In fact, Sire," says the Marquise lightly, smiling at him, "it *is* a tale about an old wife. Madame d'Angerville must have at least eighty years on her, and when she went with her husband—"

Irritation oozing off his face, the king turns away in midsentence and stalks off.

"—was quite able to predict the unfortunate accident," finishes the Marquise quickly, and smiles at the audience that remains. A hush goes through the room and all eyes follow the king as he stalks through the crowds, grimly drinking his champagne and looking as though he would like to push someone.

Suddenly, no one can talk of anything else:

"Public humiliation—it's about time. Any fool can see he's tired of her. As we all are."

"This whole friendship charade—looking shakier than the old Cardinal de Luynes' fingers."

In a corner of the Hercules Salon, I gather a crowd of admirers around me: Bissy, as attentive as always; two footmen plying me with the finest champagne; the middle-aged Comte de Livry smiling at me lavishly; a smattering of other courtiers. I am in a fine mood; my mother sent me two bolts of apple-green silk from Paris, and Alexandrine's dressmaker made me the most delightful gown, the color setting my eyes to perfection. I am having a wonderful time. In the distance I see my husband, deep in conversation with the Duc d'Harcourt.

"A plate of cherries!" I say to Bissy, and he smiles for he knows what is coming. A footman is dispatched, then returns with a large dish of fresh cherries. I show the crowd a trick I practiced when I was young: tying the cherry stems in knots with my tongue. There is much ribaldry and clapping as I spit out each perfect knot.

"A talented tongue, indeed!" someone cries in the crowd, and I curtsy, then almost topple over. I find if I drink more, I can often overcome the dizziness that happens earlier in the evening. "More champagne," I whisper to Bissy, who rushes to oblige.

Then the king appears, holding a plate of brandy butter pears in one hand, a glass of champagne in the other. He looks a little flushed and is leaning on the Marquis de Gontaut, who is propelling him to my side. I pop in another cherry stem and the king watches in delight as I produce, on the tip of my tongue, the perfect knot.

I also spy Stainville and the great Duc de Richelieu, inching closer to the crowd around me. Stainville wears a look of opaque contempt but I am pleased to see that Richelieu, a man who has studiously looked right through me since my arrival at Court, appears intrigued.

"Try this one, my dear," the king says. He throws me the heavy stem of one of his pears, which I deftly catch with my mouth. I keep my eyes on him while I struggle with the thick stem but eventually I have to give up. I sink to my knees laughing, the crowd cheering around me. "It is too thick!" I wail. "Too large for my mouth!"

The king laughs and offers me his hand to help me up. As I rise I look into his eyes and suddenly see that he *is* rather handsome, and probably still would be, without all the wine.

Was I aiming too low with the dauphin?

The Marquise sidles up, seemingly unbowed by the earlier snub.

"Rosalie is such a high-spirited girl," she says warmly, squeezing the king's arm and smiling at me. "And how thoughtful of you to help the dear girl off the floor, when it is quite clear she is incapable of doing it herself. What a delight she is."

Chapter Thirty-Six

We are in my aunt's rooms, one of the better apartments of Versailles. The least the Marquise could do, my aunt often complains, for the years of friendship she has provided her. Still, there is no kitchen and the rooms overlook only a narrow courtyard that rarely gets any sun. "I would have far preferred a set with its own water fountain," Aunt often complains. "As it is, Émilie has to beg from the Matignons or rely on those wretched water boys."

My cousin Stainville and his distasteful blobby nose, as well as the Duc de Richelieu, are gathered in the apartment with us. The powerful minister of war, the Comte d'Argenson, is also in attendance. Argenson is often by my aunt's side these days; I shudder to think they are courting. When I am old and ugly, I shall give up making love as a service of general interest so that others don't have to consider me.

Aunt Elisabeth informs me this is a family meeting, though my husband does not attend, nor the Marquis de Gontaut, nor the Duc de Biron, by rights the head of the family.

I know why these great men are here and accordingly wear my most becoming robe, the bodice low and pinned with a fichu that is the merest slip of an idea, a nominal nod to virtue. My stays push up my breasts as though willing them to escape the confines of the gown, and I note that Argenson can scarcely keep his eyes off my chest.

"Rosalie, my dear, tell our honored guests what passed between you and the king at the concert yesterday." Aunt Elisabeth smiles at the assembled men.

I incline my head and take a deep breath. I will not be nervous; these powerful men—Stainville excepted—must know that I am strong of heart and mind. I note with satisfaction that they are looking at me, and not in the way men usually look at unimportant women, with a glance that passes over them and slides quickly out the next door. I remember again Stainville's look of opaque contempt at the ball—now he must see I am worth something.

Aunt has warned me to curb my arrogance: even a hint of arrogance in a female, she says, is perceived as badly as bare breasts in church. This is something the Marquise taught her and she grudgingly has to admit she is right. Men and color combinations—no one knows them better than the Marquise. And possibly intrigue.

"Well, sirs, it was a small gathering, a select one, do note"— none of these three men was invited—"and after the piece was finished—Destouches, a trifle bold for my tastes—the king declared he was tired of sitting and would walk awhile. He asked me to accompany him, asked me directly, I must add, and without the approval of the Marquise. She hid her emotions well, but I am sure she was quite horrified when she saw us leave the room. The king and I"—that does have a nice ring to it—"walked the length of the Hall of Mirrors, twice; we chatted to the Comte de Matignon, who recently lost his favorite dog, and kindly greeted the Princesse de Rohan. We returned to the gathering at length and there the Marquise sought to introduce us to the cellist; it is my opinion that the king was not interested and only greeted the man out of politeness."

After I finish, the men discuss me amongst themselves, occasionally posing me a question. They don't ask about my husband, and they don't ask about Bissy, or Pierre either, and for that I am grateful. They would never understand—Pierre is a dog handler—and I myself don't fully understand it. I simply put it down to a weakness inspired by the full moon and the change of seasons, which can lead even the most sage-headed man—or woman—to folly.

"And her education?" asks Stainville, in a voice that matches the disdain in his eyes. He does not like me and the knowledge is confusing, for what reason would he have to *dislike* me? I am his potential glittering future, but so far there has been none of that flirtatious frisson that makes discourse with men so pleasurable.

I don't think Aunt likes Stainville either. Perhaps she is thinking the same as I am: What exactly is he doing here? Compared to Richelieu and Argenson, he is a scraggly peahen amongst roosters, and his wife a bourgeoise to boot.

"Rosalie was educated in Paris, at home; she started at l'Abbaye du Bois but the Mother Superior took against her, through no fault of my niece's, I'm sure," my aunt replies rather curtly. "Then her mother took care of her education. Rosalie is very well read in the classics, and can recite many verses of Shakesman, the English playwright, from memory."

"Perhaps you mean Shakespoint?" says Richelieu smoothly.

"Yes, as I said, *Shakespoint*. Would you like her to recite a verse or two?"

"No," the three men manage to say in unison. I feel like jumping up and starting to orate, just to annoy, but in truth I don't think I can remember any of the passages that I used to woo my maid with when I was young.

"Rosalie's oratory skills might be useful," protests Aunt Elisabeth. "The Marquise is always throwing in little quotes to her speech."

"Mmmm. For a woman, the Marquise has remarkable conversational skills," says Richelieu, looking between me and my aunt. I think, this is a man who commands armies, and plots. Sexuality fair pulses off him, like a throbbing vein, and it is rumored that with him, a woman is as assured of pleasure as if she were a man. "The Marquise keeps the king constantly amused, and she can be very charming and witty. I suspect, though this is hard to countenance, that the king values those attributes over her cu— her, ah, *physical* charms."

I think of Bissy's mooning eyes, his pleading insistence, the rush to get inside me. I know well how to please a man. The handsome face of the kennel boy comes to mind, as does Caliban's hard black body.

"It is my understanding," I say a little too forcefully, then soften as I remember my aunt's advice, "that the Marquise keeps him fastened to her by nothing more than routine. I am well known as a clever wit, and to date the king has laughed thrice in my presence. Of course, my conversation is not on the par with hers; I have a more elevated approach to the art of conversation."

Richelieu nods neutrally but Stainville doesn't move. Why won't the dratted man be charmed by me? Perhaps, I think with a sudden dawn of clarity, he is of the same persuasion as my husband. I look at him with more interest: another challenge. I have finally succeeded with François, though it did take copious amounts of wine. I wore a pair of his orange breeches, that rather excited me as well as him, and I was glad for the congress. He was tender and solicitous, explaining that he had heard that virgins feel even more pain than men on penetration. I could scarcely control my laughter; he is rather in his own little world.

"We must remember, though," adds Argenson mildly, speaking for the first time, his eyes fixed on my chest, "that the king is an educated and refined man. Entertaining him is more than pulling peach stones from your breasts, or whatever little tricks you do."

"My great-grandfather was a Maréchal de France!" I respond in astonishment. For these men to question my pedigree!

"No, Madame, we were talking not about the refinement that comes from breeding and blood, but that which comes from education and exposure to society."

It is all I can do to bite my tongue—these men are suggesting that a bourgeoise is more refined than I am!

"Your little hijinks may catch his attention but they will not keep it," says Stainville, nodding at Argenson. "And the king likes his women faithful—I would wager the Marquise's doglike devotion is a large part of her charm."

I am suddenly, unpleasantly, aware that I am on trial. The men watch me keenly, but I refuse to blush.

Aunt Elisabeth comes to my rescue: "Rosalie has *many* admirers, yet she handles them all admirably."

"Handles them?" inquires Stainville mildly. After a few tense minutes, led by the ticking of the clock on the mantel, Argenson points at me.

"The time is nigh; the Marquise grows older and sadder, and according to my men the last time the king spent the night with her was back in January. She is more minister than mistress these days."

"And petticoat politics is not something a nation can suffer," adds Richelieu. "She'll ruin the whole world if we don't ruin her first."

"The king is now bored, as he often is as winter approaches. So this is a critical time, young lady," Argenson continues, his eyes darting between my face and my breasts. "Keep your aunt, and us, informed of everything that occurs, and keep your husband beside you at all times. We are evaluating many options, mind, so stop the nonsense you have going on with . . . well, I will not sully this room, nor the proud name of Choiseul, by elaborating further."

He pauses and I bow my head to avoid his eyes. I must not blush. I must not. Oh, goodness, I hope he is referring to Bissy, a man whose pedigree dates from 1335, and not to Pierre the dog wrangler, or, God forbid, Caliban.

"I see you think you can do this alone; I tell you now you cannot."

"Of course, gentlemen," I murmur, looking up and nodding at them each in turn, triumphant that I have not blushed. One thing is certain: when I am in the king's arms, and in his heart, there will be no more insolence from these men.

"This is all very exciting," says Elisabeth, hugging me after the men are gone. "You are being primed for great things and they have placed a great deal of trust in you."

"I'm not sure they like me very much," I say, my cheeks safely burning now that they are gone. "They rather insulted me, I think."

"Nonsense. But you must be chaste, dear Rosalie, and do as they say. Keep your husband beside you, and you must stop your harmless little flirtations."

"Of course, Aunt," I murmur.

∽

"I will die," declares Bissy. I have told him the sad news: I am to be saved for someone far more important and so must end our dalliance. To my chagrin he does not resist much—he has no wish for a *lettre de cachet* and a lifetime of banishment to some remote château.

"I must be saved for someone far greater," I repeat, hoping for a little more sadness, a touch more despair. "There is someone far more important I must keep my favors for."

"My family was ennobled in 1335!" replies Bissy in astonishment, unbuttoning his coat.

"Yes, but your grandmother was a Protestant," I retort.

He takes off his coat and pulls me down with him onto the carpet.

"Dearest darling," I say, rolling over and straddling him. "It is not my choice—were it mine I would be with you night and day. As it is, I must be saved for someone far more important." But I really will miss him, I think with a pang; I doubt the king knows how to wield his tongue as Bissy does.

"You already said that," he mutters.

"We will be like Romeo and Juliet," I say, suddenly stricken with the romance of the idea. Oh, but that feels good.

"Who are they?" asks Bissy. "I know a lad Romeo de la Lande, but his wife is Louise, I believe, not Juliet. His mistress, perhaps?"

"They were star-crossed lovers, forbidden by fate to be together," I say, reaching down to unbutton his breeches. I want him to understand the tragedy of our fate, the pain of our necessary estrangement. I reach up to kiss him, but as though in anguish he pushes my face away and down toward his breeches.

"You could write a poem," I suggest before I am muffled by his member. "Something to express your sorrow." He doesn't answer but keeps his hands on my head.

"I will miss this, oh yes I will. Oooooh." His sigh is a long release of butterflies.

"A sonnet, perhaps?" I suggest, coming up for air. A relative was the poet Pontus de Tyard—surely Bissy has inherited some of the family way with words?

"Dearest, words can never—never, I say—compensate for the torment I will go through." Bissy forces my head down again. "Now, aaaaah, you must let me drown in my sorrow."

A Letter
From the Desk of the Marquise de Pompadour
Château de Versailles
December 20, 1751

Darling Abel,

A great sadness you could not return from Italy to bid farewell
to Uncle Norman; what a sorrow his death was. He was so good to
us, and to our dear mama, and now we find ourselves as orphans.
Another month and you will be home—now more than ever I crave
family around me.

You will find Versailles little changed on your return. It is still
the snakepit it always was, and intrigue continues apace. You have
doubtless heard rumors that the relationship between His Majesty and
me has changed. It has, but our friendship grows stronger every day.
My enemies are hungry and think that now is the time to unseat me.
Sometimes I fear that even those closest to me are not to be trusted.

The king is well and delighted with his grandson, though troubled
by a slight case of indigestion and Parlement's continued resistance.
What is the future? I sometimes despair. Are we to become like
Holland, or even England, where they say the king cannot sneeze
without his parliament's permission? A godless anarchy, no respect for
monarchy or for our sovereign's right to rule?

Once you are home we must find you a wife! I am glad that
no Italian beauty has snagged you, and I am thinking of a certain
Mademoiselle de Chabot—you must let me know your thoughts.

The shipment of Turin marble arrived—lovely. Do not forget my
Murano orders, and see if they have a glass lamb for Fanfan—if not,
order one made. How happy I am that your post as Director of the
King's Buildings will keep you often at Versailles.

Safe travels, Brother, and much love,

J

Chapter Thirty-Seven

Madame Henriette was even more pallid than usual and could not summon much enthusiasm when her sister suggested a sleighing party. I was happy to get outside and the snow was deep and delightful, but then Adélaïde started organizing each sleigh's passengers according to rank, then changed her mind and organized them according to age, then decided to mix the two following a formula no one quite understood. The sun was almost set by the time the horses started and everyone quite frozen.

Madame Henriette caught a chill, then coughed blood, followed by a fever, and died. She was only twenty-four and quite beautiful, so it was all rather romantic: they are saying she died of a chill, brought on by a broken heart, still mourning the Duc de Chartres. There were whispers and hopes the duke might also succumb, but alas, he did not.

Her death devastates the king. Before this latest setback—we have gone into full mourning—my flirtation with him was progressing well. Christmas, New Year's, little parties, I was always invited and by his side and I was beginning to taste the giddy potion that comes from being desired by a powerful man. I am not in love with the king—he's too old for that—but he is fine-looking and quite kind. And I adore the way all have started to notice and consider me.

Aunt Elisabeth tells me that the Marquise only thinks of me as a high-spirited young child. Is that confidence, or blindness?

But now the king is consumed by his grief and yesterday he left abruptly for Choisy without indicating a guest list. All is at a standstill, not from mourning the young princess, but from this unprecedented etiquette situation: none knows who should follow, and who should stay.

"We're going," declares Adélaïde, her face gray and puffed from too much weeping. "I can't sleep in these rooms any longer, I don't want to *ever* come back here!" She flings a cushion viciously at a small table that topples over, shattering a pair of porcelain candlesticks.

"Oh, those were Henriette's favorite! Oh, my sister!"

The Marquise de Civrac squeezes her hand and murmurs some annoying platitude while I tap my foot in impatience. How can a person have a favorite *candlestick*? Ridiculous. I have discovered I am not very good at acting—unfortunately, for it is a skill well rewarded at Versailles—and earlier this morning Adélaïde had turned to me in astonishment when she heard me humming a tune.

"It was Henriette's favorite melody," I said quickly, and weakly continued humming. Adélaïde's ear is as flat as a flounder and she did not recognize my lie, and only turned away in fresh torrents of tears.

I leave the chaos of Adélaïde's rooms and seek out Aunt Elisabeth to let her know we will be leaving. I find her with the Marquise and never have I seen that woman looking so terrible. It is a good thing the king is gone; if he were to see her like this I am sure he would exile her on the spot. Her face is ashen and her hair so loose she could be mistaken for a prostitute. She is dabbing at her eyes with a handkerchief that doesn't even match her robe.

Quite the sentimentalist, I think in surprise, for her red eyes have the look of real and recent weeping, and there is not even a whiff of soap or onions in the room. I'm surprised she cared for Madame Henriette, for Henriette certainly never cared for her.

"Madame Adélaïde is leaving this afternoon," I announce. "For Choisy. She says she can't stay a moment longer in the rooms where her sister died."

"Poor Adélaïde," says the Marquise dully. I raise my eyebrows at Aunt Elisabeth, who raises hers back: everyone knows Adélaïde despises the Marquise and likes to call her *Maman Putain*—Mother Whore—or Fried Fish behind her back.

There is a scratch at the door and the Marquise starts, but it is not what she is hoping for: a note from the king, telling her to join him at Choisy, telling her he needs her.

"He has completely abandoned her," whispers Aunt to me as the Marquise is called away to oversee the delivery of a new chandelier for her antechamber.

"Green crystals," she says sadly, following a troop of men carrying an enormous wooden box. "The crystals in daylight look divine, but at night—oh! Green makes the complexion rather sickly and wan; a dreadful mistake. And I've already reupholstered the walls to match." She trails sadly into the next room.

Aunt continues: "He always turns to his family at times of crisis. He'll recover quickly, and you'll be there, and she'll still be here. An excellent turn of events, and I shall join you and Adélaïde when my week begins. Mind you, let us know if he is thinking of summoning her, and we'll do what we can."

I spend the carriage ride to Choisy thinking that perhaps Henriette's death was a blessing in disguise. Time alone with the king, and I am a good mourner—I was an excellent comfort to my mother when our dog Schneepers died. I imagine myself comforting the king, patting him on his back, kissing him wherever he wants, rubbing him to make him forget. I wonder if Bissy will be at Choisy?

"She was so silly!" sobs Adélaïde, launching into a fresh round of wails. Most un-princesslike, I think in irritation, rubbing my freezing hands together inside my muff. "Who dies from sleighing?"

"My mother caught a cold from a carriage ride and then she died," offers the Marquise de Civrac helpfully, arranging the heavy mink blankets around Adélaïde. "And it was March no less, and not very cold. But her cloak was unsuitable, and there you have it." The carriage rolls over an iced rut and Adélaïde's head smacks the window, producing fresh wails.

Scarcely have we arrived at Choisy and settled in when news comes that the Marquise is coming. Without an invitation.

"What—first my sister dies and now the whole world turns on its head? Has she no manners, no decency?" rails Adélaïde, flinging herself and another pillow around the room. "My father will never forgive such a massive breach of etiquette!" I recover the pillow and hand it to her with sorrowful concern; it occurred to me during the carriage ride that there might be changes to Mesdames' household now that Henriette is gone. The number of ladies might be cut and I risk being left without a position. Though I loathe my duties, being one of Mesdames' ladies is very desirable and the clothes allowance, though meager, does help.

Fortunately, I do not believe Adélaïde is aware of my burgeoning dalliance with her father; she is rather self-absorbed and reserves most of her animosity, large as it is, for the Marquise. I'm glad, for I should not like that headstrong young she-boar pitted against me.

"The Marquise is a travesty," I murmur sympathetically. "At times like these, her humble roots are never more apparent. My aunt says you can put rouge on a pig, but it still remains a pig."

"I shall not greet her! I shall not! And I must find Papa and tell him to send her away. Find out where he is!" An equerry scuttles out as Adélaïde flings herself on the bed and begins to wail loudly. I'd like to roll my eyes but the Marquise de Civrac is watching me rather carefully; I still don't know what I have done to deserve her animosity. Normally I would assume it was my beauty, but she is also extraordinarily pretty, with golden hair and hazel eyes that might even be larger than mine.

The Marquise arrives at Choisy before dusk and from the minute she arrives, it is as though she was always there. She takes over the grieving king and the reins of the palace; directs accommodations for the friends and courtiers who are nervously trickling in; arranges suitable, somber entertainments—a reading of Plato, performed in respectful Greek; long walks to gather winter hawthorn berries—Henriette's favorites—and she even reproves me, gently, for wanting to amuse the king one evening with my shadow hands.

The king smiles at me, for the first time since this dreadful business began.

"We must not crush her high spirits; perhaps a little childish fun is what we need right now," he says, still smiling at me. I smile back, thinking, Childish fun—we shall see what games this child plays later.

"No," says the Marquise firmly, and I am treated to another glimpse of her soft, solid power. "This is no time for silly games. And besides, that bears little resemblance to a duck, my dear." She gestures to the wall, set with a candle to enlarge the shadows: "Your thumb is too apparent."

"Ah, you are right, my dear Marquise," says the king dutifully, "though I do think it's rather a handsome duck," he adds with a wink to me that the Marquise catches, deftly, then ignores just as easily. She extends her hand for a kiss and the king does as bidden.

"I have the most tragic story to tell you," she says softly, her voice a mournful siren drawing him in. She settles herself beside him and turns him away from the wall where I still hold my duck, defiantly. The thumb is perfectly appropriate—one could consider it a leg. "The poor Comte de Ruffec, cousin, you know, of the duke . . . ice . . . three wheels submerged . . . wild ducks . . ."

I stare at the Marquise's profile, the delicate nose, the upswept hair tied with a band of silken black posies. She is invincible, I think suddenly. Her enemies are blinded by their hopes and their hatred; the king still relies on her and probably even still loves her.

I abandon my duck and flounce away from the Marquise's suitably ghoulish story of an entire family that perished from winter chills, probably invented just for this occasion. I pick up a peach from a bowl of fruit on the side table, but see it is badly bruised—such a thing would never be allowed out of the Marquise's hothouses at Versailles. She is like this peach, I think viciously, poking at a brown squishy spot with my finger, then sucking it—old and blemished. While I am so beautiful, and the king likes laughing more than he likes sorrow. Though he does seem to like sorrow quite a bit.

I realize in astonishment that I am jealous. How ludicrous: she is old and faded and I am young and beautiful, so why should I be jealous of her?

Later I slip out and find Bissy for our tryst. He has rebounded quite well from the end of our relationship, and I still allow him my favors on occasion, to keep his sorrow and possible suicidal thoughts at bay. Though I do not think drinking poison in an agony of grief is quite his style.

In the flickering candlelight of the loft, I show him my duck, which he agrees to be quite elegant and realistic.

"But not as marvelous as this wonderful creation," he says, and shows me a shadow he learned in his regiment, a perfect oval with something moving in and out of it, and definitely not an animal.

Chapter Thirty-Eight

When the Marquise judges the time is right, we repair to her château at Bellevue. She wants to put on a play for the king; the theater she started at Versailles has stopped but there is a little stage at Bellevue.

Madame Adélaïde reluctantly—or without hesitation?—releases me that I may attend. Thus far there has been no talk of rearranging Adélaïde's household, but just in case, Aunt and I are assiduous in spreading rumors about the other ladies. We tell Argenson that we suspect the Marquise de Maillebois has six toes, and that we overheard the Duchesse de Brissac complaining she was tired of wearing black.

For the theater, the Marquise chooses an old-fashioned opera ballet, *Les Fêtes de Thalie*. The music is rather fine, especially the overture; quite a masterpiece of theater, really, but the rest is stale. The Marquise will play the Woman, and I the Girl, a very fitting role. Does she not know that the Girl always wins against the Woman? No one is interested in a woman after she turns thirty, with her graying skin and wrinkles. And she leaks. If there was a princess in a deck of cards, I think, similar to the jack, it would *always* trump the queen.

"Excellent, excellent," muses Aunt Elisabeth. "Everyone rabbits on about her intelligence, but surely she must see that you will be compared favorably to her!"

"Mmm." I am not very confident in my acting abilities and I am a little surprised that the Marquise, reputedly strict about the caliber of her actors, had thought to bestow this role upon me. But still, it will be fun, and I am glad to be away from Adélaïde and her venomous ladies.

"'Perchance, O mistress, perchance to usher here and converse with me,'" I read from the script. What silly phrases! At least it is a ballet; I have always been complimented on my graceful turn of step.

Aunt receives a letter from Argenson with news from Versailles.

"And how's your lover?" I demand. Aunt is always saying my arrogance will be my undoing, but what is arrogance if not truth stated clearly and confidently?

"You are very perceptive, my dear Rosalie, and I do believe you are aware of the change in the affections of Monsieur le Comte toward me," says Elisabeth with a coy smile, speaking of Argenson. I am disgusted to think of them together—Aunt is far too old—but she says their liaison is excellent for our little project: Argenson is one of the Marquise's most bitter enemies and he can keep us well apprised of the king's movements.

"With him in our corner," she crows, "we can hardly fail. But mind you keep our secret, my dear; the Marquise must know nothing is afoot with dear Marc and me."

"She'll never guess," I murmur. The idea is preposterous. I can't understand any man, especially one as powerful as the Comte d'Argenson, performing gallantries with old Elisabeth. Her cheeks are thick and pendulous and when she laughs they quiver like cream custard made with too much milk.

"I do believe this makes me the most powerful woman in France," Aunt says happily.

"I have to disagree; that distinction still lies with the Marquise." Unfortunately. I am becoming impatient with the pace of my courtship with the king; certainly there is flirtation, and quite a bit of it, really, but nothing has actually *happened*.

The Comte d'Argenson arrives at Bellevue with the king; the play is to be held a few days hence. Elisabeth coos and chuckles over Argenson, looking decidedly ridiculous and girlish in a too-tight peach gown with flowers in her hair. It is my opinion that women after thirty-five should not wear flowers, and Aunt is forty-six! And she should give the dress to me, for peach is one of my best colors. My father died last month—I must grieve out of propriety, but in truth I scarcely knew him—and he left far less of a fortune than my mother and I had anticipated. Not to mention my husband's family; apparently François was quite relying on my prospects. Now money is suddenly, uncomfortably, tight.

I turn back to the play with a frown.

"Don't frown, dear, it's not becoming and soon you'll have lines like old Marc here." Elisabeth strokes Argenson's face with adoration and I appreciate the rod of steel that must be inside him. He doesn't flinch, but I watch his eyes slither over to my cleavage. I massage my chest and adjust one breast, upward, then smile at him before turning back to the play.

" 'Perchance. Pray, perchance! And summon thee to my chamber.' Who speaks like that? Why can't we do something modern, by Voltaire or Marivaux?" I throw the pages down in disgust. This is a silly, silly undertaking, though I do like the costume that is being prepared for me, a pale blue gown of fine mousseline. I do believe the addition of a stomacher and perhaps some new sleeves will make a delightful summer dress.

As the night of the performance approaches my nerves increase. I am so fraught I cannot help myself with one of the Duc d'Ayen's footmen. My aunt finds out and slaps me across the face with her closed fan, saying that I should be happy she will not tell Argenson or Stainville. She calls me a hound in constant heat and confines me to our apartment for the duration.

The evening of the performance I drink almost an entire bottle of champagne to calm my nerves. The night is a disaster: two members of the symphony fall sick and the overture is flat; the king yawns four times; the Comte de Turenne forgets to carry on the stuffed duck at the appropriate time; and the Marquise does not look her best. At the last minute her gown went missing (Aunt might have had a hand in that) and she had to substitute a frilly pink concoction that looked rather silly on her. At least all the blame for the atrocious evening will not be on me. I decide that in the future, I shall leave acting to the low-class blowhards who excel at it.

Imagine, me, the great-granddaughter of a Maréchal de France, onstage! It must be my blood that is uncomfortable, I decide, rather than any lack of talent.

A Letter
From the Desk of the Marquise de Pompadour
Château de Versailles
June 15, 1752

My dear Dr. Quesnay,

How nice to receive your letter, and how glad I am you are safely arrived in Bordeaux. Your services for dear Uncle Norman were much appreciated, so there is no need to thank me for the money and gifts. And I am happy to report that I am much improved since taking the tonic you suggested before you left: Who would have thought that clams and cloves could be so cleansing?

I fear His Majesty is not so well. He is still recovering from his grief over Madame Henriette; such sorrow a man should know. And it did not help matters that they (why, my dear Quesnay, tell me why we must care what *they* say—a great puzzle I should like solved) say that dear Madame Henriette's death was a punishment for the king's sinful ways. And of course I am blamed, even though we are no longer intimate; forgive my bluntness, but you know well the situation.

I have worked hard (not too hard—I can almost hear you admonishing me to rest!) to amuse him; we performed a play at Bellevue, a first since the end of our Little Theater at Versailles. A great success and we welcomed a young addition to our usual cast: the Comtesse de Choiseul-Beaupré. She is a trifle uncouth and immature, but her lively spirits have helped His Majesty in his sorrow.

I must also tell you that I received the first book of the *Encyclopedia* today! Though it has been under such attack, I know how dear the project is to you. It was most informative and I enjoyed reading about Angola, and Asbestos. My dear friend Françoise, the Duchesse de Brancas, will be delighted to know that that chemical can help improve the complexion.

I bid you adieu; the clock has gone two and I must get my "beauty sleep," as you so eloquently call it.

J

Chapter Thirty-Nine

Back at Versailles, I discover I am not the only one impatient with the progress of events.

"We must force the issue," declares Argenson. "The king is an idle crawfish and will not move unless prodded. He's too happy with those little birds that Le Bel supplies and with his friendship with the Marquise. He may be content to have two queens he doesn't sleep with, but we are not."

"Summer is nigh," he continues, "a season when the thoughts of men and kings turn to love. The Marquise is not the only one who can stage decent theater; we will orchestrate this perfectly. Do you understand, Madame?" Argenson finishes his oration and sits down, motioning for Elisabeth to pour him another cup of tea.

"Of course," I say impatiently. "The king is already eating out of my hand." Really, trying to tell me, Rosalie de Romanet de Choiseul-Beaupré, how to conduct an assignation and a romantic liaison! Preposterous, really.

Richelieu snorts. "Yes, I heard about that little trick with the pie last week—rather messy, wasn't it?"

"And another thing," adds Stainville. "There must be nothing to add to your indiscretions. Do you hear me? You must control yourself."

"I can control myself, sir," I mutter stiffly, thinking, I am not a dog in heat. Then I remember the yelping of the dogs in the kennel—I have resumed my liaison with Pierre the dog handler. I hope they have not found out about the Duc d'Ayen's footman; I can still feel the fan of humiliation stinging across my cheek. I glare at Stainville as sweetly as I can. Such an unimportant man—what is he even doing here?

"You will be faithful to your husband."

I stifle a giggle.

"Don't giggle, girl, this is not a joke. We will put around the notion that you are madly in love with the king and that he is the only man you would be unfaithful with. That will flatter his ego: it worked for Pompadour and it will work for you."

"And mind you don't go opening your legs like a common trull," adds Richelieu. "It is imperative that you have assurance of Pompadour's exit first, otherwise you risk becoming a little bird under the eaves."

"When I wish to, I can certainly abstain, gentlemen," I say coldly. "I shall not be overcome by my passion for the king." This won't be like the Duc d'Ayen's footman—that was just a temporary insanity, over my nerves about that silly play. I have started to imagine the king, naked, and while it is not a displeasing picture, his physical charms will not impel me to rashness.

"Rosalie could never be a little bird; she is a swan," says Elisabeth proudly. "There is no danger of her being mistaken for a sparrow." She looks at Argenson in adoration. I am beginning to think that Argenson is only using Aunt, though what he hopes to gain from the liaison I am unsure.

"It is absolutely imperative you not give in. I coached Madame de Châteauroux to great effect in that area," says Richelieu. "It took the king months to break down the walls that her ambition erected, and it all worked out admirably in the end."

"Except you didn't become prime minister," observes Argenson acidly. "And she died."

A look of utter and mutual disdain passes between the two men.

"You will suggest an assignation," says Richelieu, turning away from Argenson and taking charge of the conversation, "in a romantic spot of his choosing, then suggest the Gardens, otherwise he'll be frozen in indecision, though the nights of June are already hot. Leave it to him to decide where in the Gardens—there must be an illusion of control. Or just choose a grove and be done with it. Action, now."

I write a note to the king and declare myself madly, passionately in love with him, which I am sure he would believe: he probably thinks every woman is.

My heart beats and I must see you alone in the Gardens.

Richelieu reads it. "Is this really the best you could come up with?"

"I am not a poet," I say stiffly. "The Marquise had *Voltaire* writing her love letters. And as you know, gentlemen, Voltaire is currently in Russia."

"Prussia," corrects Argenson.

I sigh dramatically. Really, these men are competitive *pedants*. Telling me how to conduct a love affair!

"Let me do it." Richelieu motions impatiently for another sheet of paper and I pass him the quill and ink.

> *My heart beats asunder,*
> *I must see you before the thunder*
> *By Diana, naked, in the Star Grove.*

"Very well," I say, blowing slowly on the letter to dry the ink. I dab rouge from my cheeks onto my lips, then kiss the note to leave a satisfactory red smudge. Argenson's tongue almost hangs out of his mouth and even Richelieu raises an eyebrow in grudging approval. Only Stainville remains unmoved.

Richelieu arranges for the note to be delivered to the king's room and placed on his pillow by a valet. I spend the night dreaming of the future. It is beginning! In my dreams I float through the rooms of the palace and come to rest in front of the door to the Marquise's magnificent apartments.

Then I open the door and walk through, and she is not there. It's only me.

Chapter Forty

Argenson inspects me and pronounces me fit for a king. How unimaginative. I simper at him and clutch my hands to my heart, or my breast.

"Come," says Elisabeth, taking the lantern from the table and lighting it with a candle. "We shall go."

"Now, Madame d'Estrades," says Argenson reprovingly, "I do not think it would be wise to be seen with our young Rosalie, as though leading her to a tryst."

Elisabeth reluctantly relinquishes my arm. "Right as usual, my love," she says. "Now remember, girl, nothing more than the breasts. Breasts only!"

"Breasts only," I repeat, then mouth the same to Argenson, who gapes at me with a drooping jaw. I hurry out with the lantern lighting the way to my future. My heart pounds with a strange mixture of anticipation and excitement, as well as, if I am to be honest, a little nervousness. It is finally beginning—the King of France and I!

I step out into the black night of the Gardens, down past the terraces and a group of men examining a white horse. The moon is not yet up and the night is soft and still. I duck into a small yew-framed alley and make my way by lantern light to the Star Grove, my excitement rising, alive to the possibilities the night will bring.

The grove is deserted and I find the statue of Diana, not naked as implied in the note but draped in a Roman costume. I set the lantern on a bench beside her and rub her cold stone cheeks, draped in cobwebs and gleaming white through the night. Ugh, I hate spiders. Diana the huntress, I think, tracing the statue's stone nose . . . the Marquise dressed as Diana to catch her king: Is this an omen or a more positive sign?

Then, a rustle of footsteps, a whispered soft order from behind a hedgerow—"Wait here, gentlemen"—and the king emerges by solitary lantern into the gloaming.

"Madame," he says, and his voice is different from the voice of majesty in the large formal rooms of the palace, different even from his voice in the carefree intimate suppers. These words and this voice are only for me, curling through the dewy night to drape me in velvet. My knees go weak and I sink down on the stone bench by the statue.

"Oh, Sire, I—I am overcome." And I am.

"Now, now," he says, coming to sit beside me. "Do not be flustered on my account." His voice is young, eager, the boy inside him bouncing in anticipation.

I look shyly into his eyes and they twinkle back at me.

"It is just, it is just . . . But I am overcome," I say again. I bury my head in my hands and wait to see what he does next. Breasts only, I must remember, but already there is a tingling between my legs and on instinct I lean in closer.

"If you permit . . . ?" He reaches over a hand and caresses the back of my neck with surprisingly lithesome fingers. Oh. I lean my head closer; soon his hands are working through my hair, and my head is inching toward the noticeable bulge in his breeches.

I take a deep breath. I'll be back, I promise, then draw myself up. Breasts only. The king disentangles himself from my hair and cups my cheeks.

"Ravishing . . . simply ravishing. A peach."

"Oh, Sire, I am overcome." Again? Really, Rosalie? I must think of something else to say, but it is the truth—I *am* overcome.

"Oh!" The king's eyes grow large. "Oh my!" He sits up rigidly, almost as if in fear, his face suddenly bone-white. He jumps off the seat, away from me. "Don't move!"

"What is it?" I say in alarm, reaching for him.

"No, no, hold still, don't move," he repeats, his breath quickening, staring at a point just over my shoulder. "Le Bel! Le Bel! Do not move, I say! Oh, goodness, the size of that thing! DO NOT MOVE!"

"What is it? Sire, you are scaring me!" I whimper, frozen in fright at the sudden change in him. What is happening?

"Oh, save us from Heaven!" With a cry the king reaches in to swat at my hair, then lets out an unkingly shriek as a large spider flies off my head and onto my arm, them promptly buries itself in the layers of ruffles at my sleeves.

I let out a scream to waken the stone statues and start squealing at the king: "Get it off me! Get it off me!"

The king, looking sickly and white, backs away as I shake my arm in terror. "Where is it, where is it, oh my God—where did it go?"

Le Bel and another man rush into the clearing, swords drawn.

"It's in there, it's in here, oh my God, get it off, get it off me." I run toward them, waving my arm frantically. "Get it off me!"

"A spider," says the king weakly, sitting down on the stone bench, then immediately jumping up, his eyes darting around in terror. "As big as a coin. Good Lord, what if there is another? Do they come in pairs?"

Le Bel rustles through my sleeve with a gloved hand, then flicks an enormous black ball out of the lace and onto my skirts, where it crouches amidst the roses. I am on the point of fainting when the other man flips the offending spider (are spiders ever *not* offending?) onto the flagstones and ends it with a loud squelch.

"By God, that was a monster," he says in admiration, holding his lantern over the black mess. "Look at the size of that thing. As big as my palm," he says in satisfaction. "Never seen the like, ever."

Le Bel, holding up an ashen-faced king, comes to admire it as well. "Is that hair on the legs? My goodness, I'd wager it was as big as a saucer."

My legs turn to rope and I crumple down to the floor. Then a horrible thought strikes. "What if there are others?" I moan, getting unsteadily to my feet. I need to get out of the dress, out of this garden, oh my God there is something crawling up my leg. I let out another shriek and whirl around like a madwoman.

"I think there is another one, another one! Please, oh God, get it off me!"

"Never," says Le Bel firmly. "A spider that size happens once in a generation."

But what if . . . oh, my God. I stare helplessly at the men, feeling imaginary spiders running up my legs and inside my skirts and worse.

"Madame." The king bows to me, still holding on to Le Bel. His voice is faint and queasy, his eyes closed. "Thank you for gracing us with your presence, but, ah, I feel the need to return to my quarters now. A slight indigestion. Forgeron, light the way. Le Bel, please see Madame de Choiseul back to her apartments and ah, ah . . ."

Well, that didn't go very well, I think, ducking my head under the water in the bath at Aunt's apartment. My dress has been picked apart by two women, roused for the occasion, and though they declared it free of spiders, I am taking no chances and insist it be washed after me in the bath.

Good Lord, the size of that thing. On my hair! On my sleeve. Then my skirt. I shudder and another imaginary spider races up my leg, under the bathwater. I jump in fright but it is only the edge of the washcloth. I peer nervously at a black speck on the wall, before realizing it is just a smudge of soot.

"Perhaps the little adventure will only increase His Majesty's ardor," says Elisabeth dubiously.

"I do not think so. I think . . . I think he might be ashamed."

"Ashamed? The king?"

"He squealed, rather like a woman. And did nothing to save me, though I was most certainly in distress. He had a sword, he could have helped."

"Mmm," considers Elisabeth. "I do not believe I have ever heard the king scream."

"No, why would he? I can't remember the last time *I* screamed. In fright," I add, thinking of Bissy's tongue flicking over me, an ecstasy so unbearable that the only way to release it was to scream loud enough to wake the whole stable, the horses neighing in fright . . . I slip under the water.

"You must never remind him of this," says Elisabeth firmly.

"Mmm? What? Remind him?" I am back in the room, away from the delights of Bissy's tongue.

"Of the spider, girl. Act like it never happened," she says briskly. "Now get out while the water is still warm. I long for a bath myself before we have to return the tub to Alexandrine."

℘

"Le Bel told me he saw the most enormous spider in the gardens last week," says the Marquise mildly, pouring us both a cup of coffee. "He said it was the size of a dinner plate." I shudder at the memory; the thing has not left my mind in five days and five nights.

"Why do you shiver so, dear Rosalie?" she asks kindly. "Did you see it?"

I gaze at her, a fraction too long. The infuriating thing about the Marquise is that you never know what she is thinking behind her smooth and elegant exterior. I notice for the first time the dark blue ring surrounding the impenetrable gray of her eyes.

"Rosalie has a horror of spiders," interjects Elisabeth, leaning in to pat my arm. "Even the word risks sending the poor girl into a queer fit."

"When I was a child," says the Marquise, daintily picking a raisin from her cake, "my mother used to put a spider—a small one, mind you—on the palm of my hand, like this." She places the raisin on her upturned palm. "And I was not to flinch or tremble." She stares down at the little raisin for a while before continuing: "Excellent training for future times when one must bear all manner of . . . adversity . . . without the slightest flinch."

"A wonderful idea," says Elisabeth, rather too enthusiastically. "We must suggest it to the nuns at Fanfan's convent!"

"I'm not sure," says the Marquise, smiling at us in her sincere, cheerful fashion, "that a box of spiders and a room of young girls is quite the thing for the peace of the convent, or the neighborhood." She pops the small raisin into her mouth and raises her elegant brows at us. "Rosalie, my dear, I must compliment you on your dress. That pale blue mousseline is delightful, and so closely resembles the costume you wore for our little theatrical effort!"

℘

The king has returned to looking me in the eye and we had a satisfying conversation and flirt over cards last week. Onward!

Shortly I receive a note asking me to meet him, this time inside. He suggests a room above the Aisle of the Princes.

"Where he brings his little birds, sometimes," says Argenson, examining the letter.

"Just make sure it's not in an attic room with cobwebs and any more of those dreadful things."

"The rooms are quite comfortable," replies Richelieu smoothly. "Though a little snug and hot in the summer. I'll have my men make sure all is in order, with clean sheets and a basin of rosemary water."

"We are *not* at that stage yet," reminds Elisabeth, her voice taut and overly loud. She has been suffering from an earache all week, and when not on duty with the Mesdames, she fills her ear with vanilla wax and keeps her head wrapped in white gauze. As well as looking quite ridiculous, her hearing and mood are suffering. "We are still on the breasts," she almost shouts.

"Still on the breasts," I mouth to Argenson, cupping mine and smiling at him.

"I'm sorry, I forgot where we are in the progress of things," says Richelieu. "The dust sheet off the sofa, then, and a plate of strawberries. Feed him one," he says, turning to me. "Do you have any tricks with strawberries? Something with the pips, perhaps?"

Is he *mocking* me?

"Suggest Friday next, after the Comédie Française and their production of *Les Nymphettes de Nîmes*. He'll be in a randy mood and ready for some excitement."

"All this creeping around," I say in irritation. "He's the *king*. He should be able to do what he wants."

"But, my dear Madame, but I thought you liked creeping around," observes Richelieu in a mild voice. I glare at him. "A useful skill for a young lady of your inclinations."

"I've already told you," says Elisabeth, far too shrilly and far too loudly, "it is not Rosalie's fault that she has so many admirers!"

ᘓᕽ

"*Ammiali, ammiala,*" I hum to myself as I climb up the stairs to the little room, following the directions provided. The ballet tonight was delightful and far more professional than that fiasco at Bellevue, and as Richelieu predicted, the king was aroused by the sight of so many dancing nymphs, their calves almost exposed. I could tell from the way his eyes kept darting over to me that he was eagerly anticipating our tryst.

He tells the Marquise that before retiring he is going to visit the dauphine, laid in bed with another pregnancy, and I quickly excuse myself after Adélaïde's *couchée*. Now the night belongs to me. To us. The night of my future, I think in anticipation as I climb the stairs.

My candle suddenly flickers out—a cheap tallow candle, one of the ridiculous economies imposed because of some war or something—and I take another from the wall sconce and continue to climb the narrow staircase, the stone steps slippery with age. The room at the top is as described, the bed with no pillows and demurely covered with a large tapestry; the sofa clean and inviting, a plate of strawberries and sliced peaches on the side table. I pop a slice into my mouth and go to pry the window open, for the room is horribly hot.

From the stairwell comes a loud thump and then a terrified woman's squeal cuts the night in two. I freeze. Who is coming up? And why the scream? I open the door and peer cautiously out into the blackness.

"Madame?" I call softly, my skin tingling. Who rises there below?

"Sire!" I hear Le Bel's voice and soon a light illuminates the stairwell. "Sire! Are you well? What happened? Oh, *mon dieu,* are you hurt?"

"Damn stairs, as slippery as a cunt, and some fool took the light from the wall." The king's voice is accusatory and sharp. Oh. I shrink back into the safety of the little room.

What should I do? I stand alert, waiting to see if he will still come up, but the minutes pass and all is dark silence. I sit down rather dejectedly on the sofa and slowly eat the peaches and strawberries, not really expecting him but still holding on to a little slice of hope. I gather the strawberry hulls and imagine making a garland with them.

But no king rises. In disappointment, and before my candle burns out completely, I creep back down the stairs.

After this second fiasco the consensus is that we wait until the Court travels to Fontainebleau. There, Richelieu will ensure I have a decent apartment where I may greet the king, and more, in perfect harmony. Perhaps all these mishaps will show the king the delights that are to be had in *not* sneaking around, I think, a trifle sourly.

Until Fontainebleau.

A Letter
From the Desk of the Marquise de Pompadour
Château du Fontainebleau
September 22, 1752

My Dearest Frannie,

I trust you are well at Choisy, and we are eagerly anticipating your arrival here at Fontainebleau. So she won't have to sleep with memories of her dead sister, Abel has arranged for a new suite for Madame Adélaïde, poor girl.

Thank you for keeping me apprised of the Comtesse de Choiseul-Beaupré's movements and disposition. We know of the king's growing attraction, but she is a fool, a diversion, something to liven him up and take his mind off his troubles—I contend that the Parlement is fair wrecking his health. If there is more to it than that—well, I am not worried, and you must not be on my account. His Majesty is a man like any other, and needs—no matter how sordid—must still be met.

The Maréchale de Mirepoix, recently returned from London, has joined us here in Fontainebleau and I do enjoy her company. She is mad about rabbits and travels with several, including an enormous white one with hair as long as a horse's tail. It is a strange passion, but oddly endearing.

I remember that Bernis used her during my education as an example of a widow marrying a man of lesser rank. Bernis called her a *fool in tulle* for bringing such a shame on herself and her family. But you know, dear Frannie, how little I care for such trifles, and luckily her second husband is now a duke and so she has been restored to her former rank.

'Til next week, dearest; I was sad to hear of the bites on your neck—certainly spiders are to be avoided, and I hope they will clear by the time you arrive. Have a safe journey and we will see you soon,

Ever in friendship,
J

Chapter Forty-One

The Court settles in at Fontaincbleau and I write to the king for our next assignation. In my note I include a secret phrase: "Discretion, always and discreet" that the king is to whisper through the door before I invite him in. Stainville's idea—I have to admit that the man has some use.

There is always the danger that the king, a sometimes superstitious man, might see our trail of failed assignations as a sign from One much higher than even Richelieu that our alliance is doomed, and so it has been agreed that once I have the desired assurances, we are to move beyond the breasts. Finally!

I dress in a light flimsy home gown, not the stiff Court skirts that bunch up in most inopportune places—cages of chastity, as they are colloquially known. I even leave off my stockings and feel delightfully naughty and naked as I wait for the king in my apartment. As Richelieu promised, I have been given two rooms to myself in the palace, overlooking the Princes' Court.

My rooms are next to the old Duc de Fitz-James, who has reminded me, perhaps eight times already, that this apartment is usually reserved for his niece the Marquise de Bouzols, who now has to make do with one room, and in the North Wing, and much to her disgust.

Aunt has decorated my salon with nasturtiums but their creeping smell bothers me and I throw as many as I can out the window before I hear the king approaching. A scratch at the door.

"Who is it?" I say coyly.

"The Lord of Discretion," comes back the hopeful voice. "No, wait, it is Discretion, always and discreet. Lord Discreet?"

"Enter, my lord."

There is a pause, then the sound of someone fumbling with the handle. Presently the door flies open, almost catching me on the side.

"There! What an adventure! What an adventure! Opening doors myself! Quite the adventure, my dear," he repeats, chuckling and bowing over my hand in greeting.

He looks around the room approvingly. "A lovely room. Well lit, tidy, no insects." He glances nervously into the corner.

"Sire." I smile at him with all the seduction I can muster, and he lights up to the possibility in my eyes, responds to the unsung symphony that is my desire. He knows that this time, the gates, and the legs, will open.

"Come and sit, Sire, and have a glass with me." I pat the sofa and pour him some wine.

The king smiles at me and takes a sip, then recoils. "What is this? Foul, most foul."

I take a sip but the swill is undrinkable. Damn that woman! Elisabeth said it was a superior vintage, but the merchant must have been treating her for a fool. Trying to be like the Marquise with her flowers and perfect drinks, and failing so utterly.

"Wait here, Sire," I say, and plant a quick kiss on his mouth. "Let me get you something more pleasurable." I skip out and wonder if I was too bold to kiss him like that, but I've already drunk another bottle while waiting for him. Oh—perhaps that was the bottle I should have kept for the king? I run down the narrow corridor to Argenson's apartment, where Aunt Elisabeth and the men are waiting. "Get me some wine, anything, anything," I say, grabbing a bottle off the table. "That stuff in there is undrinkable."

"But the tradesman said it was all the rage in Rouen!" protests Elisabeth.

All the rage in Rouen? Who cares what is happening in *Rouen*?

Back in my salon I slide smoothly onto the sofa and hold the bottle seductively out to the king.

"Could you open it with your mouth? Tongue?" he asks hopefully. "Another opening?"

I have to shake my head. "But ah, once the bottle is open . . .

It is not only my throat that is thirsty." I let my words linger and suddenly feel delightfully free and eager. Let this begin! All I need is his promise and then I in turn can promise him my many, many delights.

We drink in silence and though I rack my brain to think of conversation, I can only focus on the advice of the men: "Confirm her banishment. Ask for a signature, something on paper." I'm nervous; I'm not used to making demands, or at least demands that get in the way of pleasure. Perhaps I shouldn't have had all that wine while I was waiting?

The king finishes his glass and starts to rub my neck, and before I know what is happening I am heading south like the last time. I draw back, resisting the urge to bury myself in his enlarging lap. The king has an intoxicating scent of ambergris and almond oil, and this is more difficult than I anticipated.

I draw back and he reaches to cup my breasts, then pauses to look around.

Why is he laughing?

"Sire, why do you laugh?" I whisper.

"Just waiting for a giant rat to leap on us, or for a wall to fall down."

I giggle. "Don't worry, here we are safe." He squeezes my breasts and suddenly he is on me, pawing me, tickling my neck and pushing himself against me. I can feel his erection beneath my flimsy cotton skirt and I move my hips in greeting.

"I mustn't, I mustn't . . ." I say, grabbing at his hair and pulling off a wig, momentarily stunned—I thought the king didn't wear a wig.

"What must you not, dearest?" he says, hungrily kneading my breasts.

"Because . . . because . . ." With horror I realize I have unbuttoned his breeches—instinct, I suppose—and push him away with as much force as I can. I burst into tears, suddenly wanting Bissy, or Pierre, or Caliban. Or even that footman at Bellevue. Anyone but this man. Oh, what is wrong with me?

"I do want to be with you," I sob, but the words sound false and strained.

He mistakes my tears for ones of fright and grabs me tighter. "Do not worry. You shall be mine, all mine. You are delightful, delectable, and so very soft."

Well, it appears my tears were the right move. I smile inwardly, imagining the scene when I tell the men next door of my triumph.

"But I must . . . I must have assurance." The king is on me again and my hips are yearning against him and I find myself kissing his neck, burying myself in his hair. "My honor, my husband . . . I need . . ."

"Dearest, all that you desire," he says thickly. "I have been a different man since you came into my life. All the sorrows of this year . . . you washed them away like a laundress."

His hand has now pushed past my skirt and my one petticoat and is pawing determinedly onward.

"Oh, Sire! She must leave," I whisper, then his fingers arrive at their destination and involuntarily I open my legs and push myself slightly sideways at the pressure. Oh. "I cannot be at peace while she is here. I—I must be with you—oh, nice."

"Of course, dearest, of course. Anything you wish. Oh, how fine!"

"We must truly be together." I extricate myself from the king's finger and slip down onto the floor. I kneel in front of him and turn my bodice that he might start to undress me, my hand reaching back to massage his member that is now free of his breeches and straining toward me like a tiny cannon.

"I am so happy—we will be together. She will go?"

"She will go!" he groans, grabbing at my bodice and pushing himself against my hand. The gates are flung open and a thousand angels herald the way with their trumpets. "Oh, Heaven," he declares, coming off the sofa and burying himself in my bare breasts—where did my stays go? Then, before I have time to further my demands, he skillfully slips inside.

"She will go and we will be together," I say, in rhythm to his motions.

"We will be together," he repeats. Though his skin is a little drier than what I normally like, and his manhood is not overly impressive, I note in appreciation his strong body, from hunting no doubt, and the keen knees of a man used to the saddle.

"Oh! So soft, so very soft, pudding, peach. Ahhhh." After his satisfaction, which happened rather quickly, he kisses me chastely on the lips and declares he must leave, though he does not leave me in his heart.

"We are most pleased, Madame," he says, standing and pulling up his breeches. "Though I suffer the sharpest pangs at leaving you, the Council will not wait. And now, look, I shall open that door, yet again, and close it myself. What a marvelous time it has been."

I lie back on the carpet and stare up at the ceiling. It wasn't very . . . well, how should I say it? But that is not the point, I tell myself: this is the King of France. It would of course be almost treasonous to compare him to a dog handler, or to a slave, but it has to be said, even the footman lasted longer and had a more . . . powerful weapon. And Bissy—well, none can compare to Bissy.

They are waiting for me down the corridor, but they must not know it took such a short time. And on the floor, not even fully undressed . . . I shake off any regrets. He said he loved me and he said she would go, and he is the King of France, after all. No, I don't think he said he loved me, but he certainly said she would go. And he did say I was very fine, and soft.

I stick a finger inside me and sniff the smell of the king—yes, a dog handler and a sovereign do smell the same—then straighten my skirts and scuffle my hair. I look in a mirror to confirm that I look suitably disheveled and ravished; disorder shall be the mark of my triumph. I finish the rest of the wine, then trip carefully down the corridor.

"It is done!" I cry, bursting through the door to Argenson's apartment. "He said he loved me; he said he would send her away!"

Aunt embraces me and Argenson claps. I fling myself down onto the sofa in satisfaction.

"When?" demands Richelieu.

"Just now, sir," I say, panting on the sofa. I should like to sleep with Richelieu, even if he is old. I realize I am still very aroused— perhaps Bissy will be in his rooms? I glance at the clock on the mantel; not yet three.

"No—when is she to leave?"

"Well, sir, we didn't get to all the details . . ." I trail off, aware that I am breathing heavily. Richelieu would be *very* fine to sleep with. He looks as though he knows what I am thinking, and for a moment a slight smirk plays around his lips.

"Well," he says, turning to look at Argenson and ignoring my aunt and myself, "there we have it. The deed is done, and we shall see what fruit, if any, our labors bear."

Chapter Forty-Two

"Prudence, my love, prudence. These things take time and must be approached carefully, like . . . a battle. Plans must be made, courses of action compared, decisions finalized . . . it is a large undertaking."

It is explained to me that the king—or Louis, as I call him now—has a faint heart and is easily led. Although promises have been made and I continue to press for action, he continues to evade decisions.

I tut in frustration. "Louis, you are the *king*. All it would take is one letter, and you don't even have to write it. Argenson would be more than happy to oblige." I straddle him, then lean over and muffle his mouth and protests with my breasts (he agrees they are as angel cakes, soft and delicious). "Why not call for him *right now*, and tell him to bring a blank letter? Simple."

Louis reluctantly pushes my breasts off his face. "Nothing is that simple, my dear. Nothing. I owe the Marquise a long debt, and the bonds of history and friendship . . ." His voice trails off. I roll off him and the bed in impatience. I can't really order the king to leave, but I think I would like that. We are still at Fontainebleau; tonight Aunt Elisabeth is keeping the Marquise company at a small concert in the apartments of the Comtesse de la Marck. The king had excused himself earlier on the pretext of a tickle in his throat. We shall see how that tickles later, I think grimly.

"Would you like me to leave, dearest?" The king's voice is childish pleading and suddenly I am filled with an intense irritation. I turn away abruptly; it has only been a few weeks but sometimes I find him rather *trying*. I am not his mother. I take a deep breath, paint a smile on my face, and turn back to him.

"I would never want you to leave," I coo, twirling my pubic hair around my finger and looking at him through half-closed eyes. I open my mouth and pretend to moan in slight pleasure. Truth be told, I'd sooner be with Bissy and his tongue than beholden to the king and his rather pedestrian lovemaking, but one must make sacrifices. There are greater matters at stake: the banishment of the Marquise, an official declaration, then great riches and perhaps even a duchy for me. I suppose I must start thinking about who shall be my ministers, or perhaps I'll leave those boring decisions to Argenson.

It's too cold in the room and the bed is deliciously warm, so I climb back in. I note with pleasure he is ready again. Well, quantity over quality: a suitable approach for both lovemaking and ribbons.

"Dearest," I whisper, pulling at his ear with my mouth, my legs wrapping around his, "I'm *never* leaving."

⁊

"You're making *her* a duchess?"

The lands of Pompadour are to be elevated to a duchy, and the Marquise is to be a duchess. The Duchesse de Pompadour! There he is showering her with titles and favors, while I remain a back-corridor slut, our love still as secret as a confession.

I rail and weep at him for this foolish act, but I see too late that tears in a woman he is wooing may be attractive; in one he already has, not so much.

"A parting gift, no more, no more," he says stiffly, looking sheepish and decidedly un-kinglike. I remember the high-pitched squeal from the stairwell and sigh in impatience. I stop sobbing and get to work on his erection, my hand slicked with a heavenly scented oil that Richelieu has provided me—from a Turkish woman in Paris, he said. The king sighs again. "And she's getting tired, needs to rest and sit in dignity when it is her duuuuuuu— oh, my goodness, that feels good. What a sorcerer you are with your fingers, love."

⁊

"She knows," whispers Aunt Elisabeth to me as we attend the presentation ceremony. The Marquise, though magnificent and elegant in a beautiful dress of silver shot with gold thread, appears tired, and I might even be able to detect a hint of panic in her eyes.

She still greets me warmly and still continues to express her delight that I am so entertaining—so *childish,* she often says, her eyes glowing warmly as though complimenting me—but she knows. Of that I am sure.

"Your Majesty, we are most sensible of this great honor," says the Marquise—I mean, the Duchesse—to the king as she rises out of her perfect curtsy. The king mutters back something equally bland and formal, and I note that he is looking uncomfortable. As he should be.

"Don't worry," whispers Elisabeth, smiling at the new duchess and lifting up her train as we head off to continue the presentations in the queen's quarters. "It's a consolation prize, not an apology."

Chapter Forty-Three

"Cousin."

"To what do I owe this pleasure?" I ask imperiously. Since the triumph of my congress, I told Argenson not to include Stainville in our future plans. Argenson has no soft spot for the man—he calls him a tedious toad—and so Stainville and his bulbous nose have thankfully been absent as our project continues.

Without my invitation Stainville sits, choosing the largest armchair. Well, I'm not offering him anything to eat or drink, even though I do have a box of very fine spiced walnuts, from the Prince de Soubise, no less. As those courtiers who suspect start to appreciate me, I have been quite besieged with presents. Even the Duc d'Ayen, one of the Marquise's loyal friends, sent me a fine bolt of green-and-silver velvet, just the thing to make a padded winter jacket. Our secret is as leaky as a dam and will not hold much longer; any day now the walls will break and *everyone* will know. I smile, thinking of the acclaim.

"All that happens to you is of great interest to me, Cousin, on account of our family," he replies, looking lazily around my salon. Stainville is so unimportant he doesn't even warrant rooms at the château but has to board in town, probably with a notary or some such bourgeois horror. Perhaps a relative of his wife's.

"All that is happening to me will be of great benefit to our family, you need not fear."

"My dear Madame, I have to confess I *do* fear."

I glare at him. "And what exactly, Monsieur, do you fear?"

"The king . . . the king does not always hold to his promises. His word is a flimsy foundation upon which to build a career. I fear we may have put the cart before the horse," says Stainville, looking directly at me for the first time since his arrival. "The sweets before the soup?"

"We have done no such thing," I say, in my best imperious voice. "Things are progressing most smoothly." Why does he always make me feel as though I am on trial? I'd wager the Inquisition was never this bad.

"The Duchesse . . ."

"Who?"

"The Duchesse de Pomp— Oh, never mind. The *Marquise*." Despite her new rank, everyone still refers to her as the Marquise. "The Marquise has recently been honored—not the actions of a man who has had a change of heart."

"A consolation prize, not an apology," I snap, using Elisabeth's words. "The king—or *Louis* as he is to me—has promised that the Marquise will be dismissed. In his last letter he swore it would happen before Advent, so that we may usher in the New Year together."

Stainville's face brightens.

"Yes," I continue. "He writes me letters, with words of love and poetry."

"But that is wonderful, wonderful news, Cousin, if his letters are indeed as you say."

"Of course they are as I say! Do you think I can't read?"

"My dear, insolence is never appreciated, no matter the age or the position."

Oh, get on your high horse and ride away! I think in irritation. His insolence is not tolerated, either, but I cannot say so. Yet. Instead I say, through well-gritted teeth: "It appears, sir, that you do not believe me. "

Stainville inclines his head. "I am afraid I am doubtful." Never have I hated a man so much. "Such declarations of love, in a letter, no less, are not in keeping with the king's character. He is a very discreet man. The Lord, in fact, of Discretion."

"I think I know the king better than you!" I retort. "I understand you've hunted with him only once this year, and it's already *November*." I jump up, determined to put an end to this nonsense. I take a box from a wall cupboard in the paneling. Stainville watches me closely, his face placid yet strangely alert.

"Here." I thrust the packet of letters at him. "Read them yourself."

Slowly he peels off the first one.

"That is the latest. He declares himself infatuated and only wishes for the time when we will be alone. Alone, as in without the Marquise. Excuse me, the Duchesse. And here he says he likes my—no, wait, don't read that part—but here you can see he closes with a couplet where he declares his love for me is like a pear tree."

"Indeed. He has quite a way with words." Stainville peruses the pile in silence while I tap my foot in impatience.

"Very, very impressive," he says finally, and then leaps up and embraces me. Instinctively I react—behind the bulbous nose I have noticed he has a fine shape, and his smell is pleasing. He releases me and holds me at arm's length. "My spectacles, dearest Cousin, my spectacles. I need them to read these wonderful missives properly and give them the attention they are due. They are at my lodgings, in town. You permit me?"

It takes me a second to realize he wants to take the letters away.

"Of course. I have memorized them, regardless."

He bows and as he takes his leave there is a steely excitement in his eyes. Finally it seems he understands what I am, and what I will become. The fortunes of the Choiseul will rise, and all by my doing.

But there is something that Stainville does not know, something not alluded to in the letters. I am quite sure I am pregnant, a fact I have shared only with the king; not even Elisabeth or Argenson knows. It is quite possible that the child is the king's, so—fancy that, I think, sticking my tongue out at my departing nemesis—I shall be the mother of the king's child.

And give him what the Pompadour so utterly failed to do.

❧

I haven't actually memorized the letters and am anxious to have them back. The Court returns to Versailles but I do not hear from the king for several days, or even see Stainville. I am not invited to a little supper the Marquise puts on for the Duchesse de Brancas' birthday, and little doubts start to creep in, but then I remember the king's words and his assurances. These things *do* take time.

Fleeing the ghost of her dead sister, Madame Adélaïde settles into her new apartments. In the confusion of the move a favorite locket, encrusted with emeralds, goes missing. Acting more like a child than a princess, Adélaïde accuses the Duchesse de Brissac of having lost it and all is in an uproar as Brissac's relations demand apology and retribution. Adélaïde stubbornly refuses, even after the locket is found under the cushion of one of the bedroom chairs.

I flee the chaos and flop down on the sofa in Aunt's salon; no summons from the king today, though I did receive a note yesterday saying that if he had wings, they would be flapping for me. It's been almost a week and it is frustrating to be under the same roof yet unable to see him. And I am not going to start hanging out in the public rooms, hoping to greet him like a common courtier or sycophant as he passes by. He should send for me, or come looking for me at least.

Aunt Elisabeth rushes in, more flustered than usual. "Charlotte-Rosalie! Something dreadful has happened, dreadful!"

"What? Has Argenson woken up?" I say playfully. I no longer feel much need to be polite to those in my sway. I'm not sure Elisabeth will stay once I am in power. She's rather . . . ghoulish.

"What? No, why do you . . . No, child," she says, shaking her head as though to clear it from a cold. "A dreadful scene! An awful scene! She opened the gates of hell on his head, she wept and stormed—"

The door flies open and the king enters.

"Get out," he says curtly to Elisabeth, who leaves with a snuffle. I smile at him—finally.

"So eager, Sire, for my company? The clock not gone three," I say in my best coquette voice, then realize I have said completely the wrong thing. The king's face is dark gray and there is an odd anger pulsing off him, in such contrast to his usual good-natured indolence.

I take a step back, then gasp when I see what he has in his hand.

"Yes, Madame, you may look surprised. Indeed." He flings the bundle of letters onto the floor. He sits down heavily on the sofa and buries his head in his hands. "A fool," he says sadly, "I have been a fool."

"Wha—who gave these to you?" I demand, sinking down to the floor. I start gathering the pages with fingers I urge to not tremble. My mind races. Betrayal—but by whom?

"Madame the Marquise, I mean Madame the Duchesse, oh, you know who I mean," the king says dolefully, still staring down at his hands.

Oh! "She has spies, spies everywhere." I grab the letters and realize in horror that I am crying. "She has spies everywhere, she is a hateful woman, she is old and—"

"Enough, Madame, enough," says the king sharply, raising his head but still avoiding my eyes. He stands up. "You are young, and your youth is delightful, but you lack much maturity. You know I value discretion above all else, especially in these matters of the heart. To know that you saw fit to share my words to you— well, it is only in esteem for past memories that I am here to tell you in person, rather than by letter. Though, given the circumstances, a letter might have been more appropriate."

"No, no, Sire!" I crawl at him across the floor and attempt to nuzzle in his crotch, but with some difficulty and with a small kick he extricates himself and heads for the door.

"Oh, my love. Louis!" I wail, and the tears and the fear are real. "Our child! My love!"

He softens, hesitates by the door. "Go to Paris and have your child, then we shall see. Though, from what the Marquise told me, I have doubts it is mine." He looks up at the ceiling, raising his eyes heavenward. "I fear I have lowered myself, indeed."

"Oh my love," I wail, my voice ever higher. "Please, please—"

"Pray keep your voice down, Madame," he says coldly. "The Marquise de Flavacourt is lodged next door, and her piety must be respected. Go to Paris. You may write to me, though I shall not return the gesture. Go and let this storm diminish. Stainville has organized a coach for you. I must have peace in my kingdom, and in my house."

He raps for the footman to open the door and then he is gone, ushered out of my life, my future in tatters. Stainville, I think blankly as I sit alone on the floor, surrounded by the dratted letters and the heavy weight of remorse.

Stainville.

Stainville, that treacherous toad.

Entr'Acte

The Duchesse de Pompadour

December 1752

I am a duchess but the victory is hollow. I don't want titles; I just want the king's love. I gave him my approval, tacit and silent, and then it turned around and slapped me on the face.

It was a narrow escape, closer than I care to admit. If Stainville had not intervened, the future might have been very different. Though Stainville was discreet and declined to name names, I suspect Rosalie had powerful supporters: Elisabeth, Argenson, Richelieu? Richelieu, I would expect, Argenson too, but Elisabeth? The only proof I have is an increased attentiveness, as though to compensate for a huge mistake. Still, I cannot condemn someone for sudden affability. I will keep her close, but warily.

Stainville was a man I had thought so odious—though no relation, he used to call himself the Chevalier de Maurepas to show his support for that detested man. But then he came to me with those letters, claiming—falsely—to be concerned for his family's honor. He placed a bet and weighed that I was the wiser choice, the choice with more of a future than that feckless harlot married to his cousin.

In gratitude, I try to warm the king to him but his presence only reminds Louis of the whole sordid affair. As a sign of my appreciation, I secure for him a post in Rome.

Outwardly I am calm. I choose a large amethyst and spend many hours, thinking, as I etch out an *R*, then add *CB*. In my weaker moments I think I have had enough of this monster they call Versailles, and I imagine retiring to one of my houses. But I must be honest; I may have failings but self-deception is not one of them. Leaving Versailles would be the death of me.

I think of Pauline de Vintimille, another of Louis' mistresses, dead for over a decade now. The mobs tore her body apart; if I left Versailles, would they do the same to me? I do not think that would happen, but an angry mob is a beast that cannot be contained or predicted.

But there are many ways to die, and I know that Louis is the air I breathe, the blood that runs through my veins. I would wither away if we were apart. After so many years of fostering his dependence on me, I realize I am equally dependent on him.

I finish the amethyst and drop the stone into the fishbowl. I feel a quick stab of sympathy for the young girl: How does it feel to be banished as she was? But I'll never know, I decide grimly.

If I were less enamored of my love, I might wish for a drug to calm his appetite. But I could never deny him the pleasures of the flesh, and the debauchery now stirring in the king must be fed, and for a long time to come. His great-grandfather Louis XIV, another lusty Bourbon male, made love twice a day well into his seventies. Perhaps I need to take a more active role in managing his hunger?

I choose my next ally with care: Le Bel, the king's valet and procurer, the man with a standing order for fresh maidenhead, who keeps the king supplied with the little birds for the attic rooms. Perhaps . . . yes, perhaps. I do believe I can improve on the current system.

The house on the rue Saint-Louis is small but adequate, with a blue door and a convenient back entrance on another street. A house for the finest girls in the land, gathered here like August peaches in a basket, and all for his pleasure. Well screened, clean, with police reports from Berryer. Independent of factions and families; harmless, young, and silly. Their very baseness will be my security.

I accompany Le Bel as we inspect the house. The housekeeper, Madame Bertrand, whom Le Bel calls a most responsible woman, follows us around anxiously.

She shows us the work to date: the freshly tiled entrance hall, and the paintings of naked nymphs on the walls of the parlor, naughty but discreet, at the perfect point between politeness and perversion. I examine the beds and the feather mattresses from Ceaux, the fur-covered ottomans, the pillows, the carved mantels. Though everything is to my specifications, there is a sordidness to this house that makes me want to turn and run away. And the wall color is simply wrong, a pale mustard that gives me a headache.

"Perhaps a budget for some toys and such?" suggests Le Bel in his mild voice, fingering the soft fur of the ottoman.

"But what age are these girls to be? Surely they are beyond the age when they wish to play with dolls, or hoops?" Impatience and uncertainty make my voice harsh.

There is an uncomfortable silence and not a moment passes before I understand. I turn away to hide my sudden flush. "I would see the kitchens," I say, and make my way unsteadily down the stairs to the back of the house. I sink onto a bench, watched anxiously by the cook and a kitchen girl. I want to bury my face in my hands and heave out sobs, but instead I ask for a glass of cider.

The house is depressing. Lifeless. A tawdry harem, as base as the instincts which drive its creation. The kitchen girl who hands me the cider has a large scar across her face, no doubt from a hot poker in childhood. Such ugliness. I rejoin Le Bel and Madame Bertrand in the parlor.

"Le Bel, we need to have the walls repainted. Not this dreary mustard-gray. And get rid of that kitchen maid with the scar—so unpleasant on that already pitted skin."

Outside I draw my cloak around me and assume the anonymity of the veil as I walk the back road. I trudge wearily up the stairs of the Orangery, the afternoon sun turning the walls of the looming palace soft honey in the last of the day's light. Am I doing the right thing? Will this keep me—and my Louis—safe?

Will it be enough?

Will anything ever be enough?

Act IV

Morphise

Chapter Forty-Four

It is a large room, the walls and the ceiling and even the floor painted white. There are no curtains; winter sun and cold stream through the windows. Light, says the painter Boucher, is as important to art as breath is to man. I am lying belly-down on the curved sofa, draped with a sheet of plush blue velvet. Boucher experiments as he plans and sketches the painting; last week the sheets were crimson silk, and I know from his puffing today that he is not happy with the blue spread.

The doors open and I hear visitors ushered in.

"Monsieur le Duc de Richelieu! And Monsieur Le Bel," I hear Boucher exclaim in delight. "I am most honored to receive you in my humble atelier."

"Boucher, my man, I had to see for myself, what with the way you sing—and paint—her charms." Footsteps approach, stop beside me. "You do not exaggerate."

"I am glad you approve, sir," says Boucher in satisfaction. "She is a rare treasure."

"Indeed. Just look at these smooth cheeks," says a voice, and a gloved hand, as light and delicate as a tendril of hair, trails across my bare behind. I turn around to smile and see an older man, with an impeccable white wig and a soft gray coat the color of a mouse's belly. His shoes are of stiff silver trimmed with pearls, with high soles and even higher heels.

"So this is the little nymph we have been hearing so much about," he says, smiling down at me. "What price a pound of this? Dearer than even gold," he muses, his hand now squeezing and kneading my buttock.

"I declare it impossible for nature to have created such a beautiful creature. She is otherworldly," concurs Boucher. "I call her Morphise—from the Greek for *beautiful*."

"*Morphos* indeed. What a divine face, and look at her body. So small yet so perfect."

"Not higher than a pony's back, Duc, when standing."

"Charming, ever so charming."

I duck my face into the sheets, as though I am shy of their compliments.

"How old is she?" asks the other man, standing in the shadows.

"The mother says twelve, but I think fourteen, possibly fifteen."

"Le Bel, what do you think?" asks the first man. "Turn over, child. Look at those buds; simply delightful. And such perfect nipples."

"I call them my Apples of Venus," says the painter, "topped with the Grapes of the Gods and, ah—their nectar!" I like Monsieur Boucher; he has a kind voice and pays Mama well for my time. "Now, if you will excuse me, she must return to the correct position."

Obediently I turn back on my stomach and dangle one of my legs over the side of the sofa. I bury my head in the soft velvet and drift off as the men continue to talk about me.

"The youngest, you say?"

"Yes, of many sisters. I am sure you know the Golden Slipper, as they call the eldest one."

"Of course, of course. I assume this one's innocence is already taken?"

"Yes, that went long ago. The mother got a pretty penny for it, I'm sure. But when they're so young—the fit is still excellent, if you understand, no matter how used they may be."

The sofa is soft and there is a large glass of sweet wine on the floor and a plate of boiled snails hidden in the sheets, and as the afternoon wears on I drink and suck them from their shells. I like posing for paintings. It is far easier than entertaining men, who often insist on talking of their troubles and petty worries, and who are always probing and searching for new body parts to explore. It is certainly easier than acting. Last year my mother took me to the Opéra to audition, but at the end the director patted me on the head, sadly, and said that in my grandmother's time a pretty face was sufficient, but nowadays one had to have a little smidge of talent, no more than would fit in a teacup really, but even that was lacking in myself.

Then my mother taught me to hang my head and hide my face, in a charming way, for those situations when my acting skills do not suffice.

I doze, full of snails and wine, growing sleepy from the fire that warms me. Presently I fall asleep and dream of a large sea of velvet, wrapping around me and rocking me as a baby. When I wake up the sun has disappeared and the room is darker, and colder. I sense someone standing over me.

"Monsieur le Duc!" I exclaim, trying to sound delighted.

"Indeed," he says thickly, and pulls me up gently by one of my braids. "Undo my breeches and give me a kiss there, that's a good child." I do as he says and he sighs in satisfaction, then puts me up on the sofa and enters me from behind.

"I had to try you. Oh yes, I just had to. Mmm, yes, indeed, this is very fine. You are a delight, demoiselle, a delight. Ah." There is a small silence as he grunts over me.

"You feel very fine inside me, Monsieur; you have a large and powerful weapon," I say, as I have been taught; my mother always says politeness is the most rewarding of virtues. "I am certainly aroused." Aroused means I am excited like a man, but I scarcely see how that is possible.

"Can I have one of your buttons?" I ask, looking at his coat draped over the arm of the sofa. The buttons wink in the gloom of the late afternoon, and I reach out one hand to touch them.

"Well, those were devilishly hard to get. From Geneva . . . from . . . ahhh, just a little more, a little more." His thrusts increase in rhythm and his hand pushes down on my back with the weight of stone. "Oh yes! Yes!"

"Oh, thank you! I shall use it as a pendant on a necklace."

"No, no. Be quiet. No more talking. Yes. Yes, indeed! Oh, Huguette!" My name is not Huguette but I don't correct him as he collapses over me in a sticky mess. I lie still, then shift under him and move carefully to stroke his head. I creep my fingers under his wig and touch a bald pate; he is older than I thought.

Eventually he speaks: "No, you cannot have one of those buttons, I only have the twelve and they are a set; you'll see the ones on the cuffs, there, are slightly different. But I'll give you some coin, and I shall send you—what do you desire?" He pushes a strand of my hair aside and kisses my forehead. "You are an absolutely delightful child."

He sits up and claps loudly for a basin of water. Presently a woman brings it in, with a white cloth and a large sprig of rosemary. She lights a candle and retires. I play with his coat, rub it against my face, twinkling the buttons against the flame.

"Are these real rubies?"

"Yes. So what would you like?" he asks again, standing and indicating I should button his breeches. I catch a glimpse of it, small and squished now, scrubbed and ready to be put away. I feel like giggling, but it is a strict rule that one must never point or laugh at it, no matter how silly it looks. My sister Madeleine calls it the White Wiggly Worm, and all she has to do is say it in her funny, pompous voice to make me collapse in giggles. The duke pulls the coat from me and shakes it out, as though to rid it of bugs.

"Oh, Monsieur, to lie with you was present enough," I say, as I have been taught, "but if you are so inclined I should love a . . . a pair of gloves. Lined with rabbit fur."

Before he goes he kisses me again, then says that there is a very important gentleman he would like me to meet.

☙

Mama said it was a wonderful opportunity, and so Monsieur Le Bel has brought me here to this house. We are in the midst of the February cold and this winter is a hard one. I am glad to be gone from my parents' house in Paris, where the windowpanes are stuffed with rags and for economy there is fire in only one room. It is very quiet and peaceful here, almost like in the country or Rouen, where I was born. Paris is noisy and dirty, with the constant clatter of the boarders and the squeals from the little abattoir next door, the arguing of the lemonade sellers who live upstairs.

Madame Bertrand is the housekeeper here; she says the gentleman who will visit is a very rich man, a Polish count, a relative of the queen's no less.

"Is the queen Polish?" I ask in astonishment.

"Yes, silly child, of course she is."

"But she is the Queen of *France*."

"Never mind, dear, don't bother yourself with the queen, or the king, just with our very special gentleman the count."

"Am I to be the only one here?" I ask dubiously, going out into the hallway. I think the house rather fine; when I was younger I once stayed in a house like this, but there were other girls, and a number of little boys as well.

"Perhaps," says Madame Bertrand. "We shall see how matters unfold."

"Could my sister Brigitte come?" I say, returning to the room. Brigitte is my favorite sister and friend. I counted four bedrooms on this floor and I don't like the idea of being here all alone, with only Madame Bertrand; the glowering cook, and a kitchen girl with a fiery scar across her cheek.

"We thought you would be most comfortable here alone, at first."

I sit down on a furry stool and run my hands over it. "Ooh, lovely. Lovely."

"This shall be your bedroom, and you're not to wander into

the other rooms." The room is fine and cozy, with two large new-fashioned windows and a fireplace that burns even though it is only noon. The walls are painted in a light peach color and the bed is hung with orange draperies, patterned in gold.

"My own bed?"

"Yes, child."

Well, my own bed. I sit on the mattress, and know instantly it is feathers, not straw or stuffed rags as I am accustomed to at home. "So I shall sleep alone?" I ask. I'm not sure I like that idea. At home I share with whichever of my sisters is home that evening; most times it is only Brigitte and I, but that is enough.

"Child, don't be obtuse. If you are the only one in the house, of course you will sleep alone. But don't worry, I am sure the count will keep you very busy." Madame Bertrand chuckles and her laugh is as thin and hard as a nail, and I know, there and then, I must mind her.

⁊

Later, when it is dark, I explore the house. It is always prudent to know what hides behind closed doors—once my sister Victoire found a tiger in a room by the bedchamber of the Duc de Lauraguais, tethered, but she said it almost had her arm before the chain snapped it back. And I remember the Marquis de Thibouville, who kept a room filled with jars of spiders and long wiggly insects, including a worm with two heads that gave me nightmares for weeks.

But the tidy house reveals no unexplained insects or secrets, the first floor with two parlors and Madame Bertrand's room and the kitchens out back, the three other bedchambers on the second floor. Up in the small sloped rooms of the third floor—where Cook and the kitchen girl sleep—is an empty room. The floor is solidly boarded but there is a hole in one of the planks, perhaps where a winding winch for a chandelier once was. I kneel down and see that it gives onto one of the empty bedrooms below. It might be useful later, I think, peering down.

I explore the attic some more and find a chest, full of ancient clothes and a large fan with missing leaves. I pull out a black dress, so moth-ridden it looks like lace, and drape it over myself and pretend I am a grand lady, hiding myself from the looks of many, bringing mystery and fine secrets wherever I go.

A Letter
From the Desk of the Duchesse de Pompadour
Château de Versailles
February 15, 1753

My dearest Daughter,

Fanfan, how delighted I was to receive your letter! Your handwriting has certainly improved; I must commend Sister Anne. And how exciting your last tooth has fallen out. Yes, it is true the convent is a house of God, but Mother Superior has assured me that an exception is made for the little pagan Tooth Mouse, and that you may soon expect a coin under your pillow.

Your Uncle Abel will visit Sunday, and bring with him some pears and a blanket for your lamb, as you requested. How wonderful it is that Agnes has lasted so long! I am sure she must be quite falling apart by now, so you must thank Sister Anne for keeping the thing clean and in one piece.

Darling, your mother is buying a house in Paris, only a short ride from your convent, and I will be able to visit more often. I will prepare a room for you and you must tell me what colors you would like. I suggest pink and green.

Though of course you won't be married for several years— seven is far too young—it is never too soon to start thinking of your little husband! When you visit next month, I will bring you to the Hermitage, another of Mama's houses, near Fontainebleau, and most delightful: a country house, really, with animals (including sheep and lambs!), but all properly washed and scrubbed. I've invited a little boy I want you to meet—he is the son of the Comtesse de Vintimille, once a great friend of our king. She is dead but I do hope you will find her son charming.

All my love,
Mama

Chapter Forty-Five

"He is coming!"

I am lying on my bed, daydreaming. Idleness is a splendid thing; my sister Marguerite, whom my mother calls a lazy toad, says there is nothing finer than doing nothing. My bed is as soft as snow, the sheets just as white. I am adept at telling quality, and I know these sheets are certainly the best; they probably cost more than one hundred *livres*. If I could write, I would send a letter to Brigitte and to my mother, and tell them of the wonders of this house. But even if I could write, they do not read and Mama doesn't approve of spending money on trifles like letter readers.

"Who's coming?"

"The count!" says Madame Bertrand, bursting into the room. "We must get you ready." She looks around wildly, as though the answer to her distress is to be found on the walls, or out through the windows.

"When is he coming?" I say, starting to untie my robe. "Shall I wear that new blue dress?"

"Yes, but first we need to wash you, and make sure everything is ready and— oh! Refreshments!"

I have yet to see Madame Bertrand in such a fluster; usually she sleeps in the afternoons, but in the evenings can be quite talkative and her little black eyes—like points of ink—glow feverishly. Now she looks as though she has just been woken from a deep sleep.

"He must be very important for you to be in such a state, Madame," I say politely, but the woman only blinks at me and drags me down to the kitchen, where they are preparing a bath. As I am being bathed by Rose, the kitchen girl with the angry scar on her face, I assure Madame that I am not nervous and that she should not be either; I have had the opportunity, I explain to her, to entertain some very grand men, several dukes and once even the brother of the King of Sweden (well, that was my sister, but perhaps my lie will comfort), and that I have never disappointed.

"No, no, I do not want to imply he will find you wanting. Of course not! You are charming, charming. It's just—well, everything must be perfect. Now dry yourself and let's rub you down with that oil they sent over—now where is it? Rose! Where is the oil?"

"I don't know where you put it, Ma'am."

"Find me the oil!" roars Madame Bertrand, collapsing at the kitchen table and reaching to drink from a large earthenware jug.

When I am dried, oiled (a lovely flower smell), and dressed and my hair has been pinned up, I am told to sit in the parlor, though Madame Bertrand is not sure whether I should be there or up in my bedroom. By this point Madame Bertrand is shaking visibly, as well as drinking visibly from the large jug.

"Her favorite apple gin," whispers the kitchen girl Rose, and I grin and recognize the smell, which I could not place before, seeming so out of place in this prim and plush little house.

A man arrives and I recognize him from the painter's atelier.

"Monsieur Le Bel!" I say in my delighted voice. "A pleasure to see you again!" Oh—perhaps the count is really the Duc de Richelieu in disguise? I remember his greasy grunts, the smooth feel of his pate under his wig, the fine pair of gloves he sent as I requested.

"Ah, of course, little one, of course you remember me. You look ravishing, my dear, ravishing. I did not doubt the blue would look good on you and no petticoats"—he lifts my skirt up with his cane—"excellent, excellent. Now, this is looking very fine, to your credit, Madame," he says, looking around the parlor, his eyes resting briefly on the jug Madame Bertrand is still clutching. "But I do believe the count would prefer the visit to start in the intimacy of the bedroom. There is a fire and chairs there as well?"

"Oh yes, sir, oh yes, sir," says Madame Bertrand, bobbing frantically. "Rose! Rose! The fire in her bedroom! Everything upstairs!"

The count arrives at dusk as the town is falling silent after the bustle of the day. Madame Bertrand looks fit to faint and actually falls down as she shows the count into my bedroom, where a fire blazes and a fine cinnamon cake sits proudly on a plate. Cook says she is the finest baker in three towns, and that the count will never have tasted such heaven.

The count is older than I was expecting, but he is still a handsome man with a kind face and the soft jaw of a man in the prime of his life. He has a mass of dark brown hair, pulled back in a lace-wrapped bag, and is wearing a magnificent turquoise coat, threaded with gold and silver. I feel a rush of excitement, for I know the signs of deep wealth. That coat could have cost five thousand *livres,* I calculate. Perhaps the count is richer than even the Marquis de Lamonte, a great friend of my sister's!

"Madame is a little happy on the drink, I take it," he says easily after Madame Bertrand has picked herself up and stumbled down the stairs. He comes across the room to kiss me.

"Mother Mary!" he exclaims, lifting a candle and holding me at arms' length, his face greedy with excitement. "You are simply ravishing. So small, and petite, and what a perfect, perfect face!"

I smile up at him, then go to bury myself in his arms, affecting shyness.

"Oh, a kitten, a charming kitten!" I take the candle from his hand, blow it out slowly, then press myself against him. Suddenly he is pawing and pushing up my skirts with fevered intent, as hurried as a well-whipped horse.

Only when it is over does he ask me my name. "They never told me," he says in wonderment. "Or perhaps they did and I forgot." His voice is deep, rich and treacled. I climb out of my dress, shaking my long hair loose from its pins and draping it over my naked body. I serve him some champagne, and a small slice of the cake, and come back to the bed.

"It's Louise, if it pleases you, sir," I say with a curtsy.

"Ah, unfortunate name. No, that does not please me." The man frowns.

I laugh and straddle him. "Why is that?" I take a strand of his hair, free of grease or powder, and twirl it around my finger.

"Ah—some memories there."

"What would you like to call me?" I ask, leaning down to kiss one of his nipples. I tug at it gently and his eyes widen. "By God, you may be a kitten, but you are a sexy one at that!"

"My nickname is Morphise. That means *beautiful* in Latin." I take his other nipple in my mouth.

"You might mean Greek, but that is true. Ahhh. Now I remember—you are Irish, with an outlandish Irish name."

"Yes, sir. O'Murphy."

"Tell me of Ireland," he says in a deep, contented voice and pulls me back close to him under the luxurious covers. I snuggle by his side and tell him of the green hills, the smell of peat, the sheep and the whiskey. Though I have never been there I bring him along with me on a journey remembered from my father's tales. As I talk my words take him far, far away from his important life as a count, a life that is already beginning to etch fine lines on his forehead and around his mouth.

Chapter Forty-Six

" I think," says Thérèse, her voice rising to a conspiratorial whisper, "I think our count might be friends with the *king*." Thérèse has been brushing my hair for an hour now, dipping her comb in what she claims is argan oil, but I think it is just cooking grease from the kitchens. Thérèse's aunt is a hairdresser, and the first thing she did, upon her arrival at the house, was to show me her hair and then compare it to mine. Thérèse is very pretty but she has bad teeth; they have been painted but to an odd effect. Everything else about her is rather perfect, from her sharp, elegant features to her wide mouth and beautiful skin and her flowing cloud masses of light hair. I run my own tongue over my teeth, which are perfect and natural.

"Why do you think he is friends with the king?" I ask. Thérèse appeared last month and though the count often visits her, I note in satisfaction that my visits outnumber hers, and that hers are often only when I am indisposed.

Madame Bertrand supplied us with tapestry boards, which she wants us to work on when we are not otherwise occupied. "Imagine," she said, "how you could surprise him with a gift—a nice bag for his hair, with an embroidered bow, or a handkerchief—think how he would be delighted to receive that."

"I think he'd rather receive something else from us," Thérèse said impishly, pushing her hips forward.

Madame Bertrand's face hardened. "Little mattress thrashers," she said in disgust, "your care may be in my hands, but I would have you know I am not by nature a brothel keeper. I am the widow of a former clerk in the War Office."

"And so would that make you, Madame," asked Thérèse in

her innocent little voice, which I envy and try to copy, "a camp follower?"

Now the tapestry frames sit unused in the corner of my room like two reproaches. Madame Bertrand says she is responsible for our education ("But what would *you* teach *us?*" inquires Thérèse in her silky voice, innocent yet insolent), but when I broach learning my letters, Madame Bertrand directs me again to my tapestry board: "Stitches are a woman's writing," she says smugly, and I suspect she can't read or write herself.

"Why do you say he is friends with the king?" I ask Thérèse again, returning to the subject of the count and wincing as she works on an impossibly small braid behind my ear.

"Well, he's ever so important—you see the way Madame Bertrand curtsies to him, and how her hands shake so—well, perhaps that is the gin, but they shake even more when he comes. That man Le Bel often bows to him, and everyone knows Le Bel is very powerful and intimate with the king. They are both very deferential to our count. *Deferential* means respectful."

"I know what deferential means," I say. "The count has not been here for almost two weeks, and Rose from the kitchens told me the king and all his daughters have gone to Choisy for a week. Oh! Perhaps that explains why he has not come; he had to accompany the king."

"You see," says Thérèse triumphantly. "I told you he was important." She jabs a pin into my hair and twists. I'm not sure I like Thérèse, with her rather sly and bossy air. She has taken to marching around and giving orders, even though the count certainly prefers me.

"I'm not even sure he's Polish," I say as she coils a braid onto my head and pins it up. The oil smells like lamb; I'm sure it's from the kitchen. "His French is rather perfect."

"Well, anyone's French would seem perfect to you," Thérèse snaps back, a jab at my Rouen accent. Thérèse says I must listen to her, because she is Paris born and bred, and older.

"Not at all," I cut back. "I have been exposed to some very

high-ranking people and have a good ear for language." Thérèse was nothing before she came here, just a two-bit public girl from the Rue de Lappe whose aunt took little financial persuasion to part with her. Rose the kitchen girl told me; she is adept at listening and talking to Madame Bertrand when she has drunk too much and becomes voluble and loose. But on the subject of the count, she is closemouthed; I have to agree with Thérèse that there is more to his story than we know.

"Well perhaps, and his French is rather perfect. My *tante* had a client who was Russian—very close to Poland, you know—she had very thin hair, and her accent was difficult to understand. There! Feel that."

I run a hand over the heavy braids, piled on my head, sopping with oil.

"Are you sure all the oil is necessary?"

"Of course," Thérèse says smoothly. "My aunt had a high class of clientele and swore by this oil. I am certain he is not Polish. I actually think he's French, on account of his energy." She jams a cork into the jar of oil and wipes her hands on the sheets. "Don't move your head so, or the oil will drip off. It needs time to soak in. Only Frenchmen are ready to go again within the hour. I have heard it takes British men all day to rest, and everyone knows Polish men can only do it once a week. Still, his fucking is rather quantity over quality."

"Of course," I say, but I am confused by her words, for I am not sure how one would judge the quality of sex—it is not a pair of shoes or a coat that can be easily valued.

❧

The count comes silently, on foot or in a chair, no clatter of hooves to signal his arrival. He often arrives accompanied by Le Bel or another I do not recognize, and the other men stay in the downstairs parlor while he comes up to the bedchambers.

Thérèse is newly pregnant and has been sent to the country— to the house of a cousin, says Madame Bertrand. I am happy she is gone, of course, but I wonder what will happen to her child—will the count provide? And will she come back here after the birth?

A new girl replaced her last week, but already I sense the count is tired of her: Claire has a boldness and a sarcasm I do not think he cares for. She has glorious curly brown hair, which I know Thérèse would have fallen in love with, and an angelic beauty, just like the nymphs on the wall panels. Even though she is perhaps my age, already the street has hardened her mouth and her eyes. Mama always said that we must take care to put our hardness away, and never let it slip out. A man is hard, and a woman is soft, she would always say, in her hard voice, when one of my sisters snorted or grimaced or told a story in too shocking a language.

"This," I say to the count, "is a very fine, very particular shoe." I hold up the red-heeled little mule, soft kid leather covered with three rows of yellow satin ruffles.

"Indeed it is," he says slowly, and takes a sip of wine, watching me. He has been here all afternoon—only twice, but I'll tell Claire it was three times—and now he is lingering in the coziness of the bed; I sense he has a lot of work back at the palace and is loath to return there. Sometimes his valet will knock on the door, and whisper to Monsieur le Comte that procedure will not wait, and then he will sigh and stand up with the weariness of a grandfather, kiss me, and whisper to me that I am the only thing that keeps him alive and young. But today there is no summons and he is peaceful and torpid on the bed.

"I'll wager this pair cost you more than four hundred *livres*."

"Perhaps you are right, my dear."

"Or even six hundred. You see this, here"—I turn over the shoe and show him the red silk inside—"this is the finest craftsmanship. You see how fine the stitches are? And the lining is pure silk, a mark of true quality."

"I never realized a shoe would take such skill."

"Oh yes." I nod seriously. "Making shoes is a very skilled profession, and much care goes into the making of a pair." When my father wasn't in prison or running away from the law, he was a shoemaker, and I remember vaguely from when we were young and still living in Rouen, the smell of burnished leather in his shop, the piles of soft skins and the bucket of wooden heels.

"So how long did that one take to make, do you think?" the count asks with interest.

"Mmm . . ." I consider, turning it over in my hands. My father never made such fine shoes; his clients were not amongst the wealthy or the nobility. I hazard a guess. "About four months."

The count whistles, as I have taught him. "Four months! Fancy that. And just for a pair of shoes. Now, child, put them on."

I slip them on; the soft lining greets my toes like a friend being welcomed home. I parade about, naked, with only the red-and-yellow shoes on my feet. The count follows my progress with lazy, appreciative eyes.

"Are those the finest shoes you have ever worn, little one?"

"No," I say truthfully. "Once the Duc de Lau—oh, I shouldn't say his name, let me just say a very nice Monsieur presented me a pair edged with pearls, real ones, sewn all around the toe puff. They were most fine, but Mama unpicked the pearls to sell, and then they were rather ordinary."

I sit down on the chair by the fire and lift my legs, wiggling the shoes at him, allowing him a peek between my legs. One of the shoes falls off and then I kick the other one over to him on the bed. He chuckles and picks it up, turns it over in his hands, takes an appreciative sniff, and lobs it gently back. "Put them on again, and come and stand here."

I do as bidden and stand in front of the bed, awaiting my next instructions.

"And what would you have to match those wonderful shoes, child?" He reaches out and traces my stomach, sticks a probing finger in my belly button.

"I should like a dress, of course, made of silk and . . . and lace. With velvet trim. It should be yellow, to match the ruffles on the shoes, and with sleeves in the pagoda style."

"In the pagoda style? What does that mean?"

"Cropped and cut, here and here."

He laughs. "I'll let my valet know, and he will take care of it."

A few days later the yellow dress arrives and I parade about the house in my finery, and ask Claire over and over what she thinks of my splendid new gown.

Chapter Forty-Seven

"We must find out who he is," my sister says. Madeleine is visiting, bringing advice and the present of a paper fan from Mama. She fingers the curtains, appraises the furniture, and decides that even the fire screen must have cost a pretty penny.

"Just a pity he doesn't have a house in Paris." Madeleine is wonderfully worldly and sophisticated, and has worked as both an actress and a model. I don't think she's as pretty as I am, though; she is rather skinny and there is an uncomfortable gap between her thighs.

"He is needed at Court too much. He has much work to do, and even attends the king's *levée*," I say. Last night he came, late, when the dawn was but a few hours away. He fell into a deep sleep; I was not tired, having slept all day, and so I watched him as he snored, thinking what a fine man he was. I wondered about his wife and where he goes, in body or soul, when he leaves me.

Before the sun rose a very anxious Le Bel came to the door and sought to inform the count, in an artificially soft voice, that the man was wanted at the *levée* of the king, and that it would be noticed if he were absent. Luckily, the palace is only a short walk away.

"Yes, but if he is truly as important as you think he is, he would also have a house in Paris."

"Well, maybe he does," I say, sticking my tongue out at her. Madeleine shrugs.

"This is a pretty jacket," she says, rummaging in one of my chests, a vole in its natural habitat. "And what lovely sleeves."

"Gifts from the count," I say smugly.

"Give the jacket to me. I have a skirt it would match perfectly."

"No, but I'll sell it to you. Ten golden *louis*," I say, fixing on an outrageous price.

"Six."

"Eight."

"There, done." She tosses the coins on the bed, and from the careless way she plucked them from her pouch, I know she has more.

"Where did you get these?" I ask in astonishment, picking up the heavy coins. I jingle them in my hand. I receive many gifts, but rarely money.

"Ah, that would be telling."

"Let's go to the market," I say suddenly. The count came yesterday and he never comes two days in a row. On the days when he does not appear I am free to leave the house. "It is not as though you are prisoners here," Madame Bertrand once said to me. Of course not—why would she even say that?

Madame Bertrand is draped over a chair in the parlor.

"Don't be long," she says in a thick, faraway voice. "You never know. Take Rose. And no more than . . . no more than a . . . minute. When I was your age . . ." Her voice trails off and she stares up at the ceiling and giggles.

"*Oui,* Madame."

Outside the day is warm and lively. The Cannoneers of the Royal Artillery are camped at the edge of town and the market is bustling. I wonder if the count ever walks out in town, strolls around the streets, or visits the parks? Madeleine buys some purple ribbons and I give one of my coins to Rose. Rose holds on to it and says there is nothing at the market that interests her; I wonder when she last had a penny of her own in her hand.

We sit on a bench by the fountain in the Place d'Armes and I toss the coins in the air for distraction. A few dirty boys crouch near a bush, ready to dash forth and dive if an unsuspecting visitor tosses a coin in the fountain to make a wish. I flip the *louis* high in the air and laugh when one of the boys darts forward in expectation.

"I'm surprised you haven't been to the palace," says Madeleine, cocking her head and smiling at a passing cleric. "What?" she says in response to my shocked hiss. "His habit was fine wool without a single pill—I'll wager he has a bishop in his family."

Madame Bertrand says we mustn't go to the palace. Sometimes I feel distressed, when some days or even a week has passed; it is hard to be so near him but not able to visit. Claire accuses me of falling in love with the count, but I assure her I am not, though he is wonderfully attentive and kind. I think Claire is most in love with him; she often sighs about how soft his voice is, and the way his dark eyes twinkle like stars when he is excited.

"Madame Bertrand says we mustn't visit, for the count does not want to see us there."

"So wear a veil!" scorns Madeleine. "I must say it is a sight not to be missed." I think of the tattered black linen I found in the attic; I could wear that. Or buy a fine lace one, new even, I think, my fingers tightening over the coins in my hand.

"What is it like?" asks Rose wistfully. "The palace?" Though we live so close, she has never been inside. There are too many guards to turn away undesirables, and Rose has only one rather poor dress with too much patching to be allowed entry. I should ask the count for another dress and give it to Rose, I think suddenly.

"Well, I was once honored to visit in the company of a very fine man, a friend of mine, a duke of some distinction and standing." My sister's voice is high and pompous, and she likes to orate as though she were on the stage: "His rooms were very fine, and we went for a tour of the main staterooms. So many fine mirrors, more even than at Madame Gourdan's or Madame Sultana's—the finest houses of pleasure in Paris," she adds for Rose's edification, "and statues everywhere. He gave a party, this friend of mine, where many flavors of cordial were served, including a very fine mint and raspberry one. If you wanted more ice, you only had to ask. Versailles is very fine," she concludes in satisfaction.

"But now they say someone as beautiful"—she smiles at a man in a bright pink coat passing by, his matching scabbard swinging jauntily—"someone as beautiful as I would be in danger, for it's well known that the old woman Pompadour chases away beautiful ladies, and girls and women as well. Once she even paid a valet to cut a girl's hair!"

"I heard she pours boiling coffee on her guests' faces, if they are too beautiful," says Rose eagerly. She runs a finger along the scar on her cheek.

"Indeed; she blows pretty girls away like dust specks off a dress."

"I should like to see the king," says Rose rather wistfully, catching my tossing coin and staring down at his image. "And the queen—they say she is the most Christian woman in France. Why, look, Morphise, the king looks very like our count!"

I look at the little head, the embossed profile. "You're right. Perhaps he is brother to the king, and not a relative of the queen's."

"The king doesn't have any brothers," says Madeleine airily. "Your count's just a man with a high nose, is all."

Well . . . I lie back and sigh in containment, watch the cloud puffs float across the summer sky. But it is true, the man on the coin does look rather like our count. Perhaps they are related? I'd like to fall asleep here, but it's getting late.

"Come on, we should get back or Madame Bertrand will come out looking for us, and she hasn't done her hair today."

"I'll join you later," says Madeleine. "Look, over there, there's my gentleman with the pink sword, and he is rather smiling at me."

ↄ

"I know who you are!" I say, when the count has eaten his fill. "I know you."

"Ah, no one knows me," he replies a little sadly, watching me pirouette around the room. "By God, this wine is rotgut. Where do they get it from?"

"Try this," I say, taking the goblet from his hand and gargling a mouthful, then swallowing whole. "It improves the taste."

He laughs and does as I say, but only manages to finish half before he chokes and spits it out into the fireplace. "No, I believe it would take an hour or more of googling—gargling, you say?—to improve this wine. There should only be the finest wines in this house, not this . . . piss juice."

I don't tell him Madame Bertrand drank the consignment that came last week, and that today Rose had been sent out in a hurry to buy some replacement from the tavern around the corner.

"So, who do you think I am?" the count asks, settling back with the last pastry from the plate.

"You're a relative of the king's," I say. "I know you. Look!" I take out the coin and show him the face.

He stares at it. "This is indeed a well-known face," he says rather sadly, and then suddenly—I know. I know who our count is.

My lover—the King of France. King Louis XV of France! It scarcely seems possible, but I am sure of it. It all makes sense—Le Bel, the bowing, the scraping, the fright, the impossibly expensive coats, and all those fine shoes and presents. How my sisters will be sour when they find out! And Mother will definitely consider me the most valuable of her daughters, for I—I am the mistress of the King of France.

The mistress of the King of France.

It is rather exciting but I am not sure what to do with myself, or with my secret.

But I have to tell someone.

I tell Claire, mostly to show her that she doesn't know everything of the world, and also because she can never keep a secret. At first Claire thinks I am lying, but then she considers, and decides it to be true.

When he next comes I decide on a plan. Sometimes he likes

us both to entertain him in the parlor before he makes his decision. Today I cough several times, knowing his horror of germs and illness. Eventually he rises and extends his hand to Claire, who sneers at me in triumph. I hang my head and then when they are gone I creep up the back staircase and into the attic, to watch and listen.

"Your Majesty," says Claire, kissing him. "My king."

"My king?" The count pushes her away. From my peephole in the ceiling I can see the tops of their heads; Claire's bands of sequins in her braids wink back at me. I must wear my hair as she does hers, I think, as I am small and men can see me from above, as I see her now.

"Your Majesty," says Claire again, reaching to grab him by the lapel. "Your secret is exposed, oh Majesty! How I love you, Your Majesty."

"I believe you are mistaken," he says stiffly, pushing her away, and I know he is lying. "Mademoiselle, your words have killed my passion," he continues with cold dignity. He leaves and later they come for Claire, who screams as they carry her off to the madhouse.

"Only for a few days," says Madame Bertrand, patting my arm. "Until she clears her mind of this fanciful notion. Now, have a glass of this apple and gin, just the thing to calm our nerves after such a frightful scene. You'll tell Le Bel when he next comes that it is your drink of choice, won't you?"

⁊

But the count doesn't visit for several weeks, and then Madame Bertrand calls me into the parlor and I fear I too am going to be dismissed. Stupid Claire, I think, then remember it was I who wanted her to tell.

"Child, we have some important news to tell. Do not be shocked." Madame Bertrand takes a deep breath, then steadies herself and her voice. "Our count, our dear benefactor, is no ordinary count."

I keep my head bowed, silent. I do hope they don't send me

away. I like living here, I like this house and Rose, and above all, I like the count.

"He is not an ordinary count, in fact he is not a count at all, at least I don't think he counts—ha!—among his many titles a countship, though of course he may." She pauses, takes another sip of her apple drink. "In sum, my child, our count is the king."

I look up and widen my eyes in what I hope is innocent wonder.

"So you knew already, did you? I knew that other little sausage holder was not smart enough, but you—you're a tricky one. Well, it is good you kept your secret, for after consultation with His Majesty and his pim—ah, men responsible for his pleasure, it has been decided that to avoid scenes like the unpleasantness with Mademoiselle Claire . . . he will still visit, in secret, mind, but you will know who it is you service."

"Will Claire come back?"

"Not at all. Why?"

"Well, she thought he was the king and you said she was crazy. But she was right."

"No, Claire won't be coming back, though I am sure her bed will not be empty for long. The young David girl?" Madame Bertrand turns to the man in the corner.

"In progress, in progress," murmurs Le Bel from the shadows where he has been sitting, watching us.

∽

I practice my curtsy in my high red shoes, and when the count—no, I must call him the king now—returns, I seat him on the bed and stand in front of him. I drop my robe and sweep down in a beautiful, naked curtsy and don't once topple over.

"I have been practicing especially for you," I say in my best shy kitten voice. "Your Majesty."

"Ah, don't do that," he says easily, settling back on the bed. "You cannot know how I enjoyed the anonymity. Anonymity—the ignorance of others, who think they know everything. But a king's life can be never alone, never."

I'm not sure why he would want to be alone, but I murmur in sympathy, "It must be very difficult, to be the king." I have an overwhelming urge to giggle, so I bury my face in the pillows and my body shudders in a way which overwhelms the count—I mean the king—and soon I am in his arms, and I think, But a king is just a man like any other.

A Letter
From the Desk of the Duchesse de Pompadour
Château de Versailles
May 11, 1753

My dear Bernis,

Thank you for your news of Venice and Parma—how kind of dear Madame Infanta to bless you with a visit. Here life continues, a mix of pleasure and work. This year the Duc de Richelieu is *en charge* as First Gentleman and try as I might (and I do try hard), I cannot seem to avoid that execrable man. I suggested to the king he award his faithful friend with the governorship of Guyenne—a journey of almost two weeks in winter.

His Majesty is well though he does not travel much these days and prefers to spend his nights in town, visiting friends. He needs his amusements to offset his trials with Parlement and the bad news from the colonies—this English aggression is very vexing. It seems that one problem is just removed when another rises: troubles are indeed a Medusa. We have even talked of exiling Parlement and replacing it with a body that is more tractable and respectful to the king. A serious step, but I fear it has come to this.

Quesnay and I had a debate the other night: Where does this new insubordination come from? Some blame the *Encyclopedia*, leading men to question all that is known in this world. I fear my allegiance to the project is diminishing. To claim that animals have souls! Though sometimes, when I look at my monkey Nicolet's expressive little eyes . . . well. I shall not further my thoughts, out of respect for your ecclesiastical calling.

For another letter, perhaps one sent in a more private manner, I would discuss with you a curious idea from Kaunitz, the Austrian Foreign Minister. Perhaps a welcome overture from our traditional enemies? I find our current allies to be lacking in virtue: Frederick of Prussia makes no attempt to win my respect, and I heard he called me an unfortunate, high-rouged female.

Ever in friendship,
J

Chapter Forty-Eight

Now that I know he is the king, I am sometimes invited to the palace. I travel in a sedan chair, the windows blocked with heavy curtains, and I am carried up a back staircase to a small suite of rooms in the attic. The rooms are very luxurious, but I know there must be more to the palace they call the Wonder of Europe.

The shadow of the great Marquise de Pompadour, the king's mistress and friend, hangs all around: in the wonderful turquoise coat of the king—when I compliment it he tells me it was a gift from a dear friend; in the vases of overblooming hydrangeas in the attic rooms (the Marquise's favorite flower, Le Bel informs me); in the lines of worry that sometimes crease the king's forehead, when he tells me he has been working hard with her.

"All afternoon with the Marquise," he says, coming up the stairs and flinging himself on the bed. "Endless petitions about the falconry post, vacant yet again. We could not decide: to elevate one is to disappoint another, as the Marquise so wisely said. An intricate and troublesome business. And Parlement . . ." I rub his neck and want to ask him about her, but something holds me back.

To amuse us, the king has a bowl of little Chinese fish sent to the house on the rue Saint-Louis. They are red and gold—just like my shoes, but not as pretty. Rose thinks we should eat them, and doesn't understand when I tell her they are just for decoration. I watch the little fish swimming around the bowl, their eyes vacant glass, and I think of her. She was once just a bourgeoise with a nasty name—Poisson. *Fish*. They say she is not ashamed of her humble roots, and perhaps that is something we share. Certainly, she came from a better background than I; Mama has pretensions but I know we are far from respectable. But compared to the king her roots are humble, yet he loved her. And now I think he loves me.

A new girl, Catherine, is the daughter of a chambermaid to a great titled lady who lives in the palace. She says she once even danced in the chorus of a ballet the Pompadour arranged; she was an Indian and wore a costume made entirely of leather and feathers. Still, she has only been called to the attic rooms twice, yet I have been called five times.

Because of her connection to the palace, Catherine—a stunning girl with a quick wit and striking red hair—is an authority on all things Pompadour. She tells me that the great woman doesn't allow any beautiful ladies near the king, only little girls like us, and that we must be kept hidden away. She also tells me there are many houses like ours, dotted all around the city and the nation. I'm not sure I believe that; the king is only one man, and he does spend quite a bit of time here.

Catherine also assures us that the rumors are true, that Pompadour once poured scalding coffee over a beautiful girl's face and would do the same to us were she to think us a threat. I shudder at the thought she might take my beauty and ruin me, leave me maimed and ugly forever. And then what would I do? I would be like Rose, reduced to the kitchens.

I make a decision and that night Cook prepares a plate of delicately grilled little fish, so pretty over a bed of mashed turnips.

⌘

My sister is coming to the house! Brigitte has been ordered for the king; she is not the prettiest of my sisters, but Le Bel thinks she will do just fine, given the king's preference for me, and for sisters in general.

Even though Brigitte is older than me—almost seventeen— she still has her *baptismal innocence,* as Mama likes to say, but that is not surprising given Brigitte's crooked teeth and rather plain face. Still, the king is curious about her and so she comes to the house. She brings what she says is a letter from Mama, but it is just a black-edged piece of paper that she unfolds, and recites from memory the instructions: *Never forget your family. Ask the king for a house for us in Paris. Don't forget to mention Marguerite should anyone inquire of her—her friend the Marquis de Lamonte recently died.*

The king spends the night with Brigitte, who cries a bit the next day, and I am the one who must comfort her. "It's just men," I say, rubbing Brigitte's back, holding her as Mama held me when I was just a little girl, only ten at the time. Brigitte is lucky, for she is almost seventeen. "It's just what they like. And we must be happy that we have something they desire, for imagine if all we could do was cook and clean!"

"But I don't like being naked," wails Brigitte, and I think how young she is in some ways, how innocent. "And I didn't like him kissing me and after he kept putting his fingers inside and he didn't stop even though I cried. And it hurt."

"Being naked won't bother you soon," I say shortly, pushing down rising memories of a vast blue bed and a dribbling old man whose face I refuse to remember. "It has to happen to all of us at some time, and again, as Mama says, we must be glad we have something they desire, and so they treat us well." I suddenly feel very old, and rather tired. I hug Brigitte again.

"And . . . with your face, you should be honored it is the king who thought your maidenhead worth something . . ." I trail off. I love Brigitte, but I am sad for her: we both know it is only her connection with me that gives her any value.

The next day the king comes again, and this time he asks for both of us. Catherine's mouth drops open and her eyes are as wide as hoops as my sister and I accompany the king up to my room.

"Sinful," he mutters after he is spent, closing his eyes. Brigitte is sitting on the bed, as white as the sheets. I offer her my robe and hustle her off to the kitchen for some more cakes. "And mind you look happy when you return," I hiss to her as I push her out the door, then realize I sound just like my mother.

"Sinful, sinful, ah, what sin you cause me to commit, my dazzling little Morphise," he says, sighing, one hand over his eyes, one hand caressing my thigh.

"Plenty of time for redemption later, Sire," I say lightly. Mother taught us to say as much when men's religious qualms surface, as they often do, though less of late. Mother said when she was younger it was not unheard of for a priest to wait in the next room, for absolution when it was done.

"We must enjoy what pleasures are offered, while they are offered, and repentance comes later," I recite.

The king shakes his head and squeezes my thigh, but the next time he visits he asks me to go and fetch my sister, as well as Catherine. "But be quick, and quiet, and mind Madame Bertrand does not hear you," he says in a worried whisper.

༄

A handsome patterned gown arrives. Rose dresses me in it and sighs as she tightens the sleeves and laces the bodice. "You are soooo beautiful," she whispers, but there is only pride, no envy, in her voice. She fingers the rich fabric, a blend of silk and velvet, patterned with roses. I am wearing little panniers; the hoops lift the heavy skirts around me and my legs feel light and airy.

"You take my blue dress," I say, but she shakes her head.

"It would be too small."

"We can let it out, add a panel on each side."

"But what would be the use?" she says dolefully, finishing up the sleeves and running her fingers through the soft lace at the elbows. "It's no use. Not with this scar. Men never look at me."

"Oh, Rose, it's not all . . ." I start to say, but then I stop, for it is the most important thing in life. "Well, you shall have my blue dress, and one day we'll go to the palace together and I'll wear a veil and you'll wear the dress and they'll step aside to let us pass, thinking us two grand ladies."

Rose giggles and twirls me around. "Perfect," she says in satisfaction.

"I'll bring you something from the dinner," I say, excitement rising in me like a rush of wind. I am carried as usual in the chair but instead of going to the attic rooms I am taken to a room on the second floor of the palace, up a staircase grander than the one I usually ascend.

"Oh, but this is fabulous," I exclaim, looking around at the clusters of golden cherubs floating over the doorways, the pink-and-green tapestries that line each panel of the walls, a table seemingly made entirely of green stone.

The footman at the door snorts and says dismissively, for we are alone: "You should see the rest of the palace."

"Oh, but I have," I retort.

"Doubt it, or you wouldn't think this room so fine."

The king comes in and I fly into his arms, sticking out my tongue at the lackey as I embrace him. "Oh, King, this is beautiful."

"Not as beautiful as you, my dear," he says, shaking his head as he turns me around. "As glorious as the dawn. Now, I thought you might like to dine with some friends of mine tonight. A pearl inside an oyster's shell is wasted; what good is beauty when not shared?"

"I would love to dine with your friends," I answer politely. "I shall be on my best behavior and I can assure you I know how to behave around quality."

"Ah, don't worry about that," says the king, cupping my breasts and giving them a greedy squeeze. "It is an intimate group, and they know their king is fabulously, madly intoxicated by you."

"Intoxicated by love," I say in a playful, teasing voice. "And are you in love with me?"

"Ah, perhaps I am. Come," he says, and leads me through to an adjoining room, where the table is set and a group is waiting.

"Oh, Sire, ravishing, absolutely ravishing!"

"A veritable Greek goddess, Athena joined to Hebe, no less."

"Adorable, captivating child!"

"I certainly see the appeal; a very charming plaything," says a round little woman with a pretty face, looking at me rather coolly. "A *very* charming plaything." Her voice is disapproving, and my eyes widen; I can't imagine anyone talking to the king like this. My sister Marguerite told me that at Versailles, even the greatest of generals must be like a woman, soft and subservient, next to the king.

"Is that the Marquise de Pompadour?" I ask of the man seated next to me. He is wearing a white wig with three layers of curls at each side. Catherine follows fashions avidly and likes to point out new wig styles, and I know she would appreciate this one.

The man laughs softly. "No, that is the Maréchale de Mire-poix, recently returned from England. A great friend of the Mar-quise's. She likes rabbits," he adds disapprovingly.

"Likes rabbits? But who does not?" Cook, though thoroughly unpleasant in all regards, does make an excellent rabbit stew.

The man looks at me with a smattering of distaste. "No, she doesn't *eat* them. She raises them. Carries them around. Surprised she doesn't have one with her now."

I look at her with interest. "I should like to see her rabbits."

"Frightful creatures." The man shudders. "Vicious red eyes, and those snub noses. And droppings everywhere—pellets of filth."

"So then where is the Marquise?" I venture to ask. My curiosity has been growing but the king seems embarrassed if I mention her name. All we hear are rumors and confusions: that she is more powerful than a prime minister; that the king calls her mother; that she carries poison around to take immediately, were she to be dismissed.

"A slight indisposition, I believe, but she is often unwell. To your benefit—she would never countenance your presence, were she here." Suddenly a mask descends over his face; he realizes he has said too much.

"You are very charming," he says, returning to safer ground.

"You have an elder sister Marguerite, no, the one they call the Golden Slipper? I enjoyed her last New Year's, at a ball given by the Duchesse d'Orléans. She was fine, very fine, wore a petticoat entirely of fur." He spears a piece of asparagus and chews on it, contemplating me. "We must keep in touch," he whispers low.

I smile and start to compliment his taste, then realize I don't have to do that anymore. Not now. I stare at him and he licks his asparagus, his tongue flicking over the yellow stalk, then catches the king's eyes on him and turns his gesture into a delicate coughing fit.

"Oh, leave the room, Ayen, if you can't control yourself," says the king in irritation. "That's quite the churchyard cough." I smile in gratitude at the king and something secret and kind passes between us.

At dinner the king holds the center of attention and recounts his trials with the boar from the day before. I listen raptly, as everyone else does, but I can see the others are not really listening and much of their enthusiasm is feigned.

"This brings me such great pleasure," says the king in satisfaction when the food is but a messy memory on the table. "Come here, poppet." I get up and sit on his lap, then turn to his chest and play with his buttons so I don't have to face the courtiers. They make me uneasy, with their blank eyes and frosted smiles, their elegant coats and gowns, each one costing more money than most people would see in a year.

"Sometimes I feel like I have to skulk around," he says peevishly. "And yet I am the king." He grasps me around the waist and kisses me on the neck, his breath full of wine and longing.

"Now, Sire," says the little woman Mirepoix, speaking in her firm motherly voice, "you know you have her full blessing." How brave she must be to scold the king. I wonder if she would take me to see her rabbits? But that man said she is a great friend of the Marquise, so she would be no friend of mine.

"Now listen, hear this," says the king, not releasing his grip on me. "My little Morphise has taught me how to whistle, as a barber might. I shall give you a tune, and you must guess it." A frisson of distaste flutters through the room, then the courtiers all lean in with keen smiles plastered on their faces as the king starts the first few bars of "Awake, Sleeping Beauty."

☙

The moon is full and hangs above us like a giant silver coin, perfectly matching the grandeur of Versailles. We are up on the roofs, the hour of midnight long gone, out in the cold and shadowy realm of the night. Here there are terraces, and a small garden, and even a cage full of hens—large ruffled creatures that look very unlike the ones that scrabble around the streets.

"A present to the Marquise from Italy."

"Well, I'm sure they still taste good," I say in sympathy.

"And you see here the Maréchale de Mirepoix has taken quite a sizable space for her rabbits. Though I am not sure where the root of his feud lies, the Comte de Matignon is on a campaign to get them removed." The king sighs deeply; sometimes I think it must be very hard to be the king, with all the problems of the country on his shoulders.

I rub his arms and stare at the rabbits, their fur glowing white in the moonlight. They are enormous, unlike the skinny little hares at the market, two needed for just one pie.

"Only six last week yet today there must be more than ten. I'm not sure how that is possible, multiplying little creatures. Matignon will have more ammunition if they keep spreading like this."

"They love sex too much," I whisper in a low voice. "They love it as much as I do." My words are suddenly real, not a rote formula for arousal. Out here, in the darkness of the night, close to the stars? That is a fine idea and I feel something strange in me urging me closer to the king, almost as though I am *aroused*.

"Strong words, little one," says the king, laughing and pulling me closer. "You must not make me attempt anything indecent."

I suddenly think, Now is the time. Mother always says there

is always a proper time to reveal important news to a man and there could be no finer time than now, up here under the moonlight.

"King"—I kiss him slowly, then draw back, cup his face in my hands—"I am going to have your child."

Chapter Forty-Nine

I watch in satisfaction as Rose folds and packs my wardrobe into two trunks, the blue leather embossed with my name in gold curls, though I don't know if it says *Morphise* or *Marie Louise O'Murphy*. I have ten gowns now and some beautiful jewelry and numberless shoes. I gave one of my dresses to Rose, and one afternoon she went into the palace and watched the queen eating in public, with her daughters the princesses. She came back to the rue Saint-Louis and cried all afternoon, but when I tried to find out what was wrong, all she could say was that she never knew there was such wealth in this world.

We are going on a voyage! To the royal Château de Fontainebleau; the king has decided he cannot be without me for the month the Court will be there, and so I go, and Rose is to accompany me.

"You are my personal maid—a *lady*'s maid," I tell her, and we both giggle.

Catherine is frankly envious; she thinks herself above this house and of a higher class of people than I or the other little girls that sometimes come for a week or two, then disappear. She is always complaining to Madame Bertrand that she wants her own establishment.

"Don't get above yourself," slurs Madame Bertrand. "You're all just the same little whorelets."

The ride to Fontainebleau is long, almost a full day in a magnificent carriage pulled by four chestnut horses. The inside is lined with blue-and-silver tapestry work; like living inside a jewelry box. There is even a clock in the carriage, as well as plentiful pillows and a holder for glasses and wine.

Rose spends the entire journey with her face pressed against the window, exclaiming at all and everything she sees. It is her first time outside of the town of Versailles and she makes me feel very wise and sophisticated, for I have traveled from Rouen, a much longer journey, and have of course lived in Paris.

"Look at the stream—I think there are people in it!"

"But we have been traveling through this wood for an hour already—do you think it is the biggest forest in the world?"

"Oh, what is that?" she asks in alarm.

"That's a goat, I think."

"But it's got hair on its chin! . . . Look, Mo, a funeral." We pass a silent group of men in black and gray, carrying a rough wood coffin. We stare out at them and they stare grudgingly back.

"They probably think I am a real countess!"

"And I a real lady's maid!" says Rose in delight, touching her cheek.

The day turns to twilight as we near Fontainebleau. "I thought there would be more wolves," says Rose in disappointment. "Where are all the wolves?"

☙

Fontainebleau is not as magnificent as Versailles, of course, but it is still very beautiful. I have my own apartments and my first night I dine with the king and his friends, but then the Marquise de Pompadour arrives with the rest of the king's family.

I am allowed to walk in the gardens but in truth I prefer to be in the warmth of my little apartment, two beautiful rooms with heaven-high windows and expensive carpets, overlooking a large fishpond. How strange that I used to think the house on the rue Saint-Louis the height of luxury!

When I do walk out, in the company of Le Bel or another of the king's men, I meet some of the courtiers. Though they do not starve, their struggle for survival is clearly etched on their over-painted faces. They idle and loiter in the halls, as though outside public houses, and strut and whisper and aim to be seen. They greet me with false smiles and I can sense their distaste, floating down the corridors and out into the gardens:

"She doesn't look as grubby as I was expecting, but even a good scrubbing can't remove her gutter ways—I heard the king snapped his fingers yesterday."

"What is he going to do next, start licking his cutlery? Wearing trousers like a fieldhand?"

"I told you this was the beginning of the end. The Bible predicts it—servants dressing as masters."

"I think that was women dressing as men."

"Same difference, no? Equally unnatural?"

I prefer to stay in my rooms and play cards with Rose or sit by the window and watch the bustle in the courtyard below. Rose makes friends with the other servants and brings me all the news of the palace. Yesterday the queen—how I should like to see her!—made a pilgrimage to pray before a relic of Saint Severin and brought back a small piece of his tongue. Madame Adélaïde had a toothache that was relieved only when Dr. Quesnay, a great and powerful doctor, pulled her tooth out while a parrot distracted her.

Rose also tells me of the false rumors that drift around, about the house on the rue Saint-Louis:

"Whips and chains, my dear, and let me just say this: they are not for use on the servants."

"The Turkish ambassador advised on it, they say; they keep harems, you know, one hundred women tied up like cattle, ready to be milked at any time."

"Well, at least he is still the well-beloved somewhere."

I must receive many visitors but that trial is compensated for by the number of presents we collect: pots of jams and chocolate; fans, pearls and garters, and once even a stuffed duck, remarkably like a real one. Now the Duc d'Ayen bows to me, very respectfully, and says he has heard from a reliable source that my family is of Irish nobility. All profess their love for that distant isle and Rose tells me that the kitchens are inundated with requests for barley-cooked fish, black pudding, and heaps of potatoes made into little sham pigs; what they think of as Irish food has become fashionable.

"A relative of the Duke de Broglie, I'm sure," says Richelieu. "*Brog* is Gaelic for *shoe*," he explains, looking at me with the eyes of a lover, or a predator. I've met him several times since the king started showing me publicly, but he has never acknowledged our meeting at Boucher's studio. I wonder what the king would do if he knew.

ev)

Then one morning, she comes.

The Marquise enters my apartment without announcement and does not offer an introduction. She sits down without being asked and I take a seat before her. There is no mistaking who she is: she is very beautiful, and terribly, terribly elegant in a magnificent green gown adorned with strict rows of pink bows. She is not at all the old monster I was expecting, but one thing I know: she spent extra time on her toilette this morning. She wanted to look as perfect as she could for our meeting. For me.

I wish I had had my hair done, for it is still loose and in disarray. I may not get dressed until the evening. Sometimes the king comes in a hurry and has no time for difficult laces or stays, or petticoats that get in the way. He seems very busy these days. He is planning to ban the Parlement, he says, though the repercussions might be terrible, and it is all he can do to find five minutes for me. I'm not sure what a Parlement is. I asked the king, and he said that the Parlement was a group of scurrilous gentlemen, banded together to make his life miserable. I saw the topic irritated him, and talked of it no more.

"Well." The Marquise looks at me coolly, as if waiting for me to speak. All I can do is stare. I am reminded of the way a cat might look, before it pounces or purrs. Rose comes in and stops short.

"Oh, it's her!" she exclaims in fright.

The Marquise narrows her eyes. "I see you are still with us."

Her voice is soft and plush, not harsh as you might expect a fish-monger's daughter to be.

"Why, yes, Madame," says Rose in confusion, dropping an awkward curtsy.

"Bring us some coffee, then. Go to the east kitchens and tell them it's for me." Rose slips out and I touch my cheeks nervously and look around for something to defend myself with. The Marquise regards me as though she knows what is going through my mind.

Finally she speaks.

"How do you find your accommodations, child?"

"Very well, thank you. These rooms are beautiful."

"And the house on the rue Saint-Louis?"

"Very nice, thank you, Your Ladyship."

I want to burst out laughing. The only thing that would make this situation funnier would be if the king were here too. I duck my head and stifle a giggle.

"You've a charming way about you, don't you? Like a little kitten?" There is a tendril of something sour in her voice, float-ing under the softness. She pauses. "And tell me, how is the staff? Treating you well?"

"Yes, Madame."

"Though there is no need of explanation for my visit here, I would tell you I make it my business to know all of the king's friends; all, no matter of what sort they are. There are many in this world who wish him ill, and I must take care of him."

"I take care of him too," I retort. Suddenly I want to see her squirm and wince; underneath her elegant manners I know she is no friend of mine, and will never be. I know well the jealousy that often flows between women, and the consequences. "He says I am a comfort to him, as well as a great fuck."

She doesn't flinch and I am reminded of a graceful stone statue.

"Well," she says finally, after we have stared at each other awhile longer, "I suppose I have seen all I came to see."

"Do you want me to get undressed, Madame?" I say defiantly. "So you can finish your inspection?"

"Don't be insolent, child," she says mildly with a short laugh, as though pleased at my outburst. "And there is no need to undress; half of Paris has seen your naked form on their walls. Boucher's painting was a treat, and I believe my brother is interested in purchasing the original."

"You may know my backside, but you don't know my belly. It has a new shape now," I say, and here she does flinch, a sharp intake of breath, then she stills herself and looks down at her bejeweled hand. She twists a heavy red ring on one finger for three ticks of the clock, then looks me in the eye again. Her eyes are a beautiful gray, rimmed with the darkest blue; eyes to drown in, or swim to safety.

"No," she says quietly as she stands to leave. "I have seen all I need to. I have no doubt you are perfect, Mademoiselle. But please, never forget: you are with His Majesty, but only at my pleasure."

After she leaves I am still, then shiver, for I know I have made an enemy. But she is old and the king loves me, and here I am in these fine rooms. And I will have his child.

I do not need the Marquise's approval.

Rose sidles in, carrying a tray. "I lingered outside the door, I wouldn't serve *her* coffee. And I made sure they gave me only tepid water, what with the stories we hear!" She serves two cups but it's already cold, and we pour it out into a large vase of hydrangeas that sits on the mantel, laughing as I tell her what I said to the Pompadour.

∾

Not too soon we return to Versailles and the cozy house on the rue Saint-Louis. It is a relief to be here, away from the poisoned air and strange life of the Court. My popularity continues: the house is now crowded with people, every morning and every afternoon, though the visitors scatter like pollen in the wind when the king is announced.

It seems everyone—well almost—wants to be my friend, and when the king invites me again for a supper at Versailles, it is a larger group and the courtiers are more attentive and proclaim themselves more delighted to see me. Even the Maréchale de Mirepoix, a great friend of the Pompadour, strokes my cheek and tells me I am no longer a plaything, but a Little Queen, and then she lightly touches my stomach.

Richelieu is there, still looking at me with his penetrating eyes. Before we are seated he steers me into a corner and whispers, "I had no doubt, child, you would go far. Your face is beautiful, but your snatch is simply outstanding."

By now I am big with child. The king has promised he won't send me away when my time is come and a new nursemaid arrives just for the birth. She sizes me up, proclaims me the smallest birth she has ever attended, but vows there will be no problems. She flexes her hands and I shudder, for there is something dirty about her.

The king still visits the house on the rue Saint-Louis, to enjoy my face and my company, he says, before turning to Catherine or Brigitte or to a new girl named Marie. I wish Catherine would get pregnant and then I would press for her to be sent away, but she remains as flat as a flounder. I once searched her room to see if she had some secret or trick, but found nothing more than a box of curious round balls, made of white marble and linked by a delicate chain.

I feel the king is slipping away, just a touch, and though I can still be useful with my hands and my mouth, he rebuffs my attempts to join in with the other girls.

"It is Lent," he says rather stiffly. "You should not wish more sin upon me, dearest, than you have already. Besides, I enjoy your sister; ugliness reminds us all the more of beauty."

I smile and hang my head, but secretly I wish Brigitte would go, or get pregnant and be sent away. She told me the king said one night he loved her, though it was just before his joy, and men will say anything at that magical moment. I think she might have

done something despicably dirty with the king and now he prefers that, instead of that which is more natural between a man
and a woman.

"You should be careful of your sister," whispers Catherine, her
red hair hanging loose over her shoulders. In the past she would
have been burned as a witch; my mother always said that red was
the color of the Devil's pubic hair. "He used to love the Comtesse
de Vintimille passionately. She was the *sister* of the Comtesse de
Mailly, and the Vintimille was as ugly as sin, like your sister. I have
it on good authority; my cousin's uncle had a friend who worked
in her husband's household."

A Letter
From the Desk of the Duchesse de Pompadour
Château de Versailles
April 1, 1754

Dear Frannie,

How interesting the news of your voyage to Plombières-les-Bains was! It is wonderful that the princesses were acclaimed on their journey, for they get scarce attention here at Versailles. Do enjoy the spas—I am sure they will do wonders for your complexion.

But how I wish you were here, dear heart! I need your soothing presence. It's awful, they are calling her the Little Queen, and to show their allegiance her supporters sport all that is small, while my friends wear larger sizes. Is it through vanity or allegiance that the Marquis de Gontaut totters around in tiny heels? Is the miniature fan, no more than a hand span across, really her daughter's, as the Comtesse de Gramont claimed last night at cards?

Rumors are more dangerous than rabid dogs and the whole of it makes my head hurt. She's a child, and a prostitute; Louis cannot be serious. I remember you once observed his hobby was to be impenetrable, and as he ages he becomes even more so. I know he still loves me, or is it more dependence than love? Regardless, the intriguers see in that pregnant child a new masthead and I shan't be surprised if they make a move soon. I don't know who will be behind it, for anyone could be.

I must sign off as I have another six letters to write and four more to dictate. There is much to occupy: Machault is taking over as minister of the navy; Argenson continues as intractable as ever; the repairs to the aqueducts are causing my brother Abel no end of problems.

Safe journey back, dear friend.

J

Chapter Fifty

The pain was extreme, but in the end it all meant nothing. The baby died. A girl, they tell me, and I cry for her death and the bleakness in my heart.

I would have been a mother to the king's child.

My own mother comes to visit and shakes her head at my tears. She prepares me a tea of tart leaves, bitter and laced with ginger. She sits by me on the bed, watching with eager eyes.

"I lost four," she says briskly. "It's just the way it is. No, this is more a pity, mine were just nameless brats with no time to baptize, but yours would have been the daughter of a king. Not a son, but still—a great honor that would have secured you—us—for life. But no matter: there will be others. Remember not to show your sadness when you greet him, for tears make a man limper than a leaf."

I stare at her, wounded in my grief. The room is stuffed with roses sent from the palace, their scent overwhelming. I start crying again, for all that could have been, for all that should have been.

My mother tuts and smooths the hair from my face and picks at a pimple on my chin. "I'll leave you with this vinegar and clay mixture. Start next week and do a daily bath, down there, and it will dry you out and keep you nice and tight; you must do as I say, for no one wants a loose woman, now, do they?"

"Of course, Mama," I say dully, the tea making me nauseous, the smell of ginger mixing to ill effect with the heavy scent of the roses in the small, hot room. I wish she would go and leave me alone with my thoughts and my sorrow; I want to think about my little baby and imagine her life in Heaven.

Instead, Mother settles in and regales me with news of Paris and my sisters: the recent death of the Chevalier de Longes, another friend of Marguerite's (sometimes I think that girl is cursed, she says, her admirers dying like flies in winter); Madeleine's recent triumph with the director of the Comédie Française; the new chief of police in their neighborhood, not nearly as agreeable as the one before. She asks to see my jewels and my gowns and peruses them greedily. She pockets a ruby-studded hair comb, saying there will be more where that came from, and that the money is needed at home.

"And mind you ask for the title to that house on the rue Sainte-Appolline," she says, and plants a kiss on my head before leaving. "Such a trifle; surely it can be arranged?"

The king visits and kisses me and is all that is tender. I cry because I missed him, and because the baby died, but he doesn't seem to mind. He promises another comb to replace the one my mother took, and says that all I ask for my family will be done. He does not seem sad about the death of the baby; I suppose he already has so many daughters.

A few weeks later I am summoned to Versailles, where we sup together, alone. We make love and he declares himself as satisfied with me as ever, still as in love as ever, and tells me he missed me more than he thought possible. I feel bathed in love and all the worries and sadness of the past months disappear beneath his touch. I missed him too, I realize, really missed him.

Despite his kind words, he is in a sad mood. He says he does not want to talk, but when a man says that he often means the opposite. I coax him out of his reticence.

"It is the Marquise, the Marquise de Pompadour," he says with a sigh. "A good friend of mine."

"I know who she is," I say quietly. The whole of France knows who she is; the whole world even. I have not told the king of her visit at Fontainebleau.

"Yes, yes, of course you do, fine woman that she is. The poor woman—her little daughter is dead, died in Paris. She is, as you can imagine, devastated." The king's face is murky and gray with grief. "The poor woman," he says again. "And the child was delightful—not a beauty like her mother, but fair enough. Fanfan, she is—was—called."

Well, we have that in common, I think, but I know it is not the same. As my mother said, babies are made for fleeting times on this earth but the Marquise's little girl was almost ten years old. Not much younger than me.

I stroke the king's hair and he murmurs that I am his only comfort in this dreadful, sad world. His words wrap around me like a warm velvet cloak that will never leave me cold. He falls asleep in my arms and when he snores I ease myself out to go and sit by the window.

I look out at the darkness below and think that somewhere under this same palace roof, the Marquise is there too, roiled by grief, and then I think what the king said—that he loves me, that he missed me—and what a fantastical thing it is that I am here beside him.

I hope I am not falling in love. I might be, but my sister Marguerite says falling in love is a tragedy of the worst sort. In love you risk giving all for nothing in return; love can't be bitten like a coin or polished like a diamond.

Chapter Fifty-One

"Is this all she could do for you? Really?" sniffs my snooty visitor by way of introduction when I enter the parlor. She does not rise in greeting, so I curtsy and seat myself in front of her. She is an older woman with a gray complexion and cheeks as pendulous as breasts.

"I am"—my visitor pauses, and looks around the room in distaste—"Elisabeth, the Comtesse d'Estrades." She is wearing a striped lilac dress that doesn't fit her well and under her petticoat I spy large black boots.

"Then it is nice to meet you, Comtesse," I say, and I see she is irritated that her name did not cause more awe.

"Well, then. I shall get straight to the point, and keep this visit as short as possible."

"Would you like some tea?" I ask, remembering to be polite. "We have some lemon-flavored, a gift from the Duc d'Ayen."

"Indeed? Old Ayen? Interesting." I order some from the kitchen and when I return the woman continues talking as though I never left.

"It is no secret the king adores you."

"As I adore him," I say, and though I say it by rote it is true: never has there been such a kind gentleman. But in truth, I have seen little of him since the birth and death of my daughter; he was often away this summer and though I angled to accompany him to Fontainebleau again, and even permitted him a certain liberty he had long been hinting at, no invitation was forthcoming.

"Isn't there a servant to blow and cool this?" says the countess in irritation, gesturing to her cup.

"I could call Rose," I say doubtfully. The woman shakes her head in annoyance and violently swirls the tea in her cup. "I shall continue. Only one thing stands between you and your complete happiness."

"But I am happy here," I say. Soon it will be almost two years since I came to this house and I love this life, the luxury and the indolence and only the attentions of the king, a wonderful man, to worry about.

"Here? Don't be ridiculous, child. This—hovel. Your rightful place is at Versailles, by the king's side and—"

"But I am at his side. I was at supper there just last month!" And you weren't, I want to add, but don't.

"Don't display your gutter manners, child, by interrupting me. No, I do not mean *physically* seated beside him, though I did hear he kept you at his left all night. I refer to all this sneaking around, midnight visits to this embarrassing little house. You belong at Versailles."

I remember the courtiers at Fontainebleau, the sneers and the snide comments, the nervousness I feel when I am to dine with the king's friends. The way that Richelieu looks at me; the coded language I don't understand, the nastiness pulsing beneath the surface like an abscess about to leak over.

"Oh, I don't think . . . I don't think I should like that."

The countess tuts and takes a sip of tea, then winces as though she had just sucked on a raw lemon. I don't like it either.

"Think of all that you would have if you were publicly declared mistress. Your own house, for one. The Marquise has five houses, you know."

Oh. I didn't know that. A house of my own would certainly be nice, without Madame Bertrand or any of the other girls. I would bring Rose, and she could be my lady's maid and my housekeeper.

"You would like that," says the countess, taking another disdainful little sip. "This tastes like vinegar. Not to my liking at all."

I nod, not sure what she wants me to say, or do.

"There is only one thing that is standing between you and your future happiness. The Marquise de Pompadour."

"But couldn't the king just give me a house, my own house, now?" I think of Catherine's entreaties to Le Bel—I should just ask the king directly. "What does this have to do with the Marquise?"

The countess tuts in impatience. "He will never grant you your own home while the Marquise reigns. She would never allow it. You must," she continues, looking at me with her small raisin-black eyes, "demand the dismissal of the Marquise."

"Of the Marquise de Pompadour?" I say in astonishment. "Oh no, I could not, he loves her too much. And why would I want her gone?"

"Really, this little kitten act is charming and probably works wonders on the men, but it does nothing for me. You must stop acting so innocent."

"But . . . I could never dismiss her. She is far too powerful." I think of our meeting at Fontainebleau, of her soft words, of the smooth way she looked at me and appraised me, then rubbed me down and ate me for dinner.

"You may think she is powerful, but I know better. I am the Marquise's closest friend and confidante."

"I thought that was the Maréchale de Mirepoix."

The countess frowns and dismisses the idea with a wave of her hand. "Nonsense. And my *special* friend—I am sure you of all people will know the meaning of that—is the Comte d'Argenson, the minister of war."

"Indeed," I say, as I have often heard the king and others say when they have no interest, but are pressed upon to be polite.

"The Marquise's position is weaker than ever. Bowed with grief over her lost child, and almost without important friends. Now is the time to demand her dismissal. And mind, once you are installed, remember who helped get you there."

I look down at my hands. From her tone it is clear she thinks of me as a serving girl to do her bidding.

"Surely you do not want to stay here forever? Playing second fiddle to that wondrous child Marie?"

I stiffen. "He still visits me as often as he visits her."

"Mmmm," says the countess doubtfully.

"Well, what about Rose?" I ask.

"What rose?"

"The kitchen girl. She came with me to Fontainebleau. Could she come with me to Versailles? She has a scar on her face and is not nice to look at, but I do love her so."

A look of intense irritation passes over the countess's face. "Child, I do not think you understand the magnitude of what I am proposing to you." She leans closer, a snake to the mouse. I blink and wish I could retreat but the chair pins me down. She gazes at me hungrily.

"What is it you would have me do, Madame?" I ask politely, for I can see she will not leave until she has accomplished what she came for. Or at least until she thinks she has.

"Finally. Now, here is the plan."

⚶

That night I lie awake and think of our conversation. She is intriguing, I know it, plotting in the way of Versailles.

I think about living at Versailles, having my own apartment there, like the lovely rooms at Fontainebleau. Or perhaps I would move into the Marquise's apartments, said to be the most magnificent in the palace—Catherine was once invited in, when she was preparing to dance in the ballet, and said the decorations of the rooms were coordinated to the seasons outside.

I could move into her rooms and then I would always be at the side of the king. No menace of the Marquise, lurking in the halls, waiting to ambush me with hot coffee. And no rivalry from other girls. Catherine would be banished, I think with satisfaction, for if I succeed in displacing the Marquise, then getting rid of Catherine—and Marie—would be as easy as flicking a dead fly off a windowsill.

Perhaps . . . Sleep overcomes me, and I dream the king is in my bed. I am shivering and when he asks me why I tremble, I say that the world is cold without him holding me, and he laughs in delight and hugs me close.

Versailles . . .

Chapter Fifty-Two

"Colder than a dead fish," says the king, bursting in through the kitchen door.

"Oh, Sire, we were not expecting you!" I exclaim, secretly smiling inside for I know Catherine is indisposed this week, and Marie has a cough that won't go away, no matter how much castor oil she takes. But it seems the king came only to see me.

"Perfect timing as always, my love." We go up to my room and he leans down to kiss me, bringing all the cold of the outside world into my cozy bedroom.

"Be a good girl and take off my cloak." He sits down and rubs his hands at the fire. I kneel in front of him and massage them and cover his fingers with hot kisses.

"Let me get you some wine."

"No, I took the precaution of bringing my own." He pulls a bottle from the cloak and sets it on the table. "Richelieu swears this is the finest from Conti's own. But bring a cake or such. Something sweet!"

I run down to the kitchen, suddenly breathless—this is the day. "How is it he comes like this, unannounced?" I scowl at Cook and Rose. "Without even a word of warning."

"Madame Bertrand," indicates Cook, swirling her finger around her head. She prepares a kettle over the stove. "He'll want coffee, as well as wine?"

"Well, it is most inconvenient," I say in irritation, for I wanted to plan this better. I decided to follow the countess's advice and had been awake all day planning. "He wants something sweet. If Madame Bertrand had let us know, we could have prepared."

My eye is caught by a cloth on the table. "What's under that?"

"A cherry pie, made from dried ones, but you'd never guess it, soaked in sugar water first, to make them plump," says Cook smugly.

"It's Catherine's birthday tomorrow, and she requested it special," adds Rose.

"Good! That is just the thing. Bring it quickly, mind."

"Parlement is a beast that never dies," says the king as we sit by the fire. "They are as impossible to please as a frigid whore."

"Oh, my dearest, what troubles you have," I murmur softly, and lean over to caress his cheek.

"Yes, indeed, all this discontent and those men making outrageous demands. A voice in all affairs! The power to disapprove appointments made even by myself! This is not England, I said, and I will say it again. Argenson took more of their demands this morning."

"It sounds terrible," I murmur in sympathy. When would be a good time to set the wheels in motion? Before, between, after? I am suddenly terribly, terribly excited. I decide to wait until after—between—when the mood of a man is soft wax in a woman's hands.

"And then Argenson, he brought in the papers and I gave them to the Marquise to read, and then she told him . . ." I listen to the king drone on while I imagine entering Versailles, not in a curtained sedan chair but in a glorious carriage like the one we rode in to Fontainebleau, pulled by four horses. No—six horses. Is that even possible? I would only need four, I decide, as I am a little afraid of horses.

The coffee comes and the king is delighted with the warm pie—cherry in November! "A fine thing—nothing finer," he exclaims, and digs in while I sip my drink and watch him.

"And then Argenson refused to read Machault's brief, and while Rouillé can be a pedant, his experience in the navy . . ." but he is still talking, and suddenly I am impatient.

"Oh la la!" I say, jumping up and settling myself on his lap, taking his spoon and licking the sticky cherry off it. "All this talk of briefs is making me aroused." I lean in to kiss him and taste cherry and sugar and soon the telltale hardness shows me the time is right.

After, as we lie under the thick fur blankets, he continues to moan on about his problems. I stroke his hair until he stops, his complaining done and over. He snuffles and sighs in contentment.

"My love," he says. "These hours and nights with you—such a balm for me." I grin in delight.

Now!

"So," I say, sitting up and smiling down at him. Though the windows rattle and howl with the chill November wind, the small room is toasty and the fire warms the remains of the pie, sending the aroma of sweet cherries wafting through the air. "So, tell me, King, how is the old flirt doing? Is she still around?"

The king opens his eyes to look at me. I smile and play with my hair, as I know he likes: he once said it reminded him of a kitten playing with ribbons.

"I do not understand. Who is 'the old flirt'?" There is a hard tone to his voice but in my excitement I miss it. I see it plainly enough after, when all is done and over.

"You know who I mean, King. The old flirt, that old Pompadour. Is she still hanging around?"

There is silence and I refuse to see the darkness, coming swiftly closer.

"I would be so much happier . . ." And here I swallow in sudden nervousness, for when I imagined this scene, a hundred times, my words were smooth and seductive. Now they are awkward and wrong but I cannot stop, for I must finish what I have begun: "I would be so much happier without that old lady at Versailles, and then you and I could be together, always. You should just send her away."

The king is looking at me in shock, as though I have just committed the most heinous of crimes. And suddenly I realize I have.

Oh.

He pulls back the covers and turns away while he dresses himself awkwardly. I should help, but I am frozen in sudden fear.

"In jest," I say in a small voice as he fumbles to button his coat, panic rising in me. I try to keep my voice light. "Just a joke, King, you know I care not about the Marquise, I only care about you, and I know she is your friend . . ."

I trail off as the king stands up and turns to me.

"I will continue in my belief, Mademoiselle, that those words were not your own, but were placed in your mouth by the enemies of my dear friend. I will persist in that belief, in order to keep the sweetness of our memories alive. You have greatly displeased me."

He bows with awful finality, a formal bow that shuts all the doors and takes away all the keys. And throws those keys down a deep, deep well.

Then he is gone. I hear his footsteps on the stairs and wonder if I should run after him, but I know . . . I have done wrong. The time for forgiveness is not in the first moments, but only after when the anger has spread out and thinned away; that is the time to lick away sins and seek forgiveness. But what if I never see him again?

I sit in silence and then get up to the finish the pie; Catherine shall have no pleasure from this. But I have made a mistake. He might forgive me, eventually, but would the Marquise? I stare uneasily into the fire—will I be sent to the madhouse? Is Claire still there, and who would know where I went? I shiver and scrape the plate and suddenly I am crying, in fright and regret.

They come later that night, Le Bel and two men I don't know, burst into my room and rouse me from the bed. I can hear Rose crying on the stairs and Madame Bertrand hiccuping through a sad song. I am in my chemise and Le Bel offers me a great cloak, not mine, and they bundle me out of the house as though I were a bunch of rags, into the freezing night and the waiting carriage. We speed away and through my tears I hear

Le Bel tell me I'll get my clothes and fripperies later, but I don't know if that will be.

I am deposited at my mother's house on the rue Sainte-Appolline, where my sobs double. Oh! How I wish I could take back what I just did. If God would grant me time to do it over, then how different it would all be. My parents and Brigitte are at home and the house is dirty and mean, the bed I must share with Brigitte only a coarse mattress stuffed with old rags. I was once in the halls of Versailles and Fontainebleau, and now I lie on this horrible bed, crying in the arms of my sister, no fire to warm the room or the chill of my soul.

"But what about the rubies?" I demand in the morning, looking around the small, miserable house. "And the ten thousand *écus* Le Bel assured me the king had sent your way?"

"Ah, worries and such," says my mother, suddenly looking very old. "Madeleine's cough so bad she missed the entire season, and with the sudden death of the Comte de Leury—how could a surgeon forget a scalpel *inside* the leg, I ask you?—things have not been good for Marguerite."

I spend my hours wishing for a potion to turn back time and reverse what I did. My mother tells me I am a stupid little flea, but not to worry—once my tears are dried there will be other men and other wonderful lives waiting, and that I am still so young. The king's touch is not like the touch of other men; it enhances value rather than detracts.

"Why, Rohan has already been in touch . . . and the Duc d'Ayen has not ceased to express his interest. He even took up with Madeleine again, in a partial way, but has assured me his primary care was you."

Her words chill me and leave me sadder than before. I want to go back to the warm house on the rue Saint-Louis. I want to laze all day on my lovely bed and gossip with Rose and eat Cook's wonderful pies. Most of all I want the king's eyes on me, approving, slack, desirous. I burn when I think of Catherine's triumph and Marie's beauty, or perhaps another has already been found to fill my bed?

My belongings arrive from Versailles, and it is as Le Bel said: all of them are safely delivered. All my gowns and shoes and jewels, everything down to the small packet of red glass buttons I kept in the bottom of my trunk.

A few days later, Chief of Police Berryer visits; I remember him from when I worked in Paris. I feel small and sad. They think I am stupid but I am intelligent enough to know the finality of what happened.

"All we need from you, Mademoiselle, is the name of the person who prompted your fateful words."

I stare at him and think of Elisabeth, the Comtesse d'Estrades, with her small eyes and puffy cheeks, the moist disdain on her lips.

"The Marq—the king is prepared to be generous. A husband, Mademoiselle, with a title, and not a trumped-up one either. You will be a countess; now, how does that appeal?"

I drop my head but Berryer is quick to see the delight in my eyes. So, the ending is happy after all. I will be a countess, a real one, and married, something all my sisters aspire to but have not yet achieved. This is real, I think, and suddenly Versailles seems far away, nothing but a palace in a fairy tale. I will miss the king, of course, and I know I will cry for many more a day, but right now there is another future in front of me. A husband, a house of my own, a return to the soft and happy life. No more intrigues and plots. Me, a countess!

"Who?" I demand. They must strongly desire the information I have, to be so generous in their offer.

"The negotiations are still in progress; you can appreciate, Mademoiselle, it is but three days since your disgrace. However, I have it on good authority that the groom is a certain Comte de Beaufranchet de Something Something, a poor but noble army officer of the Auvergne, unfortunate that, but I am sure he keeps a house in Paris or Versailles. A fine lineage, dating back to the fifteenth century at least, I believe. Not the wealthiest of men, but I have no doubt he will be enchanted by you."

There is silence and I curl my toes in delight and shiver inside my robe.

"If you tell us, there will be a handsome dowry and a promotion for your husband. Despite all that has happened, the king is willing to be generous, for you and for your child."

"What child?" I ask in confusion. "My child died at birth."

"Ah, of course he did, of course he did."

"He? They told me it was a girl."

Berryer stares at me a fraction too long, then blinks. "I apologize, Mademoiselle, that I am not current on all the details of your liaison. You must appreciate that there are many important affairs I must attend to."

He's blustering, I think, as men often do when they are caught in the wrong. How strange. But the thought passes quickly, and I turn to concentrate on the future that he offers, dazzling bright before me like a ruby-red button glinting on a soft gray coat.

"Now, the details of this plot in which you were so unwilling a member, poor child," Berryer repeats. His eyes are keen, the net closing in; he can see his offer is one I want.

I think of those pendulous cheeks, the disdain and the lies. And I to be married, and a countess: a fairy tale is coming true. Perhaps Rose will come with me and her fairy tale will come true too.

Goodbye, Countess.

Entr'Acte

The Duchesse de Pompadour

1755

It is raining as I sit and write and think. The whole world rains now, at least for me; everything is ugly and gray. All my hopes and dreams died with my little girl's death. I keep my emotions hidden, as always, but inside I am as frozen and sad as ice and snow. My second great sorrow in life. A burst appendix, not even enough time for me to get there and hold her one last time. I seek what solace I can in the chapel, and though I turn to God with more fervor than I have in the past, a little voice that can't be quelled says: *Too little, too late.*

In the wake of my daughter's death I thought briefly of retiring to a convent. Weak dreams, really, for I could never be happy there, away from Louis, away from my life at Versailles. Ambition is the greatest torment, and I know it is not only my love for Louis that keeps me here.

And so I stay, and sometimes it feels as though I am besieged from all sides. Those uneducated girls were to be my salvation and my safety, but I misunderstood the power of a young girl over an aging man. After that little prostitute was banished, I wanted him to promise me that in the future they would stay in town and never again breach the walls of the palace, either in body or spirit. He evaded my subtle entreaties and I know I want something he can't or won't give. As he ages he becomes more closed off, retreating behind a mask of guilt as he seeks out diversions that are ever more unacceptable.

This time, at least, there was a satisfactory ending. It also revealed to me what I had long suspected: that even those closest to me are not to be trusted. Perhaps no one is a friend; perhaps no one ever was. Two pieces of coralline, one engraved with an *O'M,* the other with an *E*—Elisabeth received her *lettre de cachet*—nestle at the bottom of the fishbowl.

Friends into enemies, and enemies into friends. Everywhere. We are working on a new alliance with Austria, long France's staunchest foe. Together, we will stand against Prussia and its growing friendship with England. This new alliance will serve us well: British aggression against our colonies in North America and Africa is increasing, and the Prussians continue to wave their sabers around northern Europe. I fear we are heading for another war.

The negotiations are top secret and only Louis and I, Bernis in Venice, and Stainville in Rome are involved. It is a thrill to keep even the most powerful of ministers, including Argenson, in the dark and insignificant. We work directly with the Empress Maria Theresa in Vienna; she writes me letters and calls me her cousin.

Sometimes I think back to the time, so many years ago, when I made my first political request, to get rid of Orry. Now I seek to remake the boundaries of Europe, if not the world.

If only the silly girls would leave me in peace.

Act V

❧

Marie-Anne

Chapter Fifty-Three

"Oh, I am bored! So bored, bored, bored!" I fling myself onto the sofa, my arms outstretched in supplication, the soft padding breaking my fall.

"Marie-Anne de Mailly!" says my mother in a sharper voice than usual. "Get your feet off the sofa."

I partially roll over. "But I'm bored," I whine again. "What would you have me do?"

"You may be bored, but you may not stop being a lady," says my mother firmly.

I slither down the sofa until my head is almost touching the floor.

"Get your feet down, I can see the soles of your slippers and they are *filthy*."

"Only because I have but two pair," I mutter, sitting up and putting my head back. I contemplate the ceiling above; even the angels look bored. "I shall die, simply die, of boredom."

My sister, Thaïs, tells me to stop being dramatic, then resumes her intent stitching. Mother is the most placid and refined of women; sometimes she says it is hard to believe I am her daughter, and that one convent produced two such vastly different sisters.

"Why don't you help Thaïs and me with these prayer cushions?" says my mother, though she knows I hate sewing. "I promised the dauphine we would have at least two ready for the chapel on Saint Irenaeus Day."

"Noooooo," I wail. "You know I hate sewing. But, oh! How I wish I were a lady to the dauphine, or even to Mesdames. At least then I wouldn't be bored. As it is, I am nothing—nothing!"

Thaïs snorts. "I can assure you, dear sister, that being a lady to accompany Madame Adélaïde is the very definition of boredom. Even Mother has been known to complain about her service with the dauphine."

"But at least you have something to *do*. You may become friends with the other ladies, and live close with the royal family, and walk first and sit first and have an apartment at Versailles, and oh! But life is unfair!" I pick up a book on the side table, then throw it down with a shudder: *Treatise on the Treatment of Parliamentary Treaties*.

"Oh, shut up, Marie-Anne. You do talk nonsense sometimes. Mother, what do you think, the dark blue or the light blue here, on this border?"

I roll off the sofa and wander over to Thaïs. "You didn't ask my help. And why are the acanthus leaves blue? Everyone knows they are green. Sometimes brown."

Thaïs ignores me and repeats her request to our mother.

"Use the darker blue," says Mother calmly. "That is how I have done mine." She turns to me. "Darling, you would absolutely hate royal service. And you talk too much; those in service must be discreet and calm. But I promise, as I have in the past, that I will use my influence to secure you a post, once I have the slightest hope you will be a credit to our family."

"But I am discreet!" I wail. "I keep secrets; you shall *never* know what Polignac told me about his sister. And besides, Aunt Diane is the dauphine's *dame d'atour,* and she talks more than I do. You once even called her a drunk magpie because she chattered so much."

"Yes, the poor dauphine, she enjoys Christian suffering almost as much as the queen," says my mother cryptically.

"And," adds Thaïs, "it's so menial, you can't imagine. Madame Victoire never closes her mouth when she eats, she positively chomps her food like a . . . like a . . . well, like some sort of animal, I should imagine, though I do not think I have ever watched an animal eat."

"My dear wife, you must not speak so of the king's daughter," says Thaïs' husband, Montbarrey, from a window in the corner of the room, where he has been in deep contemplation of the courtyard below. "It is exactly such talk that will hinder our advancement in life. To serve the royal family is to serve our nation. We have had many talks about this, yet still you persist with this intractable attitude."

Thaïs gives her husband the briefest of glances, then returns to her sewing. "I do think the light blue here would be better, but I will follow you, Mother." Thaïs never says she regrets her marriage, but she did once call her husband a squirrel, because he climbs everything in sight, including society. Though Thaïs is the Comtesse de Montbarrey now, she never lets anyone forget she is a de Mailly.

"Have a nut," I say to Montbarrey, then start giggling at my wit.

"There are no nuts in this room, Madame," he replies with a stiff bow. "Perhaps you intended the plums?"

"Well, I think service sounds rather fun," I say, turning my attention away from Montbarrey and rolling back onto the sofa. "Better than boring old Paris, or hanging around at Court with no money for playing games or giving dinners."

"I do believe, dearest Marie-Anne," says Mother calmly, opening her sewing box, unspooling a new thread, and squinting at her needle, "that you are the type of person who is rarely satisfied where they are; you have a tendency to think the cake on the other plate is more tasty than your own. If you were in royal service, I am sure we would hear no end of complaints."

"It's not true! I like all kinds of cake! And I should be most happy if I were in royal service. But I am not and I shall just die—die, I say!—of boredom."

"No one dies of boredom," says Mother mildly. "And once again: sit up straight and straighten your cap; your hair is becoming unpinned."

"But they *do* die of boredom!"

"Who has died?"

"Well, I am sure someone has," I say uncertainly, then I am distracted by a loud smack on the window.

"A pigeon, dear Madame," says Thaïs' insufferable husband. "Now splayed on the cobbles below, being approached from one corner by a cat, from the other by a kitchen girl. Who will win, I ask you? Doubtless we will see it in some form on our table tonight."

The endless afternoon weaves on.

"I am bored, bored, bored," I say again, to no one in particular. "Only Polignac came to see me yesterday. He told me his sister was caught kissing their cook!"

"Don't spread gossip, dear."

I sigh. "Perhaps I will go back with you and Thaïs to Versailles on Sunday, but what I will do there I have *no idea*. I wonder if Milord Melfort will be there?" Melfort is another one of my admirers; English, but he hardly smells at all.

"Yes, dear," says my mother. "That reminds me, the Prince de Conti is giving a grand dinner on Wednesday, to celebrate the victory and return of the Duc de Richelieu. I was told to invite you."

"Mother! How could you forget to tell me such a thing? And something so important! And Wednesday!" A horrible thought strikes. "Mother, I have nothing to wear! Nothing! Thaïs . . . ?"

"No more loans, not after that incident with the egg sauce," Thaïs says primly. Even though I am far prettier than Thaïs—she has a rather unfortunate chin and her eyes are too close together—I sometimes envy her. Her husband is a boring midget but still, he has buckets of money and she never has to worry about what to wear. Sometimes, it is as if the world were against me.

"Unfair, unfair, unfair," I wail.

"Why is Conti inviting *Marie-Anne*?" asks Montbarrey sharply. I stop wailing to wonder the same. The Prince de Conti is the king's relative, and Richelieu is one of the grandest men at Court and is now the hero of France for having won some island or other.

"Our dearest Marie-Anne is a charming lady, a compliment to any table," says my mother, making it sound more like a warning than a compliment. She ties off her thread in satisfaction and smooths her tapestry with an elegant, bejeweled hand. "We need no more reason than that."

"I must insist, Madame," says Montbarrey, leaving his window perch to bow in front of my mother, "that you use the powers associated with your name and position to secure me an invite as well. Why, the Duc de Richelieu is one of my keenest admirers! He—"

"Don't you mean to say that *you* are one of the keenest admirers of the duke, and not the other way around?" interrupts Thaïs.

"Well, certainly, but he is also an admirer of mine. Once, last year, he—"

"Mother, I have nothing to wear!" I insist again.

"Of course you do. Your yellow silk. I'll see what I can do," says my mother to Montbarrey, not looking up from her needlework.

Another terrible thought strikes: "Mother! But I don't have any Court-wide hoops! Thaïs . . . ?"

"No."

"Thaïs, lend your sister the hoops as she wants," says my mother calmly. "At least she won't be able to spill anything on them."

"She'll find a way," mutters Thaïs darkly.

"But I wore my yellow last time I was at Versailles!" I protest.

"If, instead of complaining and slithering around on the furniture, my dearest, you chose to occupy your time in productive pursuits, you might have stitched an entire garden of flowers on your skirt, or decorated an entire bodice by this time."

"But I—"

"The yellow," says my mother firmly, raising her hand for silence. "Really, the peace of these weeks in Paris, when Thaïs and I rest from our duties at Court, must not be marred by your incessant whining and chatter. You're almost twenty-four, but you behave like a girl half your age. Now, go and find Marie, and ask her to bring more of the dark blue thread."

I trudge down the stairs to the kitchens but discover Mother has already sent Marie out to the market. I don't return to the salon but instead go upstairs to my room to contemplate the boredom of my life. The bed is too high for a satisfactory fling, so I climb on it in dejection. This summer it seems all the men of Paris are off fighting the British overseas, or getting ready to fight the British at home, or occupied at Court with thoughts of war, and the Opéra insists on showing only Italian fare, which I find dreadfully confusing.

I brighten at the thought of the dinner next week. Going to Versailles shall be fun, though I must share a bed with my sister. Thaïs likes to eat cake before sleeping and leaves the whole bed crumbed and itchy, and it feels as though we are sleeping with fleas.

The Prince de Conti's dinner will be frightfully grand. And to have invited me and not Thaïs nor my bore of a brother-in-law! And I'll see my father, and Aunt Diane and Aunt Hortense, and perhaps my husband; he wrote to say when he was coming back but I can't remember the date he indicated. I might also see the Prince de Varenne and resume our little friendship, and Polignac will certainly be there, and the Chevalier de Bissy, who was very attentive when I met him last March at the Duchesse d'Orléans' games party.

I would never be unfaithful to my husband (my mother is very insistent on this), but I like flirting and hearing sweet words whispered in my ear, and the look in men's eyes, like adorable puppies, when I smile at them. And the presents, of course, though I think I have enough ribbons and handkerchiefs, and little bottles of scent, to last me a lifetime.

I once let Polignac kiss me on the cheek, and for that I received a winter muff of raven sable—I wonder what he might gift me if I let him kiss me on the mouth, or permitted him a bodice fumble? Unfortunately, there is a line that must be crossed if one wants more gifts, and my mother is adamant that I not cross it. She threatens that if she hears even a whiff of indiscretion, I shall be banished to the country so fast the carriage will overturn.

Mother often says that a broken egg can never be made whole again. Though why one would want to put a cooked egg back in its shell, I really don't know—scrambled is certainly the best way to eat them.

Chapter Fifty-Four

"Sitting, sitting, endless sitting, I shall put up my feet, you don't mind, dear?" Aunt Diane sits on one chair and puts her feet on another, slipping off her little high-heeled shoes and wiggling her toes in relief. A dim smell of soft cheese rises up and one of her women dutifully waves a large perfumed handkerchief over them. I giggle, imagining my mother were she to see the scene.

My aunt Diane's father was a cousin of my father, the Comte de Mailly-Rubempré, but I call her Aunt. I am relieved her sister Hortense, the Marquise de Flavacourt, does not join us; Hortense adores Thaïs but never hides her disapproval of my manners. They say Hortense was a great beauty when she was younger, as was their sister Marie-Anne, my namesake, whom everyone says I look exactly like! Poor Aunt Diane was never pretty but I love her best of all—she is the only one who never complains that I talk too much.

We are in Diane's apartment at Versailles and her woman serves us a cozy supper of round noodles in beef sauce. With Aunt Diane, one never feels the need to be on guard; she is famed as a simpleton, but I think her pleasantly intelligent.

"So very exciting we shall both be attending Conti's dinner tomorrow," she says, tucking into the pasta. It's rather difficult to eat, the noodles like miniature white maggots slipping off my fork; I am glad there are no gentlemen present when I spill some down the front of my dress. At least the jacket is brown, I think as I dab at it with my linen. "At Richelieu's behest, you know; he said he wanted to meet this young lady who is the very image of Marie-Anne, and just as beautiful."

"But I've met him before, I'm sure I was presented to him, back when I married Henri."

"He's a great man, you know, they can't always remember everyone they meet and your marriage was six years ago. Why, I am sure he doesn't even remember everyone he has *slept* with," Aunt Diane giggles, and tells me a story about a dinner party the duke gave where he invited twenty-nine women, all lovers of his, and seated them all at an enormous round table. "And of course I wasn't among them, no, not at all, I mean this was in Toulouse, but if it had been here at Versailles . . ."

I giggle.

"Do you think I look like your sister Marie-Anne?" I ask. There are things in life that one can never get enough of, like kittens and candied fruit, and of course being told one is beautiful.

"You remind me of her so, though you are far sweeter and laugh more easily, both traits which only serve to increase your beauty, in my humble opinion. Ah, but she was so beautiful, just like you, my dear, and no time more so than the summer of '42 when the king fell in love with her." Aunt Diane's voice takes on a wistful tone and she sips her wine thoughtfully. "I remember it was '42 because that was the year the giant oak—from Charlemagne's time, they said!—fell down in the park."

"How romantic that sounds! The summer of '42!" I sigh.

Diane shakes her head and piles a wobble of noodles precariously on her fork, stewarding it to her mouth with a determined hand. "We were so young then, all of us, the king, Marie-Anne, everyone. Fourteen years! How the time flies."

"Aunt Diane, do you think naming someone the same makes them look alike?"

"I don't think so," says Diane with a puzzled frown. "That really wouldn't make sense, would it? Think of all the men named Louis we know! But then again, you *are* the very likeness."

We stare at each other blankly.

"Now, my dear, tell me all the gossip about your lovers. Is Polignac still attending to you?"

"Not lovers, Aunt Diane! Admirers."

"Mmm, gallants, admirers, swains, different names for different people, why, when I was young—"

I interrupt her quickly before she embarks on a long winding trip down memory lane. Though we both talk a lot, at least what I have to say is interesting. "Well, yes, Polignac is still attending me and then there is the Prince de Varennes, who is quite charming, and the Chevalier de Bissy, though he is sometimes very confusing, he was talking about his tongue and what he could do with it, but what can you do with a tongue other than talk?

"So, Aunt," I say as the plates are cleared away and a platter of strawberries is brought, "what is the gossip from you? The dauphine? Mama insists there is nothing interesting in the dauphine's household, but I am sure there must be something."

"Well, they are unfortunately more right than I care to admit, for the dauphine is certainly a woman of convention. Her husband is still devoted to her and visits every day, but his conversation and wit are not the most exciting, and of course they are very close with Mesdames, another tribe of tedious young ladies. Almost as dull as your parents, mmm, perhaps I should not say that, but I intend it as a compliment, well, not really a compliment, just an observation, but a true one . . ."

"And what about the Marquise?" I ask, for no tale of Court is complete without an account of the great Marquise and her doings. Mama and Thaïs refuse to talk of her, out of loyalty to their mistresses; they call her fish paste in a bottle, a rather curious name that neither cares to explain to me. She is now a duchess, but confusingly, everyone still calls her the Marquise.

"Ah, the Court is abuzz, half-crazed from gossip over the Marquise's newfound piety. She still maintains rouge, but eats less meat and always wears a cap and apparently spends much time on her knees, but these days in the chapel, not the bedroom. Everyone is betting whether it is real, or just another of the roles she plays. I heard the odds were that it is real, what with her little daughter's death . . ." Aunt Diane sighs and trails off. "That does something to one, you know. Well, you don't know, not yet, though God willing . . . I haven't seen your husband for a long while, was it last April, or the April before?"

"And do you think her piety is true?" I ask, steering the talk back to the Marquise and away from babies. A few years ago Diane's little girl, another Marie-Anne—would she have looked like me?—was bitten by her puppy and died; since then Aunt Diane has not been able to abide even the sound of a bark.

"Well, she does do an awful lot of embroidery," says Aunt Diane thoughtfully. "Even receives ambassadors in front of her frame. And as you know she is now a lady to the queen, something she long desired and something none thought would happen, though why a common woman might share the bed of the king but might not serve the queen at the table is an interesting question, one perhaps for the *philosophes*. As part of her new piety she even tried to reconcile with her husband, the Pope was insistent on that, but he refused, her husband I mean, not the Pope—"

"She has a husband?" I say in astonishment. "I never knew she had a husband!"

"Yes, of course, silly girl, she wouldn't be unmarried! But he lives in Paris and they have not seen each other for years, decades probably. The Holy Father wished for them to be reunited, though I'm not sure why, many women here live separately from their husbands, why, I haven't spoken to mine for years, not since that horrible incident with his flute . . . Mmm, I am not sure I understand; many things to do with the Marquise are quite a mystery."

"Does the king still love her?" I ask curiously.

"Oh yes, he loves her, but as a friend, not as a, well, you're married, you know what I mean. But that has been gossip for many years, and who knows what the truth is? The Marquise gets whatever she wants, frankly, but she is a nice enough lady."

"Mother says she is a fish in battle. I mean fish paste in a bottle. That doesn't really make sense, does it?"

"Well, your mother is rather judgmental," says Diane. "In truth I think her rather sad; not your mother, my dear, but the Marquise: What does she have left but the memory of the king's passion?" There are rumors that Aunt Diane also used to be the king's mistress, which is a funny thing to imagine, for she is as fat and ugly as a bear.

"Did your sister Marie-Anne ever meet the Marquise?"

"I don't think so," says Diane, frowning. "Of course we knew about her—we used to call her the pretty little doe in the forest—never guessing . . ." She sighs and suddenly looks older.

"Aunt," I say in my best innocent voice, which works wonders on gallants but less on aging aunts, "would you lend me your orange silk for the dinner tomorrow night?" What a fine thing it would be if men dressed as we did, for then there would be no end to the beautiful clothes I could wheedle from my admirers. Aunt Diane is much larger than I but my mother's woman is very skillful and could make anything fit me by Wednesday.

"Ah, my dear, I lent that to the Comtesse de Chilleroy, she was with child and getting frightfully large, swore she had nothing to wear to Passy. She promised to bring it back though I doubt I'll ever see it again. Let me see . . . how about the silver rose? Oh! Now, that is a good idea. It was Marie-Anne's favorite dress, but the back has been updated, as well as the sleeves. I don't wear it much; it is far too tight, everywhere."

"Oh, yes, that sounds rather fine! And pink is my best color! Well, after blue. And orange." I don't like yellow at all.

"Touffe," Aunt Diane calls, and a small worried woman gets up from a chair in the corner. "Go and find it for us and bring it here."

"Find what, Madame?"

"The pink-and-silver dress! The one with the silver bodice,

and the wine stain on the skirt. Were you not listening to us? Updated with the train?"

"No, Madame, I was not; you always tell me not to."

"Well, I don't mean that," says Diane in irritation. "Bring the dress. And then have the sugar pie from yesterday reheated, these strawberries are rather dry."

Chapter Fifty-Five

My mother's woman Marie stitches me into the pink-and-silver dress, grumbling all the while that my mother needs her to air the cupboards and there are the wax stains on the brown cotton to be seen to and the rats that got into the bed linens last week to be dealt with. She refuses to sew a bow over the wine stain, saying she will lend no hand to something so ridiculous. I do it myself, even though I detest sewing, and when I am finished it looks very fine.

Thaïs and Mother appraise me before I leave.

"What is that bow doing there? Is it to hide a stain?" asks Thaïs.

"Yes! No one will ever know, will they?"

"But I knew."

I stare at her blankly. "Well, yes, but you can't *see* the stain, can you?"

"But you know it's there," she repeats rather meanly, and turns away; even though she disdains most social functions, I think Thaïs is jealous that I have an invitation and she does not.

Mother kisses me on the forehead and reminds me not to drink too much; she will hear if I do anything embarrassing, and if I do I am going straight back to Paris, so fast I will not even have time to change my dress. "And let me look at your hands, dear, I must make sure your fingernails are clean."

My brother-in-law is green with envy, and offers to escort me to Conti's apartment, but I tell him I am going to Aunt Diane's first.

"I do not understand," he mutters, pacing up and down and shaking his sword. Montbarrey is very short, not much taller than Thaïs, and he wears shoes with high soles that give him a curious wobbly walk. "I have attended to the prince many times, many times, and he often seeks my advice on matters pertaining to the Polish succession."

"Don't you mean to say on matters pertaining to boot polish?" inquires Thaïs sweetly. Montbarrey bows at her coldly and extends his arm to escort me to Aunt Diane's.

"Oh, my darling, you look just like my sister Marie-Anne!" Aunt Diane says with a hint of wonder in her voice, hugging me hard. "And that charming bow, placed just there on your skirt! So lovely and original."

Aunt Diane takes ages on her toilette and though I love her I think it rather comical: Really, who does she think cares? She's over forty and she was never pretty even when she was young. But when she is finished she does look rather grand in an endless dark green dress, with her hair dressed close to her head in tight sheep curls. It is a fashionable style but I prefer the garland of pink silk roses that I found in Thaïs' wardrobe chest yesterday.

"Unfortunately neither the king nor the Marquise will be there; they are off with a small group at Bellevue," sniffs Diane as we mount the chairs sent for the occasion. I wonder if my admirer Polignac will be at the dinner. I haven't seen the Chevalier de Bissy yet this week, though he sent a note I didn't bother to read; his handwriting is small and scrunched.

"So this is the woman who has enchanted my nephew!" exclaims the Prince de Conti, skillfully pushing Diane aside while seeming to bow over her. I have always disliked the prince; he's not very old but he stoops like an old man, and he doesn't talk much. I distrust silent people—who knows what secrets they have hiding in their head?

"Your nephew, sir?" I reply, curtsying. I can never remember who is related to whom, one of the many faults my mother despairs over.

"Louis says he is absolutely besotted by you."

"Oh, thank you," I say. I am still utterly lost; it seems every man at Court has at least one name that is Louis.

"Indeed," says the Duc de Richelieu, sweeping toward us, resplendent in a black-and-green coat, the brocade on the cuffs a foot deep.

"Your Excellency," says Conti, "may I present Marie-Anne de Mailly, the Marquise de Coislin."

I give a rickety curtsy to the duke, who rather scares me.

"Yes, we met at your wedding, I believe," says Richelieu. "By God, the resemblance *is* rather striking. You've a slightly larger nose than the other one—her nose was perfection in a peapod—but overall the resemblance is uncanny."

I touch my nose nervously, looking back and forth between the two great men.

"Now, dear Cousin," says Richelieu calmly, taking me by the arm and steering me off into a corner, the crowds of courtiers scattering before us like a flock of pigeons. "Tell me about yourself."

Oh!

"Well, I was born at Châtillon, you know my parents, well, just my mother, she is of course the Vicomtesse de Melun, well, she was before she married my father, though I think she still is. I was at Châtillon for several years, but I can't remember much. Thaïs, that's my sister, says she can remember everything but that must be a lie, my only memory is one of the maids who smelled like wet lamb all the time, even in summer when . . ."

Conti reappears shortly, raising a hand to quiet me.

"She's a talkative one, isn't she," says Richelieu, his face starting to match his coat. He takes out an enormous green handkerchief, embroidered with gold lace, to pat his brow. "And she doesn't seem to have matured much since her wedding, more's the pity."

"Sir?"

"If I may sum up," says Conti, ignoring my puzzled look, "she is of course of historic family, one beloved by the king in so many ways; very pretty; convent educated, for what that is worth; married but no children yet, and her husband a nonentity."

A nonentity? Did I mishear? "Sirs?" I say again in confusion.

"Military slang, dear Cousin, military slang. Indicating that the Marquis de Coislin is a man of . . . ah . . . titanic honor and courage. Now, if you will excuse us, Madame, we must attend to the other guests."

Diane and I have the honor of being seated at the main table, with sixty other important guests. I find myself between the Marquise de Maillebois, who is so old I think she has forgotten how to speak, and the Duc d'Ayen, wearing a wig that looks exactly like Aunt Diane's sheep curls. He says he is enchanted by my eyes and declares them fathomless blue pools. I don't know what a fathomless is, but it sounds nice. The table is vast and long, a river of food running its length, the center studded with elegant sugar carvings dyed indigo blue, and Grecian urns filled with all manner of liqueurs.

"Forty plates so far," whispers Ayen, leaning over to position himself right by my ear, "and four services still to come!"

I think this is the most frightfully grand dinner I have ever attended, even grander than my sister's wedding feast to Montbarrey. Behind each guest a stone-faced footman is on hand, ready to jump at the slightest whim. I keep mine busy; all the best dishes are distant and just when I think I have the last of the roast stoat within my reach, the Duc de Broglie's footman whips it away from me. I send mine down the table in search of the cow udders in orange sauce and some of the delicious deer leg I think I spy.

I notice Conti's eyes on me appreciatively. I make sure to smile at him and occasionally he smiles back, baring his yellow teeth. The prince is frightfully rich; he could buy me a hundred gowns and not even know it, but oh! I don't think I could bear it if he paid me gallantries. His eyes are almost as yellow as his teeth and he reminds me of a dried sausage. Then I almost yelp in despair as I see Aunt Diane being served the last of the blood sausage in sage sauce.

After the fifth service, the table is cleared and five identical platters are brought in, laden with ground meat molded into the shape of a tower, surrounded by what looks like thick whipped cream. From a corner lively music is raised by ten cellists. The plates are ceremoniously placed before us on the table while the cellos rise in a fitting crescendo.

"Gossec, composed just for the occasion," whispers Ayen at my right side.

Conti raps for silence and raises his glass.

"In honor of our dear friend and national hero, the Duc de Richelieu, famed for his exploits and skill in scaling walls, honed escaping from jealous husbands and put to good use in capturing forts from the toady British! In his honor I present you these models of the Fort of Mahon, so elegantly captured by His Excellency."

"It was my profound duty and joy to bring honor so long deserved to our great nation," says Richelieu easily, standing up at the opposite end of the table. He is flanked by his daughter the Comtesse d'Egmont on one side, and the very pretty Comtesse de Forcalquier, whom everyone calls the Marvelous Mathilde, on the other.

"Guests, you see before you replicas, made of minced meat, of the Fort of Mahon, on one of those little islands south of Spain. They are surrounded by a new sauce I am proud to bring back, another fruitful outcome of the battle in addition to the capture of the island. And since that island is a bit of a barren rock, this might be the better contribution to our national glory." He nods as though to encourage himself and continues: "The British, as we all know, are simple barbarians—parents of present company excluded," he adds smoothly, with a nod to the Duc de Fitz-James. "On the island during the long weeks of the siege there was no cream or butter to be had. No *butter*, I repeat, if one can imagine such a travesty. But my cook is a Frenchman and a genius, and with nothing more than oil and eggs he created this luscious concoction you see before you. Ladies and gentlemen—I present you Mahon-butter."

"Why not call it just *Mahonnaise*, sir?" cries the Prince de Beauvau, in high spirits from too much wine. "After the inhabitants of the island? 'Twould be a fitting surrender to have a sauce named after them, as white and soft as their livers are!"

"Isn't it delicious?" says Ayen to me after we are served a portion. "Delightfully creamy and rich. I can imagine this with artichokes: divine."

I look at my plate dubiously. I don't mind lambs' livers, but British ones? I shudder.

A Letter
From the Desk of the Duchesse de Pompadour
Château de Versailles
August 30, 1756

My dear Stainville,

One should never celebrate the start of war, but in this case I feel we have no choice. The invasion of Saxony by the Prussians was an assault that could not be ignored. When the dauphine heard the news she rushed to the king, quite naked in only her chemise. Our Majesty has a charming fondness for young girls, and was touched by her gesture. He promised her the Prussian madman would not go unpunished.

We are eternally grateful for your help in bringing to fruition the treaty with the Austrians. You and my dear Bernis both, but if I am to be honest—a failing of mine—you were the greater asset. Of course, the treaty remains wildly unpopular here: French distrust and enmity for the Austrians runs centuries deep. Those not involved in the negotiations are all the more against it: Richelieu called it a treaty of traitors, and Conti even referred to it as a pact with the Devil. A touch of sour cream, I would think.

Thank you for your congratulations on my place with the queen. An immense honor but my duties are light; I attend only on feast days or for grand ceremonies. We are preparing for the retirement of Gilette, the Duchesse d'Antin, who has served the queen since her arrival from Poland in 1725. She is the only original lady left, and though there is no love between them, her retirement saddens the queen, reminding her as it does of the cruel passage of time.

But let me not bore you with such trivial affairs. My dear Stainville, in this time of war I think the better place for you might be in Vienna, with our new allies the Austrians. And we must make inquiries with the empress about an alliance between one of her sons and one of Our Majesty's daughters. The youngest, Madame Louise, is still nineteen—surely not too old? I fear we are the laughingstock of Europe for being blessed—cursed?—with so many old virgin princesses. That may sound a trifle harsh but I believe it the truth.

Safe travels, dear Stainville,
Pompadour

Chapter Fifty-Six

In a rather astonishing turn of events, the Prince de Conti has become my new best friend! His mistress, the Comtesse de Boufflers, sent me a large bouquet of gladioli, tied with a string of seed pearls, and Conti himself says he might be able to secure me an invitation for one of the king's private suppers. According to him, the king is sad these days because of the war, and he thinks that I—and my resemblance to my dead cousin Marie-Anne—would be just the thing to cheer him up.

Oh!

How fine it would be to be friends with the king! If he were an admirer, there might be no end of presents. The Marquise de Pompadour has the most beautiful collection of things in France, if not the whole world, and it is rumored that her magnificent *hôtel* in town was built just to accommodate her wardrobe.

Aunt Diane is excited for me. She says the king once gave her sister Marie-Anne a beautiful pearl necklace, and a castle, as well as a duchy.

"And besides, he's very handsome," she says wistfully, "the finest man in France, if not Europe."

"Really? He's rather old," I say doubtfully. "He's almost fifty! If you compare him to the Chevalier de Bissy, for example, or even Polignac . . ."

"Oh, tush," says Diane crossly. "I knew him in my youth and there was no finer man then, no finer man still." I want to ask her if the rumors are true, the dirty ones about her and her sisters and the king, but I don't dare.

"Well, I admit he has fine eyes, but his skin is rather gray and he has that mole thing on his neck, and I heard that beneath his wig he is bald as a—"

"That's not true! He doesn't even wear a wig! Where are you getting this information?"

"Well, the Marquise de Belzunce said—"

"Alexandrine is a silly cow and besides, her husband has no hair, and he's not older than thirty!"

"Are you finished, Mesdames?" asks the Prince de Conti in impatience. He is sitting across from us, watching us keenly.

"Finished what, sir?" says Aunt Diane politely.

"This—conversation, though I am not sure it even merits that word."

"We are here to listen to you, sir," says Aunt Diane kindly; her manners are rather perfect and I think her an excellent hostess. "Have another Italian meringue. This is peppermint, or was it parsley? I think I ate the last peppermint one, or did I? Well, this one's green, and I'll take the pink one—raspberry, I hope."

Conti grimly takes the green ball, then places it firmly down on his plate.

"As I was saying . . ." Conti makes a triangle under his chin with his fingers, and a wily look settles on his face. "I have no doubt the king will be captivated by our lovely Marie-Anne."

"Of course he will!" Diane pats my hand and I smile.

"I have noticed, however, that you are rather talkative," he observes, sounding too much like my mother.

"Only when there is something to say," I protest.

"Mmm, that is debatable." Conti strokes his chin with crispy yellow fingers. "Great talkers are like broken pitchers: everything runs out of them."

"I am well educated, sir," I protest in indignation. "I know when to hold my own counsel! Why, even yesterday when Thaïs asked me—"

"Yes, and that—your voice. What is it with young ladies these days? No one cares to hear your emotions in your voice. This is not the stage, you know."

"Nonsense!" says Diane. "Marie-Anne's manners are simply perfect."

Conti stands up, as though he were irritated. "Enough. I cannot . . . I cannot . . . For now, just look fine for the little supper, and perhaps try not to speak, for when you open your mouth, the resemblance disappears. You must avoid exposing your conversation skills, or lack thereof."

He leaves, muttering something about regrets, and slams the door shut before the footman can.

"What do you think he meant?" I ask Aunt Diane in astonishment. "How can my conversation be lacking, when all I do is talk? And Polignac once said my words were sweeter than honey and sugar! Well, that was my lips, though I think he also meant my words."

"I'm sure I don't know," says Aunt Diane, shaking her head and wiping pink crumbs off her chin. "He is a strange man. How I dislike silent people—who knows what is hiding in their heads?"

"Exactly!" I say, embracing my aunt.

"Now, do you think this one is lemon, or banana? Have you tried a banana, child? They are a most interesting fruit. And quite as yellow as a lemon. Until of course they mature, and then they turn a rather nasty brown color."

℘

The king greets me warmly, saying he is delighted to welcome into his circle the acquaintance of an old friend, and one with such an old name. When we rise from the table he bows over my hand with more pretty words. The Marquise de Pompadour is there and she greets me calmly, dressed in a flowing blue silk dress, a tidy little ruffled cap on her head. Oh! How elegant she is.

After the meal the tables are arranged for cards, but I have no money and must only watch. I'm glad; I'm never very good at remembering the rules and often get mixed up. The Duc d'Ayen keeps me company, and compliments me on my pretty nose. He is wearing a strange wig with a ringlet behind each ear.

"Such a pity," says the king, suddenly appearing by my side; the Duc d'Ayen evaporates instantly. "A lovely young woman as you, to grace the table could surely only be good fortune." He stares at me a little wonderingly. His hand creeps forward as though to touch my cheek, then he pulls it back at the last minute. It is true what Aunt Diane said; by the candlelight in the corner he is rather handsome and his eyes are black and deep like . . . something deep. A well?

"Come, you must stand beside me, dear, and be my luck."

I wasn't—he lost an awful lot of money—but the next afternoon he sends over a bag of golden *louis* that I might play *brelan* with them that evening. Oh, goody!

The Marquise advises me on my strategy but I can never keep the cards straight and I lose all my coins. Oh—and I spent all day perusing the stalls by the Ministers' Wing and had finally decided on a set of hair combs, made from the inside of seashells, to buy with my winnings.

"I think we might have to play *cavagnole*," the Marquise says, "to accommodate our dear Marie-Anne's muddled manners. Picking numbers is an art form I am sure even she cannot mistake." Everyone laughs, and I do too, though I am not sure what the joke is.

Since that evening, the king has invited me to several more suppers and even gave me an agate pendant, carved with a ship. Soon I notice he wears the same mooning look that my other admirers do. Aunt Diane says I must rebuff everyone else, and that I must return the pink spotted shawl that Milord Melfort sent me, which I do, ever so reluctantly.

Mother permits me a new gown and I choose a bright green silk with yellow and red flowers, very striking and modern. The king says I look like a summer field in it, and the Marquise says she has never seen an outfit where harmony was so wanting. The Marquise is the most elegant woman in France, and so a compliment from her is something to be treasured.

My little brother-in-law, Montbarrey, is now endlessly by my side; I thought he had a regiment to attend to but apparently he thinks waiting on me is more beneficial to his career. It's all rather flattering. Aunt Diane says I must not let everything go to my head, and Conti inquires if that would even be possible.

But it is true: people are starting to talk about me. About me! How exciting. Though sometimes the talk can be a little hurtful:

"She's certainly a look-alike, but a pale imitation at best."

"What is Conti thinking? Surely he knows in this new world of ours, name counts for very little?"

"She's pretty, but she'll never last."

"They say the king is smitten and hasn't even gone hunting—in town—for over a *week*."

Aunt Diane says she knew the king would love me as much as he loved her sister Marie-Anne. Then she warns me I must be careful of the Marquise.

"Oh, no, the Marquise is very kind to me. She even showed me her bowl of goldfish! I think we might be friends." Imagine me, friends with the Marquise! She has the most exquisite taste and so many gowns. If we became friends, might she lend me one?

"Well, even though the Marquise is kind to everyone, she's a little bit like a fish swimming under the surface: you never know what she is thinking. No, I'm not sure I have that right; fish are always under the surface, you can't even see them from the top of the water, can you? In sum, my dear, you mustn't trust the Marquise."

"Mmm," I say doubtfully, thinking of the kind way she smiles at me, her large gray eyes that seem to glow with sympathy.

"She doesn't like other women near the king, at least not without her approval, and the king is so dependent on her, she is almost like a part of his body. Like a third leg, no, wait, that is not the comparison I seek. A third arm, perhaps, something like an octopus but not with eight arms, why, I wonder—"

"Yes, Aunt," I say dutifully, but I'm not really listening. I daydream and imagine myself the king's mistress, by his side and without the Marquise. She is frightfully unpopular in France; it's not only my mother and sister who dislike her. All of Paris sings songs about her, about her fish name and the dreadful things she does with tradesmen and how she has single-handedly bankrupted France. She must be very silly to be so hated; I am sure I will be more popular.

I could move into her magnificent apartment and the look on Thaïs' face when she saw my rooms would be beyond compare. Of course, if I were to become the king's mistress, Montbarrey would never leave me alone, but then I suppose I could command him to leave, or make him ambassador to France or some such thing.

I pepper Diane with questions about Marie-Anne, the first one, the one the king loved as he is now beginning to love me. Diane tells me Marie-Anne adored carnations and quinces, and more than anything else, she liked reading. Diane has several trunks full of her sister's books and says I may go through them and take what I want, but I shudder and decline.

"And she was so funny, and witty. The king loved her to distraction—what a fine thing it would be to be loved like that." Diane is often sad when she talks of her sisters; only she and Aunt Hortense are left while the other three are dead. She tries to tell me about her sister Pauline but I'm not so interested in her. I heard Pauline was a green monkey, whatever that is, and didn't smell very good.

☙

Conti is leaving the Court in disgust; he has been refused command of the king's army and must retire from Court to register his disapproval. He attends on me to say goodbye.

"I should be comfortable, Madame," he says to Aunt Diane, "leaving this matter in your hands, but I have not the slightest hope that you will do what needs to be done."

"Well," says Aunt Diane, then laughs. "Conti, you are a funny one!"

The prince winces as though Diane had just tickled him.

"Now, some advice . . ." says Conti, turning to me. "Though

the king is indeed intrigued, he will soon tire of the chase. You must insist on a great deal, before you . . ." Here he pauses and strokes his nose.

"Before I what?" I ask, noticing his eyes are very yellow today, like overripe lemons.

Conti rolls them. "Really, such innocence. I suppose it is something to be prized in this most jaded circle of Hell, but there are limits. Help me, Madame," he pleads with Diane.

"I think he means before the king wants to bed you, dear."

Oh! Imagine me, sleeping with the king! I've only ever slept with my husband, of course, and it wasn't particularly nice, but I wonder if it would be different with the king. Bissy once promised me that with him the earth would move, but how can making love be like an earthquake? There was an earthquake in Lisbon last year that killed thousands of people—I shouldn't like that in the least.

"Oh no!" I say, shaking my head. "My mother would never allow it. I am not even allowed to kiss my admirers, why, when Polignac—"

"Mmm, you might be surprised on that account," says Conti cryptically, and I realize in astonishment that Mother has not sought me out once, these past weeks, to admonish me, catalogue my wrongs, or warn me against the king's attentions.

Well.

"These days the king is not one to wait. His appetite for the chase has lessened and there is a surfeit of young ladies out there. Now it is not so much a chase as a zoo, or a banquet . . ." Conti trails off. "So we must be prepared." He arches his eyebrows and looks at us as though offering an invitation, but we both stare blankly back at him. He sighs in exasperation and continues: "We must prepare and plan."

"For what?"

"I think he means for sleeping with the king, dear," says Diane again, patting my hand.

"Exactly. And before you give in to your mutual passion, you must make certain demands."

"Of course!" I exclaim. "Of course! He already knows I like pearls, and I hinted very strongly last night at the concert that I wanted a silver fan like the one the singer had. It was quite remarkable."

Conti looks confused.

"It was a silver fan, not painted silver, but actually *made* of silver, everything, even the handle, and the leaves were like lace, but also silver . . ." I look to Diane for help, as Conti does not appear to understand. "Filipee, I think it is called?"

"Madame, might I suggest you set your sights higher?"

Oh, certainly. "I should ask for a . . . a . . . a castle?" I look to Diane for approval as there is none forthcoming from Conti.

"Perhaps the most important thing would be to secure your position publicly, for which of course the Marquise must leave Versailles."

"The Marquise leave Versailles? Oh no, she would never do that! And I thought she was, um, well, I thought she didn't mind . . . a 'pitiful procuress,' I think my mother called her. And she is so nice to me, yesterday she said I was as oblivious as one of the Duchesse de Mirepoix's rabbits. I wasn't sure what that meant but I do love bunnies."

Conti looks up and squeezes his head with one stained yellow hand. "I don't normally regret things," he says, speaking to the shepherdess painted above the door, "but let me just say this: that hideous she-monster, who degrades the very tone of this Court, will never be your friend. In addition to that—ah—fan—you must also seek her dismissal. It should not be difficult: the king is entranced by you and everyone knows he just keeps her here out of habit. Even she knows it."

"She's a good woman," says Diane, looking at Conti, who nods at her. "But she is getting old, and very religious now, well, not *very* religious, but more than before and I think she would like to retire from Court and live happily in a convent, don't you?"

"I suppose most old women would like that," I say dubiously. I can't imagine the Marquise, with her elegant toilette and impeccable dress, in a dreary convent somewhere. Though perhaps she would make the cloisters as elegant as she has made Versailles, brighten the cells with floral wallpapers and paint the chapel mint-green?

"Well said, Madame, well said," agrees Conti. "It is as Madame de Lauraguais observes: the fish is ready to swim to a convent and will no doubt find happiness there. Now, before I take my leave, there is one more matter. Here is the name of a Turkish lady who offers many delights, and not of the jelly kind. She coaches women with splendid results—I myself cannot attest, but most of Paris can. The king is now used to being in the hands of—ah—professionals, and his tastes have become rather more sophisticated than in earlier years."

I stare at him blankly, then—oh! Suddenly I understand what he is talking about. I giggle and Conti grimaces. He stands up and drops a small note on the side table.

Madame Sultana, it says in a looping hand, *75 rue du Puits-de-l'Ermite.*

"I shall take my leave now," says Conti with a bow. "The door is open and I trust you have the right friends"—he looks doubtfully at Diane—"to see you safely through."

A Letter
From the Desk of the Duchesse de Pompadour
Château de Versailles
September 16, 1756

My dear Abel,

It is confirmed: we depart for Fontainebleau later than expected, and the extra time should allow you to finish the renovations to the Princes' Court before our arrival. All is in upheaval here as war starts in earnest: you can imagine the jealous jostlings for position and command. And Parlement has not rallied behind their king, but instead they continue to press for advantage, now demanding that every law that is proposed and enacted by the king's council pass before them! They are insatiable.

I am sure you have heard the rumors, but pay them no heed. Though the girl's family is like opium or gin to the king, I believe her resemblance to the Duchesse de Châteauroux is her only strength. I am not worried and you must not be either.

One last thing, and don't be angry, but your intransigence is truly vexing. You are almost thirty and think how happy our dear mother would be if you were settled and with children! Tell me your thoughts on Madame de Cadillac, recently widowed and very charming.

We shall see you at Fontainebleau in November. Please ensure that my dear friend Mirie's rooms are sufficiently far from the Comte de Matignon's; his vendetta over her rabbits is escalating, and it seems nothing placates him.

J

Chapter Fifty-Seven

"I'll be Melanie!"

"I'll be Philippine! No, wait—Philiberte!"

"Or perhaps Eglantine!"

"No, not Eglantine, that sounds like *eggplant*. I don't like them, apart from their color, of course; imagine a whole winter dress in that deep, dark purple?"

Aunt Diane and I are in the carriage on our way to Madame Sultana's, choosing secret names for our secret visit. What an adventure! Diane says she is curious—she says she knows of the place from her husband but has never been there herself.

"And what a funny name—imagine being called Sultana! Sounds rather disrespectful, but I suppose the Turks are not respectful, because they are heathens."

"Such an outlandish name," I agree.

"When I was with my husband in Saxony we met a woman called Fatimah!"

"Oh, Fattie!" We shriek with laughter.

Madame Sultana greets us and slips a keen eye out to our waiting carriage, emblazoned with the arms of Diane's husband. Oh—perhaps I should have sent the coach round the corner.

"I have long been patronized by women of the Court, Madame," she says in greeting to Diane, who can only giggle, distracted by a pair of velvet manacles on a side table.

"Tell me who?" I blurt out, but the woman only bows—like a man!—and shakes her head.

"We have been recommended to you by a man placed very highly in this kingdom," I say, to impress upon Sultana the importance of our visit. She smiles vaguely and inclines her head.

"One of the very highest." How frustrating, she is not impressed at all!

"It is in fact the *Prince de Conti*," I say finally.

Diane puts down a thin, supple leather whip, far too small for a horse, and puts her hand over mine. "Marie-Anne, we must be discreet."

"Ah, Madame, might you be Marie-Anne de Mailly de Coislin? Monsieur le Prince de Conti said you would be coming."

"I am," I say a little stiffly, not sure whether I should admit to such. It's rather too late to tell her I am just *Mélanie*.

"My pleasure, my pleasure. You must come this way, Madame de Coislin, come this way. Do you require a session as well, Madame?"

"Oh no, Diane, I mean Philiberte, is too old for that sort of thing," I tell Sultana as Diane drops a small chain studded with curious silver balls.

"Ah, might you be Madame the Duchesse de Lauraguais? How honored I am to meet you." Here the woman drops into a deep curtsy. "You husband, dear Madame, is one of my finest customers. I hold him in the highest regard—even after that unfortunate incident with the Hungarian twins . . ."

"Ah yes, that was unfortunate," agrees Diane, "but he did say they recovered nicely."

"What happened?" I ask eagerly.

"Ah, but discretion is as valuable as gold in this business," says Sultana in her infuriatingly calm voice, and I decide she's not Turkish at all; the way she rolls her words reminds me of a maid I once had, from Picardy.

I follow her down a passageway lined with velvet and we have not gone far when we hear Diane's voice booming out: "But my dear Ayen! I did not expect to see you here! And who is this, your friend? The Comte du Barry?"

❦

Montbarrey will be green with envy, I think as the footman ushers me through yet another door. There are always rumors about

smaller, even more private rooms beyond the king's private apartments, and tonight I see they are true. Are there even more private
rooms beyond this little room? One may think one is at the center, but beyond there are still more—where does it end?

Such thoughts make my head hurt, but I am quite sure there is
nothing more private than this cozy little room hung with butter-
yellow drapes. Like living inside sunshine, I think in contentment, even though it is drab October out.

"A little supper," the king says, coming in and kissing my
hand. "Very intimate, just the two of us. Quite the thing to amuse
me at the end of a long day. And oh, and how long it was! That
Prussian madman certainly knows how to distress, and my head
hurts so." He looks at me expectantly, but I am not sure what he
wants me to say or do—the only thing I know about Prussia is
that Polignac's mother was unfortunately born there.

"You permit me, Madame, to take off my coat? It is hot in
here."

I nod. I can't exactly say no to the king, can I? It's an exciting
adventure, to be alone with him. I wonder if he has ever eaten in
private like this with the Marquise? A footman helps him out of
his fine blue-striped coat, revealing a cream shirt underneath, embroidered with little acanthus leaves.

"Oh! Are those acanthus?"

"They are. You like embroidering, my dear?"

"Oh, no, I hate it. But my sister and mother are embroidering them on the dauphine's chapel cushions. Three months now."

"Indeed. Now tell me, my dear, how was your day?" The footman uncorks a bottle on the sideboard and the king pours two
glasses.

"Oh, I just ate breakfast with Thaïs, before she had to go and
replace the Duchesse de Brissac with Madame Adélaïde. And
walked around the Orangery a bit. Mother says I'm getting rather
fat and must exercise more."

The king chuckles. "How you make me laugh, my dear Madame. You are just the tonic I need, in this time of war. Now, for

supper, I shall prepare this celery soup. How I love intimate dinners at home—don't you, my dearest?" The footman lights a small
stove and the king starts stirring the pot.

"Well, yes, sometimes," I say rather dubiously. "When Mother
and my sister are not on duty at Versailles, they like to stay home,
rather than go out."

"Yes, your mother and her daughter are veritable icons of piety,"
says the king approvingly, stirring the pot and adding cream from
a small jug, then a splash of brandy. "Here, my dear, taste this."

"Mmm, I'm not sure I like celery."

He laughs again. "Ah, your honesty is as refreshing as your
youth, my dear, as fresh as the dawn. I deem it good enough, and
so we shall eat."

We seat ourselves at a small round table and the lone footman
serves us the soup. The king whispers something to him and a
plate emerges from a warming cupboard, then the footman disappears through a door hidden in the paneling. I think I hear a
key turn in a lock, then—oh! Oysters!

"Oh, I do love oysters! Milord Melfort sent me a basket last
year, and I ate all of them and had a terrible stomachache."

"These ones will only soothe your stomach, and your soul,"
assures the king, slurping one from the shell, his eyes fixed on
mine. I feel rather entranced. It is true he is quite old, but he is
still fine-looking and he does like to compliment me so.

"Tell me about your convent days, dear."

Oh!

"Well, they were frightfully fun, all the nuns were very nice except for old Sister Perpetua, who was blind and quite mean. Well,
not completely blind, her nose—"

"Indeed. The other girls—how old were you? Who was your
prettiest little friend, mmm? Tell me about her."

"Oh, that was Marie-Stéphanie, she was very pretty and had
large blue eyes, as large as . . . well, as her eyes, I suppose. She was
ever so much fun, and sometimes when we were supposed to be
sleeping she would jump on our beds."

"Ah, jump on the other girls, you say? How extraordinary! And what did her little victims do? Did they fight back?"

"Oh yes! We would hit her with our pillows, and then we would hit each other . . . I suppose you could call it a pillow fight, and once . . ."

The king listens as I prattle on, regarding me with heavy eyes and pouring me wine whenever my glass is empty. He is a wonderful listener. And imagine, me, being poured a glass of wine by the king! I can't wait to tell my mother, though she might not approve; she has warned me never, ever to drink in public, not after what happened at my wedding ceremony.

But people always underestimate me. Or is it overestimate?

After we finish eating the king invites me to sit beside him on a small sofa by the fire, and gently unpins my hair. His eyes grow deeper, as black as ink, though sometimes of course ink can be blue . . . should he be touching my hair?

"The resemblance is striking, simply striking." His voice is equal parts sorrow and wonder, overlaid with wine. "Her hair used to shine like that, shot with auburn . . . You are very beautiful, my dear, very beautiful." He leans closer and instinctively I lean back.

"Yes, thank you . . . um . . ." I duck away from the hands that are suddenly insistent on my head. I must remember Conti's advice, and the list he gave me. "I . . . I must, uh . . . I have a list?"

"You have a list?" The king's voice is a vase full of wearied amusement.

"Yes, I do." The king avidly follows my hands as I fish down in my bodice and produce the little note. I have not bothered to copy it and it still has Conti's stamp. "I, uh, must ask certain things of you, before I grant you, ah . . ." Oh! This is all rather awkward, and suddenly the words don't come. So this is what being tongue-tied is like, I think in amazement: as though my tongue is stuck to the roof of my mouth. I gape at the king as he takes the list and reads:

Dismissal of the Marquise de Pompadour
Public recognition
A place in the service of the queen
A silver pan in the Persian style

"Fan, not pan," I say quickly. I added that to Conti's list, in my own handwriting.

"The Persian style—now, what does that mean?"

"Like lace, but silver. Not silver colored, but made entirely of silver, but so fine it looks like lace. One of the dancers, a Persian, had it and I—"

"Ah, I see." There is a pause. "Well, this also reminds me of Marie-Anne," he says finally, and chuckles drily. "The other one."

"But that is a good thing? She was very beautiful, and so am I and everyone says—"

"Well, I did not love everything. She was always making demands, and it could be very tiring." The king crumples the note and skillfully flips it into the fireplace.

Oh!

"My dear," he says huskily, turning back to me and cupping my face in his hands. "You are so beautiful. So very beautiful. When I am with you, I feel young again."

"You're not so old," I say kindly. "My father is almost as old as you, but he *looks* old, you don't look old, just a little . . ."

"Mmm. Don't speak of your family, there's a dear. Some . . . some silence, perhaps." He leans in and kisses me quickly. On the lips! "You shall have your silver fan."

Oh goody! I want to ask about the other items, but now he is kissing me properly, a long, soft, and insistent kiss. He draws back slowly and tickles the nape of my neck and a shiver like pleasure rushes through my entire body. As I sink into his arms, the list burns merrily in the fire.

A Letter
From the Desk of the Duchesse de Pompadour
Château de Versailles
October 4, 1756

Dearest Claudine,

I was so relieved to receive your latest letter—it has been almost eight months since I had heard from you. And such news that you have decided to enter the cloister! A step many widowed women take and I am glad you have decided on our childhood convent at Poissy, where my aunt is now abbess. And how incredible that Sister Severa is still alive!

What sweet times we had there as children. Do you remember our bird Chester, and how we cared for him? How precious he was to us; when one doesn't have a lot, small things are more valued. Now I have dozens of birds, including a fabulous toucan from Brazil—but their songs are never as sweet as dear Chester's was. How young we were then, and how old we are now.

Thank you for inquiring about my duties with the queen. They are light; I only attend on feast days or ceremonies. Last month I secured for her the fingernail of Saint Sosipater and her gratitude was genuine. She is a Christian woman who has suffered much in her life, and now we both belong to that saddest of mothers' groups.

I wish you fortune in your endeavor, dear Claudine. Here the Duchesse de Trémoille decided to be cloistered but came out five days later, complaining of the cold and missing her morning chocolate. Everyone laughed; it seems everything here must be made into a joke.

Send me the date of your endowment—I will add to your dowry and make a gift to the convent, something I have been remiss in doing until now. And consider your request on behalf of your nephew done, he shall join Soubise's regiment.

Ever in friendship,
J

Chapter Fifty-Eight

Minister Argenson demands an audience and says he comes at the behest of the Prince de Conti to oversee the progress of our affair.

"An evil man," whispers Diane, and instantly I dislike the way his hooded eyes rove constantly over my chest, as though pulled there by an invisible string.

"Letters," he says. "Letters are what we need. Keep the king's interest by sending little notes, little *billets-doux,* so even on the days when he cannot see you, you remain foremost in his mind."

I shake my head. "My hands get terribly cramped," I say. "I am not very good at writing letters, and besides I am sure the king would rather just sleep with me than read letters. We do have ever so much fun, why, last night—"

Argenson winces and interrupts. "My dearest Madame, you must learn to curb your words. You should perhaps choose better counsel than your aunt the Duchesse de Lauraguais."

"But Aunt Diane is the dearest and most discreet woman in the entire world!"

"Perhaps you had best see if there is an entry for *discretion* in the *Encyclopedia,*" Argenson says drily. "Though banned, I could obtain a copy for you."

I shudder. I hate reading almost as passionately as I hate writing, and how many volumes are there supposed to be in that dreadful work? Oh, no. No.

Argenson proceeds with his advice: "Continue your gallantries with the king, do not mind the old woman, and leave the details of the intrigue to us. Do not attempt wit, use your other . . .

charms . . . and you should do quite well. I will keep Conti updated on the progress of our little matter."

"Why must I not use wit?" I say stiffly. "I am very witty, I would have you know. I am as witty as a . . . as witty as a Frenchman?"

Argenson appears not to hear me and takes his leave with no further words.

♥

Now I am almost every day with the king, but unfortunately so is the Marquise. The king visits her every afternoon, and she is at all his entertainments in the evenings.

But he says he loves me and tells me I am far more beautiful than she ever was. He is also very intrigued by the tricks I have learned from Madame Sultana, and makes me repeat at length all that I learned and saw there. I tell him about the mirrored ceilings; the endless feather beds, smelling of patchouli; the Marquis de Thibouville, whom I saw twice there; the plates of cucumbers by the side of every bed; the curious whips and balls, and the black woman with oil all over her body.

I've also told the king all the details of my wardrobe—I do like discussing fashion—and one day he suggests I dress in Aunt Diane's silver-and-rose dress, the one that her sister Marie-Anne owned before her. I am happy to borrow it again and when he sees me a look like a ghost comes over his face. It is a lovely autumn afternoon and we take a walk in the gardens, slowly through the alleys lined with yellowing yews. He tells me about his telescope and what he calls the "wonders of the vast blue."

"And Lacaille and Halley, and the possibilities of Uranus . . ."

I have no idea what he is talking about; it's almost as though he is speaking Greek. But I do enjoy walking with him and appreciate the low bows of the courtiers as we pass. I halloo out to everyone I know so they can see I walk with the king. We wander a bit more and the king seems to grow sadder and sadder. Back on the terraces we sit on a bench overlooking the Grand Canal and the setting sun.

"It is true as the philosophers say, that there is nothing as dead as the past. Dead, my dear, dead," he says in a low little voice and I see a tear form in the corner of one eye. Oh! I didn't know men could cry. "Such a fine line between a ghost and a memory."

"I'm not dead," I say, and giggle. Sometimes when I am nervous or don't understand what he is talking about, it is useful to giggle and blush a little. He sighs once more, then reaches out to stroke my cheek, but his face is still full of sadness as he tells me again what a comfort I am to him.

e/o

I ask the king when the Marquise will be gone; soon, soon, my dear, soon, he says, then tickles the back of my neck and tells me to be quiet, that he might drink in my beauty even more.

The Marquise is still very kind to me and even compliments me on my silver fan. I am a little confused, for does she not know the king loves me, and that she is leaving soon? But Diane says that is just the Marquise's way: she is kind to everyone, an oddity no one understands.

"I suppose it's rather nice," I say doubtfully.

"Yes, it is," agrees Diane. "The Marquise has a kind heart, though the years have hardened it somewhat. When she first came here she wanted to be loved by everyone; reminded me of my sister Louise, in fact. She had to change, you can't be nice here, I don't know why, really, no one is . . . but I still think she has a kind soul. I really believe, and I am not just saying this because of our little project, that she would be happier away from Court."

"Oh, so do I," I say brightly. "The king agrees; he says she will be gone soon, certainly after the New Year."

But one night I see that the Marquise, though she professes kindness, is not my friend. She is, in fact, my enemy.

She has arranged a night of charades, the women playing together against the men. First the Marquise acts out a scene from the myth of Icarus, using a portrait of Louis XIV—the Sun King—and a pretty allusion to flying. The Duc de Duras deduces *hubris*, and all clap at her cleverness.

I am determined to shine and make the king look at me with similar admiration, but when I unfold the slip of paper and see the task before me, my heart sinks. No! She must have arranged it thus, to give me the hardest choice. Oh, how will I ever?

I look around in despair.

"My dear, do not be distressed, for you are more powerful than you think," says the king indulgently, looking at me with satisfaction. I blush at his reference; Sultana's training has worked.

"Come now, dear Marie-Anne," says the Marquise pleasantly. "You can do it. You are very clever, you just hide your intelligence underneath a shell, as a turtle hides her beauty." She is wearing a dress of the palest gray, over a soft pink petticoat sewn with myrtle flowers; I don't think I've ever seen her wear the same gown twice.

I bite my lip; sometimes she is so nice, it can be confusing. Well, there is nothing to do but dive in. I raise one finger.

"One word," says the king triumphantly.

Oh, how can this be? I am a woman, not a—oh! Finally I let out a little *miao*, more in frustration than anything else.

"No talking!" cries the Marquis de Gontaut but is instantly shushed by the king.

"A cat! A cat, my dearest, you are excellent, simply excellent," he says, and I giggle and curtsy.

"Well, not a cat, a kitten, but thank you."

"Excellent, dearest, excellent."

"Truly, a creative interpretation." The Marquise beams and I laugh back at her, suddenly very confident. She thought to trip me up, but I showed her well.

The next night at cards, my triumph only grows stronger. We are at *brelan*, a rather difficult game, but after some coaching from Aunt Diane, I am confident in my abilities. I must remember I need three of a kind. Or is it four? But the cards smile on me, as though helping me against the Marquise.

"Ha!" I exclaim in delight. "I have a handful of kings!" I show my cards to the king, who smiles at me and confirms that it is true.

"The perfect hand," says the Marquise in her slow voice, raising a lovely eyebrow at me. Sometimes when I look at her I feel like I am looking at a painting, not a real woman. She's still very beautiful, but then I have to keep reminding myself that I am too. And I look like Marie-Anne, whom the king loved very much, and she doesn't.

"It is the best hand!" I retort in glee, Argenson's stinging words coming back to haunt me. I *am* witty.

"I have a handful of kings! Only kings!" I repeat again, and I know that this conversation will be all over the Court tomorrow, and then Argenson will know he was wrong about me. I am as witty as Voltate!

The Marquise plays her hand—a paltry two and a four—and laughs lightly and says: "I do not fear that I have not lost this round."

I fling my cards down in triumph on the table and chortle again: "A handful of kings!"

I float back to Diane's apartments to tell her; she agrees it is one of the wittiest things she has ever heard.

"Oh, you're exaggerating, dear Aunt," I say, flinging myself down on the sofa in satisfaction.

"The king is not with you tonight, will he not send for you?" asks Aunt Diane, a trifle anxiously.

"No, he says it is the wrong time of the month for him."

"What did he mean by that?"

"Well, I am not sure, I just assumed . . ."

We stare at each other blankly.

Chapter Fifty-Nine

I am with the king almost every night and soon he starts to stop by my apartment before the hunt, when usually he would visit the Marquise.

The Court is abuzz, and I can only smile in triumph.

"Interesting; forgoing his afternoon paddles with the Fish."

"Blood trumps all, you know what they say, and she is the spitting image . . ."

"Personally I think the Duchesse de Châteauroux—no blessing on her soul—would be insulted to be compared to that stupid little chit."

The king wants my advice on what to do in Silesia, for none at Court can talk of anything but the war. Really, I am not very interested—Silesia sounds like a horrible place—but Argenson says I should tell the king to fortify the troops along the eastern Elbe.

"You must fortify the troops at the Elbow," I say, stroking his head. "I mean the Elbe. The western—no I mean the eastern side?"

"And why do you say that, my dear?" he says, his eyelids fluttering in satisfaction. We are in Aunt Diane's salon; she has a very nice apartment near the state rooms and we often arrange to meet here. Diane says she doesn't mind and besides, she is in attendance on the dauphine this week. The king is lying on the sofa, his head in my lap. "Why do you say we should fortify them along the Elbe?"

"Well, because the troops need fortifying."

"Indeed. Ahhh, that feels very nice. Mouse fingers . . ." he says in a faraway voice. He shakes his head, as though to clear it. I resume my gentle stroking. "But do you not think, my dear, that the Prussians would realize what we are doing?"

"No, you mustn't worry about that," I say, running my fingers over his wig, careful not to muss his ponytail.

"And why not?"

"Well, because once the troops are fortified, they will be strong."

"Ah, my dear, your very simplicity beckons the seal of my approval."

I kiss his forehead. I like the king. He is very attentive, much more so than my husband: the king can perform very often in one night, whereas Henri only wanted to do it when he'd had some wine at dinner, and even then sometimes didn't quite finish like I think he was supposed to . . . I wonder if I am falling in love?

∾

News of my growing influence spreads and von Stahremberg, the Austrian ambassador, seeks a private audience with me.

"Oh! An honor, an honor," I say, shooing Thaïs and Montbarrey out. These days Montbarrey is assiduously at my side and cannot stop complimenting my beauty and my wit. I think I quite like him now. When ordered out, Montbarrey looks positively green and protests to Stahremberg that he is my most trusted adviser and must stay.

Stahremberg inclines his head one way to indicate he has heard, then indicates the door, and Montbarrey reluctantly wobbles out, led by Thaïs.

"And, Madame"—the ambassador bows, turning to Diane— "would you be so kind?"

"Oh no, Diane can stay!" I cry. "She is my best friend."

"Indeed, what a pleasure it must be to have a *best friend,* though I have a small idea what that expression might mean. A fault of translation, no doubt, as my French is sadly lacking. But I do insist, Madame; I would have you to myself."

Reluctantly Diane gets up. "I'm with the dauphine all tomorrow, but on Thursday you must come with me to Alexandrine's; she's giving a dinner for her new daughter-in-law, though the child is already back at her convent. Any excuse for a party, I suppose."

Stahremberg settles in, flouncing the tails of his long coat out behind him and looking at me with his small, foxy eyes. His coat is stiff wool braided with silver and his hair is combed high in a towering egg of brown powder—what an odd style.

"Do you drink coffee?" I ask doubtfully. My mother, who hates the Austrians on account of her brother being killed at Dettingen, once said the Austrians were piss-drinking fiends, so I'm not even sure they like coffee.

"Thank you, thank you, just a small cup," he says, then helps himself to a large chunk of sugar, his tiny pinky, circled by a golden ring with a hawk, lifted delicately outward.

"So, the Magnificent Vashti," he says, settling back and twirling his spoon in his drink, as though he were playing a little musical instrument. "What a pleasure to have you alone at last."

"Vashti?" I ask in confusion. Surely he knows I don't speak Austrian?

"A goddess, indeed, and reputed to be the most beautiful woman in Persia. That, Madame, is who they are comparing you to, and I can confirm that their compliments are not misplaced."

"I see," I say politely, though I don't really. I'm not sure why anyone would compare me to a Persian. An awful thought strikes: Does he know about Madame Sultana? I blush. Stahremberg is still smiling at me but his little eyes don't crinkle.

"Madame, if you permit, I shall step straight to the point. I have something of much importance to discuss. You are aware of the details of our war, no doubt, Madame?"

"Of course. We are at war," I say gravely. "Against our enemies."

"Your enemies?"

"Yes, Austria and Prussia."

"Mmm, indeed, but now it is France and Austria together, against our common enemies, the Prussians and the English."

"But Austria is our enemy."

"Not now, Madame, not now. Surely you have heard of the

Treaty of Versailles, where our two countries vowed to unite as one?"

"Of course, Monsieur. *We are at war.*"

"Yes, but not with the Austrians."

"Indeed," I say politely. "But my husband is now in Salzburg."

"Exactly. You see . . ." He pauses and takes a small, delicate sip of his coffee, then raises his eyebrows at me: "My most honored Empress Maria Theresa is eager to know she has friends at the French court, *best friends* even."

"Oh yes?" I say doubtfully. I don't know why the Empress of Austria would want friends here; they are our enemies, after all.

"We all know that your Most Catholic Majesty depends highly on the counsel of his lady friends—again, his *best friends,* if you will—and for the empress, to be the friend of his friend would bring nothing but happiness to her heart. It is my duty to understand here, at Versailles, who is the friend of the past, and who is the friend of the future, and ensure that the friends of the future are greeted as warmly as the friends of the past."

All this talk of friends is a little confusing, and I tell him so.

The ambassador starts to explain, then closes his mouth firmly and looks down at his coffee cup, and sighs as though he has just thought of something very distressing. He stirs some more, though I am sure his sugar is dissolved by now. I am about to tell him so when he puts down his cup.

"But what a lovely coffee service this is! Handles on the cups in the new English style—most convenient," he says, then lifts up the sugar bowl from the tray. "And look at these divine little legs, the curled gold—exquisite."

"Yes, isn't it! It is a gift from the Maréchale de Mirepoix, from Sèvres. Sèvres is where porcelain grows," I explain. Suddenly there are more presents than I can count, and without even flirting!

"The Maréchale de Mirepoix? Indeed." Stahremberg tries to hide his astonishment, but he doesn't do a very good job. I wonder why he is surprised? Everyone wants to be my friend, now that the king loves me: that is only natural.

"And the pure green color—magnificent!" he says, turning back to the sugar bowl—why is he so interested in it? Perhaps they don't have sugar bowls in Austria? "The delicacy of the brushstrokes—beyond compare. As fine as the strings of a lyre."

"Mmm, yes, I suppose it is quite pretty."

"And just look at the shine and the sheen, so brilliant, like green glass almost, you see on the curve here . . ." We discuss the sugar bowl at some length, then Stahremberg rises to excuse himself, saying he has a touch of indigestion, brought on by the perfection of the coffee.

"Oh, certainly. But, sir, didn't you have something important you wanted to ask me?"

"I did, Madame, but I must thank you: you have answered every question I have, and many more besides," he says smoothly, and gives me an impossibly low bow.

He leaves and I turn quite pink with pride over my first diplomatic victory. I must find Argenson so I can tell him, again, how wrong he was about me!

A Letter
From the Desk of the Duchesse de Pompadour
Château de Bellevue
October 24, 1756

My dear Richelieu,

I send you greetings from Bellevue; I do so enjoy the countryside and the locals here are simply charming. One of the gardeners has the name Armand and I instantly thought of you, my dear Duc, as it is the same as your Christian name. He even looked like you—as short as a shrub!

I must offer you my condolences that Our Majesty declined your candidacy to lead the troops. I am confident we are in good hands with the Maréchal d'Estrées—such a mature man, faithful and loyal, guided only by his rational brain, and not by any other part of his anatomy. Besides, we must remember that your year as First Gentleman of the Bedchamber starts next January. Despite your success in Minorca, I believe your talents are better suited to handing the king his candle or his slippers, rather than leading men on the battlefield?

Thank you for your news of the Marquise de Coislin, though I had thought you better able to distinguish fact from rumor. But forgive me! You are growing old, and as one descends to second infancy such mistakes become all too common, I am afraid.

Well, I must end this letter to prepare for the evening's entertainment. We have six tables of cards for tonight and I hope I shall do well; a good gambler always knows when to fold or sit the game out. But you know that: you are an excellent gambler.

I will have the pleasure of seeing you back at Versailles next week.

I remain your humble and devoted servant,
The Duchesse de Pompadour

Chapter Sixty

Argenson is becoming impatient and insists I withhold my pleasures until she is firmly banished. It has already been a month, yet still the Marquise is here.

"And don't let him tickle the back of your neck," he barks sharply, his hooded eyes fixed on Diane's bulky chest, barely covered with an enormous white fichu.

Diane looks sheepish. "He asked," she mouths to me in apology.

"Now read this letter from the Prince de Conti."

I stare at the spindly scrawl, like a spider's web, I think, and shake my head. Argenson snatches back the letter—why is he being so hateful?—and reads aloud. "'And mind you keep your wits about you and do not let him stroke the back of your neck. Demand that he declare you. Everyone must know your love.'" Argenson finishes up with a grimace. "Do you understand? Conti will be back at Court next week and we must anticipate a good outcome to share with him."

"I don't want to see him," I say sullenly. "He's only going to scold me and I am not a child. I am the most powerful woman in France and the king loves me."

"I think you may be confusing the fine line between seduction and love," remarks Argenson tightly.

That night the king sends for me.

"Darling," he says as he comes to embrace me. I duck away before he can stroke the back of my neck.

"You must declare me. Everyone must know our love," I say nervously, backing away. I still feel a little uncertain in the king's presence; he is a very intelligent man, and of course he is the king.

"Indeed," he says, pulling me back toward him, one hand on the nape of my neck.

"No, not tonight," I say, though I do want to collapse into his arms. I love the way he tickles and strokes me, and I love the smell of his nightshirt, carnations mixed with musk.

"You are indisposed?"

"No, no, I am . . . I cannot . . ." I sigh, and so does he. "I must—I have certain conditions . . . to be met, I have met conditions," I stammer.

"I see, I see," he says, sighing. "Did not the ruby earrings Le Bel gave last week please you?

"Oh yes, they were lovely, they went perfectly with the gown I wore to the Marquise de Belzunce's dinner, you know, my crimson dress with the poppies . . ." I stop. I must remember Argenson's advice. "But I want more." Oh dear, that didn't sound very proper. It would be so much nicer if the king could just understand what I wanted, rather than me having to ask.

I stare at him and he stares back, but there is no such understanding.

"Well, you must do as you see fit, my dear. And I shall do as I see fit," the king says, getting up and ringing a bell. A footman appears.

"Get Le Bel," he says, "and my coat. I'm going for a walk."

"Oh, where are you going? I could come with you." I remember our romantic stroll in the gardens, all that talk of Greek and telescopes. The little teardrop in his eye. He might need comforting again.

"No, no. That would not be a good idea. I would be alone, take a time down in the town," he says, kissing me briefly on the cheek. "Let me know when you are feeling less . . ." But he doesn't finish his sentence.

I am left sitting on the bed, feeling a little empty and foolish. What am I to tell Argenson? I really don't want to see his squinched-up eyes when he looks at me in disapproval or stares at my chest, or any more of his lectures.

After that night I don't see the king for some days, and now he has traveled to Bellevue to join the Marquise and I am not invited.

"Plumbing issues," he told me before he left, stopping by to see me in my apartment. "Something you would not understand, my dear."

⁂

"Well, the game is up," announces Conti, throwing open the doors to Diane's apartment. He bows to Argenson but ignores Montbarrey and me. Conti returned to Court last week, having decided that his disapproval was sufficiently registered. I wish he weren't here; I don't want any more lectures.

"She's a crafty one, a sly one, we must give her some credit," Conti continues, kicking over a small chair. Oh! I bristle with pride, thinking he is talking of me. Soon, however, it becomes clear he is referring to the Marquise.

"Look at this letter, supposedly from a 'Monsieur Robert.' My men have checked and he shall have our eternal enmity, but he counts on the Marquise lasting, as all foolish men do." Conti takes a letter from his pocket and unfolds it. "We know the prurient interest His Majesty takes in his subjects' letters, and this one was no doubt planted by the Marquise, and shown to the king by Janelle in the Post Office."

"Is Janelle not with us?"

"No, he is not; the man is frustratingly immune to even the most persuasive of arguments, or money."

The two men are ignoring me, making me nervous. And what does *prurient* mean? I have a sudden sense of foreboding.

"Let me read aloud the salient lines," says Conti. He stalks around the room, occasionally kicking something, and reads: " 'A mistress is a necessity, we the French can accept that . . . The Pompadour is the finest example of a French flower, a compliment to her . . .' Dah dah, more along those lines . . . then here: 'The indiscreet silliness of the girl they call the Vashti lowers the majesty of France.' "

I—lower the majesty of France? How hateful. I open my mouth to defend myself, but Argenson stops me with a raised hand. Montbarrey stiffens and comes to stand by me, ready to defend my honor. Dear Montbarrey. Perhaps *he* will be my minister of war, not foul Argenson.

"You know how he hates to be embarrassed in front of his subjects, and overly cares for their opinion," says Conti to Argenson, who nods in agreement. "Though little good it does him."

"I knew this was doomed from the beginning," says Argenson. "I should never have involved myself, debased myself . . ."

"Great sirs," says Montbarrey, standing erect beside my chair and clicking his heels together, one anxious little hand on my shoulder, "I do not like the defeat I hear in your voice, nor the disrespect implied to my sister."

"And who is this miniature man?" asks Conti in irritation.

"A brother-in-law, I think," replies Argenson.

"She has no end to useful advisers, does she?" says Conti, shaking his head. He shoo-shoos Montbarrey, who backs away in lockstep with each shoo. When he deems Montbarrey sufficiently close to the door he turns back to Argenson and continues: "The best of generals, my man, knows when to surrender. He has said she must go before he returns from Bellevue, that much is decided."

Are they talking about me? Go? Where? I look between the two men, but still no one is looking at me, or addressing me.

Argenson sighs. "That woman has the staying power of a barnacle. If this weren't 1756, I would accuse her of witchcraft."

The Prince de Conti kicks over one last chair, then stops in front of me and bows formally. "Madame de Mailly de Coislin, I must make known to you the king's pleasure. His Majesty requests you to leave Versailles and retire to Paris. At least for a while." He takes a sealed letter from his pocket and hands it to me.

They might call me silly, but I know what the letter is. The king is telling me to leave. This is . . . this is . . .

"Now, now, go and enjoy a few months there," Conti says,

more kindly than he has ever said anything to me. "You still have—ah—friends at Court and none can tell the future."

I burst into tears and flee down the hall away from Diane's rooms. As I go I hear the Court reveling in my humiliation.

"Came in as a child, going out as a child."

"Don't you mean whore, not child?"

"I know the expression is a nine days' wonder, but a thirty days' wonder also has a nice ring to it, don't you think?"

"She lasted less time than it took to wear out my new pair of slippers."

On the way to my room I collide with a servant carrying an enormous basket of candle ends. They clatter on the floor around me as I sink down in defeat. He wants me to go, I think ever so sadly between my sobs. He wants me to go. *She* wants me to go. I knew she was my enemy, that kitten play at charades—I just *knew* it. I wail and try to get up, but slip and tumble once more over the candle ends, then collapse in defeat.

My mother rides back in the carriage with me to Paris, mopping my tears and holding my head to her breast.

"Dearest, you'll be happier in Paris, away from this world. Your father and I have arranged for you to visit Marie-Stéphanie down in Châtillon; now, how would you like that?"

I sniff. It has been rather a long time since I have seen my friend; she rarely comes to Paris. But no—"I want the king," I wail. "I am so embarrassed. Mother! They said I was like a child. And Conti said I lowered the majesty of France. Well, not Conti, but some awful man who wrote it in a letter and the king read it and agreed!"

"Now, shhh, dear. You know that cruel words are just the wallpaper of that palace," she says, rocking me in rhythm to the motion of the carriage. She holds me close and I snuffle at her breast—sometimes being a child is nice. "In truth, I am glad you will no longer be there."

"They said I was a thirty-day wonder, and I don't even know what that means," I wail, letting out a huge hiccup.

"Yes, dear. But you like Châtillon, and I will write and tell my mother to visit you there; she might even bring you a new winter dress—now wouldn't you like that?"

"Yes," I say, wiping my tears.

The next week my tears are further dried by the present of a pair of shoes with a note from the king, in memory of our good times, and the offer of a house. I sit up in astonishment. Oh! My own house?

Entr'acte

The Duchesse de Pompadour

1756

Sometimes I feel my life is like that of one of those early Christian saints so beloved by our queen—perpetual combat. I am not yet thirty-five, but feel fifty. Marie-Anne, that stupid child, was banished on Saint Cecilia's Day, and as I assisted the queen in her devotional Mass, I reflected on that dear saint's life: endless persecution, torture, multiple execution attempts, the whole world against her.

He sent the child packing; my ruse with the letter worked. That giggling girl is gone but I know *she* will never be gone, the shadowy form of the mistress of years to come, my constant companion and constant threat. I carve an *MA* on a piece of jade and think of the other Marie-Anne, the Duchesse de Châteauroux. I haven't thought of her in years; even the strongest of ghosts must eventually fade. I have to admit that stupid child was interesting to look at, with her slanted, vacuous blue eyes and her rosebud mouth. Frannie told me that to look at her was to look at the first Marie-Anne.

I throw the jade into the fishbowl, violently, startling the serenity of the fish.

I cannot go on like this; I cannot. Yes, I would die away from Louis, in more ways than one, but I cannot live with the sword of Damocles constantly over my head. Enough.

He comes to me, as he always does; he is traveling on to Fontainebleau tomorrow but I will stay awhile here and rest. He sits on the bed beside me, but I don't caress his hands or comfort him, and when he talks of his discontent with the Maréchal d'Estrées, leading our troops, I offer him no comfort or words to soothe.

For the first time I regard him with something akin to coldness. He is recalcitrant, as he is when he knows he has done wrong; his eyes sheepish, the head slightly bowed. But I've seen it all before, and I do not want to see it again.

There is silence, and he sighs, pulls at his wig, and contemplates the new toilette table I have installed by the window.

"A fine piece," he remarks. "What is that wood? It is not mahogany, I think."

"Ebony," I say curtly. I take a deep breath. "I would leave, Louis. I would go away. I will retire to Bellevue or to a convent." My voice catches and I remember when I was younger, how intricately I planned such scenes. Not anymore; I am not onstage this time.

He shakes his head but does not speak.

"I cannot live like this! I cannot. These stupid girls, these plots. You must release me!"

I see he is shocked by the coldness in my voice, and I feel the old sympathy return, the desire to coddle and comfort. I bite my lip, harder than usual, and taste vermillion mixed with blood.

He gets up and wanders around, stares for a while more at the ebony table by the window.

"You mean so much to me," he says finally.

"I want to leave."

"No, you cannot . . . you cannot . . ." He stammers and grows red, can't continue. Here is a man who has spent his life shutting out the world. It pleases him greatly to be impenetrable. I know him best of any on this earth but still I don't know him, and perhaps I never will.

We stay frozen in silence awhile, and I realize I am holding my breath. Is this what I want? I start crying, small silent sobs, so wretched and undecided. All I want is peace. Why won't they let me be?

He comes to the bed and pulls me up, suddenly decisive and

firm. He embraces me and my stomach cleaves: it has been so long since I have felt his arms around me. "Dearest, you mean so much to me. You will never leave. Ever. You have my word."

I exhale and try to hold back the tears. A promise, words so long desired they have grown almost rotten with age.

"You have my promise," he whispers again, and holds me tighter.

I pull back and wipe my eyes. "You say that, Louis, but then . . . then something—someone—will change your mind."

"No," he says fiercely. "No, I will never let you go, or send you away. Be assured of that, dearest, please. I give you my word."

The promise I have been craving for years. His words should comfort me, but I can scarcely believe them. Only the naked look on his face gave me some assurance, and that night I sleep well, clinging to that part of my faith in him that is still alive.

Act VI

Duchesse

Chapter Sixty-One

I t is a cold, evil winter and the Court retreats to the Trianon, cozier and easier to heat than Versailles.

We leave behind an empty palace, as dreary and forlorn as the New Year. Only Madame Victoire, the king's third daughter, remains, sick in bed. Louis kisses me goodbye and says he is going to visit her, then spend the night in town. I wish him well and remind him of the state council the next day.

Then, the end, and the cruel reminder that rivals do not only come in human form.

A crazed madman, the incarnation of all the discomfort of the times. One fanatic who thought that by striking at the king, he could strike at the heart of all that ails our country.

Damiens attacked as the king was leaving Versailles that January afternoon, under the portico at the entrance to the Marble Court. He was hatted in the presence of the king, a strict breach of etiquette that instantly raised suspicion, but before the guards could arrest him . . . his knife pierced the king's coat right where his heart was and Louis, my darling, adored and flawed Louis, fell on the steps, the shadows of the winter dusk adding to the confusion and mayhem.

The news came to us at the Trianon that the king had been assassinated and all immediately set out for Versailles. The road was lined with carriages racing against the spreading night, some travelers alighting and running along on foot, conscious of the glorious spectacle of grief they presented.

Time quickly revealed that the king is not dead, but bleeding and in mortal danger. My relief is extreme, but so is my grief. I want nothing more than to see him, to cool his brow and kiss his lips, stanch his wound with the force of my love. But that is denied me as his family takes charge and Versailles closes around its king. I think of Marie-Anne, the first one, of how she barricaded herself in the sickroom at Metz. Here, such an action is unthinkable.

Back in my rooms, fires are hurriedly lit and friends and foe alike descend to comfort and gloat. By virtue of his profession my dear Quesnay has the entrée to the sick chamber and he acts as the lifeline between my rooms and the king's, providing updates as the crisis unfolds.

"The bed where he lies is without linen; the stewards were not ready for him to spend the night. Comfortable sheets are of the utmost urgency."

An anxious hour later: "His daughters Mesdames Adélaïde and Sophie arrived, and upon seeing their father lying on a bed without a sheet, a bare mattress in fact, they fainted dead away. And there was blood too," he adds, almost as an afterthought.

The moon unfurls over the palace and candles glisten in every window. Quesnay tells us that in the crush outside the king's bedchamber the Comte de Vivonne tore his coat, and one of the king's valets has gone mad with grief. "Then the queen arrived and she fainted, and had to be carried away. Madame Victoire, still on her sickbed, insisted on being carried to her father but the doctors forbade it and so she fainted, but in her own room."

Later: "The sheets have been replaced and the king rests comfortably. The wound is light, but poison is feared." Poison. The room sways then disappears, and when I open my eyes I am on the carpet, Nicole fanning me and my friend Mirie stroking my wrist as though I were one of her rabbits.

Then Quesnay brings the worst news of all. He takes my hand and kneels before me: "The king has requested his confessor." My blood runs colder than the dawning day outside. Those are the words I most fear, for a priest will force the king to relinquish all evidence of his sinful life; he will have to relinquish *me*.

"Did he mention me?" I whisper. Quesnay looks uncomfortable, his wig askew and tatty, his neckpiece soaked from tears.

"No, Madame, nothing like that."

Relief or just a reprieve?

The weak January sun rises over a changed world and we hear that the doctors have declared the king out of danger and the dagger unpoisoned. Louis' heavy coat sheltered him from the worst of the blade—a thick jacket padded with fox hair I had specially ordered for him.

Quickly the interrogation of the madman Damiens begins. Hearsay abounds about the heinous seed that attacked our king:

"Enraged by the parliamentarians!"

"In the sway of the Jesuits!"

"He said to beware the dauphin. Most surprised, really—one doesn't expect intrigue or plots from pudding."

"More heavenly fire raining down on this Sodom that is Versailles—no, no, not my opinion: I heard it from my priest."

Damiens worked for a member of Parlement and heard his master's discontent with the king. Somewhere in his addled brain he thought that to remove the king would be to remove the greatest obstacle to the happiness of France.

With the king out of danger, his family encircles him in a stranglehold of love. Frannie, as part of Madame Adélaïde's household, replaces Quesnay as my lifeline to the room where the center of my world lies in melancholy.

He doesn't send for me. No word for three days while I occupy the curious space between the living and the dead. I receive all those who come and visit, curiosity painted on their faces as clearly as their rouge. I do not put on an elegant face. Everyone knows my precarious situation and why bother to hide it in front of the carping courtiers, vultures in another guise?

"Oh, my darling, what a sad, sad day for you."

"Three days now? Four? No word, no word at all! Whatever is he thinking? And what are *you* thinking?"

"One look at your hair shows me you are destroyed, simply destroyed, by grief."

Every day that passes without word is a day closer to my banishment. And if banished, I decide, I will never return to Versailles. Never, no matter how he may beg and plead.

I wait, seven agonizing days. Forgotten, oblivion, the void of an empty plain.

"Never, never have I seen a man so melancholy. And unshaven," says Frannie, shaking her head, her eyes full of sympathy. "They say the wound is healed, but not the heart." I understand completely: to have a subject turn against him would be Louis' greatest sorrow. Frannie tells me the king sees his confessor every day. Perhaps my greatest rival of all is God, and the mortal fear of death and sin. Against that, his promise means nothing.

On the seventh day, Machault comes in with a face as grave as a churchyard. He bows and I dispatch everyone from the room.

"It is with no pleasure at all, Madame, that I come with my news." Machault's face is solemn but his eyes, curiously bright and darting, cannot meet mine. I thought I was prepared, but I am not.

"It would be best if you left, my lady. It is how the king would wish." As he delivers the cruel blow, Machault's eyes are fixed on his stained cuffs—a lack of care for appearance is taken as a sign of good grief. He is sad for me, I think, and without my protection—what is his future?

"Thank you, my dear friend," I say, my voice surprisingly steady. The uncertainty is over; his will is known and it will be done. I am a subject like any other, my fate in the hands of a capricious master. "Thank you. I will make the necessary arrangements."

For a while after he leaves I sit in my favorite window seat, look beyond the parterre to a row of towering yews, now covered in snow. He'll gain some popularity from this, I think, watching a sudden swirl of small birds fleeing the bushes. A brush with death, a hated mistress banished; we are in 1744 and the aftermath of Metz once again. The people will love him for this.

And so I am to leave this cruel palace where I have known the greatest of sorrows and the greatest of triumphs. The worst of dreams, the best of nightmares. What I have feared for so many years has now come to pass. And so I must go.

I rise and smooth my robe with my hands, the soft velvet assuring me that I am alive, and that I can feel.

"Nicole, have Collin bring in the trunks from town. We will start packing."

&

Mirie bustles in, without a rabbit.

"What are you doing?" she demands.

I stare at her wordlessly as Nicole and the other women continue bringing my dresses out, the four trunks open like gaping mouths to swallow my happiness.

"Stop. Immediately."

Nicole pauses, holding a pile of pink winter furs. I sit down on the sofa and begin to cry quietly.

"Jeanne, Jeanne." Mirie is beside me, the warm scent of honeysuckle cradling me. I have a friend, I think, then I sob even louder.

"Who wins at the card table?" demands Mirie, her little hand gripping my wrist.

I shake my head, unable to reply.

"The one who wins is the one who stays at the table. If you leave, you'll never win. Stay, and you have a chance."

I think of Marie-Anne, the second one, the stupid one, her arch blue eyes mocking me over her hand of kings. *I have only kings*, she said in my dreams and in my nightmares. I hate cards, but I did win there.

"Perhaps." I agree with Mirie but my voice is sad and small.

"Stop this packing. You go only if the king tells you to, and not a moment before."

"But Machault—"

"You cannot trust Machault."

"Machault is a fr—"

"No, he isn't. Believe me." She gets up, pulls a creamy lace robe from one of the chests, and throws it down over the parquet. "Stop, now! And wait for word from the king."

I submit, a leaf in the river, heading toward a pond or a waterfall, who knows? As the women unpack the trunks, I remember Machault's uneasiness, the slight embarrassment, those darting eyes that could not meet mine. So, not a friend, even though he owes everything he is to me. Should I be surprised?

Quesnay agrees with Mirie. "The fox, Madame, the fox. Was to dine with other animals and a fine spread was laid. The fox then persuaded his guests that their enemies were coming. The other animals fled, and he enjoyed the supper by himself, and all the more."

"Machault is the fox," whispers Mirie as the men come to return my trunks, empty now, to my house in town.

But still, no word. Which is worse: this oblivion he has consigned me to, or banishment? He stays in his room, every afternoon closeted with his confessor, every evening with his wife and children.

Then one night as Madame Adélaïde's ladies turned to leave with their mistress, he put his hand on Frannie's shoulder.

"Stay awhile," he said, and when they were alone he took her cloak, wrapped it around himself, and made his way down to my rooms.

I never knew what turned his mind, but when I saw him all my worries melted away. The thin crowd in my room melted away too, but at the appearance of the king they excused themselves with more politeness than they had shown all week.

I was a tangle: no makeup, my hair loosely pinned, but I had on a clean robe and a warm smile, and that was all that he needed.

Here was a man who needed mending, who needed to be stitched whole again. I embraced him tightly and we sat together until the candles guttered and the room descended into darkness. I unbuttoned his shirt to run my fingers over the wound. I traced the bandage, so small yet so close to his heart.

He clutched my hand and began to speak at last: "Oh my darling. My dearest. Such a betrayal. The doctors say the wound is light, but it is still a wound. Made by one of my own subjects, my own children."

I hold his hands and murmur the comfort he needs to hear.

"Why?" he asks in a sorrowful voice. "Why? Why would he wish me dead?"

"No! Put no merit on that man's actions; he is a madman, his brain addled by Satan." I convince the king, as I am convinced myself, that Damiens acted on nothing more than his own delusions. A week of the worst torture has not revealed otherwise. "Do not listen to your family," I say firmly. "You must listen to me, my dearest. Put him from your mind, and concentrate on your kingdom and your subjects who love you, and not on the actions of a solitary madman."

Louis kisses me tenderly on the mouth, and when he draws back, I know he is mine again. By the next day things are as normal and the great palace creaks back to life with me, again, at its center.

Quesnay tells me later that the doctors were amazed at his improvement, but I was not: the greatest tonic of all is friendship and love, one single conversation with a good friend worth more than the strongest medicine.

The whole affair is best left forgotten. I invite Louis to Bellevue for a few days and amuse him with a new mechanical table installed in the dining room, which brings food directly up from the kitchens.

"No need for servants!" he gasps in delight. "In this room, at least. Such privacy! Not even a footman, though I suppose some help turning the handle might be required."

I beam and pass him a sheet of paper and a quill. "Request what you will, dearest, and we will send it down. Then we wait, until the food appears."

"Like magic," says Louis, shaking his head in admiration. "This modern world! What do I have a craving for? Something light." He pauses, looks blank. "Perhaps a chicken, quartered?"

"Not quartered," I say hastily. "A half would be best, or even a whole."

"Indeed," agrees the king, happily scribbling away. "I shall request it with lemon and rosemary—no, with tarragon? Which would be best, dearest?"

From Gabrielle de Beauvau-Craon, Duchesse de Mirepoix
Place de Grève, Paris
March 30, 1757

Dear Jeanne,

It is done. A horrible sight and one I hope never to see again. The wretch was tortured with pincers and molten lead, then torn by four horses, then six were needed for the final quartering—the poor horses, they must have been exhausted! The crowds were enormous; I watched with a group hosted by Soubise in the Place de Grève—window seats renting for twenty *louis*! It took four dreadful hours; Frannie fainted and I must confess a bloody thigh still visits me in my dreams.

It was simply barbaric. Certainly, the king's body is sacred and any attempt against it deserves the highest punishment, but still . . . this is not 1610, the last time such a deed was done. Surely this is not who we are?

Enough. I am embarrassed by my ghoulish interest in the matter. If the king inquires, tell him I was visiting my brother Beauvau in Paris. At supper last night all agreed: the man was a lone fanatic and not in the sway of the Parlement or the dauphin—so hard to imagine that plump pudding intriguing! That reminds me, we had the most divine plum pudding; surprising, since Soubise's chef is an Englishman.

Back on Tuesday.

Much love,
Mirie

Chapter Sixty-Two

In the aftermath of the assassination attempt, the king enjoyed a brief spurt of popularity that was bittersweet, for it reminded him of what he once enjoyed and has now lost, seemingly forever. There have been too many scandals; too many mistresses; too much war and economic hardship; and too many lives of misery and humiliation for him to ever be redeemed. It started when he went back on his deathbed confession at Metz, and continued over the last decade. I too am blamed, of course, but I long ago learned to ignore the public squawking that continues no matter what I do.

This spring the Court is vandalized with upside-down fleurs-de-lis, broken crowns, obscene pamphlets littering the palace like feathers burst from an old and angry mattress. Anonymous letters flow into Versailles, saying that it should have been the king who was dismembered, calling Damiens a hero who acted for France. When the police and my spies brief me, I tremble inside. Sometimes it seems as though the country is driving fast down a road that leads to the wrong destination, the carriage too far gone to ever turn around.

Argenson insists on showing the king the worst of the letters, hoping to render the king ever more fragile and dependent. I appoint myself Louis' protector, yet another of the roles I must play. I sense a showdown coming and I return Argenson's brazenness with my own. I have faced the worst and yet still I emerge victorious: if my enemies won't give up, then they shall be vanquished.

"The king does not need to see this," I say firmly, holding the poisonous letter.

"It is my duty to keep the king abreast of all that transpires in this kingdom, now more than ever," says Argenson pompously. His eyes creep down my bodice for the merest second before flitting back to my face, with a quickness I find oddly insulting.

He does not rise from his desk and I sit down without an invitation. I am reminded of that scene with Maurepas, so many years ago, the white flowers and the smirking impudence. They say he is spending his exile in Bourges composing poetry, and possibly some of these letters.

"Not only is it my duty, it is my job," Argenson continues smugly. He believes that by frightening the king he will increase his position and importance. My spies tell me he wrote last week to Elisabeth, and promised her they would be together again soon.

Yes, you will be together, but not in the way that you would wish, I think grimly. I notice in distaste his heavy, overcurled wig that has draped his dark coat with flecks of powder. Not for the first time I think what an ugly man he is, both inside and out.

"You will not show this letter to the king."

"Ah, but, Madame, I will."

"How is this to help a man shattered in spirit? 'The time is coming, King, when the wrath of Heaven will rain . . . rage? down upon . . .' I can't read this last word, but you can imagine the rest of the sentence. I am taking this."

Argenson raises his eyebrows. "You may take it, Madame, but you must know there are many more like it. You cannot hold the king in ignorance forever. He is not a plant, to be watered and sheltered by you."

Oh, but there you are wrong, I think as I whisk the offending letter away with me. I go straight to the King's Apartments and motion for the papal envoy to leave. I don't need an update from Rome as much as I need the king's undivided attention.

"Once again, I prove to you, Argenson does not have your best interests at heart," I say, showing him the letter.

"I must know, all of them, not just that one man," says Louis, his hand shaking slightly as he reads. "How can Heaven rage down upon me? Such lies, such hatred." His voice is sad and small; last week I urged him, subtly and with some finesse, to resume his nights in town. He must have some joy in his life and Le Bel tells me there is a new girl, a dancer from the Opéra, who is entertaining him well.

"Berryer has confirmed for me that this letter is a forgery." I don't know whether it is, but that is beside the point. "Argenson delights in increasing your fright and fear; indeed, he probably wrote it himself. I have had enough of him."

"I know you do not approve of him, my darling, a fact which pains me to no end." Louis sighs. We have had many such conversations recently. "But we need experienced men such as him. It would be impolitic in this time of war to dismiss such a great man."

I stifle a snort but can't keep the impatience from my voice. "He is *not* a great man. Remember, it was you and I who orchestrated the alliance with Austria; only Bernis and Stainville helped. Argenson was as much in the dark as a chimney sweep. We don't need him."

"He is my friend."

"He is not your friend! Fox. A fox."

Louis sighs and looks to his fingernails for succor; the wound to his heart has only increased his indecisiveness.

"You cannot be surrounded by men that wish you ill. A dagger or a letter, can you not see they are both the weapons of men that seek to undermine?"

Some more prodding and eventually he does see. Away rides Argenson, with Machault beside him. Machault knew his days were numbered from the moment the king came to my apartment, and he goes without a murmur. Argenson boards a carriage to his lands in Touraine, safely in the farthest circle of oblivion, vowing he will be back. I decide that Elisabeth may join her ex-lover there; more punishment for him, really.

A garnet with an *A* and a topaz with an *M* join their brothers and sisters at the bottom of the fishbowl. It's getting rather full in there, I think, then look sadly at the piece of plain stone carved with a *D,* for Damiens.

From Louis-François-Armand de Vignerot du Plessis, Duc de
  Richelieu
Brunswick, Lower Saxony
October 2, 1757

My dear Marquise,

Were I at Versailles I would press upon you—hard—that to question
the king's judgment is tantamount to treason. Let us not add that sin
to the already capacious list of your blunders. If the king has decided
I shall replace your dear Maréchal d'Estrées, whose worth you judged
incorrectly, then you must concede to his wishes. War and wisdom are
two areas where women should never meddle.

An anecdote from the front, which I know you will find amusing:
our enemy Frederick of Prussia has named his dog after you. A
mangier bitch one could not imagine, and apparently it is a mutt,
of no lineage or pedigree. Though the Prussians are our enemies, I
consider them a most cultured race.

I must retire to sleep; the glory of France is on my accomplished
shoulders and I am sure you would not wish to distract me from my
duties and future glory.

I remain ever, your faithful and obedient servant,
Richelieu

From Étienne-François de Stainville, Comte de Stainville
Vienna, Austria
February 28, 1758

My dearest Marquise,

It was with great joy that I received your letter and the news of my recall to France. To be minister of foreign affairs would be a great honor and I am confident that together, we will guide France and the king through this vexing war. I trust the embarrassment of my cousin Rosalie's intrigue is sufficiently far in the past and will not be a hindrance to my relationship with His Majesty.

I shall be on the road by summer. I bring from the empress herself a gift for you: a magnificent writing desk. The empress speaks highly of you and takes seriously your advice. Most fitting, I contend, for you are the two most powerful women in Europe.

I understand the Austrian alliance is still unpopular in France but I am sure our eventual victory against England and Prussia will show the common man the wisdom of the treaty. On that matter, I was shocked by the replacement of the Maréchal d'Estrées with the Duc de Richelieu, and the news from the front is most concerning. My sources tell me the man was accepting bribes from Frederick of Prussia? Making illegal treaties with the British? Encouraging looting and rape as though we were Hungarians?

An immoral man, concerned only about his own aggrandizement and, if I may be so indelicate, his prick. Let us hope these latest outrages will be sufficient to wean His Majesty from him, but I fear the duke is like a venomous, jumping toad: he always bounces back.

Until June, dear Marquise.
Stainville

Chapter Sixty-Three

A glorious August day. Strong sun, a breeze as soft as a feather, the birds chirping and the insects buzzing.

"*Allez!*" cries the Duc de Burgundy, swinging his miniature sword at a stuffed dove on a string, dangled from a stick by an equerry. The dauphin's eldest son is almost eight years old, a lively and handsome boy.

"*Ayez,*" lisps his younger brother, the little Duc de Berry, stumbling slowly after Burgundy as the man with the stick yanks the dove ever higher. Two cats join the chase, clawing at the white bird as it leaps through the air.

Madame Victoire follows, with another of the dauphin's children—the little Duc de Provence, only three—clutching at her hand. A fourth boy is still in the cradle and the dauphine is pregnant yet again: the Bourbon succession is stronger than it has ever been.

We are in the gardens of the Trianon, a perfect retreat on the grounds of Versailles, only a quick carriage ride from the palace. Louis and I sit in armchairs placed on the grass beyond the more formal gardens, Louis with his feet up on a stool. The lawn is a lush carpet of green surrounded by great beds of flowers, chosen for their scent—myrtles, jasmine, gardenia. At the foot of the grass a small pond lies serene and waiting, the blue of the water mirroring the brilliant sky above.

A footman comes out with a plate of ducks' eggs, boiled to perfection. I take one and shell it for Louis. Little Berry loses interest in the bird and toddles over to us. I shell an egg for him too, but he only squeezes it in his chubby hand and throws it down. He patters back to see his aunt Victoire, now comforting little

Provence, who has fallen over and is crying on the grass. A white cat sniffs in disinterest at the messy egg on the ground, then leaps up onto Louis' lap.

I watch Louis enjoy his egg and savor the moment, here in this beautiful garden, surrounded by his family. I smile at him. "Do you remember," I say, picking up a piece of eggshell, "when I first came to Versailles, how I would crack the egg against my saucer?"

He laughs. "I do indeed. And now look at you, my love, topping the egg perfectly with a knife. Such impeccable manners; one could imagine you a princess of the blood."

"I speared it!" declares Burgundy, his little face flushed with triumph, coming over to his grandfather for approval. "You missed it, but if it was a real one it would be *dead*."

"It would indeed be dead, Monsieur," agrees his tutor, the Duc de La Vauguyon, watching from a respectful distance.

"Just like his grandpapa," observes Louis in satisfaction. "We'll be welcoming you at the hunt soon enough." Louis tousles his grandson's head and the boy takes off again, his sword drawn, running back to the dove with a slightly lopsided gait.

"Like his grandfather," I repeat, and it is true—while his father, the dauphin, is a solid, placid man, little Burgundy resembles his grandfather, both physically and in spirit. Alas, his younger brother Berry looks to be another pudding; cruel puns on blueberry jelly and blackberry custard often make the rounds.

Louis frowns, following Burgundy as he again begins his pursuit of the bird. "That limp—I would have another report from the doctors."

"Don't worry so," I say lightly, swatting a wasp away from his wig. A butterfly flutters hopefully around his waistcoat, embroidered with roses. "He's an active boy. A little fall from his rocking horse is nothing to worry about."

"Mmmm. I hope you are right, my dear, as always. What a glorious day." Louis settles back in contentment and strokes the cat on his lap. Earlier we enjoyed a simple lunch of cheese and peaches in the coolness of the marble rooms, followed by this

somnolent afternoon resting in the warmth of the day. No hunting today; an outbreak of rabies has struck the kennels, and Louis
must content himself with a partridge shoot. Later—his men are
oiling the rifles—but for now we are suspended in the peace of
the garden.

I treasure hours such as these, tucked away from the unhappy
realities of the outside world. The war against England and Prussia grinds on, our early wins eclipsed by a string of defeats that
threaten to make 1759 one of the worst in French memory. We
are fighting in our colonies in North America, in Asia, in Africa,
and of course closer to home in Europe, and suffering heavy defeats everywhere.

I sell some of my houses—including my beloved Bellevue,
back to the Crown—and join the throngs of citizens who deliver
their silver and gold for the war effort.

Last year Stainville—now elevated as the Duc de Choiseul—
replaced Bernis as minister of foreign affairs. In the wake of Argenson's departure I recalled Bernis from Venice to replace him,
but I quickly saw his aptitude was not for politics. He is now a
cardinal, a decent consolation prize.

With Stainville—Choiseul—in charge, I am sure we will
eventually turn the tide of war in our favor. He is an excellent
minister, intelligent and astute. He has his enemies—he is determined to reform the Church, and he shrewdly sees that we must
compromise with Parlement: the days of their unquestioning obe-
dience to their monarch are over. I have come to rely on him more
and more, and no longer feel the whole weight of the kingdom
on my shoulders.

I smile at Louis and shell him another egg. I watch him as
he chews on it, his eyes following the little boys at their play.
How proud he is of them, and how much happiness they bring
him. Madame Victoire—silly, sweet Victoire—hands over young
Provence, still wailing from his fall, to one of the nurses and takes
the dove on the string from the man. She dangles it in front of
Berry, giving the younger boy a chance.

"Wonderful, *mon petit*," we hear her say as Berry thrusts his little sword at the immobile dove, almost falling over with the effort.

"But I hit it when it was flying fast and I jumped like this!" announces his elder brother Burgundy, leaping for their edification.

"Poor Victoire," says Louis suddenly, shaking his head.

"Mmm," I murmur. I wonder what he means, but don't ask; he likes his secrets, and I let him have them. His four unmarried daughters are still at Versailles. Any marriage plans that might have been, are not, and now they form an odd court of aging crows led by Madame Adélaïde, who is almost thirty years old. Louis sees them every day—his closeness with them ebbs and flows but his routine remains—and I feel they are finally warming to me. Somewhat.

Madame Infanta, the king's eldest daughter and once my well-oiled enemy, is also at Versailles on the same fatuous pretext, but now she has become a friend. She hopes the spoils from this war will give her and her husband more than Parma, and she knows my influence could help decide her future.

Two footmen advance bearing a toy ship, made of cork, which they set down grandly at the edge of the pond. They bow in perfect unison as Burgundy rushes over to launch it—yes, his limp is rather pronounced. The boy pushes it off into the water and watches for a moment before losing interest and returning to his pursuit of the stuffed dove.

On the water two ducks glide curiously over to the ship and circle it. How peaceful they are, I think, admiring them as another one floats over to join them. Of course, they are paddling underneath but the outward appearance is one of serenity and calmness. I swat away a fly and chuckle: I am like those ducks, working away furiously, while on the surface showing only my serene face.

Though my old fears of dismissal have receded somewhat, I must still be vigilant, on my guard, ready for the next rival to rear her head. There was one hiccup this year—the Little Queen, Morphise, was widowed and returned to Paris. She was soon pregnant, and rumors said it was the king's. I married her off quickly, to a cousin of Uncle Norman, and she followed her new husband to his appointment in Reims. I thought about attending the wedding, but the memory of our meeting in Fontainebleau, when she mocked me with her gorgeous eyes and round belly, is still not banished from my mind.

Through Le Bel I continue to keep a sharp eye on the girls in the town house. There are also Court ladies, here and there, none lasting more than a few weeks and without powerful factions behind them. My fishbowl is ever more full of gems and stones: just last month I carved an *H,* and before that a *VC.*

"Finish this, my love," Louis says, handing me his half-eaten egg. He stretches and closes his eyes, turns his face upward to bask in the sun. As he does the years fall away and I see the handsome man I fell in love with, almost fifteen years ago, and remember the dizzying depths of our love that can still make me cry at the memory.

But now . . . we are like an old married couple. Though I may not have the security of marriage vows, I have the security of our years of love and friendship, and of his promise. And though I still adore Louis, I am more aware of his faults. I was blind when I was younger, but now I know that he is but a man: shy, indecisive, enthralled by pleasures. I know who he is, and who he is not. And that, perhaps, is love.

"I wonder if Dubois has finished preparing the guns," I say to him. "Shall I ask the man to check?"

Louis shakes his head and reaches for my hand, then leans back and closes his eyes again. "No, there is no hurry. This garden is most pleasant, and I have no desire to move."

I gently squeeze his hand and watch Madame Victoire crouching down by little Berry, holding up a worm for his inspection. She smiles at him and hugs him; the shy, awkward boy beams back in pleasure, then quickly drops the worm as Burgundy comes barreling toward them with his sword, calling out that he wants to spear it.

I am happy, I think suddenly. Happy. Still paddling furiously under the surface, but this is where I want to be. I wish I could stay like this forever with Louis, in this garden of the afternoon of our lives, holding hands, surrounded by his family and the future, at peace and content. How I would like to capture this moment, in a painting or a sculpture, to preserve it against the coming changes of time.

Chapter Sixty-Four

L e Bel found her in Grenoble, recommended by her sister. The daughter of a respectable bourgeois, she insists on her own house on the outskirts of Paris, close to the king's hunting lodge at La Muette. Le Bel made the procurement without consulting me, a fact that constantly brushes my mind with little wings of unease.

All and sundry ensure that I understand just how remarkable this young woman is.

"An animated statue—taller by a head than all the other women! A Helen, an Aphrodite!"

"Her raven hair extends to the ground, a feat all the more incredible given her height."

"I had thought your complexion fine, Marquise, or at least it was, but then, to see her skin . . . well . . ."

"A veritable Ama . . . Ama . . . what is it they call those large ladies from Brazil? Amateurs? Amarettos? No, that's a drink, surely?"

Her name is Anne Couppier de Romans, and it seems Louis is as much in love with her as it is possible for him to be. When she gives birth to a son I am ready to do naming duties but then Le Bel informs me that the king has already chosen a name for the child: Louis-Aimé de Bourbon.

Three words to worry on, for the king has never taken much interest in his bastards, which multiply every year. Two last year; goodness knows how many more this year. All are named by me and parceled out to convents and schools, sometimes their mothers alongside them, wildly content with their little pensions and their diamond hair brooches.

But now this name—Louis-Aimé de Bourbon—is like a declaration of paternity. Rumors abound that he will be legitimizing the child; that Mademoiselle de Romans will soon move into the palace and replace me, next week if not by midsummer; that the king is madly in love with both the mother and the child. Apparently she calls her son Monseigneur, as though the real child of a king, and her conceit knows no boundaries.

"Tosh," says Frannie crossly. "You know he's never been the least bit interested in any of his bastards. They are but small annoyances to him, costing as they do."

"But this—this is different." I haven't stopped shaking since I heard the news, which hit me in that most raw and private of places. "He has never before named one himself, and such a name." Louis-Aimé de Bourbon. I was thinking of Roman de Grenouille—Frog—a play on his mother's name and birthplace. It is rumored the king even signed the baptismal certificate; I must ask my men to find it and steal away that evidence of his paternity.

"Look what little interest he takes in the Comte de Luc," continues Frannie, referring to Pauline de Vintimille's son. "Already twenty and not even a regiment for him from the royal coffers! Besides, I've heard she's dreadfully arrogant; the king will soon grow tired of her. You must know your pliancy and patience are two of your greatest attributes."

I laugh lightly. But even her true words cannot stop the force of the gossip: today Mademoiselle de Romans is blessed with a new diamond necklace, tomorrow a carriage with six horses. They compare her to Helen of Troy, laud her mystical proportions, wax long and enthusiastic about her manners and her elegance.

Her elegance! A clerk's daughter from the provinces! Really, it is almost as if they were talking of a duchess.

I must see for myself. Under the guise of visiting the Sèvres factory and selecting a new coffee service, Nicole and I take my carriage to the outskirts of Paris. The set is divine, as always; the cups as thin as eggshells, painted with a pattern of blue willows in the Chinese style. Then, a short ride to the Bois de Boulogne, where daily Mademoiselle de Romans makes a spectacle of herself, nursing the king's child in public. It is a fine spring day and the areas around the forest are packed with loiterers and entertainers, folks of all stripes and merits. It was near here that I met that gypsy woman, so many lifetimes ago.

Shortly Nicole returns with the information that today she is by the walls of the Abbey of Longchamp. I pull a veil down over my face and we hasten down the path. And there she is, Mademoiselle de Romans, the woman my Louis is in love with, seated on the grass, surrounded by a crowd of curious onlookers.

The woman at the center is beautiful and radiates serenity. Her dress is a pale blue lake spread against the green grass, her only adornment a small neck ribbon affixed with a cross, a large lace fichu demurely covering her breast and the infant. Though her legendary black hair is piled neatly on her head, a single thick ringlet, raven-black, curls down her back and almost reaches the grass.

"Oh! A Madonna!" breathes Nicole, and she speaks the truth: the woman is beautiful. Her skin is as white as my Sèvres porcelain, contrasting so vividly with her black hair. And so young—they say she is no more than twenty. Half my age.

"Make way, make way," says Nicole imperiously, pushing a man with a large basket of clucking chicks out of the way. "The Princesse de Ponti comes through!"

Mademoiselle de Romans looks up, and though Nicole had announced a great lady, she does not rise or appear flustered by our approach. Quite confident for a clerk's daughter, I think sourly, and hang behind Nicole, leery of getting too close.

"Madame, if you permit," says Nicole, leaning over and lifting the fichu from her chest, to reveal the infant and a glimpse of a Heaven-white breast. "We have heard far and wide of the beauty of your son and wished to see for ourselves. They say he is the finest child in France."

The woman smiles. "Certainly I would agree, but then, I am

his mother." Her voice is slow and elegant. She lifts the babe away from her breast and hands him to Nicole.

"And what do you call him?" asks Nicole, with all the innocence in the world.

"His name is Louis-Aimé de Bourbon," says the woman calmly but firmly. Even without that lighthouse of a name, signaling his birth, the child could not be mistaken for any but my Louis' son, the eyes and chin identical. I turn away sharply and think, unbidden, of Alexandrine, my dearest Fanfan, dead now for six years.

Romans reaches to take her child back. "Might I have the pleasure of an introduction to your lady? I heard you announce the Princesse de Ponti and it would be my honor to make the acquaintance of such an illustrious person." Again her words are smooth, her composure perfect: a queen on the green grass, holding court with her minions.

"Unfortunately my mistress has a toothache and her voice is not well," says Nicole briskly. Romans smiles, a trifle sardonically, and I have an awful feeling that she knows who has come to inspect her. No. Please, no.

Nicole senses my distress and quietly leads me back to the carriage. We start for Versailles and to distract myself I unpack the box with the coffee service. I finger the chip-thin plates and hold a delicate porcelain cup, but the white reminds me of her skin, the elegant blue etching of the willow branches like the veins on her neck. What did she do for such a complexion? Frannie would be so jealous. Not only Frannie . . . I am holding the cup tightly, my fingers squeezing around the thin porcelain, and suddenly it breaks into white shards that shred my palm.

"Oh, Madame," says Nicole sadly. "Oh, Madame." She searches for something else to say but can find no words. The sadness of the world, of my life, overwhelms me.

When he visits the next day I show him the new coffee set. Though I smile and look charming in a new green spring dress, I can feel a strong sadness threatening to smother me.

"Darling, I went myself to Sèvres yesterday and chose only the most perfect pieces." The service is displayed on a cloth of pale blue linen, matching the delicate lines of the willows. Perhaps I should have the room upholstered to match? There is something so serene about that palette of blue and white.

"Only seven cups?" says Louis, picking one up and turning it over. "Quite perfect, indeed. Nice handles. Now, what do you think we should do about Bertin's proposal?" he asks, referring to the new minister of finance and his plans for yet another tax.

"One had a slight imperfection, but I have ordered another to replace it." I keep my hands inside my gloves, the bandage wound tightly. "I will pick it up myself next month." And see her again? I watch Louis closely. I recognize the familiar bounce in the step, the constant licking of the lips, his renewed interest in life.

While still at Versailles, his eldest daughter, Madame Infanta, caught smallpox and died at the end of last year. She was only thirty-three, and her death devastated Louis and spun him into a profound depression.

But now it seems he is happy again. Because of her. *R*, I think, biting my lip, I need an *R* engraved on a stone, and fast. On just a river rock: nothing special for that Romans woman.

Louis replaces the cup. "I think I should order a similar set for my Adélaïde. Her reader has introduced her to a Chinese philosopher—Confusion, I think his name is—and she is quite taken with his works. Perhaps you could take care of the details?"

"Of course," I murmur.

"Now, dearest, you decide about Bertin, and let Choiseul know. I would ride to La Muette tonight, a few gentlemen only, and spend the night there. Rochechouart tells me an albino boar was sighted—I must have it."

"Of course, dearest," I murmur again. La Muette—where *she* has a house. When he leaves the old fears return; my position is hollow, as dry as an autumn leaf, ready and set to crumble.

From Joachim de Bernis, Cardinal de Soissons
Vic-sur-Aisne, Soissons, France
September 11, 1760

My dearest Marquise,

A thousand thanks for your letter and for your good wishes. Though Soissons cannot compare to the wonders of Versailles, I find it quite pleasant, and the food surprisingly good. As one grows older, one is more content with that which does not shine so brightly: *Earthly pleasures few / When simple comforts will do.*

I am troubled by the news of Choiseul. I assure you it is not jealousy that compels me to write, but as a cardinal blessed by the Pope himself, I must take it upon myself to warn you of his godless ways; his plan to break the Church and expel the Jesuits is very troubling. Certainly, reforms are needed—out here in the provinces, one sees the true state of France—but not in so crude a manner. He—and you—will have a hard time if you alienate the Church and attempt too much compromise with Parlement.

But let us write of lighter things! You must send me all the gossip: Are Frannie and Mirie speaking to each other again, after Mirie's rabbit gave birth on Frannie's Turkish rug? I know how dear they are to you (Mirie and Frannie, I mean to say, not the rabbits), so I hope they have resolved their feud. And do tell me more about the Duchesse de Fleury not rising for the Duchesse d'Orléans—what scandal!

I submit to you humbly,
The Cardinal de Soissons

Chapter Sixty-Five

"I declare, I do not know which one to love," says the Duc d'Ayen. "We are all agreed it is the fashion to love one's sister, but which one to choose? Of the four that remain to me, one is the Devil incarnate; one drinks; another is a bore; and the last is half-mad. Which would you counsel, Sire?"

Louis roars with laughter and the rest of the guests twitter in appreciation at his wit. We are at supper in Choiseul's apartments; our host has an equal instinct for work as for pleasure, and his evenings are always lively and his table superb. Tonight we dined on sweetbreads and buttered pigeons, and I cannot but admire the elegant porcelain dinner service and the elaborate carved sugar swan, dyed pink, that graces the center of the table.

Choiseul, his wife, Honorine, and his sister Béatrice have quickly become the center of the Court. Thanks to Choiseul's adoration for Béatrice, sisters are suddenly all that is fashionable. Frannie told me yesterday they have even started calling him Ptolemy—after the pharaohs who married their sisters.

"I'm not sure I would know how to advise you," says the king, laughing and taking another swig of champagne. "Perhaps I might say choose the Devil incarnate, as the most interesting. And how would others advise Ayen on his most pressing of problems?"

"The drunkard—at least you can join her in her fun! And I'll say it again—this is fine wine." Choiseul is a particular wine connoisseur, and declared the hardest part of his years in Vienna to be the execrable Austrian wine.

"Take the simple one—great fun to toy with, like a child really. And they never get mad; you can love them as you wish," chips in the Prince de Soubise.

"Well, my choice," says the Marquis de Gontaut, "would be the bore: from my own sister I gained the decidedly useful skill of appearing to listen, while never hearing a word."

"Sisters—a category of ladies Your Majesty has great knowledge of!" declares the Prince de Beauvau, one of Mirie's twenty siblings. To please my friend I often include him in our dinners, but his wit is half-formed and he has a strong talent for saying the wrong thing. I sigh; I pressed for his admittance but will do so no longer.

At Beauvau's crass reference to sisters the king's face darkens and the mood is about to turn when Choiseul, the man responsible for this new fashion, gestures to his own sister Béatrice, the Duchesse de Gramont, to rise.

"To sisters," he says, smiling at Béatrice. "Unlike you, my dear sir"—he bows to Ayen—"I have no difficult choices to make, and can love the one I have, knowing she is as perfect as a star."

"To sisters," says Béatrice in her harsh voice, smiling coldly. Béatrice is not my favorite person. She is as ugly as sin, as she herself cheerfully admits; what is bulbous yet oddly intriguing on a man is not so on a woman. She may be witty and amusing but I sense beneath her hard exterior an even harder middle, an ice field of ambition and greed. Though she pays me assiduous court, I mistrust her as deeply as I trust her brother. She was rotting in a convent before he returned to Versailles and arranged a marriage for her: the Duc de Gramont is a drunkard and looks as though nature had intended him to be a barber. Now it is said she has a fourteen-year-old lover, rumored to be her nephew no less.

"When I was in Austria," observes Choiseul, "I had the pleasure of knowing the young daughters of the empress, and a more delightful group of sisters—now, what do we call a group of sisters? A fluster? A cackle?—you would never find."

"One of those little archduchesses for our dear Burgundy!" cries Beauvau, talking of the king's grandson. I frown; these days the king does not like talk of politics at the table, and the little boy is ailing badly: tuberculosis of the bone, his doctors have concluded.

But Louis only smiles indulgently. "Oh, I am not sure an Austrian princess would do; they may be our allies now, but such new friends . . . the people of France would never accept an Austrian as their future queen." Though a marriage between one of the empress's daughters and one of Louis' grandsons was an article of our treaty with the Austrians, Louis does not like to talk of it.

"No better way to cement the alliance, Sire," says Choiseul quickly, and I realize he is in favor of the idea. Interesting; something to be discussed with him later. His influence with Louis grows apace and any awkwardness between them is long forgotten. The war will hopefully be over soon, though there looks to be no happy outcome for France. But tonight, we may forget those worries, and concentrate on our leisure.

"Now, let me introduce the entertainment for my honored guests," Choiseul continues with an impish look. Despite the lumpiness of his face, he really is quite an attractive man. Though they say underneath his wig his hair is as orange as a carrot. "Honorine, my dear wife, since sisters are the fashion of the hour, would you allow Béatrice to do the honors?"

Honorine smiles sweetly, as she always does. Everyone loves Honorine. Times have changed, and perhaps not in all ways for the worst. Hardly anyone cares that the duchess is the granddaughter of a peasant, and I know Choiseul, a keen and intelligent man, cared little. Perhaps I had something to do with that, or perhaps it is just that the whole country, nay, the whole world, is changing. Or perhaps it is Honorine herself; she is a woman even the most malicious of men would find perfect.

Béatrice smiles and stands. "Brother," she says, then turns to the rest of the guests. "This is a game that Étienne and I invented, when we were children. We used to play it with our cousins and occasionally the servants. Now, clear the table," she orders, motioning to the footmen, who spring into action; soon the remains of the food are gone and the elaborate sugar centerpiece retired to a side table. "And more candles, more candles, for though this game depends on shadows, we must also have light."

"You intrigue me, Madame. I thought I had played all the games there were to play," observes Louis, looking at Béatrice with an expression I can't place.

"Not at all, Your Majesty, not at all. There is a world out there for you to uncover." Do her words have hidden meaning? I know she aspires to the king's bed—who does not?—but my sources tell me she has not been successful. So far. But I am not worried; his taste no longer runs to the mature.

The table is laid with four additional candelabras that light the guests' faces, now glossy with sweat and wine.

"Like being inside the sun," says Ayen, shifting his chair so his wig, styled wide at the ears, is safe from the flames.

"A fairy egg," whispers the little Comtesse d'Amblimont, all kitten curves and soft lips. And silliness—what does a fairy egg have to do with more candles and light? I hold my breath: I am feeling rather cynical tonight, and must not let my thoughts show.

"We call this game 'Murder,'" says Béatrice dramatically.

"Oh!" squeals Mirie, always ready to be shocked.

"Do not be shocked, my dear Maréchale. Ladies, no one shall die," assures Choiseul, stroking his sister's hand and gazing up at her in incestuous adoration. Incestuous—what a terrible word. But of course the rumors run there; where else would they go? There certainly is a strange bond between the two.

"No one shall die, but many shall lose," continues Béatrice with a wicked grin. "This is how we play: everyone to take a card. The person who receives the knave of diamonds, the jack of death as he is known in Italy, is the murderer."

"Oooh!"

"Such fun!"

"The knave of diamonds—I never like his red face."

Louis is alert, his morbid interests—and perhaps more—aroused. She is clever, I will grant her that. Béatrice aspires to be first in everything, a trait I understand well, and tonight she is wearing a striped red dress, the stripes running in different directions on the bodice and skirt—very fashionable. Around her neck she has tied a thin red ribbon, thinner than the usual fashion, so thin it resembles the clean cut of a knife. I wonder if she has co-ordinated her outfit with the entertainment of the evening? That is—was—my trick.

"Now . . . death is by . . ." Béatrice looks around the audience. "My friends, you must guess how the murder will occur."

"By hanging!"

"Through an excess of champagne!"

"By drawing and quartering!" cries Beauvau. I wish he were sitting beside me, that I might kick him in the ankle, or even whisper to him to leave.

"No, no, no. Death comes . . . by the wink."

"The wink?" exclaims Louis.

"Yes, the wink. As this," says Béatrice, winking at him. "If we were playing the game, Your Majesty would be . . . well, perhaps this is not the best example."

"I am but Louis Bourbon in this room," cries the king, his eyes glittering. "You may even speak of my death . . . by wink."

"Well, if you permit," says Béatrice, smiling at him and expos-ing her gray teeth. She winks at him again. "If I were the mur-derer, and if I winked at our Monsieur Louis Bourbon . . . a few seconds after receiving my wink, he must die as dramatically, or as softly, as he wishes." Louis appears to be enjoying himself but I tense, alert to a change in mood in case she has gone too far. This entertainment is risky but Béatrice and her brother follow few rules. If I were not so nervous, I might admire them.

"Ha! I think I shall like this game. I shall die—thus . . ." The king stands, doubles over and clutches his stomach, then staggers into the lap of the pretty little Amblimont, who squeals in mock terror.

"Excellent," approves Béatrice, while Mirie gasps and wails, "Sire, not even in jest!"

"Now once dead," continues Béatrice, ignoring Mirie—there is no love lost between the two, and Mirie once called the younger woman a horrifying horse—"you must retire from the table.

However, justice cannot be ignored; before being struck by the wink, keep your eyes on the others at the table, and if you catch the winker, or think you have, you may accuse. To be right is to win. But to be wrong . . . ah, that is another form of death—you are also banished from the table."

"A *lettre de cachet* for a false accusation! Splendid!" cries Louis, and I see he is enjoying himself. I must immerse myself in this stupid—and entirely inappropriate—game. I smile in delight at Béatrice and bless the whole pathetic procedure.

"Now let us play!" The king claps his hands as a gloved footman passes around the cards to the fourteen guests. I take mine— the five of spades—but no. I cannot do this. I rise and face Béatrice at the other end of the table.

"My friends, let me add to the macabre nature of this evening by withdrawing from the game, reducing the number of participants to an eerie thirteen."

"Oh, no, Marquise, don't," says Mirie, looking at me with concern.

"As in the Last Supper," says Beauvau dolefully. "And we all know how that turned out."

"Stay and play, dearest," says Louis kindly. Once my heart might have leapt at the obvious care on his face, but not tonight. "My dear, you are not feeling well?"

"No, no, I am well. Very well."

"Madame, if I am the murderer, you have my rigid promise that you will be the last to suffer my death wink." Choiseul is as gallant as ever and Honorine is full of concern. "Marquise, don't go," she whispers quietly, reaching out a soft hand.

"No, please, I shall retire . . . a slight headache, no matter, and I would leave you to your merriment." You thirteen doomed nits, I want to add, but don't. I take my leave with a curtsy and a faint smile. I know tomorrow the Court will talk of nothing else: they will invent a rivalry with Béatrice, they will say I am too old, too pious, they will conjecture and gossip to no end, but few will guess the real reason, so simple yet so unthinkable: I don't care anymore.

That knowledge is freedom, a breath of fresh air as my worries take off with wings. How strange, I muse as I walk the quiet late-night corridors back to my rooms, my equerry ahead of me with a lantern. How strange this feels. We pass a pair of men carrying an enormous branched candelabra, the crystals tinkling merrily in the shadows. As I pass them they stop and bow, still holding their charge alight. I descend to my rooms and let my women's soft, capable hands prepare me for bed.

As Nicole closes my curtains and I am alone in the peace of my chamber, the thought comes to me that if I don't care anymore, then there will be no more battles and no more fights, nothing to keep me strong.

From Abel de Poisson, Marquis de Marigny
Director of the King's Buildings
Château de Menars, Menars, Orléanais
May 5, 1761

Dear Sister,

I have finished my inspection here at Menars. It is a charming place that will certainly compensate for the sales of Bellevue and Crécy, and I would recommend the purchase. The war must surely end soon and then you will face less opposition from *them*—whoever *they* may be—in furnishing this new house to your exacting specifications.

I know you—and the king—are suffering terribly from the death of the little Duc de Burgundy. A tragedy, certainly, but we must be practical: there are three more boys in the nursery, and though the Duc de Berry is by no means the bright spark his elder brother was, in time he will rise to the demands of kingship. And any marriage plans you were making with Austria can surely be transferred to the younger boy?

Speaking of which, I must say no to Mademoiselle de Talmond-Trémoille. Her family's opposition to the interment of little Alexandrine in the crypt next to theirs was unacceptable. Have you forgotten the cruel puns about the noble bones of La Trémoille being confounded at finding themselves next to fishbones?

I received yet another unpleasant missive from the Comte de Matignon regarding the Maréchale de Mirepoix's rabbits. The issue is becoming extremely tiresome and I am not sure how to resolve it, for I suspect Matignon's motives stem more from boredom than genuine grievance. Do see how he can be placated; perhaps a new apartment for him? The Duchesse de Duras' might be free shortly, for I hear her cough has not improved.

I shall be back at Versailles within the month.

Your brother,
Abel

Chapter Sixty-Six

The king and I increasingly spend our evenings apart as the center of the Court gradually, slowly, turns toward Choiseul and Béatrice. And will they in turn, turn against me?

Perhaps.

Though my detachment increases, there is still so much business to attend to.

The walls of my private study are lacquered bright red with curtains to match. Louis calls it the womb of his heart and it is here that he increasingly spends most of his working time. This room is the scene of some of the most important decisions in Europe; just last week we debated here the terms of the treaty that will finally end the war—almost seven years now—with the British and the Prussians.

Some more sordid business, though equally important, is also carried out here.

A footman ushers in Le Bel.

"Guillaume," I say warmly. "Please, do sit." There are necessary evils in life and though I detest his vocation, I would rather have him as a friend than an enemy. He is a sensible man, and if I must have a partner in these disgusting crimes, best that it be he.

"I must thank you for coming at such short notice."

"Of course, Madame, of course." He is wary; accustomed to my ways, he knows that a private audience is a thing of importance.

"I have a report here that one of the new girls"—I check her name on the letter—"Dorothée, that she is, ah . . ." I plunge into frigid waters: "Infected."

Le Bel blanches and raises his eyes to meet mine. He is getting old, like his master, the lines riven by debauchery defining his face. I know he goes with the king to town and while the king . . . I shut down the flow of my thoughts, before they arrive at their disturbing destination.

"This is serious, Le Bel," I say, tapping my finger on the paper. "This is very, very serious."

"It is indeed." He takes the letter and reads it. Small beads of sweat sprout on his face, and a dark spreading stain on his coat shows his underarms are sweating too.

"Where is she now?" I ask.

"In town on the rue Saint-Médéric."

"Has the king seen her?"

"Not yet. Not yet. Her eyebrows were overplucked and we were waiting, a few more weeks for them to regrow . . . The king dislikes false eyebrows, or very thin ones . . ." He trails off as the enormity of what might have happened dawns on him.

Saved by a pair of eyebrows. Well, stranger things have happened.

"We must thank God for this deliverance."

"We must," agrees Le Bel, watching me warily to gauge the depths of my anger. But it is shallow, for I blame myself more.

"So get rid of her, and be careful in the future with—well, he calls himself the Comte du Barry, but he sounds more like a common procurer. According to my reports, he is a *débauché* of the worst kind, a despicable man teetering on the edges of the minor nobility. His nickname—the Roué—is most apt."

"Of course, of course." Le Bel takes the note, and the absolution, I offer. "Sartine did good work," he says, referring to the report and to the superintendent of the police; Berryer has been promoted to the Ministry of the Marine.

"He did indeed, though it should not be up to *him* to find out these things," I say pointedly. I swallow, a delicate pause before I plunge into even more frigid waters: "And how are other matters progressing?"

"Very well, Madame, very well. The Hainault girl's marriage

plans are advancing; the girl Lucie is pregnant again and will begin to show soon."

"Indeed. Make the usual arrangements with Madame Cremer." Madame Bertrand was dismissed last year after spending the funds for an entire month of provisions on one very drunken night in town at the Inn of Two Stags. "I'll do the naming, as usual."

Mademoiselle de Romans is also pregnant again, but my sources say she is out of favor with the king. It is a blessing in disguise, this rampant need for new flesh; his fickleness is my savior, allowing no girl to gain dominion over his heart. He is spreading his love so thin these days, a little here, a little there, and has lost the sense that pleasures are meant to be sampled, not gorged upon.

A pause.

"And the . . ." This one takes every ounce of strength to say. But soon this distasteful interview will be over; the rest of my day will be spent quietly with a new work by my beloved Voltaire, then in the evening a small supper with just the king and Choiseul. Béatrice has been sick these last weeks, much to my relief. The rest of my day will be enjoyable. But this . . . I take a deep breath: "And the little girl?"

I cannot bear to say her name. He is keeping a child, an enchanting little girl I have no desire to see, in one of the houses— there are several now—grooming and growing her for the day when he will become her lover. They say he visits her often, and sometimes she throws her toys at him and calls him old and ugly. The king only laughs at her impudence and takes delight in his new purchase, and the drawn-out anticipation of that future deflowering.

"Yes, Madame, little Louisette is well." Le Bel has a talent for affecting a banal tone for even the most awkward of conversations. "She is grown accustomed to her surroundings, accustomed to His Majesty. She is a high-spirited little tyke, and he—ah— seems to be pleased by that. She requests another doll, and a toy carriage."

I close my eyes and remember my faux pas when I spoke of toys, so many years ago. I was not wrong, then: it has come to pass. Was all of it—the houses, the whores, the endless girls, the *children*—a mistake?

"Certainly, get her what she wants," I say, wearily. Poor little girl, I think for a brief, slighting second, then push that thought from my mind. She will do well in this life; sympathy is wasted on those who are not hungry or dying. I dismiss Le Bel and when he is gone I sink my head against the cool marble top of my desk, feeling soiled even though I bathed before Mass.

Will God forgive me these sins?

From Françoise, Dowager Duchesse de Brancas
Château de Choisy, Choisy
April 28, 1763

Dear Jeanne,

Greetings from Choisy. We arrived yesterday and Mesdames are settling in well for a week here. It was quite distressing to see the misery on the road to the palace; the shouts and cries left me with quite a headache. Silly people—they should be celebrating the end of the war, not crying about their ills. Madame Victoire is forever foolish, and when she heard them cry they had no bread, she suggested feeding the people with piecrusts, which she dislikes and always picks off.

I am sorry to hear His Majesty remains distressed about the peace treaty, but he should remember our colonies were really good for nothing (though with Senegal gone we must find a new source for beeswax, or risk interminable chapped lips). Remind him what Voltaire said about New France: nothing but bears, beavers, and barbarians. Truer words have never been spoken—remember the dreadful tale of the Comte de Forcalquier and the beaver scalp hat?

I saw Quesnay here this morning (Madame Louise had another toothache). He is more concerned than ever about your health. You must find a way to lead a quieter life at Versailles, for the solution is not retirement to a convent or your new house at Menars! As long as the king lives, you must know your place is beside him. Without you, I am sure he would crumble like one of Madame Victoire's hated crusts.

Until next week,
Frannie

Chapter Sixty-Seven

T he war that lasted seven long years is over. Last night I dreamt Louis rode out to war, as he did when he was young, and he was victorious and the crowd wept with their love for him.

I woke feeling hollow inside. What a fantasy; I doubt they will ever cheer for him again.

France is at its lowest point. Colonies and prestige are lost, seemingly forever, and the country is bankrupt—it will take many decades to pay off our debts incurred by the costly fight.

I feel as though the end of the war in some way mirrors my own battle, for I have fought and fought, and though they may say I am victorious, what have I really won?

"Say hello to Lavender."

I pet the soft white fur, admire the little gray necklet studded with pearls.

"She's lovely, and the chain is very fine."

"You see it matches my bracelet here?" Mirie extends a plump, creamy arm, pushing back a flounce of chiffon to reveal the pearls around her wrist. She lets the rabbit down on the floor and it lops toward Nicole, hoping a piece of celery or a carrot will come its way. Mirie stops by the mantel and admires the fish.

"Is there an *R* down there, by any chance?" she asks with a wicked grin, referring to Mademoiselle de Romans. I shake my head, embarrassed as I always am when she refers to my little secret. Few know of it, but Mirie is very sharp and quickly divined what was going on.

"No, though a piece of garnet awaits. But soon—they say she

has demanded two carriages, and you know how the king hates demands."

We settle down by the fire and I pass Mirie a glass of wine; I savor these cozy nights together. The king is away hunting at Rambouillet and will spend the night there. I declined to go, for I have been coughing all week, my body racked with a strange trembling. I feel the need for the soporific of wine and I swallow a great gulp and a wave of lassitude and peace spreads through me. Quesnay be damned; I rest, and rest, yet still I ache and suffer.

Mirie kicks off her shoes and curls up on the sofa. I am wearing a snug winter robe, the plush rabbit-fur trim tickling my neck. Lavender's cousin? I think with a giggle. Mirie says on these nights, we are like widows together, and it is true. A happy place to be, free from the demands of men and convention, cozy with friends and conversation, perhaps even some gossip when the wine takes effect. But I am melancholy and thoughtful tonight; the freezing rain that beats down reminds me of winter's approach.

"I went to her, again, last week," I say, and Mirie knows I speak of the gypsy woman from my past, still in Paris and now with a yearly pension from the Crown. She started it all and she has had her reward, many times over.

"And what fine fortunes await us all in 1764?" Mirie asks lightly, refusing to meet me at the bottom of the well.

I shake my head. "I asked her about my death," I say, looking into the fire, away from the eyes of my friend and the truth.

"Oh tosh, now, Jeanne," says Mirie crossly. "You are far, far too young to be thinking such morbid thoughts. Just past forty!"

I ignore her and stare at the fire, the orange embers hypnotic, a strange feeling falling over me that someone, or something, is coming through the fireplace. A howling wind outside rattles the windows, a beast demanding to be let in. "She said I would have a good death and time to prepare. Is that not what we all want to hear?"

"Well, I know she's been right, but she has also been wrong. Coffee dregs are like clouds—you see in them what you want. Remember her prediction about Gontaut's accident? And you're not dying anytime soon. Mm, yes," Mirie says, taking a currant cake from the plate Nicole offers. "And do give one to Lavender, she is developing quite the sweet tooth."

I am buried in a small cocoon of blankets and pillows, the alcohol draining away my sorrows. Peace is I, I think, peace is I. I saw him today; he came and we chatted about the new statue of him in Paris that will be installed to commemorate the peace.

He still loves me. He still needs me.

"Bring another bottle," I say to Nicole. "A merlot?"

"Well, you can't be feeling too ill if you can drink this much," says Mirie archly, licking her fingers. "My, but I do love currants."

"My liver has never been accused." Only my heart, my lungs, everything else, seemingly.

"Early Mass with the queen," Mirie warns as Nicole opens the bottle and pours another round. "Saint Melasippus waits for no man, or woman."

"Did you know Quesnay prepared a sermon on him, last week, and presented it to the queen?"

"Yes, I heard. Rather kind of him, don't you think, to be so attentive to her interests?"

"I envy him," I say suddenly. "He is a man the queen respects."

"I always thought it a strange side of you, Jeanne," says Mirie. "Always wanting the queen's approval."

"I admire her," I say simply. "I always have. And I know some of what she suffers."

"What all women suffer," says Mirie lightly. "Why do women marry? The best way to avoid suffering is simply not to."

"So the Duc de Liancourt has not spoken?" Mirie's husband died two years ago and she has a small flood of admirers.

"He may have, but I choose not to hear him when he speaks

of marriage. My hearing is quite selective these days—a perquisite of growing older."

We both giggle, but my thoughts quickly turn somber again; I am still thinking of the queen.

"He has done her some harm, more harm than was necessary. He is sometimes a cruel man, a cold one."

Mirie is silent. She tries not to comment where the king is concerned.

"Come," I say in impatience. "You know it is true. He is not a god."

"I thought he was to you."

"He was . . . when we were younger. Ah, to say he was the center of my world would be untrue; he was quite simply my world. There was a time when his admiration meant everything to me." We sit in silence and I look down at my hands and see flashes of the past—the look in his eyes when we met in the forest of Sénart; the feel of his arm around my waist as we rode the carriage to my mother's house, that first night; the joy when I spun on the stage in front of him in my silver and green dress, with seashells in my hair.

"But now, in some ways he has lost . . ." I sigh and reveal the truth buried far inside, released by the wine: "My respect." I saw a pamphlet about me, last week. It observed, in quite a witty way, that I had been five years a whore, thirteen years a whoremonger.

"Hush, dearest, you mustn't speak so. You know you'll regret it in the morning."

"I won't remember it in the morning," I say, pouring myself another glass from the emptying bottle, the dregs swirling at the bottom like little omens. "You know, he once told me that he only feels alive, only loses his fear of death, when he is making love. I wonder: Would all men act as he does, if all restraints were removed?"

"I think they would," says Mirie, her mood turning dark to match mine. "Beasts."

I am not sure: If absolute power does what it does to men, then why is the dauphin still a true and moral man, the opposite of his father? Not every man, I think, would descend as my Louis has. Not every man. His son is stronger in his convictions and free of that fundamental weakness that leads my Louis down the path of least resistance, and greatest gratification.

"I've noticed he . . ." I struggle to find the words, from thoughts long suppressed: "That he likes unripe fruit, but I do not speak in metaphors. He enjoys white strawberries, peaches with the crunch of carrots. What does it all mean? What does any of it mean? He will answer for it in Heaven," I say, then realize I am crying, the tears flowing down my face.

"If he makes it there," says Mirie lightly, and I want to slap her. I go to do it, in half jest, but almost fall off the sofa.

"Of course he will make it," I say. "That is what confession is for. And he never hurt anyone . . ." But that is not true; I think of the broken hearts and promises, the stolen childhoods, the lies.

The fire dies down and we fall silent, lost in our own thoughts. Soon Mirie is stretched out on the sofa, her head over a pillow, fast asleep. I sit though my head spins, staring at the dying embers. I am surprised I have such energy; late nights for me are now a thing of the past. Ah, glorious wine, was there ever a finer drink? I should buy a vineyard. Grow my own grapes, make a wine of the finest color the world has ever seen, like rubies but deeper, clear but dark—suddenly I realize I am talking aloud, and giggle in surprise.

"Madame, come to bed." Nicole is by my side, prying the glass from my shaking fingers. "Dawn will break soon."

"What good are all these beautiful things?" I demand of her as I allow her capable arms to lift me up. "All of this . . ." I throw my hand around the room and marvel at how uneven the floors have become; I must get them fixed. "Morocco leather, marble from Toulouse, that clock, that porcelain duck—so perfect, so perfect, but what use are they to me now?" I knew how to live, I think suddenly, a strange thought for one who is dying.

Nicole doesn't speak, just guides me out of my robe and onto the bed.

"I'll send for the Maréchale's chair," she says calmly as she closes the curtains and I spiral down into sleep. I am on a journey, I think before darkness overcomes me. I have mounted the horse and I have started the journey, that bleak journey toward the end.

Chapter Sixty-Eight

A new doctor diagnoses me with heart troubles, in addition to my lungs; how fitting, I think ruefully. I am grown thin, emaciated as a skeleton, my skin gray and my eyes sunken, eaten by the consumption that now ravages me clean. I have aged twenty years in just a few, and when I look in the mirror these days (which is not very often), I feel more amazement than sadness at the stranger I find there. Who is she? Where is Reinette, the woman I was, the woman he loved, where has she gone?

At the end of last year I thought it was the end; many did too, but then my strength returned. These days I rarely leave my apartment, some days not even my bed. I suppress the sordid realities of vomiting and bedsores from those around me, and still insist on the fresh flowers, the scented candles and potpourris, the luxurious furs. Finally I can heed Quesnay's advice: rest, rest, and more rest.

In the cold of March, a brief respite. I feel stronger and the cough lessens and my lungs free up. Choiseul arranges a private performance by two little Austrian musical prodigies. The children are enchanting, the little girl, Maria Anna, like an angel and she reminds me of Alexandrine, as so much does these days; perhaps as death sidles alongside, it also wishes to remind me of what it offers.

Her younger brother, Wolfgang, is truly a gift from God, his small, graceful hands producing notes that could only come from Heaven. His music is so exquisite that it frightens; it is music that threatens to soar too high and too wide, to break us free of chains we never knew we had.

When I leave the concert chamber I stagger in sudden weariness and firm arms guide me to my chair. A terrible presentiment comes over me, that never again on this earth will I hear anything so beautiful. It is as though the little boy's music was sent by angels to guide me home.

The next day something is released and I retire to the bed I will never leave. As the days pass Quesnay is sad but firm: the end is near. I am on my deathbed, I think in amazement, and that small part of me that is not yet consumed by the beast rebels. No! Forty-two is too young to die. I rage against what is coming with all the strength I have left. I want to live, I want to feel the breeze on my face, the touch of a loved one, the joy of Louis' smile; I want to know what happens to all those I love as the future unfurls.

I am overcome with a desperate sadness that this world will go on without me, and I despair over all that I will miss. The world will not stop for a heartbeat when I am gone. And Versailles, this great palace that shelters me now, will continue long after me, insensate, uncaring, the epicenter of France and frivolity. Will it ever change?

I leave nothing of myself that is not of the material world. No child—not Alexandrine, nor the unborn child, that whispered cipher, the child that should have been from the love of Louis and me. No more, nevermore . . . I leave no child behind and that, as I prepare to leave this earth, is my greatest regret.

But then a tiredness like quicksand drags me down and my earthly worries are cast aside. I doze, and dream and stir, and there before me is Alexandrine and she is made of love and light, and she smiles, her hands outstretched as she beckons me toward her, toward the place where there is no more pain, and she calls to me: *Mama.*

My apartment fills with people making their farewells and paying homage. Choiseul comes; no words are necessary. He has thanked me enough and I am glad to leave him to Louis. I can only pray the king continues to recognize his worth.

Mirie comes, sobbing openly. Frannie glides in and looks at

me with a look of such tenderness that I burst into sobs that rack and hurt my chest. Dear Gontaut, Soubise, Ayen, all faithful and firm friends through the years. Their chance to betray me passed, I think, but then I stop myself: they are my friends and if plots were conceived, they were never uncovered.

Even the queen comes, an homage she knows I will find dear. I remember my presentation day as though it were yesterday: that rush of euphoria at her kindness, thinking I had her approval. But perhaps now I do.

"My dear Marquise," she says softly. Her voice is grown polished with age, no trace of the guttural accent her ladies once loved to mock. She is swathed in black, a cap over her graying hair, her eyes dampened and distant; she too is growing old, already sixty. "I wish to thank you for your years of service." She looks at me kindly.

"Madame, my one wish was to serve you."

"You have, dear Marquise, you have."

Even Richelieu comes, bearing a single daffodil: misfortune or eternal life? He offers no smirking vile words, just what sounds like a sincere wish for my recovery. We are both survivors, I think sadly, though he will outlast me. Before he leaves he arches an eyebrow at the fishbowl on the mantel—as though he knows—then bows smartly and departs.

Through the long days of darkness and dreaming, a few of the demons, with their perfect dress and their spiteful minds, come to pay me compliments and insults. They too will one day make this journey I am on, for no amount of malice can prevent that.

"My dear, so pale, what an absolutely lovely skin color, one could even say being sick becomes you!"

"Your eyes, grown even larger than before."

"A pity about your hands—looking a little knobby, aren't they?"

"Snake soup, dear Marquise, snake soup, eaten fresh—my sister swears by it."

Finally my Louis comes. He has been crying; I can read his

face like no other and I see the single streak of redness in his left eye, the faint puffiness of his cheeks. They are calling him cold but I know he is not. A lifetime of controlling his emotions in front of others—only I know what lies beneath the king's frozen mask.

He sits on my bed and strokes my hands. We are both silent, for there are no words sufficient to this occasion. Nicole brings in the box as I asked. He opens it and finds two pieces of ribbon, once fine red velvet, now crumpled and faded.

"Your first gift," I whisper, and take one of the pieces and rub it against my cheek, smell the memories and the must. I start to cry, and he bows his head.

"I take confession tomorrow, my love," I say finally, and he nods, then leans in to kiss me one last time. I close my eyes and inhale, as best I can through my scarred, useless lungs, the scent of love and life. All my memories wash over me as I breathe in one last time the man I built my life around.

"You never disappointed me. Ever. Believe me." A tear trembles in his eye. "You were my one true friend. I fear I made you unhappy."

"No. No, never," I say, and reach for his hand again, wishing I never had to let it go. "You were the best moments of my life."

"And you—you were my everything."

"Go," I whisper, releasing his hand. "Go."

He has a life to return to, one that will continue without me. I fear for him, and for France, but the time for anxiety is done. He leaves and peace falls over me. This life was a fair dream; I have had the most charmed of lives, not without great sorrows but which lives are untainted by such? I think of the gypsy woman; I think of my mother and of my darling Alexandrine. I will see them both again so soon. And Louis—was he my third great sorrow?

I take confession and the rain beats down outside, as though a great flood is coming. The room is dimly lit and faintly scented with lilies. It is a great honor to die at Versailles, for etiquette dictates that none but the royal family may die here. Tomorrow is

Easter Sunday, if I last until then. Have I done right? Have I lived my life the way it should have been lived? Do we turn to God in our later years, not through fear of death, but through increased wisdom?

And as that last terrible night embraces me in all its pain and suffering, as I prepare to leave for a palace even greater than Versailles, there is one thought that keeps me strong before I surrender:

He loved me.

He did.

Epilogue

On the 15th of April, Easter Sunday, 1764, the Marquise de Pompadour's body was taken from Versailles in a carriage pulled by six black horses. Louis XV watched from a window as the hearse rode out through the rain, tears streaming down his face. Her *cortège* disappeared into the distance and another strange chapter in the strange history of Versailles came to an end.

A Note from the Author

From relatively chaste beginnings, the floodgates of Louis XV's lust soon opened wide. *The Rivals of Versailles* highlights the stories of a few of the many women who graced Louis' bed during the middle part of his reign.

Rosalie de Romanet-Choiseul died in childbirth in 1753, just six months after being banished from Versailles and from the king's heart. She was only eighteen; her daughter and namesake died three years later. Though the timing was right, there does not appear to be any suggestion that she was the king's child.

Marie Louise O'Murphy, nicknamed Morphise in this book, was banished, married, survived, and even, after numerous men, marriages, and other adventures, lived to see the nineteenth century. Ah, poor delightful Morphise, her timing was entirely wrong: after Pompadour's death, the next official mistress was a woman with equally humble roots.

Marie-Anne de Mailly de Coislin had a long and rather exciting life, lover of kings, survivor of the Revolution, denizen of more than one country. She probably wasn't as silly as I have depicted her, but there is definite consensus that she was no match for either the first Marie-Anne, one of the great "might-have-beens" of history, or for the Marquise de Pompadour.

Finally, Jeanne-Antoinette Poisson, the Marquise de Pompadour, the little girl from the middle classes who rose to become the virtual Queen of France and quite possibly the most influential royal mistress ever. She expertly managed a capricious master and her memory lingers long in our consciousness; alongside Catherine the Great of Russia and Maria Theresa of Austria, she is considered one of the three most powerful women of the eighteenth century.

I have tried to do justice to her life, to the highs and the lows, to the impact she had on French style and history, to the enigma that she was on so many levels. Overall, I think she had quite a sad life but I believe it was the life she wanted, the only life she could ever have conceived of, and one that ultimately left her content.

Near the end of his life Louis XV, by that time a confirmed libertine, unknowable to his younger self, was asked whom he had loved most of all of the women who had graced his life and his bed.

"Marie-Anne," he replied without hesitation, referring to Marie-Anne de Mailly-Nesle, the Duchesse de Châteauroux and one of the protagonists of *The Sisters of Versailles*.

"But what about Pompadour?" came the question, to which the king replied: "No, no, I never loved her. I only kept her around because to banish her would have been her death."

Those cruel, light words of gross ingratitude contain a kernel of truth—Louis was the air that Pompadour breathed—but also came from a self-centered man for whom the passage of time had erased so much. I have no doubt that while love may not have lasted, for the almost twenty years that Reinette ruled by his side she was the most important person in his life.

After Reinette's death, Louis mourned, but privately, and the world continued onward. The final book in the trilogy, *The Enemies of Versailles,* will focus on the last years of Louis XV's reign, a pivotal decade in the history of France as it approached the revolution. The story will be told by the Comtesse du Barry, Louis XV's last official mistress, and by his eldest daughter, Madame Adélaïde.

Please visit my website www.sallychristieauthor.com for details on the research that went into this book, as well as additional information on the main and secondary characters.

Acknowledgments

Bringing a book from draft to publication is definitely a team effort. Lots of thanks and gratitude must go to my editor, Sarah Branham at Atria, and to my agent, Dan Lazar at Writers House. Thanks to Alison for once again giving me great input on the draft, and to Sylvia and Vivienne for their early feedback. Thanks to Odile Caffin-Carcy in France for answering my questions, no matter how small or silly, and to Deborah Anthony at French Travel Boutique for arranging a backstage tour of Versailles, which was invaluable in giving me much of the sensory detail that informs these pages. Thanks to the marketing and publicity team at Atria US: Andrea Smith, Jin Yu, and Jackie Jou, as well as the team at S&S Canada, including Katie Callaghan, Catherine Sim, and Andrea Seto. And of course thanks to the many helping hands behind the scenes that I never get to meet or talk with, responsible for all the copyediting and great design work, both on the cover and inside the book.